Project Tartarus

Arche

Erebus Esprit

ISBN: 978-1-963446-01-2

First Edition

Library of Congress Number:

Cover by JCalebDesign
https://www.jcalebdesign.com/

For more works by the author, visit
www.erebusesprit.com

Author's Note

Dear reader,

A content warning can be found at the back of this book and online at https://www.erebusesprit.com/project-tartarus.html.

This is a story that is very close to my heart. I've been a reader of LitRPG since 2017 and I love this genre. Throughout everything I've read, however, nothing quite hit perfect for me. While I continue to search for the book that can 'do it all,' I decided I would try to write what I felt was missing. This book became a lifeline for me during a dark and dangerous period of my life. I started writing it in October 2020 during the height of the pandemic. This world became my escape and I am very glad to be able to share it with you. I hope it can bring you some of the same joy and sorrow it's brought me, both made all the sweeter for each other's company.

You should know, dear reader, that I take inspiration from, but do not strictly adhere to depictions of, Greek Mythology and the mythology of surrounding cultures and people. This book should not be taken as a credible source for academic work in that field. It is, at its heart, a work of fiction and not intended to chronicle history or represent the cultures of that time or any other. I encourage every reader to apply critical thinking and independent research to any and all aspects of their life, especially as it comes to facts presented in this book.

Lastly, I would like to say that if you're still reading, welcome. I love this book. I loved writing this book. I hope you are able to share in some of my love for this world and these characters, dear reader. Always remember: the world is a large and dangerous place, but you don't have to go through it alone.

Erebus Esprit

TABLE OF CONTENTS

Chapter 1

Inside the Void was a beautiful nothing. A negative space. A place between places, a thing without things. It was Khaos and Kosmos, but above all it was empty. On occasion, some traveler would find their way through the Void and it would stir, rippling outward from their incursion, but before long the intruder would leave and the Void would be empty once more. Slumbering in a place outside time, far from the concerns of mortals and immortals alike.

One such incursion was different than the rest, however. It pulled at the Void, tore a sliver in it and passed through. The ripples through the nothing spread far, farther than ever before, and something at the heart of the Void stirred in response.

Change was coming.

Ψ

He was born.

Born into a world of darkness, but not one without feeling. Cold stone stung his unclad feet, harsh ridges poked into the soft fascia of his soles while a bitter wind raised gooseflesh on his arms and bit into his ears like a starving hound in search of a fresh meal. He wrapped his arms about himself. His teeth clacked together as he tried to make sense of his surroundings. Something appeared in front of him, making him flinch as his heart started beating against his ribs. It was the only visible thing in a world of swirling, biting darkness.

A rectangle bearing script hung in the center of his view. Even as he turned his head, it stayed stubbornly within his sight, refusing to vanish or even shift. Inside the rectangle were words. He recognized them as such and, though he had never seen the script, he had no trouble reading them.

Welcome, new spirit.

You have entered the world of **Tartarus**.
Your choices will define you.
Your actions will become you.
Your wit will keep you from the hordes of the Fallen.

Go forth and survive!

He didn't know what to make of that. By its phrasing it could have been advice, a warning, or a threat. Very likely it was some combination of all three. After he had finished reading it, the message blinked out of his vision, only to be replaced by another message.

Choose your Name:

____

His name? Well, at least that part was easy. His name was...
Uh oh.

His name was a formless sound reverberating off his lips and back down his throat, lost to the interminable void as nebulous as the one he found himself in. He was nameless, no sense of identity, no blueprint, and was startlingly aware of his newfound consciousness. He had no idea who he was or who he should be, or if he should even be anyone at all. If there was a purpose, a reason for his existence, he had no insight.

The message proclaimed the world as Tartarus. The word caused a slight pull inside his mind as though it was a shifting box placed precariously upon a shelf, ready at any moment to tip over and spill its contents. When he tried to draw on that feeling, it slipped away from him, the proverbial box settling into position back on the shelf, far out of his reach. It didn't help him with the problem at hand and the rectangle in front of him was still demanding an answer.

"Can I answer that later?" He clapped both hands over his mouth.

The words had felt strange, new. The act of speaking was familiar, but the words came out like they had never been formed before. He knew how to speak, knew what the words meant, but the sounds his voice made were different. The spoken words were completely foreign to him, like a dialect he'd never encountered of a language he didn't know, but he still knew their meaning. Stranger still, he knew that he had spoken actual words. The sounds had been articulate, precise. Definite words, not garbled nonsense like that of an infant learning to vocalize. The distinction served little to reassure him as he still felt, in that moment, very much like a child, new to the world and incredibly uncertain.

It occurred to him that he might be a child. It also occurred to him that it was strange he knew what a child was.

The box of words before him disappeared, unfilled, and he noticed a small, slowly blinking marker in the corner of his vision. To view it, he had to unfocus his eyes and concentrate, which brought it to the forefront of his vision and the message box reappeared.

Mentally, he willed for the message to disappear again and it faded back to the translucent, slowly blinking box in the corner of his view. Once it disappeared, he was left with a new rectangle that populated his vision.

UNDECIDED	
Level: 1 **Experience to Next Level**: 100 (0%) **Race**: Human **Age**: 27 **Height**: 183 centimeters **Weight**: 77 kilograms	**Profession**: N/A **Trade**: N/A **Traits**: N/A **Companions**: N/A **Adventuring Party**: N/A

Health: 200 / 200 100%	Stamina: 150 / 150 100%	Mana: 100 / 100 100%
Strength: 10 Dexterity: 10 Agility: 10 Fortitude: 10	Endurance: 10 Intelligence: 10 Wisdom: 10 Willpower: 10	Perception: 10 Charisma: 10 Comeliness: 1 Luck: 10

He could only assume this was some sort of profile of himself. It seemed he had been assigned attributes—physical, mental, and others—that had been further quantified down to simple numbers. Twelve sets of numbers seemed hardly capable of encompassing the entirety of a person, but it was as good a place to start as any.

He didn't really know what would encompass the entirety of a person. He did, however, learn some new things about himself. He was apparently twenty-seven, which was not a child. Probably. He was also just over one-hundred-eighty centimeters and weighed nearly eighty kilograms. The only problem being that he had no idea what those units meant.

All of his attributes had started out at ten, which was probably the baseline. Comeliness, however, had started out at a measly one, which he felt was rather unfair. Would a low Comeliness make him ugly or would it make his personality repellant? How was his Comeliness different from his Charisma, which seemed on par with everything else? He had no answers and those were not the only attributes he had questions about, but staring at them wasn't going to allow him any more insight.

With a thought, he closed the menu. In what was beginning to feel like a never-ending sequence of events, a third message box opened itself into his vision.

Inventory	

He was met with ten blank squares. Additionally, there was a silhouette of a person, mostly greyed out with the exception of the shirt and the trousers. He focused his attention on them and was met by two more messages.

Cloth Shirt	**Rarity**: Common **Quality**: Crude **Defense**: 0 **Durability**: 3/3 **Weight**: 0.2 kilograms **Comfort**: Abrasive

Cloth Pants	**Rarity**: Common **Quality**: Crude **Defense**: 0 **Durability**: 3/3 **Weight**: 0.5 kilograms **Comfort**: Abrasive

That explained the itchiness he felt. The stiff fabric resisted him as he moved, brushing against his skin. New clothes would have to be a priority. The zeroes next to 'Defense' gave him pause. What kind of place was this if simple clothes came with an armor rating? It also appeared he had space to store ten things, somehow. First, he had to find something to store. As it was, with the exception of the floating boxes, he was alone in the dark. He minimized the inventory and was met by yet another message.

> *Initializing…*
>
> *Ready for transport.*
>
> *3…*
>
> *2…*
>
> *1…*
>
> **Welcome to Tartarus.**

Chapter 2

A pinprick of light appeared in the darkness, growing swiftly until it consumed him. He clutched at his eyes, pressing his palms against them, but nothing could block out the light. It seared into him, all-consuming. He fell to his knees, curling in on himself as pain shot through his head and radiated down his arms. His throat hummed as he screamed, but he couldn't hear himself over the blood roaring in his ears. Everything was too intense. The light, the ground, even his hands pressed into his face were too much to bear.

Just when he thought he wouldn't be able to take it anymore, it faded. The afterimages of light slowly burned themselves away, giving way to a dim blackness tinged with red. Slowly, hesitantly, he pulled his hands away and tried to open his eyes. At first, he could only manage a crack and even that sent shooting pain into his eyes. With time, however, his eyes grew accustomed to the light. Tears wetted his cheeks, covered his palms.

At last able to see, he took stock of his surroundings. Beams of sunshine streamed through the canopy high above. Flowers spread their petals along the ground before him and insects buzzed around him, alighting on the trunks of enormous trees.

The ground below him was vibrant and full of dark soil. Atop it grew verdant grass, weaving paths of emerald between the trees. Flowers bloomed from the loam and undergrowth. Orange, gold, and purple buds splashed the forest, washing it with color and scent. Each tree soaked in the cool light filtering through the canopy and reflected it, seeming to glow.

The forest was beautiful, but it didn't tell him much. A notification flashed slowly and methodically in the corner of his vision, demanding he name himself, but he ignored it. It felt disingenuous to pick a name when he didn't know the first thing about himself.

He looked down at his hands, seeing the fingers displayed in front of him. His skin was tanned and dusky, his hands soft and free of callouses or markings. His arms, from what he could see, were the same. He placed his hands against the ground, feeling the moisture in the dirt, then pushed himself to his feet. He tottered for a moment, unsteady, then caught his balance. He felt energized, restless.

Not having any preference of direction and not wanting to stay still, he walked straight forward. Hours passed as he trudged through the woods, looking for any semblance of civilization. At the very least, another person to talk to or a body of water, that he might get an idea of what he looked like. The sun angled in the sky, throwing shadows in different directions, but the canopy above blocked out much of the harshness. Now that his eyes were firmly used to the light, the shade was pleasant. Through the gaps in coverage, he could see the blue sky above and the occasional wisp of white clouds.

Everything felt new but familiar, like an old friend he hadn't seen in quite some time whose face had changed with age. The birdsong, the buzzing of insects, the way his legs strained as he hiked up and down the sloped hills of the forest, the dryness of his throat as his body begged for water. Everything made sense and yet he had no idea why or how.

The scratchiness of his clothing was exacerbated by the long walk until he was almost tempted to take them off and walk naked, if not for the occasional gust of wind that sent a chill running through him. As it was, he could feel his skin becoming sensitive as the coarse material rubbed at him over and over again.

He didn't know what to make of any of his surroundings or how to find the water that his body was craving. As distracted as he was by everything, he didn't notice when the birdsong had quieted and he did not know to panic at the sound of silence in the woods, but he would learn.

It was out of sheer luck that he spotted the creature in the edges of his periphery, stalking out of the undergrowth towards him. A wolf; big, brown, and half rotted. Its face was a horror to behold. The left side showed the perfectly normal visage of a snarling wolf but the right was a mess of bone and decayed flesh. Its right eye was missing entirely, replaced by a dim flickering in the hollow recess. It was alone, which was his only cause to be thankful because its single golden eye had locked onto his own and, by the way its skin highlighted its every rib, he had no doubt that he was to be the wolf's next meal.

He did not know how he knew it was a wolf, only had the stupid realization that a wolf was in front of him, a very wrong-looking wolf, and that it was much too close for any comfort. He opened his mouth and spoke the first words that popped into mind, which came dumbly and without emotion.

"That's a wolf. That's not good."

Yellow saliva dripped from the beast's maw as it snarled and frothed, hackles raised. At the sound, his heart panicked and pounded against his ribcage. His mind cried out with fear, his eyes went wide, then he turned and ran into the underbrush, the wolf snarling as it gave chase. He could hear the wolf's guttural rasps over the blood pounding in his ears. The trees blurred as he sprinted past, but despite his best efforts, the wolf gained quickly.

"*Help!* Help me, somebody! *Anybody!* Help me!"

There was no reply, only the wind rushing past him as the wolf bore down on him. Something struck him in the back, knocking him forward onto the ground. He slid across decaying leaves and flipped over a protruding root, landing on his back with a thud. His Health, which appeared suddenly as a red bar at the bottom of his vision, barely noticed, went down by ten points. Before he could react, the wolf was on top of him, bearing down with hot, fetid breath. He brought his hands up on instinct, grabbing for the wolf's head and trying to keep it from tearing into his face. He felt his fingers sink into the creature's exposed throat, pushing past thin membranes of muscle to find esophagus and windpipe. It felt like his hand had been dipped into foul-smelling jelly, but he knew the truth was far worse. Whatever this thing was, it was completely unnatural and it was going to kill him.

Panic flared in his chest as he pushed against the wolf with everything he had. His Stamina, a green bar below his Health, dove toward zero as the muscles in his arms shook. The weight and strength of the surging wolf was too much for him to keep at bay. At any moment, his strength would fail him. The fangs crept closer and closer to his face. At any moment, they would sink into him and shake the very life from his body.

Something shot out of the thicket and whizzed past his head. The wolf let out a grunt, then sagged, no longer straining against him. He pushed it to the side and rolled over, gasping for breath. He laid there, his arms feeling dead as he stared at the wolf in confused horror. Dark blood, nearly black, was leeching from the wolf's body, mixing with the dirt. An arrow protruded from the back of the creature's neck, clearly having separated its spine with a single, well-placed shot.

He gasped for breath as he sat up, looking around for the source of the arrow.

"Some greenstick you are," a feminine voice called out from somewhere ahead of him. "Running afoul of a diseased beast after thundering through the forest like an adolescent rock troll."

He blinked a couple times. Her accent was strange, rhythmic in a way that sounded faintly musical. It took him a few moments to parse out what she had said, which he spent looking around and trying to regain his breath.

"Thank you for saving me," he wheezed once he'd finally worked out her words.

A woman entered his line of sight. Her skin was deeper than bronze, more like cherry wood, with angled features and long, pointed ears that extended up and back. Her hair was dark and came down to her shoulders, tied back to keep out of her face. She was dressed in furs and leathers dyed yellow, green, and brown. Had she been standing still, it would have been nearly impossible to pick her out from the forest surrounding them.

"Do not thank me yet. I put down the beast because she was ill. I have yet to decide about you. Perhaps I should have allowed her a final meal."

He sat up, rubbing his forehead. He felt ridges across his skin, but when he pulled his hands away, there was no blood. He saw the strange woman bend down over the dead wolf and place a hand on its side.

"All the same," he offered. "I live a bit longer thanks to you. I'm sorry, I don't know where I am. I just ended up out here. I know I don't have any right to ask it of you, but could you help me? I don't want to end up as wolf food."

The woman turned toward him and he saw she had green veins patterning her skin. Her eyes were like sparkling emeralds and incredibly intense. As she focused on him, he couldn't help but squirm under the weight of her attention. She still held her bow in one hand as she took him in. As fierce as she looked, there was something in the pull of her face that confused him. A certain softness or loosening around the eyes, some emotion he didn't quite know how to read. It didn't feel overtly dangerous but that fact alone didn't give him any comfort. Somehow, he felt this woman's presence had more intrinsic threat to it than the wolf that had nearly taken his life only moments ago.

"Humans are not welcome in Dawnwood. Still, the fact you have found your way here leaves questions to be answered. There are no human tribes nearby, so either you're a traveler, an adventurer, or a colonizer. In any case, you're as likely to spill your own blood as do anything else."

She had ignored his question or, perhaps, was still pondering it. The possibility of her leaving him behind scared him more than her aggressive attitude. He had to convince her to take him with her.

"You've done me a service. Can I repay you?"

The woman snorted.

"And tell me, Greenstick, what would you do?"

He looked around him, trying to find an answer. He had nothing on his person other than the clothes on his back. He had no skills or trades, no secret knowledge that he could share, nothing at all that would allow him to prove his value to her. His eyes landed on the dead wolf.

"You said the wolf was sick, right? If the other animals eat it, they'd get sick too, wouldn't they? I could help you bury it."

The elven woman cocked her head, narrowing her eyes at him. After several uncomfortable moments in which he held her stare with his own, his breath held firmly in his throat, she turned away.

"Very well, you can carry her for me. Do that properly and there might be a meal in it for you, assuming you're allowed to live."

"Without your help, I'd be dead. At least with you, I have a chance."

The woman snorted again. "You're a strange one, human."

"Yes," he admitted. "I suppose I am. You keep calling me human, but I don't know what you are."

The woman looked back at him in surprise, making him feel like he had said something offensive.

"You really are a greenstick. Never heard of a Daughter of the Forest before? I'm a wood elf."

He gave a weak smile, realizing that there was now very little he could say to keep her from thinking he was an idiot.

"I don't know much of anything. The earliest memories I have are of a few hours ago. I know this world is called Tartarus and I've opened up my profile, but aside from that and, apparently, the powers of speech, I'm...what did you call it? A greenstick? On my own, I'm wolf fodder."

The woman eyed him with suspicion but shrugged and slung her bow across her back. The sight surprised him. Surely she, too, had an inventory? Unless keeping the bow visible was meant to be a threat.

"I don't suppose you have a name, human?"

He grimaced. "I don't, actually."

"Well, greenstick suits you fine for now. You can call me Lyssa, at least until we get back. If Lord Cypress decides you're more trouble than you're worth, you won't have to worry about names. Now, grab the wolf and follow me."

He grabbed the front legs of the wolf and started dragging it along the ground. Lyssa didn't say much more, only telling him not to lag behind before she was off. The wolf was heavy and he had to struggle not to lose sight of her as she crept silently between the trees.

For over an hour, he trudged. His breath came short, his arms and back burned, but through it all there was a sort of giddiness deep down inside. He was alive. He was still alive. Every ache of his body, though unpleasant, reminded him that he had avoided the diseased maw of death. Every step took him closer to more people. People who might be able to explain this strange world and what he was doing in it.

He could see Lyssa glancing back at him every few minutes, though he had no doubt she always knew exactly where he was. His grunting had not exactly been as quiet as he would have hoped. Sometimes she would disappear from his view, at which point he would continue marching as straight a path as he could until he caught sight of her again, which never took long. At last, she appeared in front of him, forcing him to stop.

"You can leave her there. Another hunter will come to collect it. Now, follow me and whatever you do, don't insult anyone. Humans are not welcome here and you would do best not to draw any more unwanted attention to yourself."

He dropped the wolf's carcass with a sigh of relief, then gave Lyssa a friendly smile and gestured for her to lead on. Her eyes narrowed, but she turned and kept walking without further comment.

They approached a huge line of trees that had been grown in a gently sloping curve, like a wall of wooden trunks patched with underbrush. Lyssa walked up to the edge, then lifted her head and called out a few words in a strange language. He looked up to see several elves standing in the boughs of the trees, each of them had drawn bows and had set their sights on him. A chill ran up his spine, but one of the elves called down to Lyssa and, after a brief exchange, the underbrush pulled to the side, forming an archway.

Lyssa stepped behind him, placed a hand on his shoulder, and steered him forward through the arch. He was given the distinct impression that this was not a friendly gesture. Even as they entered the village, he had the feeling bows were still drawn and pointed at his back.

The village itself was incredible. Every structure had been grown out of living trees, woven together over centuries, if not millennia. Natural stairways, pillars, platforms, and bridges were littered throughout, connecting the different facilities to give the impression that the whole village was one massive, living organism.

Several elves sat with feet dangling over edges, high in the air, watching him as he was paraded through the twisting network of roots on the ground. The closer to the center of the village they went, the larger the trees grew until he felt like an ant walking through a world of giants. The canopy above was so high that it was more akin to an emerald sky than something connected to the ground. Stairways had been grown directly from the trees, wrapping around their trunks and leading to the interconnected platforms above. Many of the trees had also been hollowed, the recesses inside providing space for privacy and recreation.

An enormous tree grew in the middle of the village, easily ten times the size of any of the surrounding trees. The striations in its bark looked like a myriad of small pillars holding up a world of foliage. High above there was a natural archway leading into the trunk of the tree, which was where Lyssa was steering him. A staircase ran spiral around the trunk, leading up to the apparent entrance. There were plenty of people in the village, but no children. Most of the elves regarded him with open hostility, narrowing their eyes and baring sharp teeth at him in a way that could not possibly be construed as a smile. Lyssa pushed him along and soon he was up the stairs and inside the enormous tree.

He was in a large, open chamber with an empty, wooden throne at the far end. The walls were decorated with painted vines lashed together into murals depicting life and power. Surrounding the room were elves in shining armor, each glaring at him with unabashed anger. They wielded huge spears and looked more than keen to run him through. Toward the center of the room, a small group of elves in simple robes turned as he walked in, Lyssa still at his back.

She forced him to his knees in front of a tall, regal wood elf.

The elf was dressed in red leathers, a simple crown of wood rested on his brow. Red berries grew from the crown, staining red streaks into his long, brown hair. Though the elf was no larger than any of his attendants, they were all deferent to him.

"Lyssa, you have returned. And not alone."

The elf-lord spoke with a voice like a honeyed cello in the same melodic accent as Lyssa, projecting age, power, and temperament in comparison to the elven attendants who looked on with distaste, awaiting their lord's judgement.

"Lord Cypress, I found this one wandering in our woods, a diseased wolf chasing him. He claims no memories before today and has no name of which to speak. He begged the opportunity to repay me for his life so I have brought him to you for your judgement."

Lord Cypress stared down at him with hard, green eyes.

"My people have seen much in our time. We have seen the devastation wrought by humans, who have no respect for nature. We know you to be a selfish, short-sighted race bent on the destruction of all that we hold dear. By rights, I could have you killed for trespassing our lands."

Lord Cypress paused, a silence that seemed to last forever.

"That said, the actions of a species are not the crimes of an individual, nor are the actions of an individual the crimes of a species. If you truly come in peace, I will give you the opportunity to prove your intentions. No one man can repay the injustices committed against my people by yours. I will, however, allow you to prove yourself to have no ill-will toward me, my people, or this forest."

One of the elves next to Cypress furrowed her brow. She spoke quietly in a strange language, her tone controlled but angry. Lord Cypress responded in the same language, his tone commanding authority. The elves around him lowered their gazes and Cypress turned back to him.

"Do you agree to these terms?"

A message flashed in his vision.

<table>
<tr><td colspan="2" align="center">You have been offered a Quest.</td></tr>
<tr><td colspan="2" align="center">Friends of the Forest</td></tr>
<tr><td colspan="2" align="center">Lord Cypress has given you the opportunity to prove your worth to Dawnwood Village. You must accompany Lyssa on a quest given to her by Lord Cypress.</td></tr>
<tr><td align="center">Objectives
- Help Lyssa complete her quest</td><td align="center">Rewards
- 1,000 Experience
- Improved Relation with Dawnwood Village</td></tr>
<tr><td colspan="2" align="center">Failure or Refusal
- Exile from Dawnwood Village
- Possible death by execution</td></tr>
<tr><td colspan="2" align="center">Accept this Quest?</td></tr>
<tr><td align="center">Yes</td><td align="center">No</td></tr>
</table>

Briefly taken aback, he thought about it. To deny the help of the elves would almost certainly bring him to an early death in the forest and that was only if they didn't kill him outright. Clearly humans were not welcome. To help the elves would at least allow him a place to stay and an opportunity to learn about the world. It was a choice only in the abstract sense of the convention, as what he was really choosing between was life or death. As such, there really was only one option available to him.

The message disappeared as he resolved to help.

"Lord Cypress, thank you for the opportunity. I will try not to disappoint you. What do you need me to do?"

Lord Cypress turned his gaze toward Lyssa.

"As you have yet to complete the task I asked of you, you will take this human to accompany you. See to it that he is provisioned and prepared for your journey."

Lyssa made a sound like she was about to protest, but the look on Lord Cypress's face bore no room for dissent.

"Yes, my lord. I will see it done."

The elf lord nodded once, then raised a hand. Lyssa grabbed his shoulder and hauled him to his feet. He was steered out of the room, but before they left, one of the guards at the entrance muttered something in their strange language. He didn't have to speak it to know it was an insult. Lyssa didn't respond and they emerged into the glittering sunlight. He turned toward Lyssa to thank her but stopped when he saw her face. It had hardened into impassivity, but there was an undercurrent of rage, there. He felt it flow from her in a wave, strong enough to set his teeth on edge.

"Did I do something wrong?"

Her eyes cut toward him and, despite himself, he flinched. For a moment he thought she would rip his throat out like the rabid wolf. Then, with a deep breath, she visibly calmed herself.

"No. At least, not yet. My anger is not at you, Greenstick. Come on, let's get you some real clothes."

Chapter 3

Hadespera
The 1ˢᵗ of Elaphebolion
The Year 4631 in the Era of Mortals

He found himself being poked and prodded at by an elven woman who clearly had no interest in the concept of personal space. All the while, she berated him in the language of the elves. At first, he had tried to apologize for the inconvenience, but upon the first syllable, she lightly smacked him on the cheek with the back of her hand, so he decided to take the beratement in graceful silence. Or, at least, as graceful as he could manage with spindly fingers poking him and a notched cord examining his *every* measure.

When the torment was over, he breathed a sigh of relief and collapsed to the ground near a wall. The elf woman whisked off to attend to matters completely foreign to him. Lyssa, on the other hand, had apparently recovered from whatever had bothered her and her eyes shone with mirth as she looked upon his misfortune.

"At least one of us enjoyed that," he said with a scowl.

"Navinia takes her craft seriously, but she and many others here have no love for humans."

"So I've heard. You'll have to tell me why, some time."

"Let's find out if you live first, Greenstick."

"Fair enough."

Before long, Navinia had returned with two bundles of clothes in her hands. She handed both to him.

Dawnwood Linen Shirt	**Rarity**: Common **Quality**: Excellent **Defense**: 1 **Durability**: 15/15 **Weight**: 0.3 kilograms **Comfort**: Soft **Armor Type**: Clothing

Dawnwood Linen Pants	**Rarity**: Common **Quality**: Excellent **Defense**: 1 **Durability**: 15/15 **Weight**: 0.6 kilograms **Comfort**: Soft **Armor Type**: Clothing

Dawnwood Leather Boots	**Rarity**: Common **Quality**: Excellent **Defense**: 3 **Durability**: 20/20 **Weight**: 1.5 kilograms **Comfort**: Good-Fit **Armor Type**: Light

Dawnwood Leather Jerkin	**Rarity**: Common **Quality**: Excellent **Defense**: 7 **Durability**: 45/45 **Weight**: 4 kilograms **Comfort**: Good-Fit **Armor Type**: Light

Dawnwood Leather Greaves	**Rarity**: Common **Quality**: Excellent **Defense**: 4 **Durability**: 25/25 **Weight**: 1.4 kilograms **Comfort**: Good-Fit **Armor Type**: Light

Dawnwood Leather Vambraces	**Rarity**: Common **Quality**: Excellent **Defense**: 4 **Durability**: 25/25 **Weight**: 1.1 kilograms **Comfort**: Good-Fit **Armor Type**: Light

Focusing on each item gave a prompt, asking if he would like to equip the item. He accepted each and was soon wearing an outfit that looked very similar to Lyssa's, though hers was clearly of much higher quality. The cloth shirt and pants he'd worn were relocated to his inventory, but Navinia held out her hands for them. He handed them over without complaint and the elf woman walked off, muttering disdainfully.

He turned to Lyssa; arms held out to either side.

"How do I look?"

"Like a babe in his father's shoes."

She must have seen his deflated expression because she laughed. The sound didn't last long, but it was surprisingly pleasant.

"You'll get used to them, Greenstick. Now, are you ready for weapons?"

"Weapons?"

"Of course. This isn't some romantic walk through the woods or whatever your human women do. There will be danger and fighting."

He wasn't sure how to respond to that, so he nodded and let her lead the way. They walked down a long stairway until they reached the ground, then Lyssa led him to a training area. A score of archery targets were set at varying distances, some so far away that he had to squint just to find them. Several elves populated the area, practicing with swords, pikes, axes, and a variety of other weapons that he couldn't put a name to.

"I take it you're unaccustomed to such things," Lyssa remarked.

"I'm unaccustomed to everything," he said absently, spinning in slow circles and trying to take everything in.

"Let's see how you do with a bow."

He was led to one of the archery stands and a shortbow was placed in his hands. The wood was smooth, but the weapon felt odd in his grip. Archaic.

"Do you know with which eye you focus? Beginners always have one or the other."

"I don't. How do you tell?"

"A simple trick, hold on."

She backed up until she was about five strides away.

"There, now put your hands together like this." She placed her hands in front of her, arms outstretched, such that her fingers and thumbs interlocked to form a small triangle. "Hold it out so that you can see me through the gap, then bring it closer to your face, keeping me in sight the whole time."

He followed her instructions until his hands were resting against his face, his left eye completely obscured by his hand.

` "There, you're right-eyed. That means you'll want to hold the bow in your left hand, like so."

Lyssa drew her own bow and stood so that he could see exactly how she held it.

"Put your feet like this, stand sidelong your target, place the arrow such that the third fletch points away from the bow, pull to your cheek, breathe, release."

She narrated each of her actions in turn. The closest target, which was twenty paces at a glance, was left unmarred as the arrow soared over it and hit the target placed seventy paces away, neatly pinning the bullseye.

"You hold the bow in your other hand," he pointed out.

"Keenly observed. Unlike you, I'm left-eyed."

"But you just shot with your right eye."

Lyssa patted him on the head and gave him a pitying smile.

"Because I'm not a beginner, Greenstick. Now, no more blabbing. Time to practice. Shoot until your arm hurts, then we will run you through swords."

He paused, an arrow on its way to his bowstring from a standing quiver nearby.

"You mean through the exercises, right? You're not actually going to run swords through me...right?"

Lyssa did not deign to respond, instead she stood in the archery line next to him and sent arrows downrange. He sighed and tried to draw the bowstring. The arrow felt wobbly, as though it was about to fall off the string. He fumbled his hand position as he tried to get his fingers in the right position.

"Stop, you've loaded it wrong."

He hadn't noticed that Lyssa had stopped shooting to start critiquing him again. She took the arrow from him and placed it on the other side of the bow, the far side from him.

"If it stays on the close side, you'll have to adjust your hand after you nock it or turn your hand upside down as you draw, which is too advanced for you at this stage. That wastes time. Nock it to the far side of the bow and you'll be able to draw it in the same motion. There, now keep one finger above and your other two below. Your thumb should stay out of the way, or it'll knock the arrow off its path. Some methods use your thumb, but again, they are too advanced for you at this stage."

He paused and held up a hand.

"What about my pinkie?"

"Your what?"

"My little finger."

Lyssa stared at him, then brought her own hand up to show a thumb and three fingers.

"I...didn't know humans had another finger. What do you need four fingers for? Three's the perfect number for firing a bow."

"I don't know. To hold things? To stick out while drinking? I don't...I don't know why I just said that, actually."

"Just keep it out of the way. If you're being taught by an elf, you'll learn like an elf. Since you can't have the decency to possess a proper number of fingers, we'll see if we can still make a decent shot out of you."

He pulled the string back to his cheekbone, which was apparently too high as Lyssa grabbed his elbow and lowered it until his hand was resting against his jaw.

"Now aim. At your height and at this distance, you'll want to aim for the top circle of the target, or else your arrow might snag a worm as it skips over the ground."

He let out his breath and released the string. The arrow wobbled a little in flight but sunk into the very bottom of the target. It was well outside the target lines but he was thrilled to have hit something at all. A notification appeared.

You have learned a **Skill**.

Archery — Level 7

Defeat your foes at a distance or dazzle your rivals by shooting them through their axes.

Each level in this skill will improve your ability with ranged weapons of all kinds.

+2% Damage with Ranged Weapons (+14%)
+2% Accuracy with Ranged Weapons (+14%)
+1% Range with Ranged Weapons (+7%)

Instruction by an Adept Archer has improved your starting level.

His jaw dipped a little further with each word he read, still trying to comprehend what it all meant.

"I learned a skill," he said absently, still reading through the notification.

"As well you should have," Lyssa replied. "Most things you do will result in skills. The higher you level the skill, the better you are at the task. Sometimes the requirements for learning a skill are tricky to discover, but once unlocked, the task itself becomes easier. My own ability with the bow should have helped, what level did you start at?"

"Seven. My notification also called you an 'Adept Archer,' what's that mean?"

"Seven? Not the highest it could have been but at least you were paying attention. Every ten levels of a skill are given a rank to identify your relative skill-level without giving away your direct abilities. 'Adept' means that my level is in the seventies."

His eyes widened at that. "That must have taken a long time to get so high. What's the highest?"

Lyssa shrugged. "A couple centuries. Progress slows the higher you get, but some dedicated individuals can reach the rank of Legend, levels ninety through ninety-nine. Some tales tell of great heroes that could increase their abilities past that, but no one knows how or if it's even true. Right now, you should worry about trying to get your skills to at least level ten. That will break you from Beginner and put you into the Novice ranks. Should take a few hours, with instruction."

He looked down at the bow.

"Thank you. I doubt I have any real idea how valuable your instruction is but I am grateful for it all the same."

"The more detailed instruction I give, the more it increases my own Teaching skill, as well as a small bonus to the relevant skill being taught. I've heard some create institutions where they teach as many people as possible to try to increase their own abilities. If you ask me, it's just to line their pockets. Humans especially will pay exorbitant fees for the promise of faster progress. Fools. You won't learn without doing and experimenting. No more talk. Practice."

He drew another arrow from the standing quiver and was shocked at how much more natural the motion felt. The arrow felt right in his hands and the bow held firm. As he nocked the arrow to the string, he drew the bow up level and pulled the string back to his jaw. He let out his breath and released, taking care not to nudge the arrow as he did.

It flew and landed in the outermost ring, well off to the right of the bullseye, but he was ecstatic.

"I hit it! Did you see that?"

"Indeed. Next time, see if you can work it toward the center."

Three hours passed at the archery range, with the only breaks being when Lyssa critiqued his form and when they stopped to drink from a refreshment table set up nearby. When they had finished, the sun was nearing the horizon and his archery skill had increased up to Level Ten. It came with an unexpected bonus.

Archery has increased to **Level 10**.

+2% Damage with Ranged Weapons (+20%)
+2% Accuracy with Ranged Weapons (+20%)
+1% Range with Ranged Weapons (+10%)

You have reached the **Novice** rank in **Archery**.
You gain 100 experience.

You have reached **Level 2**.

As a **Human**, you receive 5 attribute points to distribute per level.

A sudden glow enveloped him. He felt a wash of golden light as all the sweat and aches of the day faded away. Even his hunger, which had started to reach the gnawing point, was gone. His shock must have shown on his face, because Lyssa took one look at him and laughed.

"Hah! You really were a greenstick. Was that the first time you've leveled up?"

He nodded, too dumbfounded to speak.

"Well, don't stand there slack-jawed, a bird will come roost in your mouth. We still have more of the day to make use of and you haven't gotten to swords yet. You can adjust your profile tonight; I wager you'll want to put some thought into where you assign your points."

"What are the best things to invest in?" he asked, feeling completely lost.

"That's entirely dependent on what you want to do with your life, though I would highly suggest paying close attention to the things that will keep you alive. What's more, to help guide your choice, you can increase nearly all of your attributes through training in addition to leveling, but you won't receive the bonus for those increases until after you sleep."

"Thanks. I suppose I'll need to give this some thought."

"Don't frown, this is a good thing, Greenstick. It means you won't be a greenstick forever."

"I do need to come up with a name, don't I?" he said wryly.

"I don't know, Greenstick suits you. It's good enough for me at least. Let's get some food. You may not be hungry anymore, but I'm starving. Swords can wait until after dinner."

Dinner was held in a communal area high in the hanging village. A wooden platform had been built out of the convergence of three trees, leaving enough space for large tables to be laid out, buffet style. The food consisted mostly of salads and cooked meat, though he spotted some stews and soups among the mix as well. Several elves came and went; some grabbed food and sat down, often chatting amongst friends, while others picked up their food and left. He filled a wooden plate with salad and a large slab of steak, then sat down across from Lyssa at a table all to themselves. She made no objection, despite the dirty looks many of the other elves were throwing his way.

"I have some questions, if you don't mind," he said after a few bites.

"Ask them and see, Greenstick."

A million questions ran through his head about the world and everything in it, but none of the most pressing questions passed his tongue in that moment. Instead, the one that came first was quite a bit more personal than he intended.

"Why don't elves like humans?"

Lyssa's face fell and her shoulders tensed. He backpedaled immediately.

"Sorry, bad question. You don't have to answer that."

Her face relaxed somewhat, but she was still tense, so he started searching for a new question.

"When I leveled up, I was told I got five attribute points to spend as a human. Do elves get a different amount?"

"Every race is different, and many subraces have their own natural specializations. Children of the Forest, like myself, get six points to distribute, but one is automatically put into Dexterity and Perception, so we have four to place where we wish. Children of the Stars, as another example, also get six, with one placed into Intelligence and Wisdom. Orcs generally get seven, with four points evenly split between Strength and Fortitude."

"That's fascinating. I don't know what all of those are, but still. Can I ask you about the journey you've been tasked with? Since I'm to help you and all, maybe I should know something about what we're doing."

"Lord Cypress has sent me to check on a disturbance we've noticed. Dawnwood is our domain, but we've received reports of something sinister building outside of it to the west. My task is to find it, observe it, and stop it if I'm able."

"He must have a lot of trust in you to send you alone to do such a thing."

"He isn't sending me alone. He's sending you with me as well. Danger is inherent in Tartarus. No place can guarantee safety, only your own strength and the bonds you make can imply it."

"So the reason you've been teaching me is..."

"Because not only will you be protecting your own life with the skills you learn, but you'll be protecting mine. Don't mistake this for trust, Greenstick, you haven't earned that. However, you have done three things that work to your favor." Lyssa held up her three fingers, keeping her thumb tucked in. "You showed wisdom and respect to nature by wanting to dispose of the diseased wolf."

Lyssa dropped one finger.

"You showed respect to Lord Cypress."

She dropped another finger.

"You have listened to my instructions without complaint or deceit."

She dropped her final finger.

"Make no mistake, I'll be watching you, and if you lead me to believe you're a danger to myself, my people, or the Dawnwood, I'll put you down like the wolf this morning."

He put up his hands in mock surrender.

"You don't have to worry about me. You saved my life. I haven't forgotten. And I don't have any reason to betray your people."

"Good, now that that's cleared, are you ready for your sword training?"

He pushed away his plate and stood up.

"More than ready. Shall we?"

Chapter 4

Hadespera
The 1ˢᵗ of Elaphebolion
The Year 4631 in the Era of Mortals

"Ough!"

He hit the ground face first, feeling the dirt ingrain itself into his cheek. His arms and legs burned, red welts littering his exposed skin. The wooden practice sword lay just beyond his fingers, dropped after Lyssa had struck the back of his hand. She had called it a xiphos when pointing out different swords to him. He grabbed the weapon and forced himself back to his feet, only to see Lyssa striking forward again. He quickly brought the sword up to parry but she changed directions, now attacking from the side. He tried to duck but was again too slow and the flat side of her blade slammed against his head.

His vision went black. When it cleared, he was on the ground again.

"You certainly know how to take a beating, Greenstick. You sure you don't want to do this more often?"

He didn't dignify the jibe with a response. Instead, he retrieved his sword and stood once more. A few of the other elves stopped practicing to come and watch. He couldn't understand their language, but he didn't have to know the words to know they were jeering at him.

Very near the beginning of their exercise, after Lyssa had shown him some footwork and hand positions associated with elven swordplay, he had received the skill 'Swordsmanship,' which had helped his learning curve immensely. He had also learned that Lyssa was a Proficient Swordswoman, meaning her skill level was somewhere in the forties. His own skill had started at three and, since he'd received it, Lyssa had stated the best learning was through practice and had been sparring with him nonstop.

Swordsmanship was not the only lesson here. She was testing him. This was a world of violence and pain; he had been told as much several times. She wanted to see how he would react to an adversary he couldn't hope to beat. She wanted to see if he would break, if he would cower, or if he would keep fighting. She wanted to see what kind of person he really was.

So did he.

He took a moment to center himself, breathing deeply through his nose before letting the air out of his mouth. He balled his fist and hit the ground, centering himself around the impact. Something in his core reacted to the sensation, spiraling through him. He lost himself in determination. His body shook with pain, but he would not let himself be consumed by it. Energy blossomed from his chest, flooding out to every extremity. Heat washed over him and with it came solidity.

He was stone.

A surprise gust rippled the grass around the training area in the light of the setting sun. The zephyr tickled his skin and he felt an almost electric spark in his muscles as he absorbed the feeling into memory. A shiver ran up his spine.

He was wind.

Warmth burgeoned through his body, unrelated to the pain of the strikes he had endured. It started in his lower chest, then spread out to his fingers and toes until the wind no longer chilled his skin.

He was fire.

Back on his feet, Lyssa approached once more. She snaked from side to side, seeking weaknesses and finding plenty in his ineptitude. By this point, he knew how she liked to attack. Her misdirections and clever feints. She would not expect him to have some of his own, so he did the thing he thought she would most expect.

He charged her.

Lyssa met his advance. The distance closed between them. He led with a thrust, the most straightforward attack he could think of, but one that would be expected of a Beginner. As soon as he felt her blade begin to move his off-line, he twisted with the motion, planting his lead foot and spinning off it. He left the ground, using his momentum to bring a tornado kick aimed at Lyssa's head. In that moment, he was victory.

The blow never landed.

Lyssa ducked the kick effortlessly and capitalized on his failure by striking him twice across the back and legs before he landed. The stinging blows made him stumble, forcing him to his knees as he hit the ground, fingers digging into the dirt to keep from landing on his face again. When he turned to face Lyssa, she held her hand up to signal a halt. The other elves dispersed now that the fight was over, muttering to themselves in their own language.

"What was that?" Lyssa's eyes shone with genuine curiosity.

He shrugged. The feeling that had surged within him had faded, leaving him tired and sore.

"I don't know. It just felt like the right thing to do in the moment."

"It was a surprise, I'll give you that. I hope you also learned that it didn't work and would have left you crippled had our fight been real."

He nodded, a grim smile on his face. She caught his eye, then returned his smile with a genuine one. He felt relief flood through him. She had understood what he had been trying to show her and, by the look of it, she approved. He looked up at the sky, almost hidden by the canopy above. Night was coming quickly, hardly noticed for the glowing stones that lit up the structures above them and the wood of the trees themselves, which glowed softly with captured light. Lyssa let him marvel at the sight for a few moments before speaking up.

"That's enough for today. It's time to rest. Tomorrow, we set out. We will train as we go, you are still weak."

He was led to a small, ground-level, hollow tree that apparently functioned as a guest house. Inside were several beds, but none were occupied. He was left alone. The inside of this tree did not glow, as some of the others did, and the only light source was the red, bioluminescent moss that grew high above, casting a gentle light down upon him. He sat down on the bed and decided it was high time he had taken a more in-depth look at his profile. First, he had his swordsmanship gains to go through.

Swordsmanship has increased to **Level 5**.

Many a tale has been told of this glorified sidearm, ensure yours is a long one.

Each level in this skill will improve your ability with swords of all kinds.

+2% Damage with Swords (+10%)

<table>
<tr><td colspan="3" align="center">**UNDECIDED**</td></tr>
<tr>
<td>

Level: 2
Experience to Next Level: 200 (0%)
Race: Human
Age: 27
Height: 183 centimeters
Weight: 77 kilograms

</td>
<td colspan="2">

Profession: N/A
Trade: N/A
Traits: N/A
Companions: N/A
Adventuring Party: N/A

</td>
</tr>
<tr><td colspan="3" align="center">You have 5 undistributed attribute points</td></tr>
<tr>
<td align="center">

Health: 200 / 200
100%

</td>
<td align="center">

Stamina: 150 / 150
100%

</td>
<td align="center">

Mana: 100 / 100
100%

</td>
</tr>
<tr>
<td align="center">

Strength: 10
Dexterity: 10
Agility: 10
Fortitude: 10

</td>
<td align="center">

Endurance: 10
Intelligence: 10
Wisdom: 10
Willpower: 10

</td>
<td align="center">

Perception: 10
Charisma: 10
Comeliness: 1
Luck: 10

</td>
</tr>
</table>

He was relieved to find that the few points of damage he had taken throughout the day, especially during the training, had healed. He hadn't been sure how quickly his minor injuries would heal, but it seemed a short amount of time and access to food was enough. His arms and legs were still covered in small, red welts that were painful to the touch, but he was glad to see that it wouldn't have a larger effect on his overall Health. Larger injuries, he was sure, would require some kind of treatment.

The unspent attribute points stared at him, begging to be assigned. Before he did that, however, he needed to know what each attribute did in further detail. He focused on his Strength attribute and tried to conjure more information about it. To his surprise, he was met with a notification.

Strength

The physical capacity to exert great force or pressure on an object or substance.

Minor effect on **Health**.
Abilities with melee weapons often rely on Strength.

It seemed pretty self-explanatory, if a little clinical. The boost to health was unexpected, but greatly appreciated. Strength seemed to be an all-around bonus, especially if he was going to get in close fights.

Dexterity

The nimbleness of extremities and accuracy of small, quick movements.

Abilities with ranged weapons often rely on Dexterity.

That was promising. Archery was his highest skill at the moment and it seemed Dexterity was directly related. The increase to coordination might have allowed him to keep his footing in swordplay, as well.

Agility

Determines physical speed and reaction times.

Speed would always be useful and reaction times could very well save his life. Even though there was no other impact to his abilities, Agility was on the contender list.

Fortitude

The hardiness of one's body to protect against detrimental effects.

Health regenerates at a rate of Fortitude per hour.
Major effect on **Health**.
Minor effect on **Stamina**.

Two direct effects on his vitals, and one of them was directly responsible for keeping him alive. He was tempted to immediately put points into Fortitude, not wanting to risk going a moment longer with the chance a low health might take this fresh gift of life from him. The impulse faded quickly. He was safe, in a village that could have easily killed him before now and could continue to do so regardless of how many points he had in Fortitude. He was not in immediate danger. He could at least wait until he had examined the rest of his attributes.

Endurance

Determines how long the body can exert itself.

Stamina regenerates at a rate of Endurance per minute.
Major effect on **Stamina**.
Minor effect on **Health**.

Another double vital gain. Endurance, it seemed, was the natural counterpart to Fortitude and was another enticing attribute to invest in.

Intelligence

The quickness and ease at which one learns and remembers.

Major effect on **Mana**.

He frowned. He had seen Mana before, twice now, as a number on his profile along with Health and Stamina, but he was no closer to understanding what it meant. It was bolded on the notification, so he focused on the word.

Mana

The ability to channel magical energies and the mystic arts.

Used to cast **spells** and is used by some **skills** and **abilities**.

That sounded much more promising, but he didn't know any magic. He wondered if improving his learning rate would improve the rate at which he leveled his skills but decided he could ask Lyssa about that later if the opportunity presented itself.

Wisdom

The inferences one makes when forced to make connections between that which is known and that which is unknown.

Mana regenerates at a rate of Wisdom per minute.

It seemed Wisdom was the natural counterpart to Intelligence, similar to how Endurance was to Fortitude. It seemed odd to be able to artificially improve his mental faculties but, after a few moments thought, it was no less odd than the ability to suddenly improve his physical attributes without exercising.

Willpower

The resiliency of one's mind; the ability to endure horror without breaking.

Spellpower and the strength of some **skills** and **abilities** rely on Willpower.

That was disconcerting. How common were atrocities that the ability to withstand them was a core attribute? The increase to spellpower was nice, but he had to wonder if that bonus was due to his mind being supposedly stronger or if it was because mages commonly endured horror. He didn't currently know any spells, so he hoped it was the former in the event he ever got the opportunity to learn.

Perception

The ability to notice that which is hidden.

He frowned at that. It seemed like a vague attribute, especially when compared to clearer attributes such as Dexterity or Agility. Would it improve his natural eyesight or would he just notice more? It was hard to tell.

Charisma

The ability to influence those around you in ways that may be beneficial to you.

His frown deepened. *'May'* be beneficial? As in, could be detrimental? Would having a high Charisma cause people to act in extremes around him? It seemed like a risk, but he couldn't deny that it was potentially powerful. After all, connections saved lives in Tartarus. His connection with Lyssa had saved him from dying a gruesome death to a half-decayed wolf in the forest that morning.

Comeliness

Alters your physical self to reflect your mental image of yourself.

He discarded that one almost immediately. He didn't know who he was yet, so his mental image of himself was blank. It occurred to him that he still didn't know what he looked like, which was likely why his Comeliness was so low.

Luck

Affects your ability to find treasure, discover weak points in your enemies, stumble upon rare and exciting things…or do none of these.

In other words, a gamble. He smiled, not expecting anything less of an attribute as abstract and nebulous as one called Luck. It was a strange thought that he would be able to directly influence his luck. Was the existence of such an attribute a manifestation of fate, or some walking chaos theory that his intent, via this attribute, had a tangible, random effect on the world around him?

He blinked. Where the hell had those thoughts come from?

He pushed it from his mind and went back to his profile. If he was being honest, he wanted to put points in all of the attributes, but something else Lyssa said wandered into his mind.

"You can increase nearly all of your attributes through practice in addition to leveling, but you won't receive the bonus for those increases until after you sleep."

It had been an extremely trying day. Between running for his life in the woods and practicing with Lyssa, he was certain there would be some changes come the following morning. It would be remiss of him to assign his attribute points before seeing how his scores naturally progressed.

With this thought affixed in his mind, he opened up his equipment list and doffed his armor. With it safely to rest in his inventory, he crawled onto one of the beds and nestled himself beneath the blankets.

A soft light filtered through openings in the tree above. From his vantage, he could see the light of two glowing moons above, one blue and one green, giving off a mixed glow. The bed felt like a sheet pulled over pine straw, but it was soft and comforting, and within moments he was fast asleep.

Ψ

In his dreams, he was being chased by tall, willowy beings wielding sticks. When he stopped, they beat him, forcing him to keep running on and on in an endless circle. When he finally collapsed, exhausted and crying, they stood around him, some pointing and laughing as others continued to beat him. One of the figures loomed over him and he saw a pair of enormous, emerald eyes. It reached for him, but before it touched him, he woke.

Ψ

Light streamed through the opening in the tree. Judging by the soft glow and the gentle bleariness he felt, he wagered it was dawn. His next thought was confusion, as he didn't know *how* he knew it was dawn if he had never seen one before.

He stopped himself from falling down that pit of questioning as he knew there were no answers. He was going to drive himself mad if he questioned every new thing he was already familiar with. Instead, he turned his attention to a softly blinking icon in the corner of his vision that alerted him to pending notifications.

Your attributes have increased.

+1 Strength
+1 Dexterity
+1 Agility
+1 Fortitude
+1 Endurance
+1 Intelligence
+1 Wisdom

He had to fight off his own surprise. He had expected a raise in a couple attributes, namely Endurance and Fortitude, but what he had received seemed ridiculous. He sat staring at the prompt for several minutes before finally dismissing it. The only explanation he could think of was that because his stats had started at ten, they were at the most basic level, Comeliness aside. That meant that they were easier to train up, having started so low. The higher they got, the harder they would probably be to train. It wouldn't make sense to be able to do the same workout every day and continue improving his attributes to infinity. The thought made him pause. Was there a cap on how high his attributes could grow? He shook his head. Too little information.

That left him with the next problem: if they were easier to train at lower levels, should he even distribute his attribute points at all? Or should he hold on to the points and try to work on his attributes through training before he assigned anything.

The two ideologies warred in his mind, but a solution came to him rather quickly. He was here to survive, to learn more about himself, and to find out what kind of world he'd landed in. He knew the path ahead was dangerous. If he was going to survive, he needed to be strong now. He would have to think in the short term in order to see the long term.

He summoned his profile and focused on the attributes he desired. He placed two points into Strength, one into Fortitude, one into Willpower, and one into Perception. Then, he examined his stats again.

Health: 240 / 240 100%	Stamina: 170 / 170 100%	Mana: 110 / 110 100%
Strength: 13 Dexterity: 11 Agility: 11 Fortitude: 12	Endurance: 11 Intelligence: 11 Wisdom: 11 Willpower: 11	Perception: 11 Charisma: 10 Comeliness: 1 Luck: 10

His muscles felt a little more toned than they had been the day before, his mind a little sharper. Whether it was real or in his head, he didn't know, but he felt better, despite the aches. He equipped his armor and left the guest house to find Lyssa approaching. He waved at her. She cocked her head at the gesture, frowning. Feeling awkward, he put his hand down.

"It's a form of greeting," he said hesitantly. "I think."

"Oh," she replied, before raising her own hand and dropping it as he had done. "Curious."

"Anyway," he said, hoping to change the subject. "When are we leaving?"

"Now. Put this on." She tossed a backpack at him.

Dutifully, he slipped it on. It was so light, he thought it was empty, but with Lyssa's prodding he checked his inventory, finding that the space of the backpack also appeared. It was a five-by-ten square pack filled with food, gear, and weaponry. Specifically, in regard to the latter, it had a shortbow, three quivers of arrows, and a xiphos.

"Come on, Greenstick, daylight's wasting," Lyssa said in response to his slack jawed expression as he processed what had just been given to him.

He startled, nodded, and followed Lyssa through the township. As they walked, he noticed none of the other elves were interested in seeing them off. In fact, the others actually seemed to be averting their gazes as he and Lyssa walked by. He also noticed, again, that there were no children in the village.

"Why do I get the feeling I'm not the sole cause of their animosity?"

Lyssa did not reply. She was straight-backed as she walked with him through the village. She did not look at the other elves, nor did she offer any of them greetings. Feeling it was the wrong time to pry, he kept quiet and hurried along.

They exited Dawnwood Village and entered the forest proper. He felt the eyes of the elves following them, felt the weight of whispers and mutterings even though he couldn't understand them. Once the tree wall was out of sight, Lyssa seemed to breathe more easily. It was a few minutes longer before she said anything.

"You are right that you are not the only one the people of my village distrust."

He frowned but didn't know what to say. Seeing that no response was forthcoming, Lyssa continued.

"Years ago, I committed a crime against my people. Do not ask me what it was. Just know that even if we accomplish our task, your association with me will mean that the others won't ever truly accept you into their society, even if they could look past your humanity. I understand if you harbor resentment toward me for that but understand I have no control over the matter."

He stroked his chin, feeling ridges beneath his fingertips.

"Fuck that."

Lyssa blinked at him in surprise. "What?"

"So you did something bad a long time ago and now they're holding it over your head forever? Fuck that. You saved me when it would have been easier for you to let the wolf have me and finish it off later. You brought me before Lord Cypress and advocated for me on my behalf when you didn't have to. You trained me, gave me equipment, and even gave me a nickname when I was nothing and no one. You accepted a mission for the betterment of your village despite knowing it would be dangerous, even deadly. If that's all that you've done for me in just one day, then I can't imagine what you've done for the village over the years and if they can't see that then *fuck them.*"

Lyssa let out a short laugh, filled with stress and genuine surprise.

"I don't think we use that term quite the same way you do."

He smiled back.

"It's versatile, like me. Now, I know you know a whole lot more about...well, everything than I do, but right now my job is to help you. So"—he held out his hand—"partners?"

She reached past his hand and clasped his forearm. "Partners."

To his surprise, a notification appeared.

Lyssanderyli has accepted your **Companion Request**.

As **Companions**, you will be able to share experience earned from killing while in close proximity, regardless of contribution. As your bond grows, you will be able to share more with each other over longer distances.

The bond between **Companions** supersedes those formed by **Adventuring Parties**.

Lyssa caught her breath and, as he glanced at her, he saw that her eyes were unfocused, staring off into empty space. For the first time, he was able to see what it looked like when someone else was reading a notification.

"Dawnwood hasn't had a Companionship form in centuries," she breathed.

"We...we didn't just get married, did we?"

Lyssa's eyes refocused to reality. More specifically, they focused on him and they were angry. She pulled her hand away and clenched it into a fist.

"We most certainly did not."

He threw up his hands and took a step back.

"All right, all right. Just checking. I'm like a newborn, a baby in dad-shoes, remember? I don't know these things."

She scoffed, but her ire dissipated.

"So," he said, hoping to move on. "What exactly does a Companionship mean for us?"

"It means we are bound by goals and motivations. It means we cannot betray one another without the other learning of it. We are aspída-adélfia, in the Elven tongue. Shield-kin."

He frowned, trying to make sense of it. "Does that make us siblings, of a sort?"

Lyssa screwed up her face. "I think for now you should try to understand it as friends who fight for one another."

"That, I can do." He gave her a wicked smile. "Lyssanderyli."

A sword appeared in her hand.

"But I wouldn't call you that, of course. Lyssa fits you *so* much better."

The sword disappeared and he let out a sigh of relief. Lyssa rolled her eyes and muttered something in Elvish that, though he couldn't understand it, certainly sounded like *'men.'*

"You will need to pick a name for yourself, Greenstick. Unless you wish to introduce yourself to the world by the title of how little you know."

He sighed. "I know, but every time I try to think about what my name should be, I draw a complete blank. There's just nothing there. I feel like I'm beating my head against a wall."

"Would you accept a name given by another?"

"You're not going to name me Greenstick, are you?"

"No. You are not an elf so I cannot give you a true elven name. Perhaps I can name you something from our philosophy. You are a new beginning. A primal point, from which anything may follow. As such, I name you Arche."

"Arche," he said the name slowly, sounding it out. "Arr-key."

Something about it felt right. He opened his pending notification.

Choose your Name:
<u>**Arche**</u>

He was Arche.

"Thank you, Lyssa."

Chapter 5

The next several days of their journey fell into a routine. They walked all day, sparred in the evening, and occasionally Lyssa would leave to hunt. Arche's Swordsmanship skill improved another three levels, putting it at Level Eight. The journeying and training were not without their own benefits, as his attributes showed. By their fourth day of travel, he'd progressed significantly from his first day waking up in the forest.

Your attributes have increased.

+1 Strength
+1 Dexterity
+1 Fortitude
+2 Endurance

As they approached evening, Lyssa signaled a halt and crouched low to the ground, her bow materializing in her hand. Arche followed suit, pulling his own bow out of his inventory and nocking an arrow to it. He had taken to carrying his sword on his hip and a quiver across his back, as retrieving items from his inventory was too slow for him to do quickly. He was not nearly as proficient at manipulating the inventory system as Lyssa was, but he was still uncomfortable carrying the bow strung over his shoulder.

"Wolves," Lyssa whispered. "Three of them."

A tinge of fear crept up Arche's back. Images of the half-rotted wolf's face floated in his mind's eye.

"What's the plan?"

"They've caught our scent and seem hungry enough to risk hunting us. You can't outrun them; we'll have to fight. Aim for the one on the right, be ready to draw your sword."

Arche peeked around a tree and saw the wolves. They were twenty-five strides away, snarling and advancing slowly.

"On my mark," Lyssa said quietly. "*Now!*"

Their bows twanged in rapid succession. Both arrows found their mark, but Arche's wasn't fatal. The wolf charged, his arrow sticking out of its chest. The uninjured wolf charged as well. Lyssa's wolf keeled over, the fletching of her arrow tickled its eye while the metal tip stuck out the back of its head. Arche dropped his bow and drew his sword as the beasts closed the gap, knowing he didn't have time for another shot. Lyssa's skill with the bow flexed itself as she loosed a second arrow as the wolves came within ten paces. It struck the third wolf in the neck, a fatal blow but not immediately.

She rolled to the side as the wolf lunged at her, both snarling at each other. Arche's attention was captured by his own wolf, which growled and snapped at him. He swung his sword but the wolf darted backwards, out of reach. Before he could bring the blade around for a second swipe, the wolf jumped, aiming for his throat. Arche dropped his shoulder and fell to the ground, turning the momentum from his missed slash into a roll as the wolf lunged.

The beast sailed overhead, but Arche managed to extend his sword and catch it across the flank as it passed him. The wolf let out a yelp of pain and turned to threaten him again. Arche came up into a short crouch, sword held at the ready. This time, when the wolf lunged for him, he stepped to the side and brought the sword down on the back of the wolf's neck. He felt a grinding vibration as the blade glanced across bone. A gentle, pulsating glow in the corner of his vision told him he had a notification waiting for him. He ignored it and looked for Lyssa, who wrenched her curved, bloody sword out of the head of the second wolf, now dead.

Golden light washed over Arche, cleaning off wolf blood and muck from days of journeying.

"You all right?" he asked, breathless.

"I am uninjured. You leveled? I didn't think this would be enough. Have you been training your skills?"

"Not really outside of our practice."

"Odd."

Lyssa placed a hand on the side of the dead wolf. As Arche watched, her arrow disappeared, along with the pelt of the wolf and much of its meat.

"What did you just do?"

"I gathered what was of use. The rest of it can be left here, to nourish the forest."

Arche looked down at his own wolf, then extended a hand and placed it on the beast's side. A notification appeared before him.

Wolf's Inventory	
1x Ruined Wolf Pelt	10 kg of Wolf Meat (Raw)
1x Arrow (Ironwood)	

With a thought, he transferred the items directly into his own inventory, watching as it filled up some of the empty spaces in his backpack. Again, he marveled at how nothing he put into the backpack made it any heavier, and as he patted it, it felt empty. Lyssa moved on to search the other wolf's body as Arche let his notifications appear.

You have slain a **Level 4 Wolf**. You gain 40 experience.
You have discovered a **Trait**! **Slayer of the Mighty** Receive a bonus to experience when you get the killing blow on an enemy that is a higher level than you are. Bonus experience = (Level difference)(100)
Slayer of the Mighty activated! You gain 200 bonus experience.

> Lyssanderyli has slain two **Wolves**.
> You gain 40 experience

> You have reached **Level 3**.
> As a **Human**, you gain 5 points to distribute per level.

That was unexpected.

"Hey, Lyssa?"

"What?"

"What's a trait?"

Lyssa grabbed Arche by his leather chest piece and lifted him up until his toes barely scraped the ground.

"Do not lie to me. Tell me why you ask."

The fierceness of her expression made his words stumble out.

"I-I discovered a trait when I killed the wolf. What's wrong?"

Lyssa stared hard into his eyes. After several seconds, she let him go. He took a step back reflexively, rubbing at his throat.

"Traits are rare. Incredibly rare. What *exactly* is the trait you discovered?"

"It's called 'Slayer of the Mighty.' It says it grants me bonus experience for killing foes of a higher level than I am."

"I've not heard of that one, but you should be very cautious. It can allow you to grow in power at incredible speed, but only with exceptional danger. Levels are not everything in Tartarus. Strategy and equipment can overcome even extraordinary gaps in levels and different species have different baselines for power."

"Don't bite off more than I can chew. Got it."

"Yes." Lyssa cocked her head. "I suppose that's one way of putting it. But having a trait often invites more trouble than it may be worth."

"How so?"

"Where there is one trait, there are often more. Any others that you discover, keep to yourself and those you trust above all others. If a Trait-Bearer kills another, they have a chance of stealing a trait. The more traits they have, the higher the chance. There are other circumstances besides, but many would resort to backstabbing even for the slightest opportunity to propel themselves forwards. You must be very careful."

"I will be, thanks. In the meantime, what do we do?"

Lyssa smiled.

"Hunt stronger prey, of course. Wolves are not the only beasts in these woods. Tomorrow, we will be out of the lands claimed by the Dawnwood and into the Sylv, which forms a majority of the rest of the Forest of Mycenae."

"The Sylv?"

"A wild place, full of monsters. You would do best to have your wits about you."

"More danger. Of course."

"Thinking of turning back?"

"Back to what, exactly? The same forest, but by myself? No, I'm with you, Lyssa."

Lyssa smiled. Arche caught a glimmer in her eye, as though her mind was suddenly far away. The sky above them was beginning to darken.

"We should make camp."

Arche nodded, looking about the forest for a flat spot.

"All right, I'll collect some firewood."

Within an hour they had a hearty cooking fire and both tents set up. Lyssa prepared the wolf meat in a copper pan while Arche used an old rag to clean his sword. Another hour passed and they were sitting with full bellies, staring at the comforting orange flames beneath a dark sky.

"This may be the safest night we have for a long while," Lyssa said, breaking the silence. "We might as well make the most of it."

She held out her hand and a bottle materialized as she pulled it from her inventory.

"Is that…?"

"Sweet wine." Lyssa took a pull from the bottle before handing it to him.

Arche took it and sniffed. It smelled like flowers, but also curled the hairs in his nose. He took a swig, then coughed. Lyssa was right, it was certainly sweet, but there was an undercurrent of bitterness that dried out his mouth. He handed the bottle back, squinting.

"Was that your first drink?" Lyssa asked, accepting the bottle.

"Of alcohol? Yeah, I think so."

"I forget so much is new to you. You just seem like a traveler from far and distant lands, with all those strange customs you use."

Arche shrugged. "I suppose I am, in a way. I'd like to find out where I'm from, some day. Who I used to be. Assuming, of course, that I actually existed before a few days ago."

"Do you ever worry about that?"

"What do you mean?"

"What if you don't like the person you used to be?"

Arche took the bottle proffered him and drank another swig, feeling the heat warm his belly and chest. The second time was slightly easier to manage now that he knew what to expect. At least he didn't cough again.

"They're just the person I *used* to be, right? Good or bad, I'm someone else, now. Besides, it doesn't help to worry about things that may have been. If I get the chance to learn what actually happened to me, I'll take it, but I can't worry about hypothetical actions I may have taken in the past. I'll go nuts."

"Fair enough," Lyssa said, before stretching and yawning. "If you don't mind taking the first watch, I'm going to get some rest. Wake me in four hours and you can have the rest of the night."

"All right, enjoy your shuteye. I'll keep the fire going. If I start shouting, we're under attack."

Lyssa retired to her tent, shutting the flap behind her for privacy. Arche stared at the fire for a while before deciding it was time, he checked his profile.

Arche	
Level: 3 **Experience to Next Level**: 220 (26%) **Race**: Human **Age**: 27 **Height**: 184 centimeters **Weight**: 78.8 kilograms	**Profession**: N/A **Trade**: N/A **Traits**: Slayer of the Mighty **Companions**: Lyssanderyli **Adventuring Party**: N/A

You have **5** undistributed attribute points

Health: 265 / 265 100%	**Stamina**: 195 / 195 100%	**Mana**: 110 / 110 100%
Strength: 14 **Dexterity**: 12 **Agility**: 11 **Fortitude**: 13	**Endurance**: 13 **Intelligence**: 11 **Wisdom**: 11 **Willpower**: 11	**Perception**: 11 **Charisma**: 10 **Comeliness**: 1 **Luck**: 10

His weight had increased slightly, so it seemed, lending credence to the idea that investing points into Strength and Fortitude had made a measurable difference. Either that, or he'd overeaten his meals. With five points to distribute, he placed one point into Strength, Dexterity, Intelligence, Willpower, and Perception. He wanted to make sure that he increased his combat capabilities, but he didn't want to neglect his mental attributes. With his allocation settled, he looked at his Skills page.

Skills		
Archery	Level 10	Novice
Swordsmanship	Level 8	Beginner

It was hard not to be disappointed by his lack of skills. He had to convince Lyssa to teach him more skills or try to discover some on his own. He also wanted to explore the world of non-combat skills and, most especially, magic. He wanted to know as much as he could, but those things would have to wait.

Arche tossed another log onto the fire, listening to it crackle as he settled against his bedroll. It was a clear night and the smoke was doing a wonderful job at keeping the bugs away, so he felt no need to set up his tent. He wondered if this kind of life was normal, or if people elsewhere lived in greater or lesser comfort. He was somewhat aware of the concept of cities, with thousands of people living practically on top of each other, but it seemed far fetched, in a way. There was so much wilderness, it seemed, in Tartarus, that it made the concept of so many people living together appear like a dream or a distant memory. Even in Dawnwood, it had not escaped his notice that most of the dwellings were high in the trees, away from the forest floor where presumably powerful predators may once have stalked.

So far, the worst thing he had come to face was wolves—really, the wolf with half a face, which made occasional appearances in his dreams—but he had the feeling that the monsters Lyssa had mentioned would be worse than any beast. He couldn't help but feel that he wasn't ready. The wolves he had fought had already come close to killing him. Levels and numbers aside, he really did feel like a child in a great, big, new world. Every new piece of information he learned came with a dozen more questions, all unlocking even more pieces of a puzzle that had no edges.

He was glad to have Lyssa with him. She could claim to have no fondness for humans all she wished, but he had a feeling that what she had done for him was more than what her own people had done for her. He'd have been dead, likely several times over, if not for her intervention. He owed her everything.

He just hoped he wouldn't let her down.

Chapter 6

The transition from the Dawnwood to the Sylv was a marked one. While the Dawnwood carried about it a lighthearted feel and was full of bright greens and oranges and softly glowing trees, the Sylv was a much darker wood. The trees were larger, on average, and the canopy grew thick and oppressive, like an arboreal ceiling through which sunlight had to fight to get through. As such, the underbrush was mostly non-existent and thin where it managed to grow. Dark leaves in various states of decay littered the forest floor. Shapes and colors ran together in the shade, making Arche feel he was lost and being watched.

Two days after they had left the Dawnwood, Arche came across his first monster. They heard it long before they saw it. Large, crashing booms shook the trees above them. Lyssa shoved him to the ground at the base of a huge tree and crouched over him, signaling him to be quiet. A creature came into view, so large that it surely must have been a giant. It towered over them, its head halfway to the canopy above and every step shook the trees around it. It was humanoid, but barely. Huge, gangly arms nearly scraped the ground, and a gut that writhed and pulsed hung over the creature's unmentionables, marking it very clearly as male.

Whatever it had eaten was still alive, pushing against the inside of the creature's stomach in a desperate bid to escape. The thought made Arche gag. The creature carried a large club in the form of a young, uprooted tree that carved deep furrows in the forest floor behind it as it moved. Lyssa shook as she crouched over Arche, using her cloak to conceal them both. They stayed that way, near the base of the tree, until they could no longer hear the footsteps in the distance.

"What the fuck was that?" Arche took deep breaths, trying to calm his pounding heart.

"A kýklops. An old one, too, by the look of him, but not one of *the* Kýklopes. We're lucky he didn't catch our scent, or we would not have survived. I haven't seen one this close to the border of Dawnwood. Not in a long time." Lyssa fell quiet.

"You think this might have something to do with your quest?" Arche asked.

"It may. It's difficult to tell. We should continue quickly, before it decides to come back."

They set off, now traveling at a soft jog to create distance between them and the kýklops. As they ran, Arche noticed a flashing notification at the edge of his vision.

You have learned a **Skill**.

Stealth — Level 6

Nobody notices the shadow on the wall until it's too late.

Each level in this skill will improve your ability to go unseen.
Every 5 levels in this skill improves your **Dexterity** by 1.

+2% Chance to Hide (+12%)
+2% Sneak Attack Chance (+12%)
+1% Sneak Attack Damage (+6%)
+1 Dexterity

Arche had the sudden impulse to pump his fist, but he managed to contain his enthusiasm to a grin. Lyssa had been making fun of his attempts to creep around the forest for days. It was also a non-combat skill, which was even better, but it made him wonder how many skills there really were. He was also surprised he had started out so high. Only his archery had started higher and that was due to Lyssa's instruction. It must have been related to the level of danger he had successfully hidden from, though how that was calculated, there was no telling.

After a half hour of jogging through the rough terrain of the forest, Arche's Stamina bar had dropped below one-quarter and he asked, between gasps, for them to slow down. They walked along as he regained both Stamina and his breath.

"How much further is this 'sinister thing' your Lord has sent us to go find?"

"If the directions I've been given are accurate, we should come across it an hour before twilight."

"How can you tell what time it is in this gloom?"

"We elves are not as limited as humans in the dark. For us, the light filtering through these trees is more than enough to see by. Even in absolute darkness, we can see a fair distance."

Arche grunted. "Lucky."

"Let's keep moving. That is, if your tiny human legs can keep up."

"I'm taller than you."

"And slower."

"Shut up."

They alternated between a fast walk and a slow jog to conserve their Stamina. Arche had made at least three internal promises to start a running regimen to train his Endurance by the time Lyssa called for them to stop again.

"What is it?"

Lyssa crouched and his mind immediately conjured images of more kýklopes.

"Something's on the wind. Something foul. I think we've found what we're looking for, be cautious."

Arche drew his bow and slowly nocked an arrow to the string. He crouched low, putting his side against a tree.

"Do you recognize it?"

Lyssa tilted her head back, breathing deeply. After a moment she wrinkled her nose and crouched lower.

"Undead," she hissed.

Arche blinked. "Like, skeletons and ghosts and whatnot?"

"Possibly, though I've not heard of a 'whatnot.' The stench of death is strong."

"What's the play?"

"What?"

Arche grit his teeth. "What's our next move?"

"Let's have a look first."

They snuck forward through the tree line, taking great care to be quiet. After about a hundred paces they found the cause of the disturbance. A massive hole in the ground, over twenty paces in diameter. Several bodies were arrayed around the hole, all humanoid. They looked undisturbed by wildlife and were laid out as though the group had simply gone to sleep. That wish was disillusioned by the fact that blood soaked their clothes and all bore horrible wounds that had long since bled dry. Some looked half-eaten.

"Are those...people?" Arche asked.

"Not anymore. This aura...I suspect necromancy."

The smell of death and rot was heavy in the air and he had to hold his nose to keep from gagging on it.

"What's that?"

"Death magic. A wicked practice. There may be mages behind this, or this area may be steeped in enough death magic for reanimation to occur of its own accord. We cannot leave it like this."

"What do you suggest we do?"

"Aim for the head. Failing that, aim to cripple. These corpses are likely slow, but there are different variants of the undead. It'll be hard to know what we're dealing with until they move. In a pinch, fire works, but it'll draw out every other monster in the region."

Arche peered out at the bodies lying around the hole.

"There has to be a dozen of them."

"Then aim well. Are you ready?"

Arche adjusted his grip and nodded. He had never felt less ready for something in his short life. He looked out upon the sprawling corpses, sizing them up, and tried to keep his knees from shaking.

"You're the better shot. I'll go for the ones that stand up, working from the right to left. You focus on the ones still on the ground, I doubt I can hit those."

Lyssa nodded. "If we get swarmed, we fall back. Chances are high that we can move faster than they can. Follow my lead and don't get separated. There may be other hunters in this forest, though their stench will have run most off."

Arche took a breath, feeling the sweat bead on his brow.

"Ready on your mark."

Lyssa nodded, stood, and loosed an arrow in a steady motion. Her first arrow tore through the head of the first corpse. It was quickly followed by two more before the rest stirred. Arche aimed carefully at one that had stood and released the drawstring. His aim was short, catching the bloated corpse of a rotting human in the mouth, but it apparently severed something as the body collapsed in a heap. The flash of a notification appeared at the edge of his vision, which he ignored. Frankly, he was just thankful that the notifications didn't pop up and obscure his vision when he was busy. He loosed another two arrows as the zombies lumbered toward them.

Lyssa shot arrow after arrow into the group at a rate much faster than anything Arche could manage. Still, six zombies were shambling toward them, not fifteen paces away.

"Lyssa," Arche growled out a warning, firing an arrow into the forehead of an approaching zombie.

Lyssa nocked, drew, and released once more, then turned to run. Arche turned with her and the two dashed into the forest. The sound of the zombies pursuing grew louder. Arche fell into a sprint, slinging his bow over his shoulder and drawing his sword from his belt, not an easy feat in the low light of the forest. Lyssa kept a hold of her bow, somehow managing to nock more arrows and fire them, spinning as she ran. Arche glanced over his shoulder. One of the zombies looked different from the others. While the others had shambled toward them upright, albeit more quickly than their gangly gaits would suggest, this one was scrabbling over the ground on all fours and was considerably faster.

"Crawler!" he hissed, jumping over a small, fallen tree.

"I can't get a clear shot on it."

"It's gaining on us. Stand and fight?"

A large oak ahead threatened to split them if they tried to go around.

"There!" Lyssa cried out.

She reached the oak first, threw her back against it, then shot another arrow. Arche could hear the crawling zombie get closer, crashing through the limited undergrowth.

"Down!"

Arche hit the ground even faster than he had in their sparring matches, his momentum sending him forward into a roll. The fast zombie had lunged for him, throwing itself into the air and sailing over him as he hit the ground. Arche popped back up to his feet and jumped, his momentum twisted him into a flip as the zombie turned back toward him. His blood was on fire from the adrenaline as he reached out with his sword. The sharp blade cut deep into the zombie's flesh, but the bones were strong and it wasn't a fatal blow. Arche landed on the other side, now on the creature's flank, as the last upright zombie emerged.

Arche approached the crawler, sword raised to finish the fight, but it reared and kicked out at him with both legs. Arche cried out and fell backwards as long toenails tore into him, carving furrows against his vambraces and into the unarmored portion of his arm. At the bottom of his vision, his Health plummeted.

Arche brought his sword around, ducking as the creature kicked again. He caught one of the zombie's arms at the elbow, severing it. The undead creature fell to the ground awkwardly, no longer able to evenly support its weight. Capitalizing on the moment, Arche lunged forward and stuck the tip of his sword into the back of the zombie's neck and out the top of its head, severing the spinal cord and piercing the brain in one powerful strike.

He turned to see that Lyssa had dispatched the last zombie with her swords. She flicked her blades to the side, black blood flying off the metal to land amidst the dead leaves. Arche took a few deep breaths and stared at the corpses, hoping they would stay dead this time. The sword slipped from his hand as he felt a wash of hot pain shoot through his left arm. He clutched at it with his right, looking down at three deep gashes that ran along his forearm. He knelt, not trusting himself to stand. Pain washed over him, then golden light. It flashed several times, more than before. When it faded, his arm was healed, the cuts closed with only thin, silver scars to show they'd ever been there. That didn't save him from Lyssa's chastisement, however.

"You were lucky. I've seen similar attacks take off limbs," she said as she inspected Arche's newly healed arm, twisting it around beneath her grip.

"I'm going to have nightmares for weeks but at least we clawed our way out of that one."

Lyssa narrowed her eyes. "Was that a joke?"

"Too soon?"

"I don't see much to laugh at, here."

Arche nodded. "Yeah. I think I use humor to cover how fucking horrifying this is. I need to sit down."

"Why don't you check your notifications. I'll bet you have a level up waiting. Four, by the look of it.

"Great idea," Arche grunted as he lowered himself next to the oak. "I'm just going to sit down by this tree and do that. Make sure I don't get eaten, would you?"

Lyssa kept her bow at the ready as Arche unfocused his eyes and called forth his notifications with a mental command.

<table>
<tr><td colspan="2" align="center">Would you like to consolidate post-battle messages?
This will reduce the amount of specific information shown.</td></tr>
<tr><td align="center">Yes</td><td align="center">No</td></tr>
</table>

Arche immediately chose 'yes', not wanting to wade through a dozen prompts about the battle.

You have slain four **Zombies**.
You have slain a **Level 8 Imbued Zombie**.
You gain 460 experience.

Slayer of the Mighty activated!
You gain 1,300 bonus experience.

Lyssanderyli has slain 7 **Zombies.**
You gain 492 experience.

You have reached **Level 7**.

As a **Human**, you gain 5 attribute points to distribute each level.
You currently have 20 undistributed attribute points.

You have learned a **Skill**.

Acrobatics — Level 1

Now you can run and jump like a majestic leopard. Go forth in style.

Each level in this skill will improve your manipulation of your body in space.
Every 5 levels in this skill improves your **Dexterity** & **Agility** by 1.

+3% Control of movement (+3%)
+1% Jump height (+1%)

Archery has increased to **Level 11**.

+2% Damage with Ranged Weapons (+22%)
+2% Accuracy with Ranged Weapons (+22%)
+1% Range with Ranged Weapons (+11%)

Swordsmanship has increased to **Level 9**.

+2% Damage with Swords (+18%)

You have learned a **Skill**.

Light Armor — Level 1

Light armor is the primary choice for mages, hunters, and thieves. It allows for high mobility and offers little interference to magic. What it lacks in its ability to turn a blade, it more than makes up for by allowing you to dodge it entirely.

Each level in this skill increases your capabilities with **Light Armor**.

+2% Defense of Light Armor (+2%)

"What level are you now?"

"Seven."

"And just shy of two weeks old. You are progressing at an accelerated rate. Truly remarkable."

"Not fast enough," Arche muttered, kicking the corpse of the zombie that had clawed him. "Wait, two weeks? It hasn't even been ten days, yet."

"Yes." Lyssa cocked her head to one side. "How long do you think a week is?"

"Seven days."

"No. Five."

"What?"

"Hadespera, Hermera, Nyxspera, Charomera, Persepera. Five days."

"What the fuck? What happened to Monday, Tuesday, and all that?"

"I don't know those words."

"My brain can't handle this right now. Hold on."

There were more notifications blinking in his vision, but Arche ignored them. His head throbbed. A drink, he needed a drink. His inventory held three full waterskins so he removed one and put it to his lips. It was cold life and gave him something to focus on. Lyssa stood nearby, brow furrowed but not angry.

"You handled yourself well out there, Greenstick. You kept your head. The acrobatics were a bit much, but it worked out in the end. You have to be careful with undead, though. The wounds they inflict can carry all sorts of diseases, magical and mundane alike."

Arche nodded, knowing that she was speaking out of concern and not out of rebuke, but he couldn't help feeling like he'd made a fool of himself. Whatever he felt, it had paid off in droves. He was now level seven and had twenty attribute points to spend.

"Hang on a sec, I'm going to spend some points."

Arche unfocused his eyes and pulled up his profile.

<table>
<tr><td colspan="3" align="center">Arche</td></tr>
<tr>
<td>Level: 7
Experience to Next Level: 168 (76%)
Race: Human
Age: 27
Height: 184 centimeters
Weight: 79 kilograms</td>
<td colspan="2">Profession: N/A
Trade: N/A
Traits: Slayer of the Mighty
Companions: Lyssanderyli
Adventuring Party: N/A</td>
</tr>
<tr><td colspan="3" align="center">You have 20 undistributed attribute points</td></tr>
<tr>
<td align="center">Health: 270 / 270
100%</td>
<td align="center">Stamina: 195 / 195
100%</td>
<td align="center">Mana: 120 / 120
100%</td>
</tr>
<tr>
<td align="center">Strength: 15
Dexterity: 14
Agility: 11
Fortitude: 13</td>
<td align="center">Endurance: 13
Intelligence: 12
Wisdom: 11
Willpower: 12</td>
<td align="center">Perception: 12
Charisma: 10
Comeliness: 1
Luck: 10</td>
</tr>
</table>

Arche put two points into Fortitude and another two into Endurance. Three points went into Strength, Dexterity, and Agility each. He placed two more points into Intelligence and Wisdom. Stroking the ridges on his chin, he decided to place another point each in Willpower and Perception. The final point he dropped into Charisma, then examined the final product.

Health: 315 / 315 100%	Stamina: 225 / 225 100%	Mana: 140 / 140 100%
Strength: 18 Dexterity: 17 Agility: 14 Fortitude: 15	Endurance: 15 Intelligence: 14 Wisdom: 13 Willpower: 13	Perception: 13 Charisma: 11 Comeliness: 1 Luck: 10

Arche flexed, feeling himself grow heavier, more solid. A wave of slight itchiness spread across his whole body, as though he were covered in thousands of crawling insects. Then the feeling was gone, just as suddenly as it had come. Arche shivered, unsettled. He felt stronger, more confident in his motions. It was difficult to tell in the lighting, but he was sure his arms were a bit more muscular as well. He stretched his fingers out, reveling in how precise the movement felt. Lyssa cocked her head to one side, a teasing glint in her eye.

"I hope you didn't spend *all* your points on physicality."

"Yep, sank every single one into Comeliness, just to impress you."

Lyssa snorted, paused, then cleared her throat.

"You...you didn't actually, did you?"

"No. It's a pointless stat for me."

"What do you mean?"

Arche waved a hand in front of his face.

"Kind of hard to make your outside match a mental picture when you don't even know what you look like."

Lyssa's face twisted violently before she wrestled her features into impassivity, but that brief moment of naked horror made Arche's heart drop into his feet.

"You don't know?"

Sweat blossomed on his brow. He rubbed at it, feeling hard ridges beneath his fingers.

"Oh fuck, what is it?"

"No, it's nothing. I should not have said."

"Damn it, Lyssa, don't do this to me. What's wrong with me?"

She looked away, refusing to meet his eyes.

"It's not a bad face. You have a square jaw, dark brown hair, and dark eyes. Your cheekbones are low, which is normal, I think, for a human. Elven faces are more slender; high cheekbones, sharp angles. Yours is less so."

"What aren't you telling me?"

Lyssa grimaced.

"You have scars, Arche. A lot of scars."

"What kind of scars?"

"It's difficult to describe. It looks like torture. You must have been under a blade for far longer than any person deserves. The damage, it's...extensive. I've never seen scars like that. You're covered in them. So many that it's a wonder you're alive. I'm truly sorry, Arche. I thought you knew."

Arche swallowed and put his back against a tree, leaning his weight against it. A hard lump had worked its way into his throat and refused to go down. He reached up and touched his face, brushing it with his fingertips. There were no beard bristles, despite the fact he hadn't ever shaved. Leveling had wiped away the grime of traveling, leaving his skin fresh. Now that he knew what to feel for, though, his fingers scraped over small lines of scars. The ridges he'd felt every time he'd touched his face. They crossed patterns over his cheeks and forehead, across his eyes and down his neck. Some were recessed, like tiny valleys in his skin. Others were keloid, raised blocks of hard skin that stopped his wandering fingertips and caught the edges of his nails.

One of his eyes blurred. He shook his head, letting his hand fall to the side. He took a deep breath, hating himself for the shakiness that came when he let it out. Someone had done this to him. Maybe whoever had was also responsible for the loss of his memories. He would find them and get his answers.

Then, he would make them pay.

"Are you all right?" Lyssa's voice was tender, none of its usual playfulness or jesting.

"No." His voice was thick. "I'm not."

"Is there something I can do?"

Arche's fist tightened around the wood of the tree.

"Find me something to kill."

Chapter 7

It was the work of ten minutes for Lyssa and Arche to dismember the bodies of all the zombies. Ten minutes to find them all and sever their limbs and heads from their torsos. Arche hadn't questioned the work. He'd simply followed Lyssa's lead in the matter. It wasn't exactly what he'd been hoping for, but the job was physical enough that he managed to work out most of his anger. For the moment, at least. When they'd finished, Lyssa explained the purpose.

"They've reanimated once. They might have done so again. Should be harder, this way, though not technically impossible. I'd burn them, but I don't want to attract other predators."

"We could toss them in the hole," Arche suggested.

The pit stretched out before him like a wound in the ground itself. Arche peered into it, then shook his head. It was pitch black inside and he could make nothing out. Lyssa, however, was looking very intently over the edge.

"See anything?"

"It's hard to tell. The ground shimmers, but it's not too far. Could be water. Could be an illusion."

"Drop a torch, then."

Lyssa opened her mouth to respond, then closed it and produced a torch and flint from her inventory. Within moments, the torch was lit and dropped into the hole. They watched as it fell, illuminating earth and rock until the torch hit the bottom with a splash.

"Well, it's water. How deep is anyone's guess," Arche said. "I didn't see anything at the bottom, did you?"

"Yes, a passageway. It seems we'll have to go down."

"And the bodies?"

"Into the deep."

Arche looked at the pile of decaying corpses and shuddered. He grabbed hold of a severed leg by the shoe, then dropped it over the edge, listening to the splash below.

"Remind me to get some gloves at some point, would you?"

"I'll do that."

By the time they'd finished, all of Arche's anger had been replaced by disgust. He wiped his hands against the grass and fallen leaves, shuddering all the while. Lyssa stood over the hole, gazing into it with her head cocked to the side.

"Now, how to get down there," she muttered.

Arche took a quick look into his inventory.

"I've got thirty whatever of rope. I'm thinking we knot it, tie it to a tree, and throw it down. That way we have an exit strategy."

Lyssa paused. "Meters."

"What?"

"You have thirty meters of rope."

"What the fuck is a meter?"

Lyssa held up her hands, palms facing each other, then sighed at his look of noncomprehension. "It should be enough."

Arche pulled the rope out of his inventory and knotted it. He passed one end of it to Lyssa, who began tying it around a nearby tree. Arche used his wingspan to measure out intervals and tied a knot at each point, then tossed the remainder into the hole. A splash echoed back at them.

"You said undead hate fire, right?" Arche asked as Lyssa rejoined him.

"Usually. It depends." She shrugged. "Some don't care at all; others detest it at a primal level. Depends on the kind of undead."

"Cool, 'cause I'm going to need a torch down there. I can barely see as it is."

Lyssa's mouth turned down at the corners, her brow furrowing. "Stealth won't be an option."

"Then let's hope no one down there is meaner than us." Arche grabbed one end of the rope and lowered himself into the hole.

The climb wasn't difficult aside from the fact he couldn't see below him. After a minute, his right foot dipped into the water. He snatched it back, cursing as he felt it seep into his boot.

"Where's the ledge? I can't see it."

"To your right." Lyssa's voice came from above. "You should be able to reach it."

Arche kicked out to the right, using his weight to swing the rope. He stretched out his foot as far as he could and felt the hard, flat surface of the platform. He shoved off the wall again, this time able to catch the ledge with his foot and drag himself over onto solid ground. Finally able to stand, he retrieved a torch from his inventory and lit it by striking a wedge of flint with a knife. The flame crackled and sparked, casting eerie shadows around him. The passageway ahead of him was hewn from grey stone, leaving behind the disturbed earth of the hole in the ground, and disappeared into darkness beyond the light of his torch.

Lyssa landed next to him, quiet as ever with bow in hand. She cocked her head, her long ears twitching. Arche kept quiet, trying not to distract her. After a few moments she nodded.

"I don't hear anything. If something is waiting for us, it isn't moving."

"Great." Arche drew his sword, holding the torch in his left hand. "Let's go find whatever necromantic sonovabitch desecrated this area."

Lyssa said nothing so he headed down the passage, torch extended to banish the gloom. The way dipped downward slightly, almost unnoticed, except for the rising chill in the air. They continued for half an hour before Arche stopped. Lyssa stopped behind him, glancing about for hidden dangers.

"What is it?" she hissed.

Arche didn't respond immediately, kneeling to look at the ground in front of them. At cursory glance it looked the same as the other stone they'd been walking on, but a tiny section stuck up a little more than the rest, less than a finger's breadth. If he hadn't been looking at his feet, wondering when perhaps they were going to break for food, he might have missed it. As Arche squinted at the stone, he saw a symbol etched into it. It was extraordinary work, full of billowing lines that blossomed upward. The air around it was odd, slightly heavy.

"I don't know, but I don't trust it. What do you make of it?"

Lyssa followed his gesture to the symbol and hissed again, this time without words.

"Traps. That's the rune for fire. Whatever you do, don't step on it."

"The rune for fire, huh?" he looked back at the stone, trying to commit the design to memory. "Well, that's just typical."

"What is?" Lyssa asked.

"My first encounter with magic and it's a trap that could have killed me."

"Don't touch it. I don't have the skill to disarm something like that and I don't have the supplies to treat the injuries it would cause."

Arche nodded and, in an exaggerated motion, stepped over the trap. Lyssa did the same, taking great care to ensure that no part of her came remotely close to interacting with the marked stone.

> You have learned a **Skill**.
>
> ### Investigation — Level 1
>
> *The act of searching is a trainable skill. The act of finding is something else entirely.*
>
> Each level in this skill improves your ability to find hidden objects and areas. Every 5 levels in this skill improves your **Intelligence** and **Perception** by 1.
>
> +1% Chance to Spot Hidden Things (+1%)
> +1% Chance to Spot Traps (+1%)
> +1% Speed of Searching (+1%)

As they continued forward, Arche kept a watchful eye on the floor, the walls, and the ceiling, looking for more traps that could kill or maim them. In total, he'd found a pressure stone, a tripwire, and a pitfall trap, and that was after only an hour of walking. There was enough hidden danger along the path to get his new skill to level two. There were more dangers that Lyssa pointed out to him, her skill in the matter clearly much higher than his, also aided by her ability to see better.

The passage wound in strange directions as they walked. It was full of sharp turns and often doubled back on itself, but all the while it led them deeper and deeper underground. It was impossible to tell the time. Late, judging by the weight behind his eyes. Arche was about to suggest they stop and rest for the evening when Lyssa stiffened next to him. He alerted immediately, heart drumming as he looked round for danger. Would it be shambling dead? Flashing blades? The necromancer?

"I hear something," Lyssa whispered.

"A threat?"

"I don't know. Voices. I can't tell what they're saying, it's echoing."

"Do undead speak?"

"Only the powerful ones."

"Shit. Should I douse the light?"

"Not yet. They are still far away. The echoes are quiet."

They continued forward much more slowly. Lyssa, as usual, had no issue being completely silent, but Arche's every step seemed to scrape no matter how lightly he tread. Lyssa moved in front of him. Though her face betrayed no emotion as she passed, he couldn't help but wonder if she was cursing him for the noise he was making. He was doing his best to obscure the light being thrown by the torch while still casting enough before him to see where he was going. They traveled another hundred paces or so before Lyssa stopped again.

"They're getting louder," she whispered.

"What are they saying?"

"They are speaking Arachnean."

"They what?"

"The language of the spiders. Whatever we are about to find, it will not be friendly. Be prepared to fight."

Arche paused and adjusted his grip on his sword.

"Did you just say 'spiders?'" His flesh crawled at the word.

"Yes. The children of Arachne. They are rife wherever it is dark. We seem to be far enough underground that her more intelligent descendants have taken up residence. This is troubling."

"What kind of spiders are we talking about, here?"

"Scared, Greenstick?"

"I'm just not super fond of creepy crawlies, apparently. What kind?"

"The giant kind."

"Now, why does that make me feel worse?"

"Pull yourself together, Arche, it's just another enemy."

"Right. Just another enormous, creepy, eight-legged-and-eyed monster. Which we will fight. With only a torch keeping us from complete and total darkness. Deep underground. With hundreds of tons of rock above our heads. Nothing to worry about."

"Are you really picking now to have compromising thoughts?"

"It's never *not* a good time to be contemplating your imminent demise at the hands of monsters."

Lyssa rolled her eyes and nocked an arrow to her bow. Arche took several deep breaths and thumped his chest a few times, trying to pull himself together. Just another monster, he could do this. He'd fought undead, this couldn't be worse, right?

Lyssa raised an eyebrow at him but he ignored her as they crept along the passage. More and more web strands hung from the walls and ceiling until spiderwebs blocked their way entirely. As they approached, Arche was able to hear the voices as well. They spoke in chitters and clacks that were wholly unnerving.

He glanced at Lyssa. Her face was a stoic mask of determination. If he could feel half as confident and fierce as she looked, he could have taken on every zombie outside single-handed. Instead, he would have to settle for the churning bundle of nerves strangling themselves in the basin of his stomach.

Arche touched his torch to the webs in front of them, which lit up in a blazing conflagration. The voices on the other side hissed and shrieked. The webs burned quickly, taking only moments to completely shrivel away into a melted, white goop. Arche moved past the smoldering webs, his sword brandished in front of him, and found himself in a large room coated with webbing.

Inside were three enormous, black, spider-like creatures. They had massive thoraxes with eight spindly legs, but where a head should be was instead the torso of a humanoid woman clad in leathery spider chitin, creating a natural protection. Their flesh was as gray as stone, nearly fading into the walls around them in the light from the torch. Each had two human arms in addition to all the spider legs and wielded spears twice Arche's height.

Most unsettling of all, however, were their faces. Each had eight beady, solid-black eyes, and all of them had turned toward Arche. Below the horror of their eyes, large spider mandibles clacked in front of mouths that would be human, if they weren't full of needle-like teeth. Arche didn't pause as he entered, as much as he would have liked to. The sheer horror of the creatures in front of him spurred his body into action and he waved his torch to fend them off, despite the fact they were ten paces away.

"Sisters," one of the creatures spat in a hissing, chittering voice that made Arche shiver. "Dinner has arrived."

Hearing the common tongue through their nightmarish mouths only made Arche want to set them on fire even more. The other two chittered and screeched, the high-pitched sounds reverberating off the walls as they advanced. Lyssa's arrow sank into one of the spider-women's legs, which was as thick as a young tree and covered in small, sharp spines, perfect for tearing.

"Arachtaurs," Lyssa spat, drawing her bow back again. "Be wary of their venom, they can inject it through their legs as well."

Arche waved his torch in front of himself in broad strokes, trying desperately to scare back the slowly advancing creatures, all the while keeping his sword high and ready. Over his shoulder, Lyssa used him for cover as she methodically targeted joints and exposed flesh.

"Help! Help me!" a frightened voice called from behind a mass of webs on the other side of the room.

One of the arachtaurs charged, forcing Arche and Lyssa to dive out of the way. They hit the ground in opposite directions. Arche's torch clattered across the floor, coming to a stop in a pile of webbing. A bright flash nearly blinded him as the whole mess went up in flames. He brought his sword up to deflect a spear thrust that nearly skewered him, then scrambled to his feet, his heart thumping painfully. Arche tried to close the distance, which would hopefully reduce the effectiveness of the spear, but the arachtaur reared and he found himself with two razor-sharp spider legs flying toward him from opposite directions.

Arche hit the ground once more and rolled to the side. As he rose, he brought his sword up and braced it against his left forearm to block an incoming swipe of the spear. The force of the blow crushed his arm against him and his breath came out in a rush as he was sent flying. His fall was broken by a mass of webs. The brief pause let him see the rest of the room.

Half of it was on fire.

Lyssa had abandoned her bow in favor of dual wielding her curved shortswords, which she called kopides. She flowed between dodging and attacking, masterfully engaging two of the arachtaurs in close combat. Arche's own arachtaur charged him, spear aimed for his heart.

Arche wrenched himself from the webs, limp from the heat of the room, and spun to the side. He avoided being turned into paste against the wall but the spear cut into his left shoulder, punching through the edge of his leather jerkin. He clenched his teeth through the pain and slashed at one of the arachtaur's legs. The blade cut deep but caught in the joint. Arche wrenched the sword as the arachtaur recoiled, ripping it free. The arachtaur let out a screech and stumbled forward as her leg detached. Arche jumped forward as the arachtaur's human half hit the ground. He landed on her back and plunged his sword into her chitin with a crunch. The arachtaur let out another scream, this one far shriller as it bucked wildly. Arche lost his grip and was thrown free, his sword still embedded. He landed hard, tumbling across the stone floor.

The arachtaur laid on the ground, groaning and trying to stand as its spider-blood spilled across the floor. The other two arachtaurs, upon seeing their sister, roared in anger and turned their attention to Arche.

"Ah, fuck," he muttered, scrambling to pull his sword free.

The sword was stuck fast and the writhing of the arachtaur forced him backwards. Weaponless, he could do nothing only watch as both arachtaurs lunged for him. They seemed to move in slow-motion, spears flashing and fangs bared. At any moment, they would tear him into pieces.

Then Lyssa was there.

Her blades spun as she took full advantage of the arachtaurs' distraction. In a flash, she severed one's arm. As the creature recoiled, she stabbed its midsection at the connection of spider and woman. Black blood sprayed and hissed among the flames.

The other arachtaur did not waver as its sister died, the spear in its hands was pointed unwaveringly toward Arche's chest. He tried to move, but his foot was caught deep in webbing and twisted at a bad angle. The spear tore into his side, barely slowed by his leather armor. The force of the impact, with the arachtaur's full weight behind it, ripped him out of the webs, bore him backwards, and slammed him into the wall.

Arche gasped.

Blood poured from his side, splashing against the webs covering the floor. He looked down at the spear, unable to comprehend what had happened. For a single moment, he felt nothing but pressure, then the pain came. It burned into him. Everything else was driven away. His vision went dark around the edges, his Health flashing dangerously low. The arachtaur leaned forward and hissed at him, but he was only dimly aware of her. Her mandibles clacked, ready to sink into his flesh. One bite and he would be dead.

Lyssa appeared, soaring up behind the arachtaur like a hero from legend. She severed the creature's head with a single stroke of her sword, letting it topple to the ground at Arche's feet. The body of the arachtaur collapsed and Arche let out a gurgle. He'd been saved from a quick death, but a slow one was still likely. Lyssa was at his side in an instant. She, too, was bathed in blood, but it was the black blood of the arachtaurs.

She gripped the spear and carefully pulled it free, then placed both hands over the wound. Arche slid to the floor, his own hands weakly grasping his wound. Lyssa spoke in a low voice, saying something in Elvish. Darkness crept over more of his vision and all sensation began to slip away. He looked up, barely able to make out Lyssa's face.

If it was going to be the last thing he saw, he was all right with that.

You have slain a **Level 17 Arachtaur**.
You gain 425 experience.

Slayer of the Mighty activated!
You gain 1,000 bonus experience.

Lyssanderyli has slain two **Arachtaurs**.
You gain 425 experience.

You have reached **Level 10**.

As a **Human**, you receive 5 attribute points to distribute per level.
You currently have 15 undistributed attribute points.

More notifications flashed, indicating skill increases, but remained minimized. A golden glow surrounded him, washing over him three times. It flooded his muscles with strength and concentrated at the wound in his side, knitting his broken flesh back together. Arche gasped as the light turned inward, reattaching split organs and shoving everything back where it was supposed to be. Lyssa breathed a sigh in relief, then hit him in the arm.

Hard.

Arche winced as his Health dropped a few points.

"Fool! Were you trying to get yourself killed? I told you to stay close to me."

"My bad," Arche gasped. "Damn, that hurt."

"You have to be more careful. You're still low-leveled, so you can reliably expect to level up after a hard fight, but soon you won't be able to rely on that to save you. You can't keep doing this."

"I'm not trying to make a habit of it. Are you all right?" Arche gestured toward the blood covering her.

She sighed, physically relaxing somewhat. "Nothing serious. I've yet to go through my prompts, but I leveled after the first one died."

"What level are you, anyway?"

Lyssa hesitated, her face twisting before she answered.

"Twenty-nine."

Arche's eyes widened. He opened his mouth to respond but was cut off by another voice.

"Hello? Is somebody out there? Help me!"

The sound came muffled from one of the corners of the room. Arche pushed his way to his feet and pulled his xiphos free from the dead arachtaur. Much of the webbing in the room had melted, but the torch still burned where it had been dropped. Arche retrieved it as well, holding both it and the sword aloft.

"Ready?"

"Ready."

They moved together toward the mess of webs at the far end of the room. Arche led the way, torch out in front of him, while Lyssa was close behind with bow nocked. As they approached the mass of webs, Arche realized they were covering a door. Someone on the other end seemed to be banging on it but the mass of webbing held it shut. He locked eyes with Lyssa, who shrugged.

"Who's there?" he called out.

The knocking stopped.

"Hello? Are you here to help me?"

"Help who?"

"Helwan is my name, good sir. I've been trapped in here for some time. If you would be so kind as to let me out?"

Arche locked eyes with Lyssa again, who nodded. Arche touched the torch to the web and turned away from the flash of heat. The flames quickly ate through the layers of webbing, revealing a thick metal door. The latch on the door lifted and swung open toward them, revealing a short creature, only a little taller than Arche's waist.

It appeared to be a man but many of its features were animalistic. The creature who called himself Helwan had large, brown, furry ears that were slightly conical, like a horse. His legs were hairy and his feet cloven goat-hooves. A small, horse-like tail, carefully braided, trailed behind him. He also wore a waistcoat that might have been colorful at one point but had long since been darkened by the grime of travel and adventure. His face was human, mostly, and sported a dark brown goatee that matched his hair, out of which grew two gently curling horns. Most off-putting of all, however, were his eyes. Large, rectangular pupils gave the short creature a wholly alien feel.

Lyssa spat in disgust.

"Satyr."

Arche looked back at her questioningly, only to find she was staring at the goat-horse-man with absolute derision, bordering on open hatred. Helwan, on the other hand, had a look of astonishment and adoration upon the satyr's face. Helwan stepped forward, kneeling with a hand on his chest, completely ignoring Arche.

"My lady, I am Helwan Panysk. Musician, mage, and megaloscholar. It is my utmost pleasure to have met you."

He reached for Lyssa's hand, presumably to kiss it. Lyssa drew her bow and placed the tip of the arrow against the satyr's forehead.

"Allow me to make something very clear to you, satyr. You touch me and you die. Is that understood?"

Some of Helwan's timidity returned as Lyssa's razor-sharp arrow pricked his forehead, drawing a small bead of blood.

"Y-yes, understood very well, my lady!"

Arche threw up his hands in confusion, still holding the torch and sword.

"What the fuck?"

"Perverts of the forest," Lyssa spat. "The sooner this one is out of our company, the better it will be. Better yet, I'll kill him now and save us both the trouble."

"I mean no offense, dear lady. I merely wanted to show you the depths of my gratitude for saving me from those fearful monsters."

"Keep your depths to yourself, goat."

"Whoa!" Arche interjected, moving to place himself somewhat between the two of them. "Let's all just settle down and remember why we're here in the first place."

He paused, then looked at Helwan.

"Why are you here?"

Helwan hesitated, then produced a scrap of parchment from his inventory.

"I discovered this map hidden within the forgotten stacks of the Lyceum Apokryfos library, marking a hidden path to this site, deep below the surface. As a megaloscholar, I could not pass up the opportunity to explore a potentially great historic find. If I could be the first to write about it, why, I could have my name lauded about the great academic halls. Who knows what secrets or magics could be found here?"

"And you didn't expect to find monsters?"

"Ah," the satyr looked sheepish. "I did. I had hired an adventuring group to protect me. They, uh, they were not quite up to the task, and I locked myself away in this room for safety. When the fighting was over, the group was gone and I found myself trapped. I can only presume they are dead or fled."

Arche paused, looked at Lyssa, then looked back at Helwan.

"How many were there?"

"Oh, perhaps a dozen in total."

"Well, that explains the zombies we found."

Helwan blinked in surprise.

"Zombies? They turned into zombies?"

"Yeah, pretty fast ones, too. What kind of mage did you say you were?"

"Oh, well, ah, you see, I'm more of a historian, really, but I have an interest in a large display of magical arts, histories, artifacts. I've been trained in gaiamancy and phosphomancy but can't say that I'm especially gifted in either approach."

"What about necromancy?"

"I have studied a little bit of it, but only academically. It's a foul branch of magic and my curiosity was only that of the very young and foolhardy. Once I learned how terrible it actually was, I swore away all study of it." Helwan cringed away at the admission, as if ashamed.

Arche glanced at Lyssa to gauge her reaction. It had changed, ever so slightly, from disgust to revulsion.

"All right, all right," he said, sheathing his sword and pinching the bridge of his nose. "Let's just calm down, everybody, and talk this through. Helwan, why don't you tell us exactly what you're doing here and what happened to you."

"I, erm, I already told you. I found this map and wanted to write–"

"I may be younger than I look, Helwan, but I don't believe you would pay for twelve armed and capable individuals to accompany you on an extremely dangerous academic pursuit just to write a paper. You're looking for something. What is it? From the beginning."

Helwan glanced back and forth between Arche and Lyssa. His strange, rectangular pupils bouncing. Finally, he let out a sigh.

"This may take some time; it would be best if everyone made themselves comfortable. Your torch, sir, looks to be running low. Perhaps you would be inclined to use my light?"

The satyr produced a lantern from his inventory. Inside the lantern was a glowing orange orb that, upon a cursory glance, could have been firelight, but did not flicker or waver as the lantern moved about. It was also much more effective than Arche's torch, illuminating the entire room in steady light.

"What is that?" Arche asked, looking at the lantern intently.

"This is an Everlit Lantern. A larger, less expensive version of an Everlit Locket. Both are made by my employer, Bits and Baubles Enterprises."

Helwan paused, evidently expecting some kind of reaction out of Arche and Lyssa. They stared at him blank-faced until he coughed and continued.

"Yes, well, Bits and Baubles is a manufactory and repository of enchanted items but they also send teams out for the collection of rare magical artifacts."

"I imagine there's a lot of money in that," Arche said.

"Indeed. Now, I discovered the map to this place like I said. There was a riddle in old dwarvish about a collapsed mine with a great treasure and great danger hidden away below. As I'm sure you both know, the only thing dwarves value more than their precious metals is magic. So I took it upon myself to come and retrieve the artifact and present it to my employer, Lady Rune Oyl."

"Hang on," Arche said, raising a hand. "You weren't even tasked by your boss to come here? You just decided you were going to follow some ancient riddle and map to a place you knew nothing about, on the off chance that it had magical treasure that you could then bring back to *maybe* get a promotion from your boss?"

"That's quite reductive but is the general gist of things, yes."

"I'm almost impressed. That explains why you came here, but not what's happened since."

Helwan's face fell.

"Yes. We found the entrance; I imagine you found it too. A large, excavated hole in the ground, pool at the bottom. Anyway, we made our way along it until we came to this room. Here, we were set upon by the three arachtaurs you were so kind to take care of for me. They fought my companions while I fled and hid in that room. I conjured an illusion to throw the arachtaurs off my trail, but I was trapped when they put a fresh coating of web in the room. I was there for five days, surviving on the rations I brought with me. I tried a few spells to release myself from that room, but nothing worked. Furthermore, I must have made too much noise because they started screeching and talking to one another right outside my door. If you two had not shown when you did, I would be dead. For that, you both have my everlasting gratitude."

Helwan bowed low, the gesture made awkward as he was still sitting.

"May I ask the names of my rescuers?"

"I'm Arche, this is Lyssa."

"It is my honor to have made your acquaintances."

Arche turned to Lyssa.

"What do you think? Is he telling the truth?"

She scowled. For several long moments, Arche thought she was going to kill the satyr and be done with it, then she lowered her bow.

"There is some truth, at least, to his words. As much as it pains me to admit it, a mage will be useful as we continue."

"Most excellent!" Helwan exclaimed. "You shall not regret the addition of my company, I guarantee it!"

"I already regret the addition of your company, satyr. You should know that I do not intend to allow powerful artifacts to fall into your possession, regardless of your spun tales."

Helwan deflated slightly. "I understand. My apologies for earlier, Lady Lyssa. I am not ignorant of the reputation my kind have throughout Tartarus. However, I hope that the common notions of my heritage do not sully all your thoughts of me. I can hardly make up for the sins of my forebears, but I can, perhaps, do some good here."

Arche was reminded of Lord Cypress and the similar argument that saved his own life from execution.

"As for the artifact, my oversight at Bits and Baubles is not one that would be forgiven lightly, even if I had presented the item. Reputation means much to Lady Oyl and I didn't exactly go through proper channels to procure travel here. To that extent, I have no great impetus to claim the item for myself. All I ask is that I might be allowed to study it. I have a few identification spells in my repertoire that may prove useful."

"A word, Arche?" Lyssa asked.

Arche stood and they walked to the other side of the room, farther than what Arche thought was necessary but, then again, he didn't know how good a satyr's hearing was.

"I don't trust him," Lyssa said.

"You said yourself that he was telling the truth."

"I said there was some truth to what he said. That's not to say he won't abandon us or actively work against us if we travel together."

"It's a risk, certainly. But think of the potential benefits of having a magic wielder down here. We faced three arachtaurs that have already killed a dozen adventurers. They nearly killed me and certainly would have, had it not been for you. You've saved me several times already. What if you need saving next time and I'm not enough? It might help to have some magic in our corner."

Lyssa shifted her weight, folding her arms in front of her.

"I don't like the idea of traveling with a satyr."

"You've said similar things about traveling with a human. What's the matter with satyrs? You called them perverts of the forest. What is this about?"

She grimaced.

"They're sexual predators, generally speaking. Ancient tales across Tartarus speak of satyrs that would chase women through the forests. Humans, elves, dryads. It didn't matter what they were. If they caught the women..." Lyssa trailed off, clenching and unclenching her fists.

Arche was at a loss.

"I...I don't know what to say. That's disgusting beyond words."

"It's unforgivable. In my village, our women are warned about satyrs. Our histories are full of their monstrous actions. They are one of the many reasons our women are taught to fight. In centuries past, they would be shot on sight for trespassing into our territories. Tartarus has changed since then, but elven memory runs deep. He,"—she pointed at Helwan—"is from the city. There is nothing of a forest satyr about him. For a satyr to live in the city and not have been killed or imprisoned, he must have overcome his nature. I do not know what kind of people reside in these cities, but I doubt even they would tolerate those kinds of actions. Still, the idea of traveling with a satyr? Sleeping near one? I'd rather kill him now and be done with it."

"I can't condone killing him, but it's your choice whether or not he joins us. This is your quest, after all."

Lyssa nodded, her eyes full of indecision. They stood in silence for several moments, then she shook her head.

"If he was hired by a woman, that speaks enough to his character. Fine. But please, keep an eye on him."

"Of course."

They returned to see Helwan was in the process of cleaning a pan flute.

"You're not planning on playing that right now, are you?" Arche asked.

"What? Oh, no! No, I think the quieter we are the better. I just like to occupy my hands. Helps calm me down."

"We have decided to allow you to join us," Lyssa said. "On the condition that you do as we tell you. Know that I do not trust you and if you do anything to suggest you are working against us, I will kill you without hesitation. If you have been honest with us, we will consider allowing you to study whatever artifacts we come across, but do not give you the right to keep such items. Do you understand and agree to these terms?"

Helwan scrambled to his feet in order to bow properly.

"Oh! Yes. Yes, I do."

A notification appeared in Arche's vision.

Helwan Panysk has agreed to join your **Adventuring Party**.

"Good. Now that we have that settled, we can set up camp for the night."

Chapter 8

Without the proper materials or necessary ventilation for a true campfire, the three happenstance adventurers gathered around the Everlit Lantern. Though the lantern provided no warmth in the cold depths, the darkness it banished was enough to keep their spirits steady.

Helwan, evidently stressed by the day's events, had fallen fast asleep sprawled out on a bedroll. Lyssa and Arche sat against a wall, side by side. She poured both of them a bowl of hot soup, produced from a container in her inventory. Arche was thrilled to find that objects stored in the inventory kept their temperature in addition to not spoiling.

"What happens if you don't store something directly in your inventory?"

"What do you mean?" Lyssa asked, scraping the bottom of her bowl with a spoon.

"The bag you gave me added more space to my inventory, but what if I were to physically pick something up and put it inside the bag. Would it automatically go to an inventory slot, or would it stay in the bag?"

"It stays in the bag."

"Oh." Arche ducked his head, feeling like an idiot.

The corners of Lyssa's mouth twitched as she eyed him.

"In millennia past, legend has it that our inventory space was entirely physical. You had to carry everything with you. However, something changed in the time since and the world became more like we know it today."

"You mean with the levels and everything else?"

"Yes. Some of our earliest stories indicate that there was no such metric. People had to demonstrate how skilled they were, they had to exercise to grow stronger with no clear idea of how much they had improved. Some blame the Titans for the shift, but I'm not so sure."

Arche blinked.

"Wait, Titans? What are those?"

Lyssa shuddered. "I should not have spoken so flippantly. They are not a good topic for discussion, deep underground as we are. Old superstitions say that if you mention them too often, you gain their attention. The last thing we need right now is more trouble."

"I'll agree to that. It's strange, though. So much of life and living seems familiar to me, despite everything, but the levels and the skills and the attributes, the whole system is completely foreign."

Silence filled the space between them as they ate. Arche used the time to go over the skill gain notifications.

Acrobatics has increased to **Level 7.**

+3% Control of Movement (+21%)
+1% Jump Height (+7%)
+1 Dexterity
+1 Agility

Swordsmanship has increased to **Level 13**.

+2% Damage with Swords (+26%)

You have reached the rank of **Novice Swordsman.**
You gain 100 experience.

Archery has increased to **Level 12**.

+2% Damage with Ranged Weapons (+24%)
+2% Accuracy with Ranged Weapons (+24%)
+1% Range with Ranged Weapons (+12%)

Stealth has increased to **Level 8**.

+2% Chance to Hide (+16%)
+2% Sneak Attack Chance (+16%)
+1% Sneak Attack Damage (+8%)

You have learned a **Skill**.

Persuasion — Level 1

Your ideas are great, and now others will think so, too.

Each level in this skill improves your ability to talk others around to your viewpoint. Every 5 levels in this skill improves your **Charisma** by 1.

+1% Persuasion Chance (+1%)

A new skill, new rank in swordsmanship, and an improvement to his attributes. It had been a very productive, if very dangerous, day. Arche pulled open his profile to check his changes.

<table>
<tr><td colspan="3" align="center">Arche</td></tr>
<tr>
<td>Level: 10
Experience to Next Level: 918 (8%)
Race: Human
Age: 27
Height: 185 centimeters
Weight: 80.5 kilograms</td>
<td colspan="2">Profession: N/A
Trade: N/A
Traits: Slayer of the Mighty
Companions: Lyssanderyli
Adventuring Party: Helwan Panysk</td>
</tr>
<tr><td colspan="3" align="center">You have 15 undistributed attribute points</td></tr>
<tr>
<td align="center">Health: 315 / 315
100%</td>
<td align="center">Stamina: 225 / 225
100%</td>
<td align="center">Mana: 140 / 140
100%</td>
</tr>
<tr>
<td align="center">Strength: 18
Dexterity: 18
Agility: 15
Fortitude: 15</td>
<td align="center">Endurance: 15
Intelligence: 14
Wisdom: 13
Willpower: 13</td>
<td align="center">Perception: 13
Charisma: 11
Comeliness: 1
Luck: 10</td>
</tr>
</table>

Fifteen points to distribute, thanks to one near-death experience. Arche's thoughts flicked back to the last three fights. He had attempted to use his bow twice to limited success but had been forced to rely on his sword every time. His physical traits were improving but he was still outclassed by everything he came up against. That needed to change but the 'how' was giving him trouble. Strength was certain, Fortitude was just as necessary, but after that, what?

Three points went into Strength and Fortitude each. In the fight with the arachtaurs, he had managed to dodge the strike of their spears until the end, when he had been caught by the webbing. He'd only been able to do that because of his speed and reactions. Two points went into Agility.

Seven points left.

Lyssa's warning about placing all his points in physical attributes came back to him, so he examined his mental stats. Each had their own allure, and he didn't want to skip any of them, so he put one point each into Intelligence, Wisdom, Willpower, Perception, and Charisma. With two points left and no hard ideas on where to place them, his eyes were drawn to the two attributes he had thus far neglected: Comeliness and Luck.

Arche ran a finger along his face, feeling the raised scars that traced his cheeks and forehead. Comeliness was an attractive option for someone in his situation but it still felt like the wrong choice. He didn't have a solid self-image and, after Lyssa's words, he dreaded the idea of looking. Luck, similarly, was so ambiguous that he hardly felt he could justify spending points on it when the other attributes were very clear on how they would keep him alive.

With more than a little reluctance, Arche pulled himself away from the two attributes and placed his last two points placed into Intelligence and Charisma.

Health: 360 / 360 100%	Stamina: 240 / 240 100%	Mana: 160 / 160 100%
Strength: 21 Dexterity: 18 Agility: 17 Fortitude: 18	Endurance: 15 Intelligence: 16 Wisdom: 14 Willpower: 14	Perception: 14 Charisma: 13 Comeliness: 1 Luck: 10

There was a clear bias toward his physical attributes but he could focus more on mental if and when he learned magic. In the meantime, the physical would keep him alive. That would have to be enough.

Arche glanced at Lyssa, intending to ask her more about attributes and their effects, only to find she had fallen asleep, her empty bowl sitting on the ground next to her. The sight brought a smile to his face. It was the most peaceful he'd ever seen her. With the wave of a hand, he produced a blanket from his inventory and draped it over her. Not far away, Helwan kicked a leg in his sleep. It had been a risk, letting the satyr join them. He hoped it was the right choice. There was little point in worrying about it, the decision was made. As long as Helwan didn't give them further reason not to trust him, Arche would follow Lord Cypress's lead and not hold Helwan's species against him.

The next few hours crept by until it was time to wake Lyssa for her watch. Arche was grateful for the chance to sleep. The day had taken its toll on him.

Ψ

Arche woke to Lyssa shaking him by the shoulders. He was panting and covered in sweat, hand scrabbling at his right hip for a weapon that wasn't there. The sounds of screams and explosions echoed in his ears.

"Arche, calm down."

Battles of blade and fire swirled in his mind. It was several moments before he recognized where he was and who was around him. His body shook with adrenaline, with the need to fight. Helwan was also awake, standing several paces away and looking at him with more than a little apprehension. Arche gulped air, trying to soothe his frayed nerves. He readjusted the sword on his belt, the weight on his left hip bringing some small comfort.

"Sorry. Sorry, I'm all right. Just a bad dream."

It had been more than just bad. He had been a faceless thing, unable to speak, unable to scream. He had clutched at somebody, a man in strange garb, trying to beg his help but couldn't form the words. The man had recoiled from him, screaming, and run away. The air itself howled and shrieked in turn. People shouted over the anguished laments of the dying. Fire bloomed from people's hands and others were torn apart, their blood mixing into the sand. Where his face should have been was only pain and his blood poured from it, joining the rest, only to be drunk by the ground below.

"Just a bad dream."

Arche clenched his fists and stood, gathering his bedroll and blanket back into his inventory, more as an excuse to do something than anything else. Lyssa and Helwan watched him for a few moments longer, then turned back to their own tasks. He'd never dreamed anything like that before. His dreams had always been vague, nebulous, and faded quickly after waking. They'd never been so vivid, so terrifyingly real.

Arche tried to banish it from his mind. He needed to focus on the task at hand. They were hunting the source of some evil and there was likely danger ahead. This place had already nearly killed him once. He had to be on his guard.

"Do we have any idea what to expect next?" he asked. "My knowledge of arachtaurs is limited. Will there be more?"

"Arachtaurs," Helwan said with the steady voice of a seasoned lecturer, "are not as prolific as their tiny, eight-legged ancestors. They live in modified familial units, often underground or in areas with very little light due to the photosensitivity of their eyes. If there are others, I don't think it would be more than what you two have already faced. They are fiercely territorial and often the siblings will kill and eat their parents as a rite of passage into adulthood."

Arche raised an eyebrow and looked at Lyssa, who nodded and shrugged in a manner that said, '*more or less.*'

"Right," he said. "What about that artifact? Did your ancient dwarven poem give any idea what it could be?"

Helwan stroked his goatee with one hand while his other hand found the end of his horse-like tail and swished it in slow circles.

"I spent weeks pouring over it, but dwarves are notoriously complex and clever. They don't like to share their treasure and any reference to something of value is hidden behind layers of code and reference."

"Yes or no, Helwan."

"Given your experience with my former compatriots, I am willing to wager it is an artifact of necromancy filling the air and, therefore, ambient Mana with powerful necromantic energies."

Now it was Arche's turn to stroke his chin.

"So you're saying this artifact can bolster a necromancer's abilities?"

"If it is indeed what I believe it to be, absolutely."

"And what was your experience with necromancy, again?"

"I, erm, well, my interest was of a purely *academic* variety, I assure you."

"Have you ever brought anything back from the dead?"

Helwan brought himself up proudly.

"I'll have you know I successfully reanimated a drosophila once, under controlled circumstances."

"A what?"

"A fruit fly."

"Anything else?"

"I, erm, blacked out shortly afterward." Helwan's pride vanished as quickly as it appeared.

"Great. What exactly *can* you do in terms of magic?"

"I–"

Steel scraped against stone and culminated in a wet plopping noise. Arche and Helwan whirled about to find Lyssa in the process of decapitating the dead arachtaurs with her sword. When she was done dismembering the corpses, she rejoined them.

"Just fixing a problem before it reanimates."

"Good thinking," Arche said, eyes fixed on the black, bloody ichor seeping out of an arachtaur's neck stump. "Well, I think that does it for my appetite. We ready to get moving?"

They set off down the only passageway left available to them. Arche took the Everlit Lantern and fastened it to his chest so he wouldn't have to waste a hand to hold it. The lantern had a dial on the top which, when twisted, lowered a hood to conceal the light, a function Arche regarded as ingenious, and he resolved to get one at his earliest convenience.

It wasn't long before they came to a fork in the passage. Arche and Lyssa stopped, trying to determine which way to go, but it was Helwan who made the choice for them.

"It's that way," Helwan said, pointing to the left. "I can feel the Mana it's emitting."

"How close are we?" Lyssa asked.

"Hard to say. A few hundred meters, more or less."

Arche gave Lyssa a tired look.

"Not too far," she clarified, eliciting a puzzled look from Helwan.

"Let's keep going. Be on your guards." Arche set off before the satyr could ask questions.

Helwan walked in the middle, giving directions whenever they came to a junction, and Lyssa brought up their rear to keep an eye on the satyr and ensure they weren't attacked from behind. Despite the traps they had encountered on the outskirts of the underground facility, Arche hadn't found any since they had fought the arachtaurs. It made some sense, as the dwarves probably wouldn't want traps covering the areas they lived and moved in, but it also made him paranoid that they were barely avoiding dangers they didn't know were there.

At the last split in the corridor, Helwan pointed towards a large, metal door at the end of the hall.

"It's in there. Can you two really not feel it?"

Arche paused, trying to sense anything that seemed out of the ordinary. He got nothing more than the musty scent of still air and damp ground.

"Nope. Let's go."

As they approached the door, Arche could see that it had been intricately designed. Three symbols adorned the door, each interconnected in a pattern that almost seemed to flow, despite the cool metal. Front and center was a trident, the metal blue and green, resembling the sea. Above the trident was a lightning bolt, golden and white in a mist of intricacies that looked like clouds. The final, below the trident, was a bident aiming downward and colored red and black. There was also a mist of intricacies, but instead of clouds these looked like pools of blood. Across the door was some form of runic script.

"A puzzle door?" Arche said aloud, not entirely sure of the concept.

"In ancient dwarvish," Helwan said excitedly. "Oh, this is wonderful! I must examine this fully, copy the words! I'll need a rubbing of these symbols, too. I've never seen anything like this!"

Arche grabbed the back of Helwan's collar as the satyr stepped forward.

"Careful. A big door protecting a powerful magical artifact? I don't think you should touch it until we figure out how to open it."

Helwan's eyes grew wide and he swallowed hard.

"Quite wise, Master Arche. Quite wise indeed. Yes, I think I can see well enough from here."

"Can you translate?" Lyssa asked.

"I believe so. It might take some time, but yes, I think I can."

"Good. Do it now. Arche, set down the lantern and come over here."

Something in her tone delayed any argument. Arche unfastened the Everlit Lantern and joined her, sword in hand.

"We're being tracked," Lyssa said quietly. "I can hear them, echoing through the stone."

Arche glanced at her long ears, wondering briefly just how good her hearing was that she was able to pick out the noises before Helwan's horse-like ears could. He immediately shoved those thoughts away as unimportant and nodded at her.

"Do you know what it is?"

Lyssa shook her head. "No. The echo is distorting it. I think it's bipedal, just one creature, but I could be wrong. Not more than three unless they're walking in unison."

"So not an arachtaur, then."

"Likely not, no."

Arche examined their hallway. They were at one end with the puzzle door, five paces away from the probable death trap. Another fifteen paces was the turn-off point where they had entered into the passage, and another forty beyond that was the other end of the hall, which turned sharply out of sight. The passage itself was two paces wide, enough for Lyssa and him to stand comfortably next to each other, though fighting would be difficult without an overreliance on stabbing attacks.

"It's just one thing after another in this place, isn't it?"

Lyssa said nothing as she drew an arrow and nocked it to her bow. She left it slack and let out a slow breath. Arche stretched, warming up his arms and legs.

"How long do we have?"

"Five minutes, perhaps?"

"Helwan, how long is this going to take?"

"I don't know!"

"Just work quickly. We're on a deadline."

Helwan glanced back at them, seeing them both preparing for a fight.

"What's going on?"

"Focus, Helwan! Get us through that door," Lyssa ordered.

The satyr went back to furiously scribbling notes onto a scrap of parchment. Arche looked through his inventory for anything that could be used as a trap. Most of the contents were food or camping supplies. His bow was there, along with his quivers of arrows, but nothing else.

"You don't have any oil, do you? Caltrops? Ball bearings?"

"No," Lyssa said. "Nothing like that."

"Damn. I'm out of ideas, then. Looks like we'll have to fight on even footing."

"Your mind is keen for strategy."

Arche snorted. "Hardly. Not that it's doing us any favors right now, anyway."

"I wanted to tell you, I'm sorry for having judged you when we met. You've proven yourself a trustworthy friend, and an ally to my people. For that, I thank you."

Arche frowned and glanced sidelong at Lyssa.

"Why are you talking like we're about to die?"

Lyssa let out a shaky breath and met his eyes. He saw the twisting of fear in her face and it chilled him to his core.

"Because I have identified the creature that hunts us. A revenant."

Arche waited, but when no further information was forthcoming, he gave a small cough. Lyssa took the hint.

"A powerful creature of undeath. My people know them as the Persistent because they never sway in their conviction to a task. I know of no way to kill one. They can shrug off mortal blows, regenerate themselves over time. Even if we manage to defeat it now, it will continue to come for us."

Arche said nothing, only watched her. She looked away from him, casting her eyes instead to the floor. Her knuckles were bright as she gripped her bow, hands shaking ever so slightly.

"Well, aren't you a bucket of sunshine today?"

Lyssa did not answer.

"Look, if we're going to go down, let's go down swinging. I don't know about you, but I'm not ready to die just yet. Helwan! How's that door coming?"

"I've translated some of it. It makes references to ancient powerful creatures, a whole family of them by the look of it, denoted by these symbols. I don't know yet to what end."

"Keep working." Arche put a hand on Lyssa's shoulder, forcing her to look at him. "We are not dying today."

She gave a soft smile that did not reach her eyes. "I hope you're right. Because it's almost here."

Arche looked down the hall and strained to listen. Finally, he heard what she was talking about. Over the scratching of Helwan's quill there was the echo of shuffling feet and low groaning. Arche picked up his xiphos and waited for the monster to appear.

He didn't have to wait long. It resembled a man, if an emaciated one. Its clothing was old and torn in places, though it must have once been incredibly expensive. The revenant had gray, marbled skin that stretched tightly across bones with very little muscle. Its hair was snow white and wispy, framing glowing, blood-red eyes. The revenant's teeth, which it bared, were long and pointed, like fangs. Arche had some vague idea of what a dwarf looked like, but this creature resembled a corrupted elf more than any other creature, with its long, gaunt ears and angular features.

"Time to dance," Arche muttered, stepping forward so Lyssa would have the space to fire her bow.

Despite his bravado, he could feel the familiar thumping of his heart in his chest, but it wasn't nearly as horrifying as some of the other creatures he'd fought. That Lyssa was scared of this thing meant that he should be terrified, but after his near-death at the hands of the arachtaurs, it felt like just another monster.

When anything can kill you, the ones that can do it well aren't especially scary.

The revenant ambled forward, picking up speed with every step. An inhuman roar burst from its throat as it spread its arms wide, giving a good view of its abnormally long fingernails. Arche matched its roar with one of his own and waited for Lyssa to shoot twice before he charged to meet it. Lyssa's arrows plunged into the revenant's torso, but the creature didn't even flinch.

Arche closed on the revenant, then jumped to the side as it swiped at him. The speed at which the shambling creature moved was surprising, but Arche was quicker. He kicked off the wall and swung his sword at the revenant's exposed arm. The blade cut skin but turned away at the creature's bones. Arche rolled to the side to avoid another swipe, which put the creature between him and his allies. It turned with him and Lyssa's arrows sank into its back but to no avail. The few times she had aimed at its head, the arrows only scattered off.

"Its bones are too hard. We can't break them!"

Arche worked his sword defensively, deflecting the creature's swipes, always wary for it to lash out with its head to try and bite him with its large fangs. Instead, the creature kept trying to grasp him by the throat. Arche moved to the side and grabbed the arm with his free hand, then he twisted his body and threw the revenant over his shoulder onto the ground. If the undead creature could feel surprised, he was sure it would have been gaping at him, but instead it just started reaching upward for him with its other arm. Arche let go and dragged the blade of his sword across the revenant's throat, not that the action did anything more than make him feel better.

Arche backed away toward Lyssa and Helwan as the revenant climbed to its feet. A prompt had begun flashing in the corner of his vision, which he ignored.

"Helwan!" Arche growled.

"I've almost got it. The symbols all relate to kings of an ancient family. The riddle refers to the one that rules Tartarus!"

"Well, which one is it?"

"I don't know! Tartarus doesn't have one ruler! There's a lot of kingdoms!"

Arche parried one of the revenant's arms away with his sword but wasn't fast enough to avoid the other arm. Lyssa's blade redirected the limb high as she joined him in the fray.

"Figure it out, Helwan!"

Arche backed off as Lyssa took his place, using her dual swords to deflect both of the revenant's swiping claws. He looked back to Helwan, who was gripping his horns and staring at the door.

"I–I don't..."

"Shut it! You're a mage, right? Go help Lyssa!"

Helwan stumbled backward as Arche sheathed his sword and looked at the door. It stood as imposing and stoic as ever. A lightning bolt, a trident, and a bident. Each symbol as infuriating as the last. Arche glanced back at the others. Lyssa had been knocked down by the force of the revenant's blows; it was towering over her, ready to deliver a killing blow. Helwan finished the final words of an incantation and a beam of light shot from his hands, causing the revenant to stagger backwards and fall to one knee. Twisting vines grew from the floor, entangling the revenant's limbs to hold it down. Arche heard a loud snap as one of the vines tore in half. The revenant was rising to its feet, its movement barely slowed.

Arche turned back to the door, thinking quickly. Somewhere in the back of his mind, some buried instinct whispered an answer, too nebulous for words. Too nebulous, in fact, to wonder where the thought even came from. Still, it wasn't like he had a better idea. Arche lifted his hand and pressed the lowermost symbol, the one of a bident. The door grinded over the stone as it opened.

"Come on!"

Helwan was the first to turn and sprint through the door, grabbing the Everlit Lantern off the ground as he passed. Lyssa wasn't far behind, but the revenant was back on both feet and heading toward them. It was quick now, much quicker than it had been at the start of the fight. Arche watched with mounting horror.

Lyssa wasn't going to make it.

Her eyes were wide with terror. Green blood dripped down one of her legs from a wound as she limped for all she was worth. The revenant gained on her with every step, claws outstretched, seeking to rend her flesh into pulp.

Blood pounded in Arche's ears. The fear on her face broke something deep in him. He moved forward, dashing toward Lyssa and the monster. He passed her, saw her turn her head and try to stop as the revenant turned its focus to Arche, but she twisted on her injured leg and her momentum carried her forward into the room as she fell. The revenant swung at him but Arche felt no fear. Something surged deep within his chest. Strength and warmth flooded outward from his center, seeping into every part of his body.

Stone, wind, fire, victory, and something else.

The world flickered around him. He was everything and nothing. He was the world and all that moved within it. He was life and he was death. He was power and rage and the strength to shatter every cursed thing.

Ruby light flooded the dark hall. Arche's left hand rose and caught the revenant by the wrist, stopping its swipe mid-motion. His other hand curled into a fist and he struck the revenant's chest. Something passed between them. An invisible force extended from his center, through his fist, and into the revenant. The revenant was launched backwards, sliding along the stone floor all the way to the far end of the passage.

Arche wasted no time in turning and running toward the door, where Lyssa and Helwan were holding it open for him. He sprinted toward them, his movements extraordinarily quick. Midstride, he felt a rush of vertigo and all his strength leeched out of his body.

He made it the last few steps past the doorway, then he hit the ground and knew no more.

Chapter 9

"But I don't understand, how did he solve the puzzle?"

"That's hardly the most important question right now, Helwan."

"You're right, of course. He glowed! Have you ever seen someone glow like that? I felt his Mana surge, but that certainly wasn't like any spell I've ever seen."

"The process nearly killed him, he's lucky he made it as far as he did."

"Indeed. Mana Burnout is the bane of all young mages, though with his power I'm surprised it's still an issue for him. Will he wake up soon?"

Arche groaned. "With you two making all that racket, how am I to sleep?"

He opened his eyes and found that Lyssa was leaning over him, wiping his forehead with a cool rag. She looked relieved, though her eyes still shone with worry. Helwan paced nearby, wringing his hands.

Arche felt like he had been trampled by an ox. Or, perhaps, a kýklops. His head pulsed with each beat of his heart. Trying to concentrate only made his head pound worse as the room swayed in front of him.

"What happened?"

"You did something that bottomed out your Mana. What you're experiencing is called Mana Burnout. Typically, it's young mages that have to worry most about that sort of thing. I thought you didn't know any magic," Helwan answered.

"I don't."

"And yet here you are."

Arche checked his vitals.

Health: 360 / 360 100%	**Stamina:** 240 / 240 100%	**Mana:** 15 / 160 9%
Mana Burnout: 18:42		

"How long was I out?"

"Just over ten minutes," Lyssa said. "What's your Mana at?"

"Fifteen. I thought I'd have regenerated more by now."

"Normally, you would have. Mana is based on your mental attributes, but during burnout there are punishments. All of your vitals will regenerate more slowly."

"How much more slowly? I've got almost twenty minutes left before it's gone, you might as well explain it to me."

Lyssa gave a conspicuous look toward Helwan, which Arche waved off.

"Going to have to trust him eventually, right? His light blast pretty much saved you, after all. Besides, he might help me get answers."

Lyssa's squinted, clearly not happy at the situation, but spoke anyway.

"Mana Burnout happens when you run out of Mana. It lasts longer the more Mana you use and the faster you use it. Yours seems to last about half an hour, which is light compared to what it could have been. In some cases, it can be fatal. Your vitals will replenish at one-tenth their usual rate. Normally, you regenerate the value of the associated attribute every minute, with the exception of Health. At base ten Wisdom, you would regenerate ten Mana per minute, or one point every six seconds. During burnout, you regenerate at one-tenth that speed, getting only one point in that minute."

Arche nodded his understanding as Helwan looked between them, frowning.

"This is basic information," Helwan finally asked. "Why don't you know this?"

"I'm an amnesiac. Total memory loss of everything before a week ago. I'm still learning about this world and its mechanics."

"Strange," Helwan said quietly, almost under his breath. "Amnesia rarely erases all memories."

"Nonetheless, everything is brand new to me."

Helwan narrowed his eyes.

"How did you solve the door?"

Arche blinked. He had no idea how to explain the feeling he had, so he went for his backup reason.

"Well, erm, dwarves are on the smaller side, aren't they?"

Lyssa nodded.

"I figured if they had a magic door where you had to pick the symbol that would let you through, they'd use the one easiest to reach."

Lyssa and Helwan stared at him in shock.

"You realize if you were wrong, we could have all died."

"I didn't see an alternative. We were getting our asses kicked. I had a hunch, I went with it."

Lyssa muttered something quietly in elvish. Helwan stared down at his hands, as if realizing how close to death's door they had all come. Arche eased himself off the floor and look around the room. It swam before him, but his headache was beginning to soothe. The timer still had ten minutes left. Arche placed a hand against his pounding head. This must be what a hangover felt like, curse it all.

The room they were in was made of fine stone. It was also lit, which surprised him. The rest of the underground complex had been in pitched darkness, the only light came from torches or the Everlit Lantern. In this room, however, pillars were adorned with sconces that burned a bright blue, casting an ethereal sheen on everything in the room.

Treasures piled high between the pillars. Golden trinkets, precious jewels, statues, figurines, paintings, piles of coins, and adornments of a kind so alien that Arche couldn't think of a proper name for them. In the center of the room, on a marble pedestal, a single staff of dark metal was embedded into the stone's very center.

Something about it drew Arche's attention immediately.

"What is that?"

"The reason we're here, I'd wager," Lyssa said, following his gaze.

"What, we've been here for fifteen minutes and neither of you went to have a look?"

"I'm afraid it's not quite that simple," Helwan said, gesturing toward the treasure on the floor. "The whole area is under a powerful enchantment. Do you see these runes, adorning the stones?"

Arche turned his gaze toward the pillars. Now that they had been pointed out to him, he clearly saw writings carved into each pillar. He looked back at the treasure horde and, from what little he could see of the stone floor, also saw writing adorning it.

"I don't know much about magic—well, anything, really—but I imagine that anything that requires that much effort is probably dangerous."

"Well reasoned. Yes, if anyone so much as touches any of the treasure here, their life-force will be siphoned. That staff is emitting quite a bit of necromantic energy. It's possible it's empowering the enchantment."

"So, what you're saying is that this treasure isn't just the dwarves' horde, it's also the trap itself?"

"Yes, for as long as it remains in the circle."

"Can you dispel it?"

"Oh, goodness, no! It would take half a dozen master enchanters weeks to undo a ritual as powerful as this and I am no enchanter. Not even my gaiamancy would be enough to counteract the effects of the spell if I were to command the stone beneath to change."

Arche held up one hand and began counting off his fingers.

"We can't take any of it or we'll die. We can't leave the artifact or we fail the quest. If we go out the way we came in, the revenant will kill us." He shook his head. "We've got to figure out some way of solving this. The dwarves wouldn't have set up a massive death trap without some way of deactivating it. Look around, there might be a lever or a clue somewhere that we can use."

He tried to take a step and stumbled, the world spinning in front of him. Lyssa caught him by the arm and lowered him into a sitting position.

"On second thought, I'm just going to sit here and wait for my burnout to end. Ow."

Lyssa and Helwan split up to explore the room. Arche's stomach grumbled and he recalled his skipped breakfast. He pulled some bread out of his inventory, wincing at the pain the mental effort brought forth. After a moment's thought, he also produced some of the cooked wolf meat they had and made himself a sandwich. It was good, but dry. He felt it was missing something, he just didn't know what.

The flashing of unread notifications caught his attention as he closed his eyes.

You have learned a **Skill**.

Unarmed Combat — Level 1

Punch and kick your way to a brighter, bloodier tomorrow.

Each level in this skill improves your ability at fighting without a weapon.

+4% Damage while Unarmed (+4%)
+0.5% Natural Armor (+0.5%)

You have learned a **Skill**.

Divine Body — Level 1

Two new skills. Unarmed combat felt like something to experiment with more. Something about it was attractive, but he couldn't quite verbalize why. When he fought with his hands, it felt familiar. The Divine Body skill was the complete opposite. He had no idea what that was about. The outline of the notification was a radically different color from any other he'd received so far. Whereas the rest of his notifications were a translucent gray, this one was a royal purple.

He had no clue what the color signified and the lack of skill description, combined with still another five minutes on his Mana Burnout timer, was a thorough argument against immediate experimentation.

"Just more questions," he muttered, dismissing the notifications.

His current Mana had risen to a whopping thirty-three in all the time he'd been waiting, a mere twenty percent of his total. His Stamina had dropped with his exertion of walking around and was now sitting at around seventy percent, which explained why he felt so winded. Arche closed his eyes and pressed his fingers against his temples.

"Lesson learned. Mana Burnout's a bitch."

"I've got something!"

Lyssa was standing next to one of the walls, her hand resting on what appeared to be a normal section of stone. Arche took a breath and forced himself back to his feet, using the wall to guide him around toward her.

"There's something here," she said, unable to keep the excitement out of her voice.

Next to her fingers was a small indentation in the masonry, easily mistaken for a stray chisel scrape. As Arche peered closer at it, however, he made it the slightest hint of a seam, outlining a small circle.

"Well spotted," Helwan praised. "Dwarven culture is famous for their hidden secrets. We should make sure we're ready for whatever might happen when this is pressed."

"Agreed, so don't press it yet," Arche said, his voice betraying his weariness. "Let's figure out our next steps. Say we press the button, the ritual powers down, we get the artifact. All right, then what? Do we take more treasure? Do we leave it now that we know how to get to it?"

Lyssa shrugged. "The mundane items are of little use to me. My people don't trade like the outsiders do. Magical items could be useful, but more difficult to find in this heap."

"I have some debts," Helwan said in a quiet voice, his eyes downcast. "That a couple of these treasures could pay off, and then some."

"What's the potential that this stuff is cursed?"

"Curses delve into a type of magic that the dwarves consider heinous. Even in the early periods of their history, they valued secrecy and privacy, but were not outwardly malevolent. Traps and protections, yes, but they would not purposefully curse their own artifacts. Anything of dwarven make should be fine unless it was cursed by other means."

"So, if we can get the treasure, there shouldn't be anything supernatural about it? It's not going to force us to walk the land and sail the sea, unable to eat or sleep or die until every last piece is returned?"

Helwan frowned. "That's a, erm, a very specific and very powerful sounding curse, Master Arche. I think I can say with some certainty that it won't do that."

"All right, cool. So we grab some treasure and any magic items we find. What if taking the staff doesn't depower the revenant? How do we deal with Sir Kills-a-lot outside the door?"

"What if we lure him inside, then trap him in here?" Lyssa asked.

"Not a bad plan, but it means we'll have to deal with him again if we want to come back here."

"Better to make it out, first, and have the option of coming back later," she pointed out.

"True enough. Helwan, any other ideas?"

The satyr shook his head. "No. My Ray of Light spell was only enough to stun it for a moment and barely accomplished that."

"All right. If, for whatever reason, we can't trap it, run like hell."

"Like what?" Lyssa asked.

"Just run for your lives."

Arche took a deep breath and the pulsing sensation in his head faded away to nothing. His Mana Burnout had finally elapsed and his Mana ticked up every few seconds.

"Burnout's over. Give me a couple minutes and I'll be good to go. Helwan, you said earlier that you could feel the magic that this thing is emitting. Can you locate other magic items the same way?"

"To an extent. I have a spell that gives me general directions of magic, but with as much magic in the air as there is right now, anything less powerful than the artifact would be masked."

"I guess that makes sense. Coming back seems more and more like the best option."

"If we can kill an unkillable monster," Lyssa's voice dripped with bitterness as she looked at the door.

Arche raised an eyebrow at her, then shot a pointed look at Helwan. The satyr caught the look and nodded, nervously straightening his waistcoat.

"I'm going to study the architecture a bit more. Perhaps find something we may have missed. Over there."

Arche waited until the satyr was out of earshot before turning back to Lyssa, who had her arms crossed tight.

"You all right?" he asked quietly.

Lyssa stared at the door. The back had an identical pattern to the front. Three strange symbols, full of hidden meaning.

"No," she said at last. "I...I gave up, out there. Without even fighting. I always thought I would die with a weapon in my hand and defiance on my lips. But when faced with that reality, I gave up. I saw the end coming and I flinched."

"That's not what I saw."

Lyssa's brow furrowed, but Arche pushed forward anyway.

"I saw a person who was scared, who thought they were going to die, who fought regardless. I may have been the first to face the revenant, but you're the first who struck him. You fought in spite of that fear and in spite of defeat, and we're all alive because of it. That's not shame, Lyssa, that's courage, and we'd all be better off if we had half of yours."

"You didn't even flinch when you fought it."

"That's mostly stupidity and ignorance, and don't get me wrong, I was scared fucking shitless by the end. I don't know this world; I don't know what battles to stand my ground and what battles to run from. But you do. You could have run down that other passageway and left us far behind. You're fast enough. It may not have been a way out, but it could have given you a few more minutes. You don't have to see what happened the same way I do, but don't for a second think that I resent you for what you did back there."

"I...thank you, Arche."

He held out his hand to her and she clasped his forearm, her skin warm against his. Helwan wandered back and waited for them by the hidden button.

Arche checked his vitals again.

Health: 360 / 360	Stamina: 240 / 240	Mana: 108 / 150
100%	100%	72%

"All right, let's see what happens."

Helwan pressed the button and the room went dark. The blue flames sconces were snuffed simultaneously. The only light came from the Everlit Lantern, which Helwan held gingerly in his other hand.

"Uh, Helwan?"

"It worked," the satyr said quietly.

"Are you sure? That was definitely the button for the ritual? And not some weird light switch?"

"A light...switch?"

"Never mind. Only one way to find out."

Arche stepped forward, crossing the boundary of the ritual, and kicked a golden plate. He kept an eye on his vitals, but they didn't start falling.

"All right, we're good."

"That was reckless," Lyssa admonished.

"Stupidity and ignorance, remember?"

She rolled her eyes but he caught a smile at the edge of her mouth. They made their way through the hoard to the staff on the pedestal.

"All right, is *this* going to be the thing that kills me if I touch it?" Arche asked.

Helwan shrugged. "I honestly don't know. I'm well beyond my depth here."

"Truer words, my friend, could not be spoken for any of us."

"It's my quest, as you pointed out," Lyssa said. "I'll accept the risk."

Lyssa placed her hand against the dark metal of the staff and tried to lift it out of the stone. Nothing happened. She gripped it in both hands and gave a mighty heave, the veins and muscles in her arms bulging, but still nothing.

Seeing nothing horrible happen to her, Helwan stepped forward and looked at the pedestal, searching for any writing.

"What a strange sort of stone. I don't believe I've ever seen one like it."

"Isn't it just black marble?" Arche asked.

"No. I do not believe so."

"Quit gossiping and help me," Lyssa grunted.

Helwan placed his hands near the base of the staff and heaved with her, but the strange staff refused to budge. Finally, they both backed away, panting slightly from the effort and throwing the staff dirty looks. Arche, on the other hand, could not tear his eyes away from it. Standing this close, he thought he could feel the Mana that Helwan had mentioned. It was hypnotic, capturing all of his attention. The staff was begging to be freed, to be used.

Arche stepped forward, hand outstretched. The staff was drawing him in. It tugged at something inside of him, beckoning him closer. The hair on his arms and neck stood upright, then a spark of lightning arced from the staff and zapped his hand.

"Ow, fuck!"

Even as he said the words, a prompt appeared.

You have discovered **[REDACTED]**	
Will you claim it?	
Yes	Yes

The notification disappeared almost as soon as it appeared, barely giving him time to read it. He cradled his hand, which throbbed painfully like he had just grabbed a hot coal. The notification was purple, just like his new skill. Perhaps there was a connection.

"What happened?" Lyssa asked.

Arche reached out and touched the staff again. Nothing shocked him this time, so he tried lifting it. The staff moved easily. Part of it was embedded inside the pedestal, so he had to lift it even farther than he had expected.

"It's a spear?"

He held it sidelong in his hands, revealing a metal, bladed tip. The spear was longer than he was tall, and holding it brought a notification.

<table>
<tr><td colspan="2">You have claimed the [REDACTED].
Some of its properties will now be made known to you.</td></tr>
<tr><td>[REDACTED]</td><td>Quality: Godforged
Rarity: Mythic
Durability: 15,000 / 15,000
Weight: 6 kilograms
Length: 4 meters
Status: Dormant, Bound, ?</td></tr>
</table>

"Oh, wow," Arche said. "That's cool. I don't know what it means but it's cool."

He read the description to the others, both of whom gasped.

"It said you claimed it? Not that you found it or received it, but that you claimed it?" Helwan asked. "And that it's bound? To you? *Redacted?*"

"Mythic rarity?" Lyssa murmured. "Such a thing truly exists?"

"Look, I don't understand it either, but let's wait until we get out of here, yeah?"

He tried to store it into his inventory but was met by a notification.

<table>
<tr><td>[REDACTED] cannot be stored in Inventory.</td></tr>
</table>

"Looks like I have to carry it out of here, it can't be stored in inventory. Why does it have to be so big?" Arche paused. "I could have phrased that better."

"Focus on the size you want it to be. Bound weapons tend to associate with dimensional magic, that might be why you can't store it in your inventory," Helwan said.

Arche looked at the spear in his hand. It towered above him at over twice his height. He closed his eyes and imagined it being as tall as he was. His Mana began to drop, his vitals still visible even with his eyes closed. After fifty Mana was expended, it leveled out, and Arche opened his eyes to see that the spear had shortened in length. By the feel of it, it had lightened somewhat as well, though it was still much heavier than his sword.

"Incredible," Lyssa breathed. "What did you say it was called?"

"I don't know. It just says 'redacted.'"

"A mystery, much like you."

"Agreed. So we have the artifact. Next step, look for magic items and take some treasure."

They gathered up as much as they could fit into their inventories. Arche left a couple spaces empty, just in case, and put a couple smaller items into the bag physically. As far as he could tell, none of it looked magical, but a small treasure trove could come in handy in other ways. Helwan could take a more in-depth look to find any enchanted items once they left the dwarven tunnels, and the revenant, behind.

When they had gathered their fill, Arche stood by the door, breathing deeply.

"What are the odds we just open the door and it's gone?" he asked half-heartedly.

Lyssa put her ear to the door and listened, holding up one hand for silence.

"Not good. I can hear him scratching against the door."

Arche hefted the spear and gave it a few practice thrusts, half-heartedly hoping it would be enough for him to learn whatever skill was related to fighting with spears. It was not. He looked expectantly at Lyssa.

"I don't know anything about spear-fighting. Only staves." Lyssa forestalled his question. "You'll have to wait until we get back to Dawnwood before you get a proper teacher."

Arche sighed and nodded at the others. Helwan held the Everlit Lantern at the ready, casting a wide light over all of them. Lyssa touched the bident symbol and the door opened, grinding against the stone floor. An angry, rasping cry filled the air as a bony arm stuck itself through the gap.

"Back, back!" Lyssa cried out as the revenant forced its way into the room.

Arche raised his spear awkwardly, unsure of how to hold it. Seeing the revenant again made his palms slick with sweat and the dark metal of the spear wasn't helping his grip. The revenant, who had appeared relatively emotionless before, was much more animated. Its face twisted in hatred as it stretched clawed fingers out toward Arche, despite Lyssa being closer. He could see there was an indentation in the revenant's chest where the bone had caved a little, about the size of his fist.

"Come back for more, did you?" Arche taunted, putting as much bravado into his voice as he could.

The creature lunged for him, to little effect as it hadn't brought itself entirely into the room yet. Arche backed off and the others followed his lead.

"He's pissed at me," Arche said. "I'll distract him while you two get out."

"Arche, no!"

Further conversation was cut short as the revenant pulled itself entirely into the room and lurched toward Arche. The first thing he noticed was that it was *much* faster than before. He gripped the spear tightly with both hands, holding it out in front of himself like a quarterstaff. The revenant swiped at him, fangs bared and screaming. Arche screamed right back, though whether it was out of defiance or the fear sweeping through him, he wasn't quite sure.

Claw crashed against dark metal. He hadn't been sure that the spear would be up to the task as the revenant's sharpened claws could gouge stone, but it appeared fifteen-thousand durability actually meant something. Arche ducked out of the way of the revenant's second attack, a vicious swipe that would have taken his head clean off. The third attack came unexpectedly as the revenant lunged toward him with gnashing fangs. It moved inside his guard before he could react and bit deep into his shoulder, its teeth puncturing straight through his leather jerkin. Arche cried out in pain as his Health dropped thirty percent. The revenant twisted its head as it tore away, dealing even more damage as a spray of red blood painted the floor.

Arche's fell onto his back and the revenant fell with him, biting and gnashing at his face. He shoved the spear widthways into the creature's mouth, barely keeping the snapping teeth from tearing off his nose. The pain in his right shoulder was maddening even through the adrenaline, and the extra weight pressing down on him brought tears to his eyes, blinding him. The revenant pressed against him, inching closer and closer with each snap despite the length of metal in its mouth.

A sword pommel slammed against the side of the revenant's head and the weight was gone. Arche grabbed the proffered arm and let it pull him to his feet. The heavy spear hung loosely in his grip, one end resting against the ground, as his free hand clutched his wounded shoulder. Blinking the tears from his eyes, he saw Lyssa standing between him and the revenant, swords drawn. She turned her head to look at him over her shoulder.

"Go!"

Arche didn't have the strength or the courage to disobey. He moved for the door, dragging the spear behind him. Helwan appeared in front of him, moving his fingers in nimble, well-practiced gestures. The satyr intoned a word of power and green light enshrouded the revenant. Flora spawned across it, bright flowers and moss sprouted from its skin and bones. The revenant moaned, the sound unlike the angry shrieks from before, and its movements slowed. Lyssa capitalized on the moment by striking. Her movements were precise, and her blades were deadly accurate. She attacked the revenant's joints, aiming to sever a limb by avoiding the hardened bones. The revenant was forced to a kneeling position to protect its legs from her strikes.

The fresh plant life began to darken and wither, and with it the revenant roared its anger. It lunged forward, slashing at Lyssa's own legs, but she danced backwards out of the way. Helwan took Arche under his uninjured arm and half-dragged him toward the door. They were almost to it when Lyssa lost the creature's focus. It saw Arche nearly out of its clutches and let out an otherworldly screech.

The revenant charged forward in a lurching run, completely ignoring Lyssa. She broke away and moved back, still trying to impose herself between them and the undead. She brought both swords up but the revenant barreled into her, knocking her to the ground, and continued toward Arche with single-minded determination.

Arche slipped from Helwan's grasp and turned. He knelt and raised the spear, setting the butt against the ground and pointed the tip at the oncoming revenant. His right hand hung at his side, utterly useless with his torn shoulder. Helwan grabbed the spear on the other side and held it steady with him. The revenant had too much momentum to change directions and ran directly into the tip of the spear. Bone crunched as the tip plunged into the creature's fractured chest. The look of rage on the revenant's face barely wavered as it saw the length of metal protruding from its sternum. Arche stood and kicked the revenant free of the spear. It fell backwards to the ground, its movements suddenly slow and groggy.

Lyssa reached them a moment later and dragged Arche out of the room as Helwan shut the door behind them, trapping the revenant inside.

Arche noticed a notification in his vision and opened it, hoping for an after-battle experience count.

You have learned a **Skill**.

Spearmanship — Level 1

The weapon of choice for warriors across millennia.

Each level in this skill will improve your ability with spears.

+2% Damage with Spears (+2%)

Arche dismissed the notification with annoyance. No experience meant the revenant still lived, in a manner of speaking. Even the satisfaction of learning a new skill was dulled by the horrible pain in his shoulder.

"Remove your shirt," Lyssa ordered, pulling out a bandage.

Arche inventoried his leather jerkin and linen shirt, biting back a hiss of pain. Blood streaked his torso. Lyssa poured cool water over the mass of torn flesh, then applied bandages and wrapped his shoulder with gauze.

"You are not invincible," she hissed at him when she had finished. "I had hoped your previous injuries would have taught you that, but you continue to rely on leveling to fix your wounds."

Arche couldn't answer. Now that the battle fervor had worn off, his shoulder felt like it had been slathered with molten flame. It was all he could do to keep from howling his agony.

Lyssa watched him for a moment, her gaze calculating. Then she produced a large, yellow flower and tore it into several pieces. As quick as thinking, she tilted his head back with one hand and forced the flower bits into his mouth with the other.

"Chew into a paste, then swallow."

At the first taste, Arche wanted to vomit. The flower was bitter beyond belief and he could feel his gorge rising as the flavor seeped into his tongue. Through effort of will and her hand still covering his mouth, he did as he was told and chewed until the texture was paste. It took Arche two swallows to get it down. The first had nearly brought the vomit up anyway but he managed to clench his teeth and keep himself under control. Finally satisfied, Lyssa removed her hand from his face. A notification appeared.

You've ingested **Unidentified Flower**.

Pain reduced by 20%.

"You're not going to be able to move your arm for a while. We need to immobilize it to ensure it heals properly if you can't level beforehand."

The inferno of his shoulder dulled into a bonfire. He still wanted to scream, but now he could talk.

"If it heals properly and I level up later, will it fix itself?"

"Doubtful. Healed injuries are rarely affected by leveling. Certain injuries and illnesses can be similarly unaffected. This is why you must be *careful*, Greenstick."

Arche poked at his bandage, earning his hand a smack.

"Point taken; lesson learned."

Once he had reequipped his clothes, Lyssa used a spare shirt to fasten a sling, looping the fabric around his neck. Arche turned, squatted, and bent over, but the movement didn't aggravate his shoulder at all.

"Thanks. I really appreciate it. So who remembers how to get out of here?"

Helwan shrugged, his ears drooping. Lyssa just chuckled and took the lead.

"Greenstick mistake. *Always* remember where the exits are."

Chapter 10

The journey through the halls was uneventful. Lyssa led the way, bow at the ready in case there were any other dark surprises waiting for them. Helwan walked behind using the Everlit Lantern, watching for the revenant. Arche spent the entire walk hoping that some easy, high-level foe would jump out at them so he could get enough experience to level up. No such luck was had.

It was dark by the time the three of them made it out of the dwarven complex. Arche had been completely incapable of climbing out on his own and had to be hoisted by Lyssa. He had seen her fight and been on the receiving end of her blade, but he was still stunned at the incongruous strength the lithe elf had. In moments, she had him out of the hole and sitting on the ground as if he weighed no more than a sack of flour. He was almost a head taller than she was, but there was no doubt in his mind she could tear him apart if she really wanted to.

Upon finally leaving the hole, however, he received a notification.

Beginner Dungeoneer,

You have fought your way through the depths of the **Necropolis of Pygmaia**, but you have not delved through all the depths have to offer.

Your dungeoneering experience has been modified to reflect this.

You have learned a **Skill**.

Dungeoneering — Level 7

Where there are dungeons, there are dungeoneers. Far more of the former than the latter.

Each level in this skill will improve your knowledge of dungeons and how to survive them. Every 5 levels in this skill improves your **Perception** and **Luck** by 1.

+1% Chance of Spotting Hidden Things (+7%)
+1% Chance of Spotting Hidden Enemies (+7%)
+1% Chance of Spotting Traps (+7%)
+1 Perception
+1 Luck

A dungeon. Monsters, traps, and treasure, all part of a quest. Arche's head spun. A foggy awareness stirred somewhere in his subconscious, like the briefest glimpse of a fish in dark water before it disappears from sight. All he was left with was a vague sense of familiarity and the bizarre desire to start laughing and crying at the absurdity of it all.

Somehow, someway, the world had gone mad. And he'd gone right along with it.

Still, one had to accept the facts as they were and a new skill, especially one that provided Perception and Luck, was a welcome addition to his list. The starting level was relatively high but that was likely an indication of the level, or perhaps quality, of the dungeon. It had slain a dozen well-armed adventurers at least, and though he didn't know what their levels were before they had died, it was no small feat that he and Lyssa had survived. Arche was once again grateful to have Lyssa as a companion. Her skill in battle was without a doubt the principle factor of their survival.

They made camp for the evening, well away from the entrance to the dungeon. The thought of the revenant or some other monster crawling up after them had hastened their steps away. Once settled, Helwan gathered nearby herbs and roots while Arche and Lyssa prepared a fire and set up tents. Lyssa inspected Arche's bandages, but decided it wasn't yet time for them to be changed.

Once dinner was eaten and all was quiet for the evening, Lyssa taught Arche how to wield a sword with his left hand and walked him through a simple sword dance until he could repeat it on his own. It was supposed to improve his dexterity and sword skills, and could be done with the sword in either hand or even a sword in both, but his clumsy attempts did little to improve his skill or mood. He practiced until he could barely hold the sword, but no notification of skill gain appeared. Sweating from exertion and with Helwan and Lyssa taking the watches for the evening, Arche settled down into the world of dreams.

Ψ

The world of dreams, it appeared, was full of blood.

Arche drowned in an ocean of it; was pelted by a storm of it. His only respite was the occasional corpse that bobbed in the red. Each one disfigured and charred, as though burned, but how one could be burned in an ocean was unknowable. Those that had faces were masks of despair and agony, and they stared at him as though he were the cause of their suffering. Arche pushed them away and crested over a wave, only to see that corpses littered the ocean like dead fish all the way to the horizon.

Something grabbed his foot and he was sucked under the surface, deep into the blood. Arche struggled but the grasp on him was too strong. Blood forced its way past his lips and down his throat. He tasted it, choked on it, as his body screamed for air. Something moved in the crimson. He couldn't see it but he felt its presence. It bore down on him, crushing him from all sides. It was like a mountain had been placed over his chest as he was pulled ever deeper.

Something approached, pushing apart the blood as it hunted.

It knew of him. It was *stalking* him. Amidst all that blood, he was known. He was the only one left alive and it knew it. It was the ultimate predator and it had caught his scent.

There was no escape.

Ψ

Arche awoke drenched with sweat. He rose swiftly into a sitting position, his shoulder shrieking in protest. Arche clutched at it, wincing as reality settled back upon him. Lyssa was on watch, sitting by the fire. She didn't move as Arche exited his tent and sat next to the flames, trying to banish the images from his mind.

"Another bad dream?" she asked quietly.

He didn't answer. The sensation of drowning, of being hunted, was too fresh in his mind. The wind blew through their camp, howling against the trees and stoking the flames. Arche shuddered. A moment later, a blanket hit his head. His blanket. Arche pulled it away and looked at Lyssa, who was busying herself by poking the fire. The sky above them was beginning to lighten, thin tendrils of purple appearing in the east among the clouds and canopy. Arche flexed his hand and checked his vitals.

Health: 301 / 360	Stamina: 240 / 240	Mana: 160 / 160
84%	100%	100%

His Health was still down from full, which made sense given the fact he was still injured, but it had risen significantly while he slept. Lyssa checked the wound for him and removed the sling.

"You'll be fine. Don't move it overmuch or it will hurt, but you should be able to use the arm now."

"This seems like it's healing more quickly than it should." Arche prodded the wound with his fingertips. "Is this normal?"

The scabs were beginning to give way to new skin.

"The higher your Fortitude, the faster your wounds will heal and the greater resistance you have to poisons and venoms. It also helps prevent more serious injuries. Most things heal within a few days. Quicker if you get plenty of rest, but fast healing opens the opportunity for things to heal incorrectly before they can be seen by a professional."

"So another day and I should be all right?"

"More or less. Your wound will scar, that's inevitable."

Arche looked at his mess of a shoulder and shrugged.

"Something tried to bite my arm off. If I got away with a few scars, I'd say I was pretty lucky. It's not like it was my face."

Uneasy silence followed his poor attempt at a joke. Arche coughed, uncomfortable, and packed away his tent.

Ψ

The journey back to Dawnwood was quiet. No trolls, wolves, or kýklopes waylaid them and by the time Arche had full mobility back in his shoulder, they were in Dawnwood Forest. Lyssa's keen sense of direction and her haste in pushing them through the Sylv shaved days off their return. At the end of the fifth day of travel, the trees lining Dawnwood Village were finally within sight.

Arche's second approach to the village was reminiscent of his first, though this time he wasn't the only one at whom bows were pointed. Helwan's ears drooped all the way back and he was clutching onto his horse-like tail with both hands, holding it nervously over his stomach like a blanket half-wrapped around himself.

The treetop elves Arche could see were looking at the satyr with unconcealed derision. More than one bared teeth in a snarl, their hands shaking as if itching to kill him. If he'd had any reservations about the animosity he'd been shown as a human, it paled in comparison to what Helwan was dealing with. Arche put his hand on the satyr's shoulder and walked with him, trying to offer some small comfort to the frightened satyr. Lyssa walked behind them, a signal to the other elves that she was in control of the situation.

Their progress was stopped at the entrance itself. A tall male elf blocked their path, redwood skin and regal features. He stared impetuously at Arche and Helwan.

"Inventory your spear, human."

"I can't," Arche said.

"I did not tell you to speak. I told you to put away your weapon."

The elf drew his sword, a beautiful xiphos with an embossed leaf design, and leveled it toward Arche.

"I vouch for him, Velgilar," Lyssa said, stepping forward between them. "He can keep the spear in my company."

The elf drew an eyebrow up and turned his sword toward Helwan.

"And do you also vouch for this one? Dallying with a human is one thing but consorting with satyrs? It seems there is no end to your disgrace, Lyssanderyli."

"I vouch for him," Arche interjected.

Velgilar spat something in elvish before switching back to the common speech.

"You are human. Your word, like your life, is meaningless. I would hear it from her."

Arche and Helwan looked to Lyssa. Arche saw the muscles in Lyssa's back tense and, for a moment, thought she might strike the tall elf.

"I vouch for him." The words came through gritted teeth.

Velgilar gave a smile that sent a shiver down Arche's spine.

"Then let it be known. First you debase yourself with humans, now with vermin."

Lyssa stepped forward, so quickly that not even the elves had time to react, until she was almost touching Velgilar, teeth bared in a feral snarl. Arche was once again surprised at the sharpness of elven teeth. For a people who lived off what the land provided, it seemed their mouths were made for the rending of meat. Velgilar stiffened, his own teeth bared in response but there was no hiding the fear in his eyes. His pupils had constricted until they were near vertical slits.

The action and reaction were so strikingly non-human that Arche had to remind himself that these *weren't* humans. These were elves and he knew frighteningly little of their customs.

Lyssa growled something in elven and Velgilar's redwood face paled considerably. The elf took a slow step to the side, allowing them to pass. His eyes dropped to the ground and, though defiance was still written on his face, the elf made a point of not looking at them. Lyssa walked forward into the village, Arche and Helwan following close behind.

The elves of the village were much more blatant with their observations this time. Several watched them pass with open mouths, gawking at Helwan, who was doing his best to be as small and unmenacing as possible. Lyssa ignored the attention and led them to the enormous tree that served as the village center. Lord Cypress met them outside, a retinue of three elves accompanying him.

He stood tall, a flowing robe the color of autumn blended him into the tall grass, as though he were also a monument of the forest. His face was hard and impassive as he observed them, taking in everything and giving away nothing. Arche shifted his feet. He didn't like being stared at like that. Even the open hostility the other elves were showing was better, he didn't have to worry about where he stood with them. This felt like his soul was being bared open and it didn't feel right that someone else should be looking at it before he could.

The elves that accompanied Lord Cypress were a sour bunch. Tall, willowy, and proud, all three. Two had the skin of dark wood, while the third, the only other woman in attendance besides Lyssa, was more yellow, like cut oak. All were dressed in flowing garments of seasonal array, not at all like the form-fitting armor of the hunters. Arche had no doubt that these were elven leaders, perhaps under Lord Cypress, perhaps beside him. Two of them fixed their displeasure on Helwan, who had been displaying interest in nothing but his cloven feet for quite a while, whereas the oak-skinned lady elf took Arche's measure.

If the downward twist of her mouth was anything to go by, it seemed she didn't like what she found.

"You have returned. And not alone."

Lyssa knelt, startling Arche. He glanced sideways at Helwan but the satyr appeared not to have noticed, so intense was his focus on his hooves. Arche hesitated, then followed suit, nudging Helwan to do the same. The satyr decided to take it a step further, fully laying down on the grass, his knees tucked beneath him.

"I trust that you are successful in the task I set you?"

Cypress spoke the common language, probably for Arche's benefit, but it was Lyssa who answered.

"Yes, Lord Cypress. The disturbance was the site of dwarven ruins. We found and fought several undead, three arachtaurs, and one of the Persistent, which we managed to trap. In the dwarven treasure room, this spear was affixed to a pedestal and was assessed by the satyr, whom we rescued from the arachtaurs, to have powerful necromantic properties. We believe this to be the cause of the disturbances."

"Yes, he was right on that account. You, human, place this on the spear." Lord Cypress removed a wooden bracelet from his arm and tossed it to Arche.

Arche caught it and a prompt appeared.

Bracelet of Privacy	**Rarity**: Rare **Quality**: Excellent **Durability**: 55 / 55 **Weight**: 0.2 kilograms **Effect**: Magical Dampening
Magical Dampening Attaching this item to a person or object will dampen their emission of magical energies, making them more difficult to detect and track through magical means and reduce the effect on ambient Mana in the area.	

Arche slipped the bracelet around the shaft of the spear and was met by a prompt.

Do you want to attach the **Bracelet of Privacy** to **[REDACTED]**?	
Yes	**No**

Arche indicated 'yes' and the bracelet snapped onto the shaft, molding its size and color to be nearly indistinguishable from the dark metal of the spear itself.

"You two have done well in completing this task. I can see the weapon is powerful, as I can also see that you have bound it to yourself, Arche. You have set yourself on a dangerous road, perhaps unwittingly. Nonetheless, you have done what was asked."

Lord Cypress raised a hand and yet another prompt appeared in Arche's vision.

You have completed the **Quest**:

Friends of the Forest

Reward

- 1,000 Experience
- Improved relation with Dawnwood

Your reputation with Dawnwood has improved from **Neutral (0)** to **Friendly (+1,000)**.
Citizens of Dawnwood will regard you as a friend of their people.
Individuals may still harbor grudges against you.

You have reached **Level 11**.

As a **Human**, you gain 5 attribute points to distribute per level.

Arche opened his mouth, but Lord Cypress silenced him with a wave of his hand. "Delay your words, human, I am not finished."

The elf-lord's gaze landed upon Helwan, who shuddered under its weight.

"A satyr. Helwan, is it?"

Helwan flinched at hearing his name. Arche frowned but said nothing as Cypress continued.

"You should know, Helwan, that you are the first satyr that has ever been allowed entry into Dawnwood. Your kind tried once, long ago, to commit atrocities against my people that some here still remember. I understand you are something of a mage and of a scholar. These are good endeavors for a satyr. They imply you have the ability to think. I suggest you use that ability in any interactions you may have with my people here. I will allow you one night's shelter, then you will be escorted to the edges of our lands, nearest whichever land or city you call home, and you will be allowed to leave with your life intact. Return and you will not find me to be so hospitable."

"I thank you for your hospitality, lord." Helwan's voice was muffled slightly on account of his face being pressed against the ground.

Lord Cypress eyed the satyr for a moment, then nodded.

"Ryalon, escort Helwan to the guest quarters. Ensure no one troubles him. He is our guest for the night and will be treated as such."

An elf emerged from behind a tree and stepped forward. He hoisted Helwan to his feet and pushed him in the direction of the guest tree. Helwan shot a fearful look at Lyssa and Arche but accepted that he had no choice in the matter.

One of the elves at Lord Cypress's side said something in elvish. Anger rippled across the elf-lord's face, gone in an instant. Arche felt his stomach twist as the three accompanying elves fixed all their gazes on him. Cypress turned to face the elves and said something. The three scowled, one of the male elves even going so far as to bare his teeth, but they all inclined their heads and walked away.

"Now," Lord Cypress said, turning his attention back to Lyssa and Arche. "We have matters to discuss. Follow."

He turned and climbed the steps that led to the primary hollow of the huge tree. Arche hesitated, unsure if he was included, then followed Lyssa. The guards stayed at the foot of the tree, leaving the three of them alone inside. Lord Cypress made his way to a table that was covered by a large map. Arche came to a stop next to Lyssa, who looked similarly puzzled at their situation.

"The council has convened, Lyssa," Lord Cypress said quietly, speaking in the common tongue.

Lyssa sucked air through clenched teeth. Arche looked between them but neither paid him any attention.

"Their decision?"

"I explained the situation and the mediation measures. They were not sympathetic. They are going forward with their initial motion."

A vein in Arche's forehead pulsed. Why invite him along if they were going to dance around the subject?

"I see. How long do I have?"

"One day to prepare yourself. I have the details arranged. The addition of the satyr was unexpected, but easily incorporated. You will escort the satyr to the edge of our lands on the morrow. Please, watch yourself in his company. I can't...just watch yourself. On the map is a list of your options."

"Would someone please tell me what's going on?" Arche interrupted.

Both elves looked at him, as if realizing he was in the room for the first time. Cypress furrowed his brow but Lyssa spoke first.

"I told you that I committed a crime against my people. I broke one of my people's most important laws. I have been paying for it since, but now the sentence has come. As of tomorrow, I am exiled."

"Wait, *what?*"

"The decision is out of my hands," Cypress said. "The council holds a status that not even I can dispute, and given my connection to you, I was only allowed an advisory role. Arche, thank you for your assistance. You have more than proven yourself to us. You are not included in the banishment and may stay in Dawnwood if you wish, but I will not lie to you. Your humanity will not incline anyone in your favor."

Arche took a few moments to process what was being said.

"Arche, you don't have to follow me. You'll be safe in Dawnwood." Lyssa did not look at him as she spoke. "The elves here will provide for you. In time, you will earn their trust, as you did mine. You can make a home here."

A home. A place to belong. Surrounded by elves who hated him for what he was. And for it, he would have to abandon the one person who had actually helped him.

"'No place can guarantee safety, only your own strength and the bonds you make can imply it.' You taught me that. I haven't forgotten." At last, she met his eye. He held it for a moment, then shifted his gaze to Cypress. "Thank you for the offer, but no. Where she goes, I go."

"I had hoped you would say something to that extent." Relief showed plain on Cypress's face. "It is good to know she will have a steadfast companion."

Lyssa's face grew guarded but her eyes betrayed an emotion Arche couldn't identify. Somehow happy, sad, and bereft.

"There's a fledgling village not far from here. A few days' walk from the border of Dawnwood. It lies east, in the valley of Mount Hyperion. The village is rudimentary at best but has a mixed populace. I think you would find the best results there. Your experience and your"— Cypress cut his eyes toward Arche—"enthusiasm may make you valuable to them."

Arche threw up his hands in protest but Lyssa cut him off before he could say something regrettable.

"Thank you. I know you tried your hardest. Will I ever see you again?" Her voice was calm and level, and as perilous as a knife's edge.

"Not for some time. When word gets out about the council's decision, these woods will no longer be safe for you. I will do all I can but, as you well know, my influence is dwindling with each passing season. Do not worry for me. Keep a watchful eye about yourself. You are exiled, Lyssa. You know what this means."

"I understand. We will head to the village." Lyssa inclined her head, then turned on her heel and walked away.

Arche watched her leave, turned back to Lord Cypress, back to Lyssa, then back to Cypress again.

"Wha...?"

"Lyssa will explain everything when she is ready," Lord Cypress said. "For now, we should discuss that spear. Set it on the table."

Arche bit back a sigh and did as he was told.

"Tell me how you found this. *Exactly* how you found this."

"It was like Lyssa said. We found our way into the dwarven treasure room, deactivated a trap on the treasure. This was stuck into a pedestal at the very center. I thought it was a staff at first. Lyssa tried to pull it free, then Helwan, but it wouldn't budge until I touched it. What is it? Every time I try to look at it, it just says the name is redacted."

"It is an artifact from a time before time, when Tartarus was young and scarcely populated. It is called the Tridory, the spear of three. It was entrusted to a champion in ancient tales, then sealed by those who feared its power. I can tell it is dormant now, but not even I know what may be unleashed if it is to be awakened. To think it rested so close to Dawnwood for all this time is...disturbing."

"All right. That's a lot. Should I leave it with you?"

"No!" Lord Cypress's eyes went wide. "No. In the wrong hands, the dangers could be cataclysmic. I cannot keep it. I would be tempted to use it. I know myself too well. I hold too much anger and grief in my heart to ever trust myself with such power. You found it, you have bonded it. I believe you are meant to have it. Above all, keep it safe from those who would wish to wield it."

"What can it do?"

"That's something you'll have to find out for yourself. I have no further answers."

Arche picked the spear up. Its weight was still considerable, much more than he felt was comfortable for a weapon.

"You still have no memories of your life before you came to us, do you?"

Arche shook his head.

"No. Try as I might, I'm a blank slate."

"A hard thing, to start a life over. Harder still when you are so ignorant of the world. I am going to give you something which will make your time easier, because of the deed you have done for my people that I fear I have not adequately rewarded. Treasure it and use it wisely, for the giving of it does not come without cost."

Lord Cypress crossed to the other side of the table and placed his palm against Arche's forehead. Arche waited, more than a little uncertain. He didn't have to wait long.

> You have learned a **Skill**.
>
> **Examine — Level 1**
>
> *Looking at things rarely tells the full story, but your gaze is more piercing than most.*
>
> Each level in this skill improves the speed and each rank improves the extent to which you can view another person's profile. This skill can also be used to examine the properties of objects.
> Every 5 levels in this skill improves your **Perception** by 1.
>
> +2% Examine Speed (+2%)

Arche blinked away the notification and frowned.

"This is how you knew Helwan's name and those other things, isn't it?"

Cypress ignored the question.

"Do not speak of this to anyone. Most will be unable to discern your prying gaze but those who become aware of it will likely not respond favorably. Be careful whom you Examine."

"Thank you, Lord Cypress. This is quite a gift."

"One more thing, Arche. A word of warning. If you forget all else, remember this."

"Yes? Erm, lord?"

"Keep my daughter safe."

Chapter 11

Arche's head spun. Lord Cypress's daughter. How had he not put that together? He rubbed his temples, laying on a bed in the elves' guest tree. Dim, red light washed over him from the glowing moss above, making a mockery of sunlight as he reflected on the day's events. Helwan, on the other hand, had cheered up considerably. He was holding the Tridory and was muttering to himself about potential meanings for the different writings that were patterned into the metal shaft.

"There are several buttons here," Helwan murmured, breaking Arche out of his own thoughts.

"What?"

"Here, built into the grip. Three buttons, and another on the opposite side. The whole spear seems to be one continuous piece of metal except for these buttons. It's a strange metal, not one that I recognize. I'm not entirely certain what the buttons do but simply pressing them doesn't seem to be enough."

"Then what is?"

"I haven't the faintest idea."

"More questions!" Arche moaned, falling back onto the bed and staring up into the wooden ceiling far above. "Is that all life is? Just a series of questions and questions, and any time you get an answer all it does is spawn more questions?"

"Well," Helwan chuckled. "The life of a megaloscholar, perhaps."

"What does that even mean? I'd never heard that word before you used it."

"It is a clever word of my own devising. It means a scholar that has accelerated above the rest, one whose accomplishments precede them. A giant amongst men, to put it in other terms."

"And do your accomplishments precede you?"

Helwan's ears flattened nervously. In the red light, it was impossible to tell if he was blushing.

"Well, in the right circumstances, among the right population, there are some who may know me. I suppose I'll have plenty of time to work on that when I get back to the city."

"True," Arche said, trying to keep his voice casual. "Or you could come to a startup village. I'm sure your knowledge of the arcane and the obscure would come in handy."

Helwan sat up straight.

"What are you talking about?"

"There's a village a few days away that Lyssa and I are going to check out. You could come with us."

"Come with you? You want me to stay?"

"Yeah, why not? Could be fun."

Helwan's mouth opened and closed soundlessly.

"What exactly do you mean by 'check out'?"

Arche snorted.

"I know this may come as a shock but it turns out Dawnwood isn't exactly accepting of outsiders. Point of the matter is we're leaving, me and Lyssa both, and if there's nothing keeping you in whatever city you're from, you could come with us."

"I...I don't know what to say."

"Yes? No? I'd love to? Fuck off? Any of those would work."

Helwan blinked several times before answering.

"I will consider it, though I'm worried some of my debts may cause trouble if I don't show up to pay them off." Helwan said at last. "What kind of village is it? Human?"

"Mixed, so I hear."

"Curious. Mixed settlements don't often live long. Even in the big city, people like to live with their own kind. Little communities pop up inside a bigger one and those that don't belong are made to feel it."

"What is the city like? I feel like I know but I've never been to one."

"Oh, well let's see. There are buildings everywhere. They aren't like the trees here, though some are made of wood. Mostly, they're built from stone, brick, metal, and glass. All kinds of materials. And the people! Oh, they're everywhere. The streets are full of them. They bustle about from place to place, working and leisuring, selling and buying. It's a crowded place in every sense, but there's so much culture there. Histories, magic, services, the most beautiful women. Oh, and the *dancing*. It was a port town initially, you see. Now, hundreds of ships go in and out every day and the air smells like salt no matter where you are. It's unlike any other place."

"I hope I get to see it someday." Arche smiled.

"I think everyone should have the opportunity someday but it is not for everyone. Some can't get used to the artificiality of it, especially after a life spent in nature."

Arche shrugged.

"This is only my second night here, actually. Most of my life I actually spent traveling in the woods."

Helwan could not have looked more surprised if Arche had admitted he was a satyr in disguise.

"When you say, 'most of your life,' what do you mean?"

"Let's see...better part of the last three weeks?"

They stared at each other for a moment, then threw their heads back with laughter. It felt good to laugh after the stress of the past week. Tension that Arche hadn't even noticed was draining away. For the first time in what was quite honestly his entire life, he felt like he could take a break. There was no imminent danger, no threat to life or limb. He could relax for a night.

Helwan went back to studying the Tridory and Arche made himself comfortable on his bed. With eyes closed, he pulled up his profile.

Arche		
Level: 11 **Experience to Next Level**: 1,018 (7%) **Race**: Human **Age**: 27 **Height**: 185 centimeters **Weight**: 81.8 kilograms		**Profession**: N/A **Trade**: N/A **Traits**: Slayer of the Mighty **Companions**: Lyssanderyli **Adventuring Party**: Helwan Panysk
You have **5** undistributed attribute points.		
Health: 360 / 360 100%	**Stamina**: 240 / 240 100%	**Mana**: 160 / 160 100%
Strength: 21 **Dexterity**: 18 **Agility**: 17 **Fortitude**: 18	**Endurance**: 15 **Intelligence**: 16 **Wisdom**: 14 **Willpower**: 14	**Perception**: 15 **Charisma**: 13 **Comeliness**: 1 **Luck**: 11

"Time to distribute, again," he muttered.

His eyes flicked over each of his attributes in turn. He was fairly balanced, all things considered. His mental stats were a little lower than he would like but considering the fact he didn't know any magic and had only used the Divine Body skill once, Mana didn't feel like a priority.

"Wait, Helwan." Arche sat upright. "You know magic, right?"

"I am familiar with a few different schools, yes," the satyr replied.

"Can you teach me anything?"

Helwan's face instantly took on a guarded expression with a twist of wistfulness.

"What you ask is no small feat, my friend. I only have one branch of magic that I can impart, gaiamancy, but I must admit I am hesitant. It takes most people several years to gain the proficiency to teach magic, and that is not something that is often done for free. It is also not something done quickly. Typically, it takes months of guided meditation to get your Mana to a point usable for spellwork. Species with intrinsic magic, such as satyrs, often learn their natural branches of magic easily, but it can still take a long time to learn new branches."

"Don't worry about it. I get it, I think. Not something someone can learn in just one night."

"Correct, not without access to some rather extraordinarily rare materials. I will say that magic is a very expensive progression. Lower-level spells can be cast through proper distribution of word, gesture, and intent, but the more powerful a spell is, the higher its cost, sometimes requiring material components that can be rare and dangerous to acquire or handle."

"Of course, why have something super powerful *and* easily accessible?"

Arche turned his attention back to his profile. The Tridory was currently too heavy a weapon for him to properly wield, even at its reduced size. Improving his Strength might make him better at handling it. On the other hand, his Divine Body skill had given him an incredible burst of power for a few moments; enough that he had cracked the revenant's ribcage with nothing but his fist. That made his Mana, and by association his Intelligence, a mighty lure. It was tempting to split the five points he had into both

Strength and Intelligence, but that was too risky of a gamble. Instead, he put one point into each, leaving him with three points to place in his other attributes.

Those three points would be needed to further balance his physical and mental attributes. His Endurance had fallen behind the pack, but Agility and Fortitude were still alluring. Arche decided to place one point into Endurance, not wanting his Stamina to fall too far behind.

The last two points would go into his mental stats. His Willpower had helped him in the fight with the arachtaurs, the memory sparked a shudder as he recalled the gruesomeness of their features. He was also certain it had helped him put forward the brave face needed to convince Lyssa that the revenant was a creature that could be overcome, though he stood by what he'd said about ignorance and stupidity. Charisma had also been vital in that conversation and was clearly important for social interactions. It could be even more important in the coming days when they reached the mixed village, helping them build relationships with the people there. Perception would also be important, as it had helped to find traps in the dwarven ruins and might help them survive out in the wild.

Arche fought the urge to laugh maniacally at the sheer size of it all. He wanted to spend points on everything, become the best all around. He was sure he wasn't the only one who felt that way but he didn't have the luxury of dumping points into everything. He placed his last two points into Perception and Charisma. Now that Arche knew what to look for, the boost to his Strength and Intelligence were readily apparent. His muscles felt a little broader, filling out the parameters of the new shirt he'd been given. His mind felt a little sharper, ready to process new information and solve new problems. He pulled up his profile again, wanting to test a hypothesis he'd had for a while.

Arche	
Level: 11 **Experience to Next Level**: 1,018 (7%) **Race**: Human **Age**: 27 **Height**: 185 centimeters **Weight**: 82 kilograms	**Profession**: N/A **Trade**: N/A **Traits**: Slayer of the Mighty **Companions**: Lyssanderyli **Adventuring Party**: Helwan Panysk

Health: 370 / 370 100%	Stamina: 250 / 250 100%	Mana: 170 / 170 100%
Strength: 22 **Dexterity**: 18 **Agility**: 17 **Fortitude**: 18	**Endurance**: 16 **Intelligence**: 17 **Wisdom**: 14 **Willpower**: 14	**Perception**: 16 **Charisma**: 14 **Comeliness**: 1 **Luck**: 11

No doubt about it. He was getting heavier. He was pretty sure it was tied to his Strength but he couldn't shake the feeling that there was another factor as well. He would need to pay more attention to that in the future. He was also growing taller, if his memory served him from when he'd first come to Tartarus. If only the measurements were in a format he understood. It seemed his body was physically adapting to accommodate his increased attributes. The height boost felt odd, however. Arche wondered if he would eventually grow to superhuman proportions if he could improve his Strength high enough and entertained an image of himself running through a forest while the same height as the trees.

Helwan wrote notes on the other side of the room, scribbling down thoughts and sketching images of the Tridory. Arche watched him surreptitiously, thinking of the skill Lord Cypress had given to him. The skill guided him in how to activate it. Arche tried to focus on Helwan and unfocus his eyes at the same time. The first time only succeeded in making his head hurt but the second time he managed to unfocus and refocus in succession and saw text over Helwan's head that listed his full name. Focusing further revealed a limited profile that appeared as notification.

Helwan Panysk	
Level: 17 **Race**: Satyr **Age**: ? **Height**: ? **Weight**: ?	**Profession**: ? **Trade**: ? **Traits**: ? **Companions**: ? **Adventuring Party**: Arche, Lyssanderyli
Health: 375 / 375 100%	**Stamina**: 210 / 210 **Mana**: 440 / 440 100% 100%

The information was basic, but what surprised Arche most was how close he was in level to Helwan. He had assumed that he was low-leveled given that he'd only started a few weeks ago, but here was Helwan only six levels above him. He probably wasn't as far behind as he had thought. Though, he had to consider that there likely wasn't as much fighting being done in cities as there was in a dangerous quest to ancient dwarven ruins.

He was also surprised at the amount of Mana Helwan commanded. It was nearly three times his own, meaning Helwan had invested heavily into his mental stats. That made sense, considering the satyr was both a mage and a scholar. Examine had used five Mana, which interested him because it wasn't a spell. It was the second skill he had that required Mana to use but at least this one was unlikely to kill him from Mana Burnout.

Arche turned his attention to the Tridory, which was still in Helwan's hands, and tried to Examine it. It was easier this time now that he knew what to do.

Tridory	**Rarity**: Mythic **Quality**: Godforged **Durability**: 15,000/15,000 **Weight**: 4 kilograms **Length**: 1.8 meters **Traits**: Dormant, Bound, Size-Altered, ?
As you are bound to the item you are trying to examine, information that is normally beyond your skill level is available	

That didn't tell him much that he didn't know, though it did confirm that the reduction in length had caused a decrease in weight. It was still abominably heavy.

Arche looked through his inventory, emptying items out onto his bed to make it easier to pick through them. Picking them up was enough to elicit a small notification that hovered next to the grabbed object, displaying its name, weight, and other relevant information. He was almost starting to get bored when a small ruby ring elicited a notification that got Arche's heart pumping.

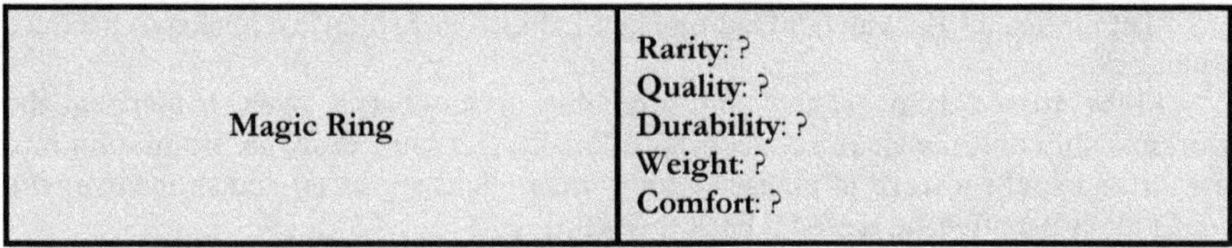

Magic Ring	Rarity: ? Quality: ? Durability: ? Weight: ? Comfort: ?

There was no additional information other than the revelation that the ring was magical. Testing a hunch, Arche tried to use his Examine skill on the ring, hoping it would reveal the item's secrets. Now familiar with the strange eye-trick required for the skill, Arche got it to work on his first try.

Ruby Ring of Lesser Life	Rarity: Uncommon Quality: Masterwork Durability: 50 / 50 Weight: 0.1 kilograms Comfort: Resizing Traits: +5 Fortitude, +5 Endurance

Arche almost choked. The ring gave a boost to his attributes equal to two entire levels. He slipped the ring onto his right hand and pulled up his profile. The ring magically adjusted to fit his finger perfectly.

Health: 445 / 445 100%	Stamina: 325 / 325 100%	Mana: 170 / 170 100%
Strength: 22 Dexterity: 18 Agility: 17 Fortitude: 23 (18)	Endurance: 21 (16) Intelligence: 17 Wisdom: 14 Willpower: 14	Perception: 16 Charisma: 14 Comeliness: 1 Luck: 11

The affected attributes glowed a soft green. Arche let out a small sigh of satisfaction, feeling better than he had in a while. An improved Fortitude and Endurance seemed to translate to improved feelings of physical wellness.

Arche quickly searched through the other items he had grabbed, but nothing else was magical. He did, however, have a veritable trove of silver and gold at his disposal. Helwan sniffed the air and turned to look at Arche, narrowing his eyes.

"Did you do something magical?"

"I found out that one of the things I took had a magical effect," Arche said, raising his hand to show off his new ring.

"So you decided to put it on without considering the idea that a ring kept in a treasure horde might have been cursed?"

Arche lowered his hand slowly, feeling his heart start to hammer in his chest.

"I thought you said the dwarves didn't do curses. I asked *specifically.*"

"I said they didn't curse their own treasure. I didn't say that all of it was theirs."

"Fuck."

Arche grabbed the ring with his other hand and pulled hard. It slid from his finger easily and his attributes reverted to normal, giving him a small sensation of discomfort.

"Let me see it," Helwan held out one hand, the other fishing in a pocket to produce a monocle.

Arche tossed it over and the satyr began looking it over, inspecting the workmanship and the small runic designs. Finally, the satyr drew an incantation into the air and spoke a word of power. A soft, orange light appeared and shone over the ring. Finally satisfied, he tossed it back to Arche.

"It's not cursed. You got lucky. Remember this the next time you activate a magical item, though. Sometimes they bite. Sometimes you're lucky if that's all they do."

Arche put the ring on again and breathed a sigh of relief.

"All right, all right, point taken. What was that spell you just cast?"

"Reveal Magic. A lower level phosphomancy spell, but effective for quickly studying magical items and, before you ask, no, I can't teach it to you. Like I said, I'm not a high enough level and you are not skilled enough."

Arche raised his hands defensively. "I know, I wasn't going to; I'm just trying to learn more about magic."

"A pursuit that many have dedicated their lives to over the millennia. Knowledge of the arcane is closely guarded by the lyceums and libraries that house magical acolytes."

"A paywall, in other words."

"Yes, I suppose that would be a term for it, if it means what I think it does."

"It's a good thing we have access to a treasure hoard, then."

"Yes, well, we should be careful. Greed is as big a reason for people to kill as anything else. It would be prudent not to flash our newfound wealth to the wrong people."

"Damn, I was hoping to add a crown to my aesthetic. Guess that'll have to wait."

Helwan chuckled and went back to studying the Tridory. Arche laid back on the bed and closed his eyes. A notification waited for him.

Examine has increased to **Level 2**.

+2% Examine Speed (+4%)

Arche smiled and went to sleep.

Chapter 12

Persepera
The 15th of Elaphebolion
The Year 4631 in the Era of Mortals

Rain broke over Dawnwood. Water soaked the wood, the grass, and the people. Many of the elves stayed inside their trees, not wanting to face the downpour. A few seemed to be enjoying it, chasing each other through the wet as they raced along the bridges far above the forest floor. It was the first time Arche had seen elves having fun and that it happened on such a dreary day was unsettling. They three were to be banished, but up above, the elves of Dawnwood were enjoying themselves.

Arche, and Helwan trudged through the mud toward the edge of the village, both completely soaked through. As outsiders without an escort, they were barred from the upper levels and forced to remain on the ground. Arche alone probably could have gotten through but he refused to leave Helwan behind. Every elf they passed made it clear they would rather kill Helwan than suffer a satyr in their home for a minute longer.

Lyssa met them at the line of trees that acted as a palisade for the village. She had a thick, green, traveling cloak wrapped over her armor and had the hood pulled high, masking much of her face. As they reached her, she tossed two packs to them without a word, then turned and left Dawnwood. Not a single elf was present to see them off, other than the guards in the trees above who menaced them with drawn bows. Not even Lord Cypress was present.

Arche and Helwan exchanged a glance before shouldering their packs and hurrying after her. Arche looked through his pack as they walked, finding it filled with food and, to his delight, a cloak just like Lyssa's. Without wasting any time, he put it on. The pelting of the rain softened, rebuffed by the heavy fabric, and some magic or craftsmanship of the elves made the majority of the water run off onto the ground.

The rain continued all morning. The foliage above seemed to consolidate the water among huge leaves until the weight of it pushed it to the forest floor in huge curtains. More than once, Arche had been unfortunate enough to be in the landing zone. Twice it had knocked him off his feet, sending him tumbling into the mud. Both times, Helwan had helped him back up, his own cloak wrapped tightly around him. Before lunchtime, Arche's new cloak was muddied, soaked, and had a small tear in the side where a thorn bush had caught him as he passed.

Lyssa stayed about twenty strides ahead of them. She hadn't said a word all morning but she hadn't left them behind, either. Arche knew from experience that she could easily disappear into the forest and there would be nothing they could do about it. He couldn't begin to understand what she was going through but he was grateful she hadn't left them.

Come lunchtime, the rain finally abated. They stopped and hung up their sopping clothes, using the inventory interface to instantly change into dry ones. Lyssa hung a shirt over a tree limb but kept her cloak on and her hood up. Lunch was simple. Oil-drizzled bread, cheese, olives, and slices of cooked deer meat. Lyssa kept to herself throughout the meal, quiet and distant. She kept her face down and refused to meet Arche's eyes. His few attempts at conversation were met with single-word answers. They finished their meal in uneasy silence and continued walking.

When they stopped for the night, Arche asked Helwan to help him train with spears. After a small amount of wheedling, the satyr agreed. They outlined a large circle with fallen tree branches and stepped inside. Arche held a long piece of straight wood and Helwan held a walking stick uncertainly in his hands.

Helwan thrust outward, his steps unsteady and his grip weak. Arche stepped to the side and batted Helwan's thrust out of the way. His riposte sent a swipe toward the satyr's head but he pulled it back when it was clear that Helwan wasn't able to block it.

They continued for ten minutes until Lyssa stood from her place by the fire and walked over. Wordlessly, she took the walking stick from Helwan and pushed him out of the circle. Helwan, grateful for the break, hustled over to collapse next to the fire, a mess of sweat. Lyssa held the stick horizontally in front of her, knees bent into a wide stance.

"I thought you said you weren't trained with spears," Arche said.

"I wasn't. I was trained with staves."

"With wha—?"

Before he'd finished his question, she had taken his feet out from under him. He landed on his back with a painful thud.

"Ow."

Arche pushed himself to his feet and rubbed his shoulder. Lyssa had already reset her stance.

"Not again," he whispered.

They circled each other. Lyssa's grasp on her stick was centered, allowing her to use either end to attack or defend but greatly inhibiting her reach. Arche's grip, on the other hand, favored one end of the stick, keeping the other end pointed forward, but allowed him only one end of the weapon to strike or parry with. He stabbed forward a few times, gauging the feel of the motion. Lyssa rebuffed him easily, but he found that he could rein in the thrust and try again with relatively little risk due to his reach.

Next, he tried swinging the stick. This proved more difficult, due mostly to the length, but it did force Lyssa to block or dodge the swings. The momentum of the swing often left him open for her to close the distance and attack where it was difficult for him to use the spear effectively. He learned between bruises that he would need to be ready to access his sword at a moment's notice if an enemy got too close. Lyssa knew this and made him practice dropping the spear and drawing his xiphos from his side-scabbard at a moment's notice. When he could reliably drop the spear and parry with the sword, they moved on.

Lyssa drilled him in footwork, which was often punctuated by jabbing at his feet with pointy sticks. She marked a point on a tree and had him thrust toward it with the Tridory, working on his accuracy with the point of the spear. Lastly, he held the Tridory in one hand and practiced thrusting and slashing. The weight of it made him feel slow and awkward, but he was starting to get a sense for how it moved. When he had finished, he checked the progression notification he'd been ignoring.

Spearmanship has increased to **Level 3**.

+2% Damage with Spears (+6%)

It wasn't much improved from the measly level one he'd earned by letting the revenant run into his spear, but it was still progress. His skill wasn't progressing as quickly as it had with the bow or the sword, but he suspected Lyssa's Teaching skill had been the reason those skills had skyrocketed as fast as they had. Giving it a few swings, the Tridory felt much more comfortable in his hands than it had when he'd started training, but he was still off-balance using it. That meant more practice and more points dedicated to Strength and Dexterity.

When his spear training was done, Arche collapsed onto the loam next to the fire. His whole body ached. Helwan served their evening meal, a stew made from wolf meat, onions, and juniper, along with some wild vegetables he had picked along the way. After dinner, Lyssa drilled Arche in swordsmanship. Starting first with footwork drills, she progressed along to teaching him additional grips that would allow him greater control while swinging and thrusting his leaf-shaped xiphos. When he could no longer hold the blade steady, she called for a halt.

They all gathered around the fire. Bruised and tired, but full, warm, and finally dry after the morning deluge. Helwan told a story of a satyress who shaved the legs of all who slept in her grove to get back at her husband, who had accidentally set fire to her legs while trying to cook some mushrooms. Satyrs apparently took great pride in the hairiness of their legs, which was why they often wore nothing to cover up their lower half. What Helwan had no doubt intended as a scary campfire story was instead rewarded with Arche's raucous laughter. Even Lyssa spared a chuckle. Rather than be disappointed by the reaction, Helwan joined in with them. It was good to laugh. It seemed there had scarcely been a reason to, as of late.

Arche took the second watch that night, letting Helwan stay up first. When the satyr roused him for his turn, a peal of thunder sounded in the distance. An hour later, the rain began once more. A few drops at first, but then the torrent came down in a crash, rustling leaves. The campfire sputtered as the water landed on hot coals. Arche pulled up the hood of the cloak he had been given. He had nothing he could use to cover the fire, so he let it be drowned by the rain and peered out into the darkness, listening for any noises among the crashing of rain against leaves. He scuffle behind him, somewhere close, and turned his head sharply. His body tensed, one hand reaching for the handle of the Tridory. He saw Lyssa, still wrapped in her cloak, making her way toward him.

"Storm wake you up?" he asked quietly.

"I thought you could use the company," She replied. "And perhaps an explanation."

She sat down across from him, her back to a tree. He couldn't make out her face in the gloom, but he was certain she could see him.

"You don't have—"

"I want to. I…need to. You made the decision to come with me, you should know why. The full extent of my actions, and yours. Did Lord Cypress explain any of it to you?"

"No. But he did tell me that you're his daughter."

Lyssa nodded.

"I should have expected as much."

"I don't get it. If you're his daughter, why did he send you on such a dangerous quest? You could have been killed."

"Penance. The latest attempt to pay back my crime before I was properly sentenced. An effort that ultimately did not succeed."

Lightning flashed, lighting up the forest and letting Arche see her for a moment. Her face was wet from the rain and twisted with pain.

"Elven children are rare. Not every daughter of the forest is capable of bearing children, nor is every son capable of siring them. My people can live for centuries, perhaps millennia. No elf in memory has died from age. Our barrenness is nature's balance but not even nature can plan for war. Over time, my people have had our numbers thinned. As wood elves, we have always found our place to be in the great forests and woods of Tartarus, away from the struggles and politics of the other races. We thought ourselves above such things. Isolated. Safe. We were not."

Lyssa cleared her throat and pulled the cloak tighter around herself.

"I was born as the younger of twins. My brother, Gregorinandiir, was heir to our village. He was a skilled fighter, already an Adept Swordsman by our fourth decade. I don't think I need to impress upon you how rare twins are among my people. We were seen as a sign, a portend granted by Tartarus itself for good tidings. Gregori was good with our people. He understood them, connected with them in a way that I never could. They trusted him and would come to him with problems that did not warrant our father's attention. I did not have my brother's gift. My talents lie in archery, so when it came time for us to pick our Professions, I chose the path of the Huntress."

Arche heard her sniffle, barely audible over the pouring rain.

"One day, my brother asked to go hunting with me. I agreed but I was jealous of him, of the way my people cared for him and not for me. I led him beyond the borders of our territory. He objected but I convinced him that a great hunter could not stalk the same paths forever. Unwillingly, he followed me out of the safety of Dawnwood. We followed the trail of a gigaboar; a large, tusked creature that carries enough meat to last the entire village through winter. We failed to realize that a monster was also stalking the gigaboar. As we engaged with the creature, we were attacked by one of the Kýklopes. Similar to the one we saw together, but much larger. My brother yelled for me to run, but I was angry. It was my hunt and I wasn't prepared to let it go without a fight. I could not face that shame in front of my brother. I attacked the Kýklops, forcing my brother also to engage. He refused to leave me behind.

"We were outmatched, a fact I refused to recognize at the time. Throughout the fight, my brother called for me to run. I did not heed him. His sword, which he always used to wreak devastation, was like a splinter to the creature. Gregori's luck ran out first, and he was caught in the Kýklops's hand. Throughout the fight I had been trying to hit the Kýklops's eye, which is said to hold the center of their life force. I failed, as it covered that weakness with its hand. Nothing I did came anywhere near to hurting it. Never in my life have I been so useless. As it grabbed my brother, I hoped to have an opportunity to fell the monster once and for all. I was down to my final arrow. As it lifted Gregori skyward, I knew the dark truth of the matter. I could not slay it. I wasn't strong enough and my brother, now firmly in its clutches, would die a very painful and agonizing death. As jealous as I was of him, he was my brother. I loved him. I knew that whatever fate befell him would be weighed upon my head. So I did him the last kindness of which I was capable. With my final arrow, I killed my brother."

Lightning flashed again, the light making it impossible to tell whether it was rain or tears that were streaking down Lyssa's face. Her voice was steady, but raw. Her melodic speech low and mournful.

"I do not recall much of what happened next. In that instant, my heart was sundered and my spirit lost. I was struck by the Kýklops, a backhanded blow, and lost consciousness. I awoke in the village, found by other hunters who had noticed our absence and tracked us. I was not the only one brought back. They found my brother, half-eaten, with my arrow sticking out of his neck."

"It wasn't your fault," Arche said softly, but Lyssa shook her head.

"For an elf to kill one of their own kind is the most heinous crime we have. It isn't allowed under any circumstances, not even in ones that would seem merciful. For a crime such as mine required the Council, a coalition of lords across the Forest of Mycenia and into the territories beyond. Father recommended that I attempt penance for my crime before my sentencing, that it might lessen the punishment. The quest we undertook was only the latest in a long line of atonement. Attempts that were ultimately meaningless."

"How long ago did it happen?"

"Ten years. It may seem long to a human, but not so to an elf. It took nearly half as long for me to recover from my own injuries. I did warn you that some are too severe to heal with Fortitude alone."

"What exactly is your punishment? I get the banishment part but you make it sound like it's more than that."

"It *is* more. No elf of the Forest Tribes can offer me assistance. In their eyes, I am no longer a daughter of the forest. If I return, I risk imprisonment or worse. Lord Cypress ushering us out as he did was an attempt to spare me from what this sentencing entails."

"What does it entail?"

Lyssa pulled back the hood of her cloak and looked Arche in the eye. Her hair had been cut short, barely enough to run a hand through, but the worst of it was her ears. Bloody bandages pressed what was left of her ears to her head. They'd been clipped, cut down by more than half.

"They came for me this morning, before the first breath of morning light. Our elders made my father watch."

Rainwater splashed into Arche's agape mouth.

"That's...barbaric. I'm so sorry."

"It is the way of things. The crime is irredeemable, the punishment is the same. All who see me shall know my crime. Shall know my shame."

"You can never go home again."

"That is what 'exile' means."

"I can't imagine how hard this must be for you."

"Do you still stand by your decision? Knowing what I am, what I've done?"

Lightning flashed again, offering them just enough light for Arche to lock eyes with her.

"After all you've done for me? Without hesitation. Where you go, I'll follow. I'm with you 'til the end."

"And I, you. Should I someday be worthy of that loyalty. You should rest now. I will continue the watch."

"Are you sure?"

"Go, I doubt you can see much anyway. I will keep watch until dawn."

Arche stood, hesitated for a moment, then left for his tent.

Lyssa looked up at the sky, feeling the rain on her face. Lightning flashed again, but she didn't flinch. She stared into the heavens, eyes piercing into the dark clouds and beyond. Her lips moved, a whisper in elvish. Lightning answered her and thunder roared over the forest.

Chapter 13

The next several days were quiet. Lyssa had taken to scouting ahead, using her superior talents of stealth and hunting to scout out monsters. Arche and Helwan kept travel conversation to a minimum, not wanting to draw undue attention to themselves. The near run-in with the kýklops the last time they had ventured into the Sylv was still heavy on Arche's mind, especially after Lyssa's story, and he didn't want to imagine what kind of devastation such a creature could deal when provoked.

On their fifth day of travel, they emerged from the Sylv and into a valley. A river wound through the land, bisecting the valley as it flowed down from an enormous mountain to the north. The valley itself was a rolling field of meadow and grassland, with trees dotting the area sporadically. Hills and minor cliffs broke the land, hiding much, but dark shapes near the river outlined the fledgling village.

Village, as it turned out, was a generous title. As they approached, there was only one permanent structure made from hewn wood. The rest were tents and there were dozens of them. The village was nestled between two steep hills, giving it some concealment from the north and south, but leaving the entire village vulnerable if an adversary force took the high ground. If he were to plan an attack on the village, their placement would make them an easy target for bows to shoot from the hills with impunity.

Lyssa cursed, breaking Arche out of his violent thoughts. Arche tried to follow her gaze past the village to the eastern side of the valley, but his Perception wasn't high enough to give him an idea of what she was looking at.

"Those fools," Lyssa murmured. "Oh, no."

She broke into a run. A moment later, Arche and Helwan gave chase. They were still a considerable distance away from the village but the difference in ability made itself clear quickly. Lyssa outstripped them both, pulling away with every step. Arche strained himself, looking at the far edge of the valley and could finally see the cause of her concern. Vaguely humanoid creatures of mottled gray skin galloped over the grass straight for the village, which had yet to notice the approaching threat.

"Fuck," he groaned. "Be careful, Helwan, we're running into a fight!"

Arche put on an extra burst of speed, trying to catch up to Lyssa, but only ended up separating himself from Helwan, who was already panting from exertion. Lyssa reached the river in impressive time and didn't slow down. To Arche's eyes, it looked like she ran up a tree by the bank and disappeared into the boughs. A moment later, Lyssa sailed through the air, over the wide expanse of river, and landed with a roll on the far bank. Arche skidded to a stop at the water's edge half a minute later. He couldn't replicate Lyssa's actions, so he didn't even try. Instead, he hefted the Tridory and threw it as far as he could. It sailed over the slow-moving water, wobbling in its flight, and landed on the far bank, thirty strides away, sticking out of the ground. A prompt flashed in the corner of Arche's vision, but he ignored it. Instead, he quickly inventoried the majority of his clothing and dove into the river.

The water enveloped him. His heart seized with panic and he started thrashing. It occurred to him, as he moved in limbo between the surface and the riverbed, that he didn't actually know how to swim. A deep pressure settled onto his chest as the water grew colder around him. A repressed memory fought its way to the forefront of his mind and he kicked hard with his feet, bringing him horizontal. He reached out with his arms and started dragging them to the side awkwardly. His lungs burned and his Stamina bar was close to bottoming out, already drained from his headlong sprint. His movements became more desperate as the pressure in his chest started to build. The riverbed brushed against his chest and face and he realized through the rising panic that he had sunk all the way to the bottom.

His body begged him to breathe but he was surrounded by nothing but murky water that stung his eyes. His stamina bar blinked red as it dropped to single-digits. Pain racked his throat and chest as his health started to fall. He opened his mouth to scream but water rushed in and drowned the noise. A last, desperate thought occurred, and he tried to summon the feeling of determination and anger he had when he'd fought the revenant. Something inside him stirred and responded to the command. Crimson light flashed beneath the water. His Health and Stamina shot upward as his Mana flew down toward zero.

Silently, he asked the universe not to let him die there and jumped.

Arche broke the surface of the river and kept going. As soon as he had jumped, he had let go of the Divine Body skill, but his momentum was enough to carry him out of the water and through the air. He landed on his knees on solid ground and began retching water. Still half-panicked, he checked his vitals.

Health: 445 / 445	Stamina: 142 / 325	Mana: 28 / 170
100%	44%	16%

Arche expunged the last of the water and took a glorious inhale of breath. He had landed next to the Tridory and was lucky not to have impaled himself on the metal spike at the butt of the spear. Helwan had reached the river and was shouting his name. Arche waved a hand to show he was all right and used the spear to pull himself to his feet. Thanks to the sudden regeneration granted by his Divine Body skill—which was an unexpected and greatly appreciated feature—he felt physically all right, but his mind was thick and foggy from the loss of Mana.

Someone screamed.

It sounded far away. Blood thundered in his ears as he forced himself to concentrate. The need to find Lyssa drove him on, centering his clouded mind as he staggered further up the bank toward the settlement. Helwan shouted something behind him but Arche wasn't paying attention. The satyr's voice was soon drowned out by screams coming from the village ahead. Arche shook his head, trying to clear himself. Pausing only to equip his clothing and armor, Arche hefted the Tridory and started running.

Pandemonium gripped the village.

More kinds of people than Arche knew how to recognize were screaming and shouting, some running for the river while others equipped armor and weapons. Arche caught a glimpse of Lyssa arguing with someone in gleaming armor next to the wooden building.

A black arrow ripped through the canvas tent next to him. Arche threw himself to the side as three more plugged the ground where he'd been.

"To the river!" he shouted, trying to corral the screaming people toward where Helwan was still standing on the far bank.

Dark figures poured through the gap in the hills toward the village. In the press of bodies, Arche lost sight of Lyssa. He hefted the Tridory and ran toward a gap where villagers were engaging with the attackers. Now that he was closer, he could see them more distinctly. They were generally humanoid, in that they typically had two arms, two legs, and a head, but that simple baseline was by no means the standard. Several were disfigured and misshaped. Some of the creatures had too many legs, others had too many arms. More than a few had upwards of a half dozen heads that sprouted from their torsos at odd angles. A small portion weren't humanoid at all, but looked instead like monstrous animals, the only indication of them being the same kind of creature was the gray, mottled skin and short fur they all shared.

Arche joined three armed villagers near the forefront and stood with them, interposed between the oncoming horde and the fleeing villagers. He raised his spear toward the incoming threat. He used the few moments before battle to Examine one of the creatures running toward them.

Kyrzzgtk		
Level: 12 **Race**: Beastmar **Age**: ? **Height**: ? **Weight**: ?	**Profession**: ? **Trade**: ? **Traits**: ? **Companions**: ? **Adventuring Party**: ?	
Health: 390 / 390 100%	**Stamina**: 170 / 300 56%	**Mana**: 100 / 100 100%

"Beastmar?"

There was no time to look into it further. A dozen beastmar approached. Most wielded no weapons, armed instead with a variety of claws and horns. The three fighters—a human woman, an elven man, and a massive lizard-person—readied themselves next to Arche.

"Hold the line!" he shouted. "Fight for all you're worth. Hold the line!"

If the others had questions about who he was and why he was there, they didn't voice them. The beastmar Arche had Examined, the one called Kyrzzgtk, charged him. As beastmar went, this one had several legs and had quickly outpaced its allies. It no doubt intended to run Arche over, trampling him with no less than eight legs, some of which ended in clawed feet, others in hooves.

At the last moment, Arche lunged forward and to the side. His spear plunged through the beastmar's chest. It let out an animalistic howl of pain but didn't stop, even as the tip of the spear exited the creature's back. The Tridory was wrenched from Arche's hand as the beastmar fell to the ground and slid. Reactively, he drew his xiphos and stepped back. The three fighters beside him engaged their own enemies. Arche slashed at a beastmar as it came close, catching it in the side.

The beastmar that had taken his spear lay dead several paces away, its momentum having carried it too far for Arche to retrieve the Tridory without abandoning his position. The beastmar now facing him had incredibly long arms with sharp protrusions in each joint. His sword was barely effective against the odd, carapace-like skin that served as a natural protection on the creature's extremities. His every strike was rebuffed, the delay in killing the creature only gave the beastmar more time to swarm and overwhelm him.

As the edge of his blade glanced off the beastmar's skin again, Arche wished he had the Tridory in hand. The sharp spear would have made short work of this monster. A spasm of pain ran through his mind as his already low Mana dropped five points and the Tridory rushed toward him. Arche was so surprised that instead of catching the Tridory, he fell onto his back trying to get out of the way, losing any focus he'd had. The spear's inertia carried it forward the last few paces, slamming point-first into the beastmar's hip. Arche quickly scrambled to his feet and struck the beastmar's neck while it tried to pull the Tridory free. It took two strikes, but he was able to deal it a killing blow. Quickly sheathing his xiphos, Arche wrenched the Tridory out and turned to face the next enemy.

The spear vibrated in his hand, almost like a living thing, but he didn't have time to worry about that as a new beastmar captured his attention. One of its claws pressed against a wound on its side, trying to keep its insides from becoming outsides. It snarled its challenge at him, a challenge that seemed to say that even though it was wounded, it didn't regard Arche as a threat. Seeing that the others were being overrun by sheer numbers, Arche wasted no time. He took a large step forward, thrusting several times in a maneuver he had practiced with Lyssa. The beastmar dodged the first two strikes, but the third caught it in the throat and the creature died with a bloody gurgle.

"No!"

Arche turned to see that one of the beastmar had broken past their line and was currently running toward the crowd of unarmed villagers that were in the process of fording the river. Arche took a deep breath and whispered a prayer for luck.

"No whammies, no whammies, no whammies."

He hefted the spear into an overhand grip and threw it.

The metallic shaft of the Tridory caught the light as it sailed through the air, wobbling heavily. Arche's heart rested firmly in his throat, but the spear sailed true. It struck the back of the sprinting beastmar and pinned it to the ground. Arche pulled his xiphos back out of his scabbard and turned to face the rest of the beastmar threatening them. The three fighters had retreated a few steps and reformed their line, protecting each other's flanks while rebuffing the beastmar, each having no less than two trying to slay them.

Arche swept in like a tornado to equalize the field. He came in low behind one of the beastmar, sliding on his elven greaves to slash at the creature's heels. He came back to his feet as the next beastmar swiped at him with a multitude of its claws. Arche jumped, body twisting in a somersault as his xiphos separated the beastmar's head from its shoulders. A large tail hit him as he landed, knocking him to the side and taking off ten percent of his Health. Arche gritted his teeth through the sudden pain in his side, reckoning the strike had bruised a rib, and rolled away as the beastmar slammed its tail into the ground where he'd landed. He was about to engage it when a green-fletched arrow took it through the throat.

"Lyssa," he breathed, but he didn't have time to look for the huntress as the next beastmar bore down on him.

This one was multiheaded, with over a dozen faces protruding from its torso like some sort of botched experiment. He had failed to notice this one during his initial assessment as it wielded a large, double-bladed axe and a shield that had strange curves, almost like an hourglass. It roared at him through its plethora of mouths and Arche roared back, partially out of pain and shock, partially because he didn't know how else to respond. Any witty response he might have given had been driven well out of his mind by the pain in his side and the pulsing headache of low Mana.

Arche spun to the side to avoid a vertical chop and responded with a diagonal slash that met the creature's shield. The shield punched out and caught Arche in the face. He tasted wet copper as his nose cracked and blood poured. His Health dropped another five percent.

Arche stepped back as the beastmar advanced and swung its massive axe once again. Arche ducked low and rolled to the side to avoid another shield bash. He grabbed a handful of dirt and threw it at the creature's litany of heads. The shield moved to intercept the dirt and Arche used the distraction to drive his sword into the beastmar's leg. The creature howled in pain through a dozen mouths. Arche ripped the sword free and spun, dancing around the creature. He stabbed it through the back, then slipped past to its other side and severed the beastmar's weapon hand for good measure. As if to cement his victory, golden light washed over him, healing his nose and cleaning the blood off his clothes.

The beastmar suitably dispatched, Arche checked on the other fighters. The strange elven man was supporting the human woman, who had sustained a head wound, and the lizard-person was guarding them. Over a dozen dead beastmar littered the ground around them. The last of the villagers had crossed the river to the west bank. Helwan was helping them move up the slope and out of harm's way. Arche searched the battlefield for Lyssa as he retrieved his spear, trying to catch some sign of the elf. He finally spotted her atop one of the adjacent hills, silhouetted in the light of the sun and shooting arrows into the beastmar as they charged the hill. Whenever one that wielded a shield would make its approach, she would fire a carefully aimed arrow into its exposed foot and another into its heart or throat when it tripped. She was like an avatar of death but she stood alone and the beastmar horde showed no signs of stopping. It was only a matter of time before they overwhelmed her.

Arche ran for the hill, not bothering to pace himself. Thanks to the level up, his Stamina had been fully replenished. He used his spear to strike at three different beastmar as he ran, allowing the villagers that still fought the opportunity to finish them off. Arche reached the hill and pounded his way up the slope, scrabbling at the ground with his hands when it grew too steep to run.

"You took your time," Lyssa said when he had reached the top, felling another beastmar with an arrow to the forehead.

"You didn't," he replied between gasping breaths. "Hard to watch each other's backs when you go dashing off like a mad woman."

Lyssa sent an arrow through the heart of an approaching beastmar and wounded a second one behind it. Perhaps there was a better time and place to chide someone so proficient in dealing death. Golden light encompassed Arche a second time, washing away fresh blood splatter and replenishing his spent vitals once more.

Arche used the Tridory to fend off the approaching beastmar, stabbing at them and forcing them back down the hill. Three beastmar fell beneath his spear before a horn blared. The tempo of the battle changed immediately as the beastmar turned and made their retreat. Several were carrying villagers away. Most dead, but some struggled against their captors, screaming for help. Their cries echoed in Arche's ears. A small pocket of fighting villagers gave chase, but the beastmar quickly outpaced them. Lyssa didn't stop her rain of death even as the beastmar ran away, felling several at incredible distances. Golden light surged through Arche again. When it faded, he felt a terrible emptiness in his chest as he and Lyssa stared into the distance at the fleeing beastmar. Perhaps two dozen villagers had been taken.

"Are you hurt?"

"Superficial wounds only. Nothing that can't be healed. You?"

"Nothing that three levels couldn't get me through," he replied, the empty feeling in his chest was growing stronger with each passing moment. "Don't suppose a shield to the face made me prettier, eh?"

Lyssa did not deign his attempt at a joke with a response, so Arche took the moment to sift through some of the vast list of notifications waiting on him. Anything for a distraction.

You have slain **7 Beastmar**.
You gain 1,620 experience.

Slayer of the Mighty activated!
You gain 1,000 bonus experience.

Lyssanderyli has slain **19 Beastmar**.
You gain 1,640 experience.

You have helped slay **8 Beastmar**.
You have gained 320 experience.

You have reached **Level 14**.

As a **Human**, you receive 5 attribute points to distribute per level.
You currently have 15 undistributed attribute points.

Now that his injuries were healed and his vitals restored to full, there were other concerns, like tending to the wounded and introducing themselves to the villagers. Lyssa apparently intended to start with the latter as she stomped down the hill toward the man in armor Arche had seen her talking to earlier.

He followed, not certain if he was heading toward another fight. Many of the wounded villagers were being washed with golden light as the fighters went through and killed the wounded beastmar that had been left behind. Arche watched in surprise at the amount of people leveling up. To come to what he assumed was a remote region to start a village, he had also assumed the villagers would all be high-leveled, perhaps close to Lyssa, but as he looked at their faces, he could see the fear and shock settling in.

These people had no idea what they were doing, they were just trying to survive.

Lyssa walked up to the armored man, Arche on her left loosely gripping the gore-covered Tridory. The cleanliness aspect of leveling did not, apparently, apply to magic spears.

"Satisfied now?" she spat.

The man was tall, almost as tall as Arche, and quite handsome. He was human, with curly dark hair over full brows. His breastplate gleamed and shone like silver and he wore a dark blue cape that reached almost to the ground. A kopis with a golden handle rested in a beautiful dark leather sheath. Arche noted that there wasn't a speck of blood on the man's outfit, nor did the man sport a single scratch. It was possible that the man had simply leveled, but for all his looks he didn't strike Arche as a warrior. Something in the pompous angle in which he jutted his chin didn't seem like the type to get his hands dirty. The man's well-proportioned face twisted into a sneer as he turned the attention of his bright blue eyes onto Lyssa.

"Congratulations, you are not a liar. You do not, however, get to walk into my village and start making demands of me. You are an issue that I will deal with later. For now, there are matters to which I must attend. When my people are no longer bleeding into the ground, you will be questioned. Wait until then."

Without waiting for a response, the man turned and left, his attendees whispering to him. Arche narrowed his eyes and used Examine as the man left.

Callias Buteo		
Level: 19 **Race**: Human **Age**: ? **Height**: ? **Weight**: ?	**Profession**: ? **Trade**: ? **Traits**: ? **Companions**: ? **Adventuring Party**: ?	
Health: 240 / 240 100%	**Stamina**: 180 / 180 100%	**Mana**: 100 / 100 100%

"Well, he seems nice," Arche said.

"He ignored my warnings and tried to have me apprehended just for approaching him."

"What a dick."

They turned their attention to the rest of the village. Several wounded laid on the ground, raising their lamentations as their blood trickled into the grass. An incredibly diminutive woman was ordering several of the uninjured villagers about between the wounded, clearly setting up a triage. Lyssa approached a man that had a black-fletched arrow sticking out of his leg and began bandaging him.

Arche wanted to help but he didn't know where to start. His only experience with wound care had been when Lyssa had treated his shoulder and that wasn't something he knew how to replicate.

"I'm going to go find Helwan, make sure he's all right."

Lyssa nodded.

"I'll be here," she said. "Helping where I can."

Arche set off, jogging through the crowd. He spotted Helwan across the river without much difficulty. It might have been a mixed village but there were no other satyrs. A group of small children were dancing around him and he was dancing in the middle, hopping from leg to leg as he played his pan pipes. It was an odd sight, joy and laughter so close to so much pain and death.

Arche caught the satyr's attention from across the river and waved him over, deciding against fording the river after his last experience. Helwan trilled a final note and said something to the children, who ran and jumped into the river, squealing and laughing. It set Arche's teeth on edge.

With a wave of his hand, Helwan inventoried the pipes and also ran into the river, jumping far out over it and landing in a cannonball. Arche was genuinely impressed, as the satyr had managed to clear half the river with a single bound. He supposed it had something to do with the goat legs. Helwan surfaced and swam effortlessly over to the far banks.

"Good to see you in one piece, friend," the satyr said, smiling. "Though you should probably clean your spear."

Arche looked down at the Tridory, still covered in gore.

"You should see the other guys."

"I'm sure I will. Is Lyssa all right?"

"She's fine, she's helping the wounded. I was just getting in the way, so I thought I'd come see how you were. Did any of the beastmar get through?"

"No, thanks in no small part to your efforts. I saw you hurl that spear. Incredible. Once the villagers had crossed the river, we got them organized away from the fighting. Wasn't long after that until the fighting was over. I may have mentioned your names, embellished a story or two to explain why we were here and why we were helping."

Helwan's genuine optimism was infectious. Already, Arche could feel some of the emptiness in his chest abate, if only a little bit.

"I hope nothing too tall. If we're going to join these people, I'd rather not lie to them."

"Lies of omission, only. Well, maybe some exaggerations of deeds, but it's not like you two haven't done incredible things in the short time that I've known you."

"Stop it, I'm blushing." Arche affixed the straightest face he could manage, then cracked a small smile. "Anyway, just wanted to give you a heads up, the leader here's a jerk, so we should try to help out where we can and get to know the people."

"I should make myself useful, then. I don't excel in wound care but I know enough. I'll catch up with you later."

"Wait, what am I supposed to do?"

Helwan gestured towards the aftermath of the rampage.

"Whatever you can. You'll find no shortage of need, here."

Helwan turned and walked off, leaving Arche quite alone. Without the first idea of where to begin, Arche let out a loud sigh and turned back to the rest of the village. The single permanent structure of the village, what appeared to be a wooden house, had taken some damage. Claw marks gouged the wood in several areas and at least one beam would need to be completely replaced. A few beastmar laid dead next to the door. Several of the tents had been trampled and torn, and people were already trying to fix them. He wandered over and began helping the villagers fix the tents. At the least, it was something physical he could do.

Most of them focused only on fixing their own tents. The villagers seemed surprised at his help. Or, perhaps, they were surprised at him. More than one shied away as he approached. At first, he thought it was because he was a stranger, then he realized how he must look to them. A heavily scarred stranger dressed like a wood elf, always wielding a large, black-metal spear. He must have looked a right terror, but they accepted his help, nonetheless. He made a point to introduce himself to each of them, but none seemed willing to talk more than a few words. He couldn't blame them, considering what they'd all just been through.

After the fifth tent he helped erect, he was approached by three armed villagers, the same three he had fought alongside against the beastmar. The elf was the first to greet him.

"Hail, stranger. We wanted to share our appreciation for what you did back there."

The elf smiled at him beneath the hood of a gray cloak, flashing blue skin and piercing, black eyes. He had a long, slender blade in a scabbard at his waist and had fancy, leather armor.

"Just glad I could help. The name's Arche."

"Vikterandor." The elf extended an arm. "But my friends call me Vik. After what you did, count yourself among that number."

"Well met." Arche clasped Vik's forearm as Lyssa had done to him.

"This is Elpida." Vik gestured to the human.

The woman never took her eyes off Arche's face, even as he turned to look at her. She still wore the iron cuirass she'd fought in but had inventoried her weapons. Her straw-colored hair was pulled into a bun and one side of her face was stained red from a head wound, now tightly bandaged. She nodded to him without speaking. Her eyes gave no quarter as she took the measure of him. He could easily have been their next enemy with how hard she was staring at him.

"A pleasure to meet you," Arche said, acutely aware of the scars lining his face.

Vik shifted his feet and turned to introduce the lizard-person. It was a subtle move that nudged Elpida with his scabbard. She blinked, her face softening a fraction, and looked away. Arche wiped at his forehead with the back of his hand, trying to blame the sudden redness of his cheeks on physical exertion.

"I can introduce myself," the giant lizard person rumbled in a voice like wet thunder. "I am Gigator the Maeotian."

Gigator was a huge monolith of strength and scale. He stood easily head, shoulders, and head again over Arche. Dark green scutes of a great water lizard made lifted protrusions all along his body. Instead of extending an arm as the elf had done, Gigator inclined his head low, still towering far above Arche. He spoke again from this position.

"You fight with fervor and conviction. It is an honor to know you, warrior."

Arche smiled in mild bewilderment but returned the gesture.

"The honor is all mine, Gigator. You must forgive me if I seem rude; I haven't met a Maeotian before."

"All you need know of him is that he prefers his meat fresh," Vik said, smiling beneath his hood. "You travel with the wood elf and the satyr, do you not? Interesting company you keep. Some would say unheard of."

"I do. We were hoping to find a place here, though I have my concerns about your leader."

"Callias does like to think himself the dashing hero." Vik scratched his chin. "Though the only dashing he's done is away from danger."

"He's rich. Enough so that he has funded this entire expedition, as well as hired all of us to provide protection," Gigator added.

"Wow." Arche raised his eyebrows. "Deep pockets."

"Indeed. If you are looking for ways to be helpful, come with us. We need to secure the perimeter and take care of the dead."

Arche looked back at the rest of the village, which was managing fine without him.

"Yeah, all right."

Chapter 14

The village was back up and running surprisingly quickly. Arche and the others slowly swept across the dead beastmar, stabbing each corpse to make sure it was dead. Arche could have done the job easily by using his Examine skill, but it would have been difficult to explain and Lord Cypress had more or less warned him not to tell anyone about it. When they had determined a beastmar was dead, its body was dragged away from camp for disposal. Others had joined them for the effort, mostly the village guards, and they had soon gathered the corpses a fair distance away from the village proper.

Night was falling quickly. One guard stepped forward with a lit torch, arm cocked to throw it onto the pile, when Arche stopped the man's hand.

"We should burn them tomorrow. It's getting dark and a pile this big will signal everything for miles."

The man frowned but stepped back.

"Initiative is a trait that many applaud, young man, but I detest it among my ranks. It makes people disobedient. If orders are going to be doled out to my people, they had best well come from me."

Arche turned to find Callias, still dressed immaculately. He thought the 'young man' comment was especially odd, as Callias himself looked to be relatively young, probably in his early to mid-twenties, but he let it go.

"It's a bad move. The Sylv is home to powerful monsters. The beastmar are not the worst to call this place home. If you light this up, it may attract attention we're not ready for."

"Learn your place," Callias spat. "If we don't burn the bodies, then the smell of their decomposition will no doubt attract scavengers who will strew them about the entire valley. I won't risk the safety of my people by wasting guards on the bodies of the enemy. If you are so insistent that we wait until morning then you can be the one to stay here."

Arche stuck the Tridory into the ground and crossed his arms. Callias sneered a smile at him, clearly applauding himself. He turned to walk away, but Arche called out to him, loud enough for everyone around to hear.

"When do you plan to go after the captured?"

"What did you say?" Callias whirled on him.

"The beastmar captured some of your villagers. Alive. Surely you have a plan to rescue them, don't you?"

An uncomfortable murmur passed through the small crowd. Callias glanced around, then waved one hand dismissively.

"If the beastmar have them, then they are already dead. I won't waste more lives trying to bring them back."

"If the beastmar were going to kill them, why go to the trouble of capturing so many alive? They need help. Who else is going to give it to them?"

Callias's expression darkened.

"If I say they're dead, then they're dead. You would do well not to question me, boy."

"Would that your own people show you the same respect you show them."

Callias stiffened, his eyes blazing with hot fury.

"I don't know who you think you are, but I will not take criticism from some common leper."

"I'm not a—"

"Enough, you bore me. I won't be paying you for what you did today, no matter what you argue. I know the only thing you adventurers care for is money. We have no contract. If you're still alive or still here come morning, speak to the steward. He might be able to make some use of you, impossible as that may seem. If you're not, then you had best leave my village, and quickly. Accidents happen in the frontier, you know."

Without waiting for a response, Callias walked away, some of his retinue going with him. Arche rolled his eyes and turned to Vik.

"Can you find me a shovel? If I'm going to be up, I might as well get started on a burial pit. That is, unless we want to just leave a barbecue out in the middle of the valley."

Vik waited until Callias was out of earshot before replying.

"Pompous prick. Do not worry, my new friend. You won't spend the night alone."

"Why does everyone follow him? Money is good, but certainly it's not as useful out here."

Elpida answered, speaking for the first time since Arche had known her.

"Most of the people here are indebted to him. His family has its fortune from moneylending and most here are tradesfolk who have fallen on hard times. Artisans, crafters, traders. A few farmers here and there whose crops didn't have enough yield. This land is rich in resources and he intends to capitalize. Once he establishes the village, he expects to turn a fortune. The people here can't afford to refuse him."

"You three?"

"Gambling debts." Vik shrugged. "The pay here is good enough."

"He paid my release fee from the fighting pits, so I work for him to pay it back," Gigator said.

Elpida looked to the side and didn't answer. Vik and Gigator seemed to take that in stride, so Arche didn't push. The answers seemed plausible enough, but there was an itch in his stomach. They weren't giving him the whole story. Still, he was still a stranger to them, and he supposed it had been a rather personal question. Vik produced a shovel from his inventory and handed it to Arche.

"We'll be back later with some food. Don't worry, I'll tell your friends where you are."

"Thanks, I appreciate it."

Arche was left by himself in the dark. Alone with a massive pile of slain beastmar. He wrinkled his nose at the smell and started digging. As he did, he began sorting through his notifications.

You have learned a **Skill**.

Spear Throwing — Level 1

A spear is useful for its reach. With a little technique, it can reach further than expected.

Each level in this skill improves your ability to throw spears and spear-like objects.
Every 5 levels in this skill improves your **Strength** and **Dexterity** by 1.
This is a **subskill** of **Spearmanship**.

+3% Accuracy of Thrown Spears (+3%)
+2% Range of Thrown Spears (+2%)

Arche paused, rereading the description of the new skill. He focused on the word 'subskill' and another notification appeared.

Subskill

A subskill is a specialization that exists within another skill.
A subskill cannot be leveled past the host skill's level, but experience earned for the subskill is also earned for the host skill.

Arche resumed digging with a smile.

You have learned a **Skill**.

Swimming — Level 1

Water, or similar substances, cover the majority of Tartarus. Swimming is not the recommended form of travel, however.

Each level in this skill improves your ability to not drown when submerged. Every 5 levels in this skill improves your **Strength** and **Endurance** by 1.

+2% Speed of Swimming (+2%)
-0.5% Stamina Drain while Swimming (-0.5%)

Arche paused again.
"Are these notifications getting *snarky* with me?"

Divine Body has increased to **Level 2**.

You have learned a **Skill**:

Leadership — Level 2

Some are natural leaders, others are made. What matters is the quality, not the origin.

Each level in this skill will improve your chances of getting others to follow you. Every 5 levels in this skill improves your **Wisdom** and **Charisma** by 1.

+1% Persuasion Chance (+2%)
+1% Reputation Gains (+2%)
-0.5% Reputation Losses (-1%)

You have discovered a feature of the **Tridory**:

Return

You can summon the **Tridory** to you at a rate of 1 Mana per meter.
Bond further with the **Tridory** to discover other features.

Arche stopped digging for a third time. His hole was only a foot deep but he was completely distracted by the last notification. He looked to where the Tridory still stuck out of the ground and hesitantly extended a hand. He remembered wishing the spear would come back to him in battle and the surprise he'd felt when it worked, but it had felt like a fluke. Some battle shock obscuring the truth of things.

He willed the spear to come to him and, to his surprise, it bent toward his hand and shot out of the ground. He caught it by the grip easily, as though the Tridory was being pulled to his hand by that point specifically. His Mana dropped two points, an almost imperceptible amount that would be replenished in less than nine seconds with his current Wisdom score.

Was there a limitation to how far he could summon the spear or was the limit his own Mana pool? He had no way to reliably test that theory without risking revealing the feature to everyone in the village. He was certain that if Callias Buteo discovered that he had a magic spear, the pompous ass would do everything in his power to confiscate it. He supposed he could go off by himself to some remote part of the valley, but that would be just as likely to get him killed as it would to give him answers. Arche sunk the Tridory back into the ground and rubbed at his palm. He needed a way of carrying it around that didn't require him to hold it all the time.

Spearmanship has increased to **Level 11**.

+2% Damage with Spears (+22%)

You have reached the rank of **Novice** in **Spearmanship**.
You gain 100 experience.

Swordsmanship has increased to **Level 14**.

+2% Damage with Swords (+28%)

Acrobatics has increased to **Level 8**.

+3% Control of Movement (+24%)
+1% Jump Height (+8%)

Light Armor has increased to **Level 4**.

+2% Defense with Light Armor (+8%)

You have learned a **Skill**.

Digging — Level 1

Diggy diggy—wait, you're not a dwarf!

Each level in this skill improves your ability to dig holes.
Every 5 levels in this skill improves your **Strength** and **Endurance** by 1.
This is a **subskill** of **Menial Labor**.

+3% Digging Speed (+3%)
+1% Soil Manipulation (+1%)
-0.5% Stamina Drain while Digging (-0.5%)

You have learned a **Skill**:

Menial Labor — Level 1

Work harder, not smarter.

Each level in this skill improves your ability to do a wide variety of physical tasks.

+1% Efficiency at Menial Tasks (+1%)
+1% Speed at Menial Tasks (+1%)
-0.5% Stamina Drain during Menial Tasks (-0.5%)

The hole was as deep as Arche's waist when he took a break. He sat with his feet dangling over the edge. The idea that 'digging' was a skill made him snort, but it made as much sense as anything in Tartarus. Arche wondered what a Master at digging would look like and chuckled at the thought of a person swimming through the ground like water.

Night fell fully on the valley, though one almost couldn't tell. The small, green moon in the sky was full and the larger blue moon was missing only a crescent. They bathed the entire valley in cyan light. Arche stared up at the sky for a long time, wondering what was out there, among the stars. It felt so open and unguarded after all his time in the forest. Constellations flickered, meteors flashed across the sky, and through it all the two moons shone down like the multicolored eyes of some celestial being. The world was a bigger place than he could imagine and the sky only served to highlight how little of it he'd actually seen. After he'd drunk his fill of the sky and considerably widened the hole, he took a break. It was as good a time as any to assign his new attribute points.

<table>
<tr><td colspan="3" align="center">Arche</td></tr>
<tr>
<td>Level: 14
Experience to Next Level: 238 (83%)
Race: Human
Age: 27
Height: 185 centimeters
Weight: 82 kilograms</td>
<td colspan="2">Profession: N/A
Trade: N/A
Traits: Slayer of the Mighty
Companions: Lyssanderyli
Adventuring Party: Helwan Panysk</td>
</tr>
<tr><td colspan="3" align="center">You have 15 undistributed attribute points</td></tr>
<tr>
<td align="center">Health: 445 / 445
100%</td>
<td align="center">Stamina: 271 / 325
83%</td>
<td align="center">Mana: 170 / 170
100%</td>
</tr>
<tr>
<td align="center">Strength: 22
Dexterity: 18
Agility: 17
Fortitude: 23 (18)</td>
<td align="center">Endurance: 21 (16)
Intelligence: 17
Wisdom: 14
Willpower: 14</td>
<td align="center">Perception: 16
Charisma: 14
Comeliness: 1
Luck: 11</td>
</tr>
</table>

Fifteen points to assign, and twelve places to assign them. The choice never seemed to get any easier. Still, he was happy to have the chance to improve himself. Despite the fact he still didn't know any spells, the prospect of being able to use his Divine Body skill more was tempting. Now that he had more of an idea of what it could do, all he wanted to do was experiment more. With that thought in mind, he invested two points into Intelligence and Wisdom each.

The next part was difficult for him but he gritted his teeth and did it anyway, investing a full four points into Charisma. Seven points left, it was time to shore up his physical stats. The Tridory still felt unwieldy in his grip and if his foot race with Lyssa had proved anything, it was how much slower he was compared to competent fighters. He placed two points into Dexterity, two into Agility, and the final three into Strength.

<table>
<tr>
<td align="center">Health: 460 / 460
100%</td>
<td align="center">Stamina: 283 / 325
87%</td>
<td align="center">Mana: 190 / 190
100%</td>
</tr>
<tr>
<td align="center">Strength: 25
Dexterity: 20
Agility: 19
Fortitude: 23 (18)</td>
<td align="center">Endurance: 21 (16)
Intelligence: 19
Wisdom: 16
Willpower: 14</td>
<td align="center">Perception: 16
Charisma: 18
Comeliness: 1
Luck: 11</td>
</tr>
</table>

The investiture into Charisma would help him make allies, or so he hoped. Considering how badly his last two interactions with Callias had gone, he would need all the allies he could get. Now that the housekeeping was done, it was time to reattack the gardening.

An hour and four levels in both Digging and Menial Labor later, he was interrupted by Lyssa.

"What are you doing?"

Arche stopped and looked up out of the hole he'd dug. It was now up to his chest, though not much wider or longer than his shoulders. He had removed his armor and his shirt, hoping to avoid sullying them with sweat and dirt.

"I'm digging a mass grave. For them to place the beastmar bodies into."

"I can see that. *Why* are you doing it?"

Arche clambered out of the hole and saw that she was covered in dried blood. Red blood, to his relief. She looked as though she had been more than hands-deep in a couple of the people in the triage.

"Two reasons," he said. "The first is that I don't think it would be wise to leave a giant pile of burned bodies out in the open like an all-you-can-eat buffet for any nearby monsters."

Lyssa blinked and shook her head, clearly not understanding the simile. Arche pressed on anyway.

"The second being that I would want the same effort done for me."

"They wouldn't do the same for you. They would eat you."

"Then that gives me the moral high ground, don't you think?"

"Barely four weeks old and now you're spouting philosophy at me."

"I blame you. You named me after a philosophical abstract, didn't you?"

"It's foolish."

"I disagree."

Lyssa snorted and produced a platter of food from her inventory.

"I brought you some food. Your new friend, Vik, told me where to find you. I wanted to apologize for leaving you. We should have stayed together. I saw the beastmar coming and no warning had been raised. My instincts acted before my mind. If something had happened to you or Helwan, I would have been completely distracted."

Arche held up a hand to stop her.

"Don't apologize. You were absolutely right to do what you did. You saved lives, gave those people enough time to prepare for the attack. It would have been a slaughter if you'd waited for us."

"Still, you could have been killed. We both could have been. All for my recklessness."

"You know, I think a certain wood elf once told me that the journey is often dangerous and that I should be prepared for that danger and not walk through the woods like some human woman."

Lyssa let out an actual chuckle.

"That was a horrible paraphrase."

"Am I wrong?"

Arche poured water over his hands, rubbing the dirt from beneath his fingernails before he ate. There wasn't much, a few thin slices of meat, a handful of olives, and a salad of pepper slices, but there was also a small flagon of mead that they took turns sipping from. What was left wanting from dinner they supplemented with their own supplies, wolf meat and sweet wine that conjured a memory from the weeks before.

The memory seemed almost hollow now that he was surrounded by so much death. He stared at the pile of beastmar. Black blood congealed throughout the mass; wounds gaped like a broken taboo. Dozens of beastmar were piled high not twenty strides away and Arche was sitting and eating and laughing. The realization of it made his stomach turn.

"Is this what life is like?"

Lyssa tilted her head, brow furrowed in confusion.

"Battle after battle, conflict after conflict, with everything else happening in the breaths between fights?" Arche gestured to the pile of beastmar corpses. "Is that our fate? Are we going to end up like them one of these days? Wasted flesh and wasted life?"

Lyssa didn't say anything for a long minute.

"Long ago, before my people secluded themselves to the forest, there was a society of elves who dedicated themselves to making war. They lived for battle, constantly training and constantly starting conflict. They came to be feared throughout Tartarus for their brutality and their skill, but they did not last long. Throughout their many conflicts, their numbers dwindled. Elves are long-lived but not easily replaced. In less than a hundred years, they went from three hundred elves to only three."

She paused to take a swig of wine, then handed him the flagon.

"When it was only the three of them left, they turned their blades on each other. Two of them were struck down, their blood joining the fallen, but the last survived with grievous wounds. Before he succumbed to his injuries, he left writings for those who would come after."

"What did he write?"

"Seek peace and fight to defend it. Raise your weapon only for what you believe in." Lyssa paused, her throat flexing and unflexing as though the words were stuck. "Spill not the blood of your kin, for it is the ruin of us all."

Arche stared at the bodies of the slain.

"Battle can be your life," Lyssa said. "Or it can be part of it. Ultimately, it is your choice what kind of life you will lead and what the meaning of it is. Death is part of life, there is no escaping it, but a life is not defined by its end, it is defined by its measure."

It wasn't the reassurance he had hoped for, but her words helped lessen the empty feeling that had settled inside his chest. He began to feel a little more himself, whoever that might be.

"I would not have expected a Huntress to be wise in philosophy."

"My life has been defined by the death of those around me. I have had time to consider these things."

"You're wrong there." Arche wiped his hands on the grass. "If my life is a product of what I dedicate it to, then so is yours. Many of these people would be dead, if not for you. I would be dead, several times over. That accounts for something."

Lyssa fixed her eyes on the moons. It was her turn to be silent and think.

"By the way, I learned a few new things." He did his best to keep his voice calm and disinterested.

"Oh? Like what?" Lyssa took another swig of wine.

Arche gave a mysterious smile and held his hand out to the side. The Tridory launched itself toward him from several paces away and he caught it without looking. Lyssa spat wine in a fine mist, turning Arche's smile into a full grin.

"What the *fuck?*"

"Hey! You're learning!"

"How did you do that?"

"By complete accident, the first time. I finally had time to go through all my notifications out here and found out that one of the features of the spear is something called 'Return' which allows me to summon it for a small Mana cost."

"That's incredible. I don't know of any weapons that have an ability like this."

"I guess I'm just that special."

"Who else knows about this?"

"No one, I think. I used it once in the battle, but I don't think anyone saw and it wasn't half as slick. I figure the only people who might have seen were the three I was fighting alongside. Vik, Elpida, and Gigator, but they've been friendly so far and no one's said anything."

Lyssa nodded. Her gaze turned back to the sea of tents sequestered near the river. Now that night was upon them, many had strung up candles or lanterns outside their tents, giving the whole community a soft, golden glow reminiscent of fireflies.

"This place is different than I had hoped. It's full of people. People I do not understand."

Arche looked sideways at her and realized she probably hadn't met many people outside of her village before him.

"How are you holding up? We haven't really talked in a minute."

Lyssa shrugged.

"I don't know. I've known this was coming for years, but it still doesn't feel real. Dawnwood is all I've ever known; now I can never return. This village seemed like the best choice, but I don't know that I can join a community that would subjugate itself to a man like *that.*"

"What if we showed them a different way?"

Lyssa frowned.

"What do you mean?"

"I've been talking to Vik and his gang. By the sound of it, most people here are only following Callias because he's paying them or holding them in some kind of debt. If we can wipe away that debt, maybe we can undercut his whole operation, force him to step down and establish a better way of life for the people here. Right now, it seems like he calls all the shots and is only acting in his own self-interests."

"How would we get the money to pay for such things?"

"The treasure from the dwarven ruins. I never got rid of my share and Helwan still has his. If the three of us pool it together, I'm sure it's worth more than whatever that prick has with him. If we can free enough people from their debt, we might be able to sway the people against him."

"Who would they follow? You?"

Arche paused. The idea of running his own village was tempting, but the sheer responsibility of it all was too much to fathom. His own goals would be constantly overshadowed by administrative issues and the needs of the people.

"I don't know. I don't think I'd be a very good leader. I'm just saying, if we don't like the way things are, we could try to change it. Maybe you could lead."

"Doubtful. My father and my"—she took a steadying breath—"brother were both gifted leaders. But me? I wouldn't know where to begin. What if we just made things worse?"

"One, I don't believe that. I'm not really sure how old you are, but if your dad is even half as good as you say he is, you must have learned something from him over the years, even if you don't know it. Two, how could things be worse than a leader who's so adverse to listening to advice that he'd rather let all of his people get ambushed and eaten by monsters?"

"You make some good points, I'll give you that, Greenstick."

"I'm not even saying that we become the leaders of the village. Maybe they have someone else lined up who'd be perfect for the job. I'm only saying that if we can bring a better life to these people, we should probably try. Just think about it."

"I will. That's all I can promise for now."

Persuasion has increased to **Level 2**.

+1% Persuasion Chance (+2%)

You have received a **Quest**:

Rise and Fall

Lord Callias Buteo has proved himself a poor leader, relying on fear and finance to gain the loyalty of his townspeople. Replace him and set forth a new age of opportunity.

Objectives	Rewards
- Remove Callias Buteo from power - Establish a form of government for the village - Have a member of your party lead the village (*Optional*)	- 10,000 Experience - Increased Relation with the village of Buton - Leadership of a village (*Optional*)

"I can't believe he named the village after himself," Arche muttered. "And the worst part of his name, too."

"If I agree and if we succeed, that's the first thing to change."

"Deal." Arche dismissed the notification. "In the meantime, we should avoid taking any of Callias's money. Help the people, refuse the pay. We can last on our own supplies or do our own hunting if it comes to it."

"Trying to win another moral victory?"

"Not exactly. I'm trying to show him that we can't be bought. That not everyone cares about his stupid money as much as he does."

Arche finished the last of his meal and stood. He picked up the shovel and jumped back into the hole. It wasn't going to dig itself, after all.

Chapter 15

Dawn broke over the trees. Pink sky peeked through amber clouds like rosy fingers reaching for the night. Arche wiped the sweat from his face and looked out over the valley. He hadn't slept and every last muscle ached, but he'd gotten the job done. He'd also propelled himself all the way to level twelve in both Menial Labor and Digging, leaving him a measly thirty-eight experience away from Level Fifteen.

Lyssa sat on the ground nearby, cleaning the dirt from her nails. She had called him an idiot a dozen times at least over the course of the night, and probably worse things in the language of the elves, but she had helped him anyway. A few monsters had crept out of the woods to investigate, but a few well-placed arrows caused them to scurry back into safety. Lyssa had slept while he worked and took over when he was too exhausted to go further. The effects of a full night of manual labor were hard to ignore, but there was vindication in a job well done.

Exhausted — Tier 1

-50% Vitals Regeneration
+15% Chance to Make Mistakes
+50% Stamina Drain of Physical Tasks

People were rising in the village and several were already approaching. Callias led them, but Arche spotted Vik, Elpida, and Gigator among others he didn't know. Helwan was also amid the burgeoning crowd.

"So you've proved you can dig a hole. We're all very impressed," Callias said in a flat voice. "Torch it."

One of the guards stepped forward and hurled a lit torch onto the pile of bodies. The beastmar ignited quickly, blazing brightly in the light of the morning sun. Arche was forced to take a step away from the sudden blast of heat.

"You think you've proved something here?" Callias asked. "I assure you, you've only proven your own stupidity."

Arche narrowed his eyes. A small voice in the back of his mind told him to let it go, but he was too tired and too annoyed to listen to it.

"You sure talk a whole lot to say nothing, don't you? As unenlightening as our conversations are, I have better ways to waste my time. Now, if you'll excuse me, I'm going to go take a bath and a nap."

"You think you talk to me like that and just walk away?" Callias snarled. "I am in command, here."

"Well, yeah. I'm not one of your people, as you're quick to remind me, and unless you're going to have your guards there try to kill me for mildly sassing you, I'll speak and think how I please. Of course, if you *did* sic your guards on me, that would only prove my point."

"And what point is that?"

"That you care more about your image and your money than anything or anyone in this town."

Callias sputtered at him, more shocked than anything, but Arche could tell rage was coming. The crowd was suddenly a lot more interested in the exchange, excited whispers filling the air. Lyssa stepped up next to him.

"Careful," she whispered. "We're outnumbered."

"By all means," Callias said at last. "Please, continue to talk however you wish. But know that you will receive no aid from me. Good luck surviving when your supplies run low, when winter sets in, when you have no coin to trade."

"You forget, Callias. I am not from your city. I have lived in these woods. You will get your people killed by your own greed and ignorance. You've been here, what, a week by my estimate? How many times have you been attacked?"

"Twice!" someone called out.

"Twice," Arche echoed, layering the word with as much contempt as he could muster. "And yet you still camp out in the worst vantage in the entire valley and refuse to even place a watch. If I didn't know any better, I'd say you were *trying* to get these people killed."

"Insults are one thing, commoner, but accusations are another. Kneel and apologize now, and that will be the end of it."

Arche took two steps forward. The guards flanking Callias drew their swords, each one a bundle of caution and nerves. Arche gave a mirthless smile.

"I kneel for no man, least of all whatever you are."

Callias, to his credit, refused to be intimidated.

"You will learn your place or you will find none here."

Arche turned and left, heading toward the river. The crowd parted for him, too astonished to say anything.

"I'm not finished with you!" Callias called after him.

"But I'm bored of you. If you really want to continue this, you can berate me while I bathe."

Callias took a step after him, as though he intended to do just that, but quickly thought better of it. Instead, the village lord stormed off toward the village proper. Lyssa caught up to Arche easily and fell into step beside him.

"That was foolish."

"True, but damn if it didn't feel good. Do you want to spend the next however many years bowing and scraping for a pompous asshat like that? I'm not putting up with it."

"I haven't even agreed to your idea."

"What idea?" Helwan asked as he joined them, followed by Vik, Elpida, and Gigator.

"Bold move, kid," Vik said, his mouth curving in a smile from beneath his hood.

"Your words showed scales." Gigator nodded his approval.

"You're an idiot," Elpida grunted.

"Something we agree on." Lyssa nodded.

Arche looked back and forth between the small crowd. "Are you *all* coming to watch me bathe? Because at this point, I feel like I need to start charging people."

Five pairs of eyes rolled at him.

"Come find us later, kid," Vik said. "I think we've got something to discuss."

The three fighters left, leaving Arche alone with Lyssa and Helwan.

"What idea?" Helwan repeated himself.

"Arche wants to start a revolution," Lyssa said.

"That's a bit of an overstatement."

They reached the river. Arche side-eyed his friends, but they apparently had no intentions of giving him any privacy so he pulled open his inventory and started depositing his armor and clothing into it. Wearing only his pants, he gave a running leap, tucking his arms around his knees and inventorying the last of his clothing as he hit the water.

He surged down into the dark, his feet quickly finding smooth stone at the bottom of the river. The cold was overpowering, especially so in his exhausted state, but the water was a balm to his aching muscles. The previous fear he had experienced during his last swimming attempt was still there, lurking under the surface, but he managed to keep the rising feeling of pressure in his chest at bay by staying close enough to the bank that he could stand. Initially, the water came up to his navel, but that felt too exposed so he kept moving inward until the water came up to the middle of his chest.

"I'm *not* going to start a revolution. I'm going to get Callias removed from power."

"That's, erm, certainly a bold strategy," Helwan said delicately. "The people here seem to be scared of him. It seems he has some powerful connections back in Ship's Shape."

"What's that?"

"Oh, that's the city I'm from. They're from the same place."

Arche narrowed his eyes at the satyr.

"You're bullshitting me."

"I beg your pardon!"

"No way it's called that."

"It most certainly is!"

Lyssa sat down and dipped her feet in the water. "In any case, I have not agreed to the plan."

"You don't think Arche would make a good leader?"

"Actually," Arche cut in. "I don't want to be the new leader. If one of us has got to do it, we should make Lyssa be in charge."

"Now that's a much, much better idea."

"Hey!"

"I mean no offense, but Lyssa is clearly the calmer mind when it comes to decision making."

"And yet I'm still offended. Never mind. How did your night go?"

Helwan dusted the shoulders of his tunic proudly.

"I have, in fact, established myself amongst the people as a musician, a mage, and a megaloscholar."

Arche summoned his shirt from the day before and began rinsing it in the river, trying to rid it of blood both red and black. "Sounds like they like you. Anyone give you trouble?"

Helwan shook his head. "No, not yet. There have been some looks, but I think for the most part I've been accepted. How long that will last if you draw their lord's ire, I don't know."

Arche gave Helwan a flat look.

"You know I'm on your side, whatever action you decide to take," the satyr said quickly. "You two saved my life, after all. I haven't forgotten that I'd be spider food if it weren't for you."

"Enough! Enough with the moroseness! I think we've all saved each other's lives a half dozen times by now. We're all square. Now, if you'll excuse me, I'm going to wash the rest of the mud out of my shirt and take a nap, and not necessarily in that order."

"I'll go stake out some prime camping territory, then. Do try not to have Callias arrest you until you've freshened up," Helwan said as he began walking away.

"That depends on him!" Arche called back.

He inventoried his shirt and sank into the river up to his neck, letting his eyes close.

The current ran all around him. It pulled at him, making him dig his toes into the soft mud at the bottom of the river. A small, intrusive thought whispered to let the current pull him under, to drift along the river and see where it would take him. He fought that urge as the water surged against his hair, arms idling just below the surface.

> **Swimming** has increased to **Level 2**.
>
> -0.5% Stamina Drain while Swimming (-1%)
> +2% Swimming Speed (+4%)

Arche snorted. Other than his less-than-graceful entrance his feet hadn't left the riverbed and he had no desire to go any deeper into the river.

"Something funny?"

Arche opened his eyes and turned around. Lyssa had also entered the river. He hadn't realized she was still there, let alone had joined him. Now she was standing in water just below her jawline, not ten strides away, just as naked as he was. It was so unexpected that he could do nothing more than gape.

"I…I…uh…"

Words failed him. He blinked, then turned away. A strange heat flooded through him despite the cold of the water, leaving him decidedly uncomfortable.

"What are you doing?" he asked, his voice a few octaves higher than normal.

"I fought all day and dug all night. I need a bath as much as you do."

"Okay, I get that, but why are you doing it right *here*?"

Arche heard a small splash behind him and shuddered. His mind filling with a thousand images he didn't necessarily want to picture.

"Why shouldn't I be here? This is where the water is, no?"

Arche ground his teeth, realizing that there was no way to be tactful about the situation.

"You're naked. I'm naked. That doesn't make you uncomfortable?"

"I am a daughter of the forest. We live in nature and know the natural element in all things. You mortals may hold shame in the self, but we do not."

"It's not always about shame, sometimes it's just about privacy. No one likes to be reduced to a piece of meat."

Behind him, Lyssa's voice took on a slight edge.

"Is that how you view me, Greenstick? A 'piece of meat?'"

It was a trap. Arche knew it was a trap, but he was trying to be genuine and he was so thoroughly thrown off guard that he blundered forward anyway.

"No. I think of you as my friend. Someone I trust, someone whose culture I barely understand, and someone I respect too much to be comfortable around while naked."

There was another small splash behind him and Arche screwed his eyes shut.

"Oh, so you would only disrobe with those whom you don't respect? Perhaps I should call Callias down to bathe in my stead. Then you might be comfortable."

"Come on, you know that's not what I mean. Besides, you mean to tell me you're not at all uncomfortable with me being right here? What if Helwan was here?"

"You are something entirely separate."

"What, your 'companion?'"

"No. An idiot."

Arche snorted and tried to focus on rubbing the dirt out of his pores. Whatever her claims about shame or the lack thereof, it felt intrusive to look at her. It seemed he had found an uncrossable schism between elven culture and his own, whatever that may be. Regardless, he wanted a private bath, so he let the current pull him a little farther down the river. Not out of sight, but far enough at least that he and Lyssa were in no danger of accidentally bumping into one another.

If that happened, he would never live his embarrassment down.

The feeling of floating in the water was one Arche had to grow accustomed to, the simple thought of it making his heartbeat faster. He walked a few more steps and found a dip where he was barely treading water. He wasn't quite ready to go underwater again, but he was more prepared than he'd been the last time he'd gone swimming.

> **Swimming** has increased to **Level 3**.
>
> +2% Swimming Speed (+6%)
> -0.5% Stamina Drain while Swimming (-1.5%)

He found a spot near the bank where the ground fell away and the current spun him in soft circles. He floated on his back, eyes closed as the weariness and weight of the past two days struck him. Before he knew it, he was fast asleep.

Fire licked his flesh. He was consumed by it. An inferno roared in every direction. The heat blasted at him, piercing his flesh and cracking his bones. Every sensation was agony. Arche sunk further into the flaming depths, unable to struggle free. The scent of cooked meat filled his nose, then his nose melted and he could smell nothing. His skin hissed and bubbled, falling away from his charred bones in great, hulking husks of flesh. His vision went dark as his eyes melted, but around him the fire burned ever brighter afterimages into his mind.

"Arche!"

He awoke, gasping and sputtering. Water forced its way up and out of his throat in uncontrollable spasms. He was lying on his side on the riverbank, half out of the water, and trembling like a tree branch in a storm. Lyssa stood over him. She was dressed, to his great relief, in a simple green tunic that ran down to her knees, a cord tied the fabric to her at the waist and above the stomach. Concern was etched into her features.

"What happened?" he gasped.

"You fell asleep and drifted beneath the water. Are you all right?"

Arche thought back to the dream. His every hair was on end, his body quivering from the memory of it. Falling asleep in water, he'd dreamed of consuming fire. Strange.

"It seems Tartarus is committed to scaring me into an early grave. Can you let me get some clothes on?"

Lyssa raised an eyebrow but obliged him by turning her back. Arche sat up and opened his inventory. His shirt was still wet from the earlier wash—which was to be expected as items in the inventory retained their state from when they entered—but he figured it would dry out as the day went on. When he had finished, Lyssa had turned back around.

Arche had never seen her without her leathers. There was something vaguely foreign about the sight of her looking like an ordinary elven woman instead of as the armored, highly capable huntress he knew her to be. The two, he had to remind himself, were not mutually exclusive.

A shiver ran down his body. It was hard to catch his breath.

"What's wrong?"

"Nothing. Bad dream."

"You've been having a lot of those, lately."

"Doesn't mean I'm any closer to figuring out why."

"Well, you should get some rest. Proper rest."

Arche stood and summoned the Tridory. It flew toward him from farther up the bank. His Mana dropped twenty points from the effort, causing a flicker of discomfort.

"You should be careful how brazen you are with that ability."

Arche leaned heavily against the spear. She was right, of course, but he was too tired to care.

"Go on," Lyssa said. "I'm not quite done here."

Arche stumbled into camp, trying to find somewhere to set up his tent or roll out his bedroll. His exhaustion debuff hadn't disappeared with the little bit of sleep he'd gotten. The near drowning had interfered with that, no doubt. He found an empty space and was about to retrieve his tent from his inventory when Helwan grabbed his arm.

"Wha—?" Arche started to say, but Helwan ignored him and led him through the canvas jungle.

They stopped in front of an unassuming tent.

"You're practically dead on your feet," the satyr told him. "Give me your tent and I'll set it up next to mine. For now, use mine and sleep it off."

Arche was too tired to protest. He crawled inside the tent, laid the Tridory down next to a bedroll, and fell asleep still fully clothed and dripping water.

Ψ

Arche sat up, his heart pounding. He was surrounded by an ash-laden field. Hills and plains stretched the horizon around him and before them were the burned and hollowed husks of what once must have been a bright and verdant forest. Dark, translucent husks of humanoid forms drifted all around him, each with a small green flame the size of a candle floating within their shadowy silhouettes. They seemed to appear and fade; one moment, almost tangible, the next, practically invisible. Arche stood, reaching for his spear.

It was nowhere to be found.

He tried to access his inventory, but nothing happened. He tried accessing his profile, his vitals, anything, but nothing happened. He turned as one of the humanoid shades passed near him and saw a figure kneeling. Unlike the shades, this one was solid.

"Who are you?" His voice came out more timid than he intended.

The figure reached out and touched a prone shade, cupping the green candle with both hands as the silhouette dissipated into nothingness. One hand moved around the flame in a steady motion, then the figure gently tossed the green flame into the air as though he were letting go of a bird. The flame flew off toward the horizon, a glinting coin somehow suspended from it by a dark thread.

The figure stood and turned toward Arche. It was dressed in all black. Black metal in interlocking plates adorned the figure's torso and legs, a black cape billowed dramatically behind it. An amorphous helmet covered its face, constantly shifting between human expressions and a smooth metallic surface. The only thing revealed were its eyes, which had pinprick white pupils in a dark sea of black sclera.

"You should not be here."

The figure took a step forward.

Arche felt a cold within his stomach and looked down to see that his form was translucent, much the same as the shades that flitted about beside him, though more defined. He looked back at the figure, which had stopped in front of him, eyeing him.

"Who are you? What did you do?"

"You've gained awareness." The figure ignored Arche's questions. *"A trick of the Moirai? Or perhaps Hypnos has singled you out. It matters not. I will speak to the Oneiroi of this. Forget what you have seen here. Lingering on it will not bring your soul peace."*

Ψ

Arche woke with a cold knot in his stomach. His clothes were soaked and his limbs felt leaden. Sweat from the nightmare had mixed with river water to soak through the bedroll. Curling his lip in disgust at himself, he slowly extricated himself from the wet clothes and put on a simple shirt and pants. The fabric was stiff, but dry. He hung the wet clothes on a thin cord strung between the poles of the tent, hoping that they would dry quickly. He didn't have many clothes and didn't really want the ones he did have to mold or sour.

Daylight poured in through a small opening at the front of the tent, telling him that he had not slept the entire day away. Arche held his hand out and found the comforting grip of the Tridory, the weight of it pulling him fully into reality.

"It was a dream," he told himself. "Just a dream."

It didn't matter how many times he said it. He couldn't quite believe it.

Chapter 16

With an uneasy weight settled onto his shoulders, Arche visited Vik, Elpida, and Gigator. The bulk of the day was behind him and his sleep hadn't been particularly restful, but it was enough to rid him of his exhaustion debuff and get his attribute bonuses for all his hard work.

You have gained:

+1 Strength
+1 Endurance

Arche found Vik and the others sitting at a table in the open, playing some sort of game involving rocks on a lattice-style mat. Gigator sat on one side of the table, Elpida on the other. The latter was frowning heavily.

"What are they doing?" Arche asked Vik, who stood nearby, watching the game play out.

"They're playing petteia." Vik said it like the answer was obvious.

Rather than expose his ignorance once again, Arche waited and watched. Elpida had a series of light-colored rocks on her side of the grid, and Gigator had a number of dark rocks on his. They took turns moving their rocks across the board in straight lines, either vertical or horizontal. Gigator maneuvered one of his dark rocks adjacent to one of Elpida's light rocks, sandwiching it between another dark rock he had placed on a previous turn. Elpida cursed and removed her stone from the board. Something about the game seemed oddly familiar to Arche, but the movements and the rules were as strange to him as everything else.

Arche watched them play. Two small piles of coins were sitting next to the board they were playing on. The coins were a dull grey metal. Arche Examined them, realizing he hadn't actually seen what kind of currency Tartarus used.

Obol	**Rarity**: Common/Currency **Durability**: 5 / 5 **Weight**: 0.002 kilograms

Arche mouthed the word, *obol.* Now he knew what the money was called, but he still had no idea how much it was worth or if it was the only kind of coin. Realizing that he hadn't yet Examined his newfound friends, he made a show of interest in the game as he watched the players.

Elpida Giannakopoulou	
Level: 19 Race: Human Age: ? Height: ? Weight: ?	Profession: ? Trade: ? Traits: ? Companions: ? Adventuring Party: ?
Health: 810 / 810 100%	**Stamina**: 705 / 705 100% **Mana**: 120 / 120 100%

Arche baulked at her vitals. He recognized that she was a few levels higher than he was, but her vitals were staggering. Judging by her Mana, it looked like she was almost entirely physically based, which explained the heavier style of armor that she wore. He turned his eyes to Gigator, wondering how the large lizard person would compare.

Gigator Sávrandras	
Level: 21 Race: Sauros Age: ? Height: ? Weight: ?	Profession: ? Trade: ? Traits: ? Companions: ? Adventuring Party: ?
Health: 1,040 / 1,040 100%	**Stamina**: 780 / 780 100% **Mana**: 110 / 110 100%

> **Examine** has increased to **Level 3**.
>
> +2% Examine Speed (+6%)

It was enough to make Arche feel self-conscious about his own attributes. Part of him was surprised that he was anywhere near their levels, but their vitals put his to shame in almost all regards. It was one more sign that he still had a long way to go ahead of him. There was only one member of the trio left. Not sure what to expect, Arche Examined Vik.

> Vikterandor has resisted the effects of **Examine**.

Arche froze. Vik turned sly eyes in his direction and winked at him. No one else Arche had Examined had resisted the effect or even signaled that they knew what was happening. Vik hadn't shown anger, but if the strange elf could resist his Examine skill, he could also hide his emotions.

At the table, Elpida cursed long and loud in a grunting language that Arche didn't understand, bringing his attention back to the game at hand. Gigator had reduced

Elpida's forces down to a single stone, which apparently meant she had lost. Gigator let out a booming laugh that had more than a bit of serpentine hiss in it.

"Every time! I don't understand!" Elpida slammed her fist on the table.

The pieces bounced, threatening to spill onto the ground. Gigator was too busy gathering up the pile of obols. Vik let out a chuckle, slapping Arche on the shoulder.

"Let's take a walk, friend. I'm sure Elpida wants a redemption match."

Arche hefted the Tridory and walked next to Vik as they made their way up one of the hills that surrounded the village. When they were reasonably alone, Vik spoke.

"I notice you never put away your spear. I don't think I've ever seen its equal. Where did you get it?"

Arche couldn't think of a convincing lie, so he decided to be vague about the truth.

"The bottom of a dwarven ruin, behind several monsters and traps. What about your sword? I'm not familiar with that style."

Vik drew his sword and held it in both hands, by handle and blade. Even in the light of the sun, Arche could see that the metal glowed a faint blue and the grip was masked by a beautiful swept basket hilt. The blade was skinnier than any Arche had seen, barely thicker than one of Lyssa's arrows, and almost resembled a spike more than a sword. Still, the single edge was undeniably sharp and no doubt enhanced by magic.

"Starpoint has been my companion for many years."

The hairs on Arche's arms stood on end as Vik held the sword, but the strange elf sheathed it without further incident.

"You're a strange one, Arche. I've been around Tartarus a few times, but something strikes me about you. There's a naïveté to you that doesn't befit an adult. Care to explain?"

Arche bit his lip, deciding how much to share. Vik hadn't given him any reason to distrust the elf outright, but Arche still felt like he was hiding something.

"I have amnesia. Total mind wipe. Before a couple weeks ago, it's like I didn't exist."

"Fascinating. Do you know how rare that kind of amnesia is?"

Arche gave a weak smile. "No, I don't. I didn't even remember my name. Lyssa gave me this one."

"I was going to ask if you knew what your name meant. It's an elvish concept."

"She told me it means 'beginning.'"

"Yes and no. It's a point of philosophy, actually. Not just a beginning, but rather *the* beginning. The fundamental beginning. It's more of an abstract than an actual thing, you understand."

"I'm not sure I follow."

Vik chuckled. "Don't feel bad. Wiser men than you have come to blows over smaller things. I want you to see things from my perspective, for a moment. A human who walks Tartarus seemingly for the first time, who wields a strange, clearly magical spear, has befriended both a banished wood elf and a satyr—which, mind you, the fact that she hasn't killed him already is shocking in its own right—comes out of nowhere to warn our intrepid little village of an immediate attack and fights them off with impressive skill and tenacity. Then, just when I think the human might be out of surprises, I notice he's trying to get a peek at my profile with a rare skill normally only utilized by heads of state, spies, and assassins."

Arche shifted uncomfortably, not sure where this was leading. Vik smiled at him.

"You're going to stage a coup, aren't you?"

"What? No!"

"Hah! You'll have to improve your Deception, lad, that wouldn't have convinced a child."

Arche let out a heavy breath. "How did you know?"

"You wear your intentions on your chest. I knew from the first time you spoke to Callias that you wouldn't stand him, let alone kneel to him. Don't get me wrong, I'm not going to stop you. I'm simply curious if you've thought this through."

"I haven't actually committed to it, yet. I'm still trying to get my friends on board."

"That's not surprising. But let's say you do take down Callias. What about the villagers? Who will support them? How will you gather supplies? Do you know how to outfit a village? What infrastructure is needed?"

The more Vik spoke, the more Arche felt out of his depth.

"I don't, no."

"Normally I would ask you if you'd ever done something like this before, but given your memory situation I'm going to take that answer as a 'no.'"

Arche felt a small spark of anger grow in his chest.

"What's your point, Vik? Are you trying to talk me out of it?"

"Not in the least. I'm trying to let you know how important allies will be. I'll let you in on a secret: I lied earlier. None of my group are indebted to Callias. That's our cover in case people get nosy."

"Your...cover?"

"Aye. You see, lad, we three used to be pirates. Relax, we're long since reformed. Point being that we were looking for somewhere to settle, get a new start away from the old life and any who might find us. This seemed like a decent enough place, out in the middle of nowhere, away from your usual law and order types. Plus, Callias was willing to pay for any muscle he could get. He knows very little of our situation, which didn't sit well with him, but he needed capable fighters and not enough were in his debt. Now, I knew he was a terrible leader from the beginning, but I didn't know the depths of his ineptitude."

"How do you know I won't be inept?"

"Because you're not looking to place yourself on the seat." Vik waved a hand to dismiss Arche's impending questions. "Read it in your face. You're not that kind of ambitious and I am an excellent judge of character."

"What's your point in all this, then? What do you want?"

"Is it not obvious? Security. I think you have the guts to pull off your plans and I want to make sure there's a place for me and mine in the new village order. If you set yourself against Callias, you'll need allies. And if you set your pretty friend at the forefront, you'll need advisors."

"And how do I know I can trust you?" Arche said, locking eyes with the elf.

Vik smirked and lowered his hood, revealing startlingly blue skin and dark hair covered in tiny, white dots, like stars among the night sky.

"Because I'm a moon elf and I give you my word that neither I nor mine will take any actions against you, so long as you take none against me or mine."

Arche was about to ask what Vik's being a moon elf had to do with anything when he received a notification.

<table>
<tr><td colspan="2">Vikterandor has made you an **Oath**.

One's word, once given, is binding. As a moon elf, Vikterandor's word is doubly so. Breaking an oath has extreme consequences. If you accept his oath, you will be held to the same standards as though you were a moon elf.

Do you accept this Oath?</td></tr>
<tr><td>Yes</td><td>No</td></tr>
</table>

Arche dismissed the window. What a moon elf had to do with making an oath, he had no idea, but he knew how he felt about it.

"Trust is not a contract, it's a leap of faith. I'm grateful that you would go to such a risk for us, but I won't ask you to bind yourself to it. If you really want to help us, I won't ask you to take an oath. I can't speak for Lyssa, in fact she's more prepared to speak for me, but if you truly wish to help us, then I will trust you at your word until you give me a reason not to."

> **Leadership** has increased to **Level 3**.
>
> +1% Persuasion Chance (+3%)
> +1% Reputation Gains (+3%)
> -0.5% Reputation Losses (-1.5%)

Arche blinked away the notification and met Vik's eyes. For the first time that Arche had known him, Vik looked genuinely surprised. The elf stared at him, his head cocked to one side in a fashion Arche had often seen Lyssa do.

"I just made you a binding vow and you reject it based on a loose belief that I will keep my word regardless of consequence? All this *after* trying to sneak glances at my profile and finding out I'm a former pirate?"

Arche smiled and held out his hand. "Yeah, sums it up."

Vik let out a disbelieving chuckle and clasped Arche's forearm. "You're a strange one, kid, but I like you."

"So people keep telling me. Welcome aboard, Vik."

"We'll see. In the meantime, I think we should get both of our groups together. Explain what's happened and decide how to move forward."

"Agreed. We should do so quickly. I think Callias is planning retribution for my 'impertinence.' The sooner we decide how to proceed, the less we'll be taken by surprise."

"I look forward to working together, lad. Who knows? Someday I might even let you get a look at my profile."

Vik winked, then vanished.

One moment the elf had been standing there, the next, he was gone. Arche startled and fell backwards, landing on the grass. He looked around, but the moon elf was nowhere to be found.

"What the fuck?"

He had the sneaking suspicion that Vik was still somewhere nearby, laughing at him.

"Asshole!"

Arche grumbled to himself as he stood and dusted off the seat of his pants. What really concerned him was why Vik would show him this ability. Was this meant as a warning? A threat? Or was the moon elf messing with him? Was this a boast of his capability or a hint that Vik was aware of some of the things Arche himself could do? A million questions bloomed, each as valid as the next and none with easy answers.

Arche was left alone in the light of the dipping sun. Dark would be upon them within the hour. Arche stabbed the Tridory into the ground next to him and stared out over the village from his vantage point on the hill. There were a couple hundred villagers in total. Maybe a fifth of those were guards; former soldiers or mercenaries that Callias had hired for protection. The rest were crafters, traders, farmers, or common folk looking for a better life. Many were still repairing damage to their tents from the previous battle as a handful of small children chased each other through the camp.

Callias refused to enact even simple safety measures for the people that trusted him with their very lives. Instead of keeping an effective watch against the treeline to the valley, most of the guards were stationed around the single permanent structure that had been built; a large, wooden house that served the dual purpose of administrative estate and personal lodgings for one Callias Buteo.

It made Arche's blood boil.

He couldn't stand by and do nothing. That was the impetus for this entire harebrained idea. He couldn't stand to watch Callias get the entire village killed. Inaction was complicity. He had to do something.

Lyssa would come around to the idea, he was sure of it. If she didn't, he would respect her decision, but he had to act. Even if they didn't stay, someone else needed to take charge. He could at least give the village the opportunity to pick their own leader. He wasn't sure how widespread that concept was within Tartarus, but to him, not having a say in one's leadership, even a small say, felt wrong. These people were putting their lives in the hands of whoever led the village, that trust needed to be recognized and respected.

Arche realized he didn't actually know what claim that Callias had to the land. He had been given the impression that the land was being settled, but he didn't know whether it was claimed by a particular kingdom or country. That could complicate things exponentially, but he doubted any kingdom would hold solid claim to lands that were so wild and filled with monsters. Even if such claims were held, they'd be near impossible to enforce. The difficulty would be in establishing a territory that was defensible and self-sustaining.

The valley itself could prove a lush environment, but drastic changes needed to be made and they would need resources. Wood was in abundance, but they would have to carve into the mountain for stone or create a quarry. Such an expedition would likely be expensive and laborious, not to mention dangerous.

It was a monumental task, to start a settlement, but Arche knew it would be for the best. As the daughter of the lord of Dawnwood, Lyssa would have been exposed to civic leadership from a young age. She would know what needed to be done. Probably. He certainly didn't.

For now, he had some privacy and intended to use it to train.

"Are you still there, Vik?" he asked aloud.

There was no reply, so Arche had to trust that the moon elf wasn't spying on him. He stood, hefting the Tridory. He hadn't had a chance to experiment with the weapon in private, nor had he a chance to use his Divine Body skill without an audience.

He headed down the hill, out of sight of the village. Satisfied that he was alone, he hefted the spear in an overhand grip. He focused on his connection with the spear and felt it thrum in his hands. It felt like a living thing, humming in anticipation. Foolishness, of course. He was sure Lyssa would laugh at him. Whatever connection he had to the weapon, however, it clearly responded to him. He threw it, aiming for a tree that stood about ten paces away. It wasn't a great throw, the aft of the spear rose up midair, but it hit the trunk near the roots. Arche held out his hand and the spear flew back to him at the expenditure of seven Mana.

The spear had gotten easier to wield as his Strength increased, making him wonder if there was some sort of requirement to the weapon. It made sense to him, but he was annoyed that the Tridory hadn't told him what he needed to effectively wield it. As it was, it felt much heavier than any other weapon he had used. Without a high combination of Strength and Endurance, he was certain swinging it about would quickly eat through all of his Stamina.

He continued throwing the spear and summoning it back to his hand until both his Stamina and Mana were nearing half. He was sweating from the exertion and his arm felt ready to fall off, but he was rewarded from the effort.

Spear Throwing has increased to **Level 5**.

+3% Accuracy of Thrown Spears (+15%)
+2% Range of Thrown Spears (+10%)
+1 Strength
+1 Dexterity

Spearmanship has increased to **Level 12**.

+2% Damage with Spears (+24%)

That was a decent increase, and though the subskill was still at the Beginner rank, his accuracy and technique improved with every throw. Next came the dangerous part. Arche took a deep breath and tapped into his Divine Body.

His Mana dove and his Stamina shot up as light flooded from his skin. By rough estimate, he was burning through about fifty Mana per second. Almost as quickly as he activated the skill, he stopped it. His Mana bar blinked red, the number in the low teens, but he had prevented himself from running dry and risking Mana Burnout.

He waited for his Mana to regenerate over the next several minutes, then activated the skill again, trying to focus on the feeling of Mana flooding through his body. He could feel it suffuse all of him. Cautiously, he tried pushing it from his center into his arms. He felt the Mana react to his will. At first, it resisted his pressure, but after working and molding it inside of himself, it began to coalesce down his arms and into his fingers, causing them to glow even brighter.

Divine Body has increased to **Level 4**.

He'd skipped an entire level with it, which seemed to imply that if he experimented with his skills, he could earn more experience than simple repetition.

"I'm an idiot," he muttered, rubbing his eyes as he fought off an impending Mana headache. "Of *course* new methods would provide more experience."

He waited the ten minutes it took to refill his Mana, noticing that his usage of Divine Body had refilled his Stamina by almost a hundred points. He repeated the process a few times over the next hour as the sun dipped behind the lip of the valley.

Arche found he could slow the rate at which his Mana was consumed, the most being to a rate of about forty Mana per second, and that his Stamina rose by the same amount. He wasn't sure if it affected his Health regeneration at the same rate, but he also wasn't willing to purposely hurt himself to find out. That experiment would have to wait for the next time he inevitably got injured. As it was, he'd made considerable progress.

Divine Body has increased to **Level 8**.

Arche sat with his back against the tree he'd used for target practice. A side effect of his Divine Body skill was that he emitted golden light when he used it; now that it was dark, he didn't think he'd be able to practice the skill without someone coming to investigate the glowing lights over the hill. He held the spear in his lap, wondering about the three buttons that Helwan had pointed out to him. He tried to focus on the bond he had with the spear. It vibrated in response. He pressed the topmost button.

Nothing happened.

Remembering that Helwan had mentioned a button on the opposite side, near where his thumb rested in the grip. He pressed it with his thumb and hit the first button again. Still, nothing happened.

Disappointed, he tried pressing the second button and nearly jumped out of his own skin when the spear whirred and shifted in his hand. The blade of the spear broke in half and separated, forming a bident that resembled a huge cattle prod.

"Whoa!"

Arche dropped the Tridory.

It remained in its new bident form, laying in the dirt as though rebuking him for his reaction. Arche picked it up and examined the separation in the fading light, wishing he had an Everlit Lantern. The two prongs were perfect mirrors, now separated by two hands length, each occupying a place on a crossbeam.

Curious, Arche pressed the third button and a new prong came out of the center, bladed on both sides. The bident was now a proper trident. He marveled at it, taking a few practice thrusts. The weight and balance hadn't changed at all, meaning that a sudden change wouldn't throw off his rhythm in the middle of a fight. That confused Arche. The balance *should* have changed, but it hadn't. Arche started pressing the buttons again, this time watching the rest of the spear, trying to note any changes. As he cycled the buttons, bands of metal formed and unformed near the spike at the butt of the spear, the sauroter, counterbalancing the change in shape.

Arche adjusted his grip on the trident and tried the fourth button again.

The middle prong of the trident launched from the spear and embedded itself into the hillside, twenty strides away.

Arche stared at the spear, now a bident again, and then at the prong in the dirt.

Out of curiosity, he focused on his connection to the spear and reached out toward the prong with his mind, trying to recall it with the Return ability. The prong flew backwards out of the dirt, kicking up a spray of rocks and soil, and reconnected with the top of the trident, sliding into place as if it was an uninterrupted part of the whole weapon. He gave the trident an experimental twirl, playing around with switching the forms mid strike. The change was quick, near instantaneous, and no matter how closely he watched he could see no hint of a seam of mechanical parts. Whoever had built the Tridory had clearly designed it to be versatile and durable.

Arche grinned. The bloodthirsty part of him wanted to test out the spear's new functions in combat. With any luck, however, that wouldn't be for some time yet. Still, Lyssa's warning was still as true as it ever was.

Tartarus was a dangerous place, but he was one step closer to being ready.

Chapter 17

Arche was on his way back to the village when he spotted a leg dangling from a tree next to the river. At first, he had mistaken it for a branch and wouldn't have paid it any mind, but it had moved and caught the light of the moons.

Arche cracked a smile and wandered over, trying to be as quiet as he could. He stopped at the base of the tree and leaned against the trunk in a nonchalant manner.

"I didn't realize 'wood elf' was so literal. You all right up there?"

"I didn't realize you were trying to sneak. It sounded like another beastmar attack. I'm surprised the village hasn't sounded the alarm," Lyssa retorted.

Arche chuckled.

"That would explain why my Stealth level is so low. Seriously, though, are you all right?"

He grabbed a low limb of the tree and scrabbled up the trunk into some of the taller branches.

You have learned a **Skill**.

Climbing — Level 1

At long last you have the ability to see past the limitations of your own meager stature.

Each level in this skill improves your ability to scale surfaces.
Every 5 levels in this skill improves your **Strength** and **Dexterity** by 1.

+1% Speed of Climbing (+1%)
-1% Stamina Drain while Climbing (-1%)

Arche's eyes narrowed. He'd take all the skills he could get, but the snark was something he could do without,.

"I'm okay," Lyssa said, bringing his attention back to the present as he settled in against a tree limb near her. "I suppose I'm just missing Dawnwood. These people are so different from what I'm used to."

"I can imagine. I haven't even really met them yet; mostly just been talking to Vik and his friends. How are you holding up?"

"I don't know. I'm trying not to think about it."

"Ah." Arche nodded sagely. "Repression. Smart. Keep the feelings inside in the hope that one day you'll die and won't have to deal with them."

Lyssa snorted.

"Of course," Arche continued, swinging his feet back and forth. "That might not be the best plan for an elf, so if you want to talk about it, I'm here."

He didn't really expect her to say anything but he was content to simply share the view of the valley in moonslight with her. A bird swooped and skimmed the surface of the river. Its claws broke the surface, then reappeared a moment later clutching a wriggling fish. It struggled desperately, red blood dripping into the grass from the piercing wounds in its side. The bird flapped quickly back toward the forest, to the safety of a nest, but it was too slow. Another bird intercepted it, ramming into it with such force that the fishing bird was stunned and plummeted toward the ground. The other bird caught it and carried it away, the fish still trapped in the first bird's claws.

After a few minutes of quiet, Lyssa broke the silence.

"I don't want to accept what happened. I can't."

Arche didn't have the first idea what to say to that, so he kept quiet. Thankfully, Lyssa wasn't done.

"I know they didn't care for me, especially after what happened, but not one of them thought about what I went through. My brother is dead and it's my fault."

"No, it's not."

"Yes, it is, Arche. I was the one who pushed forward, out of the safety of our territory. He wanted to turn back, but he wouldn't leave me. He was there because of me, taking a stupid risk *because* of me. I killed him; even if it hadn't been my arrow that had ended his life, I killed him. In every way that matters, I killed him."

She sniffled and wiped her face. Arche opened his mouth to argue, but he realized there was no point. Nothing he could say would change her mind. No words would bring her brother back.

"All right."

She looked over at him, her eyes reflecting the light of the moons; one blue, one green.

"All right," he repeated. "So what are you going to do? You've got three options from where I'm sitting. Three outcomes. You can focus on the past until you can see nothing else, drowning in your own misery, or you can find a way to press forward and move on to the next point in your life. That's not to say you forget what happened, but you find a way to make your peace with it."

"What's the third option?"

"Death and taxes."

She tilted her head to the side. "What?"

"The only certain things in life. Personally, I recommend the second option, but the decision is ultimately yours."

She didn't answer. Arche looked at the light of the moons reflecting in the water of the river. Without the forest to block the moonslight, he could still make out a decent amount of the area around him, despite not having racial night-sight like Lyssa.

"Why do you want to save this village?"

Arche blew out his cheeks and scratched his head. He hadn't expected the conversation to go there, but it was a fair question. He'd been pushing to get rid of Callias. It seemed like the obvious thing to do but saying that wasn't good enough.

"Callias will get these people killed. I can't stand by and let that happen."

"And if you succeed, what happens to them?"

"We'll let them choose their own leader. Democracy and all that."

Lyssa's head tilted to the other side.

"I like the sound of that. Sometimes, you give good advice, Greenstick. I do need to find a way forward. Maybe this village can be my way out."

Arche grinned. "Let's find out, together."

> **Leadership** has increased to **Level 4**.
>
> +1% Persuasion Chance (+4%)
> +1% Reputation Gains (+4%)
> -0.5% Reputation Losses (-2%)

"By the way, before I forget, Vik volunteered his group to help us."

"What? When did this happen?"

Arche peered out at the moons from beneath the tree's foliage. "Two hours ago? Maybe three? Hard to tell. He said he wants security for his trio, so he promised he wouldn't oppose us if we didn't oppose him."

If Lyssa had been anything other than a high-level, highly skilled wood elf, she would have fallen from the tree.

"You two seem to have bonded closely in the last two days."

"I don't quite know what to make of him, actually. There's a lot he's keeping secret, but I believe him when he says he'll help us. I didn't accept his oath, though."

"You denied the Oath of a son of the moon?" Lyssa's voice had turned sharp.

Arche blinked in surprise. "You knew what he was?"

"Of course I knew, Greenstick, we're *elves.* That's not the point. He made you an Oath? You're sure?"

"Yeah. I got a notification and everything. It said it was some sort of binding contract."

"And you turned it down?"

"Yeah. It didn't feel right. What he had swore was fine, but it felt too much like holding a blade above someone's head. If we're going to make allies, I don't think it's right to hold cosmic consequences over them."

"You don't understand the significance of what he offered you."

"Oh, for sure. No idea."

"Moon elves are used to make the most binding of contracts. Oaths in Tartarus carry consequences, but a moon elf's heritage amplifies that. You said 'cosmic consequences' but I don't think you realize how true that is. Having a moon elf handle a contract practically guarantees that both sides will keep their word."

"You make them sound like tools." Arche frowned.

"Many moon elves have been enslaved and used like tools. It's no wonder that he wears that hood at all times. If he made you a vow of his own volition and you turned him down, well, to say such a thing is unheard of is an understatement."

"I still don't understand. Did I do the right thing or did I fuck up?"

"He risked his agency in this matter, you gave it back to him. Trust that you did the right thing."

"Cool. I'll add that to the list titled: 'Went Better Than Expected.'"

Lyssa smirked and jumped down from the tree, landing without a sound on the soft earth below.

"Oh, we're leaving now. All right." Arche jumped down and landed with a heavy thud.

"I think it's time we integrated with these people you seem so intent on saving."

As they approached the village, Arche could see the glow of a fire burning. Music wafted over to them, the sound of instruments and singing. People were clapping and stomping their feet. They picked up their speed, trying to find out what was going on, and found that Helwan had apparently started a party. He was dancing wildly in the middle of a large group of people, playing his pan pipes expertly. Some of the other villagers had stringed instruments and drums and had joined in, and one elven woman had even started to sing. There was cheering and laughter and Arche found it hard not to join in on the fun. People were twirling about as they danced to the music and ale flowed from several tapped kegs.

Arche made a detour to Helwan's tent and dropped off the Tridory, not wanting to carry a large weapon into the party. He still had his sword in his inventory if anything happened, but the happiness of the party was infectious. When he rejoined the crowd, several strangers went up to him to clasp his forearm and thank him. He took it in stride, not really sure what they were thanking him for, but smiling and nodding all the same. Helwan had finished his song and dance and let the other musicians take over. He made his way to Arche, grinning.

"A party! A real live party. Oh, ever since I spent those days locked in that room, I didn't think I'd ever see one of these again. Come, my friend!"

"What are we celebrating?"

"Life! We celebrate life!"

Arche laughed and joined the satyr amongst the throng of dancing people. He didn't particularly know how to dance, but his Dexterity was high enough that whatever he was doing at least looked intentional.

You have learned a **Skill**.

Dancing — Level 1

Grace and expression, or wild flailing. Your choice.

Each level in this skill improves your ability to rock your body.
Every 5 levels in this skill improves your **Dexterity** by 1.
This is a **subskill** of **Performance**.

+1% Fluidity of Motion (+1%)
+1% Body Control (+1%)

You have learned a **Skill**.

Performance — Level 1

Being the center of attention isn't always as easy as it looks.

Each level in this skill improves your ability to physically perform, whether it be music, dance, or a demonstration of martial prowess. Every 5 levels in this skill improves your **Charisma** by 1.

+0.5% Overall Performance (+0.5%)

The grin on Arche's face grew as he committed to having a good time. He had no idea what he was doing but that was half the fun. His body twisted left, then right. He crouched and waved his hands around; his shoulders swayed and his hips bounced. Several of the other dancers were watching him with bemused expressions, but he chose to believe that at least some of the looks were begrudging respect for his moves. Heat crawled into his face, making him flushed and giddy. He was getting into the swing of things when another stranger came up to thank him.

"What's going on?" he asked Helwan, swinging his arms and snapping his fingers.

"I've been spreading word about you. How you came to help yesterday and how you stood up to Callias. You've left an impression on them."

The satyr folded his arms across his chest and was dropping down into squats in time with the beat of the music, kicking his goat hooves out whenever he got low.

Someone brought out drinks and Arche grabbed a mug and drained it. A strong sense of bitter currants hit him and he coughed, but thankfully none of it found its way back up. He spied Vik and Gigator dancing near the musicians. Vik was doing a lithe, graceful sort of dance that made him look boneless with how he flowed in time to the music. Gigator, on the other hand, had taken a wide stance and was thrashing his head and tail about to the drumbeat, encouraging the musicians to play ever faster. Elpida, it seemed, was in no mood for dancing and instead stood near Lyssa, who had skirted around the dance floor. The two appeared to be engaged in quiet conversation, though what they could be discussing, Arche had no idea.

The music sped up, shifting seamlessly through songs. Arche danced, flailed, twirled, and jumped with the others. If he was getting looks before, nobody cared enough to notice as everyone freed themselves to the wildness of the dance.

Helwan leaped through the air, his pan pipes leading the music onward. Arche didn't know if it was magic or music or both, but he was having the time of his life. Even Lyssa and Elpida, who had kept away from the mosh, found themselves sucked into the frenzy of it all. Drinks found their way into Arche's hands, whether passed by Helwan or by grateful strangers. Several clashed their mugs against his and he found he had to drink quickly to keep from spilling it everywhere.

Someone brought out a firkin and a cheer went up. Arche danced his way over, noticing that his Performance and Dancing skills had reached level two. Someone filled up a cup and handed it to him. When he threw it back, the harsh sting—worse than any wine he'd ever tasted—made him gag and cough. Someone smacked him on the back and people laughed. Tears were running from his eyes as he waved off the good-natured inquiries.

"I wasn't expecting liquor!"

"Liquor!" roared the thick, short man in front of him. "Away with your human piss. This here be felsbier, a dwarf's drink!"

A cheer rose from other short men, presumably dwarves, gathered around him. Arche poured himself another glass and raised a toast.

"To felsbier!"

"To felsbier!" a score of dwarves shouted back.

"You seem a brawny enough fellow, how about a contest?"

Arche turned to see he was being addressed by another dwarf.

"What did you have in mind?" he asked, eyes already beginning to drift from drink and excitement.

"Like any true measure, we'll see who's the better by a comparison of balls."

"Fuckin' *huh?*"

One of the dwarves pressed a smooth, metal sphere the size of an apple into his hands. They cleared a pathway through the crowd to give them a corridor out of the party. Another dwarf dug his heel into the ground, marking out a line.

"Just stay behind this line and throw the ball as far as you can. I'll go first and you just do like me if you can."

The metal ball pulled Arche's hands toward the ground but its weight wasn't impossible to handle. His vision swam, but he managed to focus long enough to Examine it.

	Rarity: Common
Ballast Ball	Quality: Good
	Durability: 50 / 50
	Weight: 15 kilograms

"That's a lot," Arche mumbled. "Fifteen whole whatevers."

The dwarf stood several feet away from the line and took a slow walk toward it, spinning with the ballast ball held close to his cheek. When the dwarf reached the line, he launching the ball forward. The ballast ball sailed through the air and landed with a *thunk* in the side of the hill. A dwarf who had positioned himself on the hill ran over to stand on the impact site, measuring distance with his thumb.

"Twenty-five meters!" the dwarf shouted.

Arche tried to whistle, but only succeeded in blowing stinking breath out of his mouth. He hefted the ballast ball in one hand, knowing instinctively that if he tried to twirl around like the dwarf had then the only thing sent flying would be the contents of his stomach. A sly smile broke across his face. All he needed was a split second and there was plenty of light from the bonfire.

He might be able to get away with it.

Arche stood a few steps away from the line, holding the ball low with both hands. He skipped forward, brought his hands up, then back as he transitioned the ball to one hand. As he landed, he brought his arm up and forward to throw as hard as he could. At the same time, he activated his Divine Body ability, just for a moment. A moment was all he needed.

Two things happened in very quick succession.

First, he flashed like a red sun. Most of the people nearby flinched at the sudden radiance and looked away. Second, the ballast ball sailed clear over the hill and disappeared into the gloom beyond. The music paused as everyone tried to figure out what had happened. The measuring dwarf, who was standing on the hill they were throwing at, disappeared and reappeared a minute later, holding the ballast ball.

"Sixty meters!" the dwarf called out.

The crowd erupted.

Arche was immediately jostled and shaken by every dwarf in the entire village. Each of them wanted to shake his hand and challenge him, which he barely had the wherewithal to decline.

"If anyone wans-a beat me, beat mah record firs'," he shouted, his words slipping over themselves. "I'm-a grab a drink!"

Someone pressed a cup into his hand and he drank it down, then turned back to the party, ready to dance again despite the rolling heat coming off his body. He felt a hand on his shoulder and the last thing he saw was a pretty smile, gently waving locks of golden hair, and brown eyes that could make all his worries go away.

Chapter 18

Arche woke to the stench of vomit.

Pain thrummed through him, consolidated mostly in his head, but seasoned with a stabbing pain in his side. There was a pressure behind his eyes that threatened to explode at any moment, pulsing steadily with his heart. Arche cracked his eyes open and the world swayed unrecognizably in front of him, giving his already weakened stomach an extra turn.

He forced his eyes to open fully, straining against the sunlight, and realized that the world wasn't just strange, it was upside down. Or, more accurately, he was upside down. Something gripped his right leg, snaking around his ankle and, as he focused on it, he saw a rope held him up, tied to the bough of a tree high above. He was also shirtless and had a knife sticking out of his side.

That explained the stabbing pain, at least.

"Ugh, why do I feel like I'm back in college?" he muttered.

"As if someone like you ever attended the Lyceum."

A woman's voice, full of scorn and derision. Too full, actually, it couldn't have been more forced.

Arche twisted about, trying to get a look. The move cost him a couple points of Health as his skin twisted around the blade, sending a fresh wave of pain through him. The woman leaned against a nearby tree, dressed in blue scale armor that had been crafted from some creature Arche couldn't even begin to identify. He struggled to Examine her. It took longer than it should have, thanks to his muddled mind, but it opened eventually.

Theresa Eliades		
Level: 23 **Race**: Human **Age**: ? **Height**: ? **Weight**: ?	**Profession**: ? **Trade**: ? **Traits**: ? **Companions**: ? **Adventuring Party**: ?	
Health: 420 / 420 100%	**Stamina**: 375 / 375 100%	**Mana**: 260 / 260 100%

She had flaxen hair tied back into a bun and was playing with a dagger, flipping it end over end in one hand as she regarded him. He stared back, confused. She turned away, instead fixing her gaze on the forest nearby, but as he craned his head, he could see that she had deep, brown eyes.

"You," he muttered. "Wait. Did we...?"

She sneered at him.

"You wish. Granted, the rest of the village is still laboring under that delusion, so don't think anyone's coming for you."

"Wouldn't dream of it, but if it's not too much trouble, could you explain why"—he gestured loosely to himself with his bound hands—"all this? Seems like a lot of effort."

Her eyes narrowed, but she shrugged and answered anyway.

"I agree, and I argued as much, but Callias didn't want you murdered outright. You're meant to look like an accident, so we're just going to wait for a monster to come and mangle you out of your misery."

Arche ground his teeth and glanced around. They were surrounded by trees, which meant they were in the Sylv. A roaming monster could no doubt put him out of his misery, especially as he was. His vitals didn't give him much hope, either.

Health: 290 / 420 69%	Stamina: 280 / 280 100%	Mana: 190 / 190 100%
Hungover — Tier 1: 02:46:29		

His injury was worse than he'd thought, but still manageable. As long as he didn't move too much, he wasn't even losing Health from the knife in his side. That part was likely equal parts pain and lure. His max Health and Stamina were lower than what he remembered, meaning she must have removed his ring. What surprised him most was that she had left the knife in him. Sure, his hands were tied, but they weren't tied behind his back. He supposed she felt he wasn't much of a threat even if he got his hands on the knife.

According to his inventory, he'd been cleaned out. He couldn't recall taking anything out, so either she could access his inventory or he'd *really* gone too hard with the felsbier. The latter was likely true, regardless. The hangover debuff explained his headache and rather horrible cottonmouth but he had a bigger question on his lips than the desperate need for water.

"Callias put you up to this? I can't say I'm surprised, but I'm surprised you admit it. What if I make a miraculous escape?"

Theresa shrugged again.

"Not likely. I'm here to ensure you die. As for the village fool, he didn't pay me to keep his name out of it. He assumes he inspires more loyalty than he does."

"Then why bother telling me?"

"I don't like having enemies. I've got nothing against you, really. If, and that's a big if, you get out of this, I don't want you coming after me. Why waste time on me when you could just as easily go for the guy in charge, right?"

Arche stared at her from his inverted position, his mouth twisted open in surprise.

"You abducted me, put a knife in me, and are waiting for some random monster to come tear me apart, and you're really trying to give me the 'it's just business, no hard feelings' about it?"

Theresa shrugged.

"Take it how you will. It won't make much difference in a few minutes. Won't be long now until something comes along."

"If you don't care for him, why do you take his money?"

"Enough. I'm not interested in small chat."

"It might be my last conversation. Not exactly small for me."

The assassin didn't respond. She had finished playing with the dagger and instead crossed her arms, still refusing to look at him. Try as he might, he couldn't hear any approaching monsters, which meant he had some time left to try talking before he had to resort to more drastic measures.

"You don't like your job very much, do you?"

"What would you know about it?" she snapped at him.

"Not much," he admitted. "But your secrets are safe with a dead man, right? You don't look like you want to be here any more than I do, and that's saying something. I mean, normally I would expect a little more enthusiasm out of a hired killer."

Her eyes flashed toward him, full of anger.

"I'm not a hired killer."

"Ah." Arche managed a grunt, wincing as it shaved away a few more points of Health. "My mistake. It must have been someone else who dragged me here, used me as a knife-sharpener, and strung me up a tree."

"You're still alive aren't you?"

"You're still waiting for me to die, aren't you?"

She looked away. Interesting.

"What?" he asked. "Too proud to look at your handiwork? If you're going to kill me, you could at least look me in the eye."

Theresa clenched her jaw and met his gaze. Arche did his best to let all animosity out of his face. He locked eyes with her and refused to blink. After a few moments, Theresa cursed and turned away.

"Malaka, I knew this was a bad idea," she muttered.

"It's not too late," Arche said. "You don't have to do this. Let me down, help me get back to the village. We both know Callias is an idiot. You don't have to subjugate yourself to him."

"He runs this village. He holds all the money, the guards, the power. To turn against him is to have the whole village turn against you. I would never make it back to the city on my own. Not that much good is waiting for me, there. As long as he thinks I'm in his pocket, I'm safe. A lone woman, this far from civilization. The chances are not good."

"It doesn't have to be that way. You still get to make a choice."

"It's the way it always is." She set her jaw. "I don't want this, but I don't see a way out. For what it's worth, I'm sorry."

Arche heard a rustle. It was far away, but it was unnatural. A chill ran through him. Something had caught his scent. Theresa didn't seem to notice.

"You've never done this before, have you?" Arche asked. "Killed someone, I mean."

"I should have gagged you," she muttered.

"I should have told you my safe word." Arche's chuckle turned into a pained gasp as his Health dropped a few more points.

"Look, Theresa, it's clear you're in over your head. If you're really in trouble, maybe I can help, but I can't do anything if you leave me here."

She kicked off the tree and stepped in front of him, her dagger held to his throat.

"How did you know my name?"

"Really not the point I'm trying to make, here. Look, offer ends if I'm dead. I can't say my friends will be as understanding."

There was the glint of uncertainty in her eyes. He latched onto it.

"Does Callias really strike you as the sort to leave loose ends? He'll probably have you killed once you get back anyway. I can take him down, but not without your help. You won't be on your own. The only way we get through this is together."

Her face stiffened and Arche caught his breath. Slowly, she lowered the dagger.

Persuasion has increased to **Level 3**.

+1% Persuasion Chance (+3%)

"If I help you and you fail, I'm dead."

"Chances are good you'd be dead regardless, so why not have a few friends by your side?"

She hesitated again, brow knitting as she weighed her options.

"How do I know you won't try to kill me if I free you?" she asked.

"I'd rather have a new friend than a dead enemy, but at the end of the day that choice is yours."

Theresa said nothing. She deliberated the choice for several long moments. Sweat and blood dripped from Arche to the forest floor as he waited for her to make her decision. Finally, she nodded.

"Fine."

"Great! Now, if you don't mind, this position really isn't great for my hangover."

She raised the dagger to cut the rope when something large and red burst through the bushes and tackled her to the side. Theresa screamed as the creature let loose a heavy roar.

"Oh, come *on!*" Arche snarled.

He took a deep breath and gritted his teeth, then grabbed the knife in his side and yanked it out. He almost lost consciousness from the pain as his Health dropped another sixty points. Not wanting to lose momentum or give in to the sudden rush of wooziness, Arche forced his injured side to bend as he grabbed the rope around his leg. With a quick slash, he severed the rope, using the hanging end to twist himself over to land on his feet.

Acrobatics has increased to **Level 9**.

+3% Control of Movement (+27%)
+1% Jump Height (+9%)

Arche's leg buckled, but he caught himself before sprawling across the ground. He blinked, trying to clear the pain of the hangover. The skill increase should have delivered quietly while he was in combat, but the aftereffects of the drinks must have screwed with the way they filtered in. He dismissed it, twisting the knife back and forth against the rope around his wrists as he stumbled toward Theresa and the creature that had tackled her. It was enormous, easily twice his size, and the only weapon Arche had was the knife.

The creature had the shaggy mane of a lion and large, bat-like wings. It stood on hind legs, with a powerful, crimson-furred body nearly twice Arche's height. The most pressing danger, however, was a long scorpion-esque tail that waved in the air, daring Arche to approach. Arche pulled up short and Examined the creature.

Rakor	
Level: 27 **Race**: Mantikhoras **Age**: ? **Height**: ? **Weight**: ?	**Profession**: ? **Trade**: ? **Traits**: ? **Companions**: ? **Adventuring Party**: ?

Health: 1,700 / 1,700 100%	**Stamina**: 1,550 / 1,665 93%	**Mana**: 120 / 120 100%

Arche swallowed. The creature was stronger than anything he had faced, with the possible exception of the revenant. The rope came free, falling to the ground. Arche twisted the knife into a reverse grip and brought his fists up.

"Hey, ugly!"

Remarkably, the mantikhoras turned and looked at him with a face that was uncomfortably human. It resembled a man in his forties with an incredibly flat features and a deep, crimson beard. There was a wicked intelligence in its red eyes. As the creature turned toward him, Arche saw Theresa on the ground. The armor covering her side was torn, jagged blue scales were bent and twisted as blood spilled over and pooled on the ground.

The mantikhoras flexed its claws, muscles rippling as it prepared to pounce. When it did move, it was blindingly fast. Arche threw himself to the side, dodging the claws by a hair's breadth. Even as the monster moved past him, the scorpion tail lunged for his chest. Arche threw his torso backward, succeeding in doing three-quarters of a backflip, narrowly avoiding the stabbing tail before landing face-first on the ground. He winced as his Health dropped a few points, now hovering around fifty percent.

Acrobatics has increased to **Level 10**.

+3% Control of Movement (+30%)
+1% Jump Height (+10%)
+1 Dexterity
+1 Agility

You have reached the **Rank** of **Novice** in **Acrobatics**.
You gain 100 experience.

You have reached **Level 15**.

As a Human, you gain **5** points to distribute each level.

Professions are now available to you.
Further leveling will be disabled until you earn a **profession**.
Any experience you earn will be held until you earn a **profession**.

Golden light flooded Arche, collecting in the wound in his side. The dull ache in his mind from the hangover was also gone, but any levity from that was short-lived. The notifications flashed and disappeared almost instantly. Arche rolled to the side and came back to his feet.

The mantikhoras growled, the threatening rumble of a big cat, and swiped a paw at him. Arche dashed in, trying to close the distance and make some use of his knife. He ducked the paw and stabbed at it as it went by. The sharp blade caught the mantikhoras's arm and tore a hole, but the skin was thick and resisted the knife's edge. Still, the mantikhoras grunted in pain. The scorpion tail lunged forward as quick as thought. In a stroke of luck, Arche brought the dagger up to deflect the sharpened point of the stinger but the force of it knocked him back.

He hit a tree and his back spasmed with pain. The impact shaved ten percent off his Health. The mantikhoras eyed him warily. Arche could see the cut on the creature's arm was dripping orange blood and was held to the mantikhoras's chest defensively. He must have done more damage with the knife than he'd thought, but the mantikhoras's health still dwarfed his own four times over.

Arche ducked a thrust from the creature's pincer tail but couldn't avoid the backhand that sent him flying. His Health dropped to sixty percent, but he managed to twist himself in midair and land on his feet, sliding against the loam of the forest.

Despite the pain in his everywhere, Arche felt light on his feet. The mantikhoras was huge and faster than he would have expected, but its sheer size slowed it down. As a smaller opponent, Arche's inferior agility was augmented by the simple fact his range of motion didn't extend as far. The mantikhoras was taking advantage of its better range by keeping him at a distance, where it could strike more easily with its scorpion tail, but Arche's eyes settled on the bat-like wings that spread to either side of the enraged mantikhoras. They were thick, covered in crimson fur, but looked exceedingly vulnerable to sharp knives.

Arche crouched and pulled his tried-but-true tactic of leaping over an enemy when they least expected it. Surprise registered on the mantikhoras's face as Arche twisted forward. It worked beautifully, with one small exception.

Arche was, in fact, not faster than a striking scorpion.

The stinger slammed into Arche's shoulder as his knife carved through the base of one wing. The force of it completely reversed his momentum and drove him toward the ground. Out of pure instinct he brought his knife up and slashed at the tail. He had expected the tail to be hard with some kind of exoskeleton, as if it belonged to an actual scorpion, but he was surprised to find it quite fleshy and his knife tore through it with ease.

The mantikhoras let out a scream at a much higher pitch than the angry roars it had showcased before. Arche hit the ground hard. One hand went to his pierced shoulder as he saw his health had dropped by an astounding two-hundred-twenty points. With barely thirty percent of his Health remaining, he felt ready to pass out. The normally red Health bar was tinged a sickly green, resembling puke more than the deep green of his Stamina. He watched his health tick down as the status effect washed over him.

> You are **Envenomated**.
>
> Lose 1 Health every 3 seconds.
>
> **Envenomated**: 4:59:57

Arche grit his teeth. Even if he killed the Mantikhoras, the venom was too potent for him to survive. He didn't know exactly how much damage would be done over five hours, but it was probably somewhere in the thousands. In other words, too damn much. A quick glance down told him that the veins around the puncture had turned black. The venom clotted the blood, leaving a strangely clean wound that tugged at him as he moved. The pain came a moment later, flaring through him. The puncture felt like a brand, making even his breath seem inflamed and hot in his chest and throat.

The mantikhoras clutched its tail, nearly severed by Arche's slice. Its eyes were filled with pain and rage.

"You will die," the mantikhoras rumbled with a voice that made the trees quiver. "You will water the weeds of my forest with your blood. I will spread your remains from every mountaintop. You will not be prey, you will be meat, and treated with no more respect than maggots."

Arche forced himself into a standing position, holding the knife in a standard grip as he struggled to focus on the mantikhoras. The fight was leaving him quickly but he could at least die on his feet.

"Try me, bitch."

The mantikhoras pounced, moving more quickly than Arche could react. It seized Arche in a massive claw and pinned him against a tree by the chest. Arche felt something in his back crunch and his health dropped to ten percent. Breathing was suddenly a lot more difficult. Darkness crept into the edges of his vision until he could barely see.

Death was close.

He knew it. The mantikhoras knew it. Hell, even Theresa, who was probably dead already, knew it. The monster opened its mouth wide, revealing sharp fangs and a forked tongue. Arche white-knuckled his knife and forced himself to stay conscious. With the last vestiges of willpower, he activated his Divine Body skill.

The effect was immediate.

Arche's Health and Stamina surged as his body glowed with red light. Torn skin knit itself back together, leaving him itchy all over. His knife plunged into the arm pinning him to the tree. The mantikhoras surged forward, trying to bite his head off, and Arche surged forward as well, slamming his head into the monster's mouth with a crunch.

He felt the impact on his forehead but there was no pain. The mantikhoras, on the other hand, reeled from the blow. One of its claws covered its face, the other was limp at its side, the dagger still embedded between the bones of its forearm. Arche fell to the ground, trying to control the flow of Mana. He needed it to last as long as possible but it was flowing out far too quickly. In a few moments, his Mana would bottom out and he would be at the mantikhoras's mercy.

The mantikhoras bellowed in rage and rushed him. Its maw was bloody and some of its fangs laid on the ground, knocked free by Arche's forehead. Arche pushed himself up and tucked forward, propelling himself in a flipping dropkick that he could never have pulled off without the physical augmentation of Divine Body. He hit the mantikhoras at surprising speed and, though it likely outweighed him several times over, sent it flying.

Arche landed on his feet and jumped after the monster, crossing the considerable distance with a single bound. The mantikhoras bared its teeth at him, but he paid the threat no mind. He curled his fists and hit the creature in the face three times. On the final blow, the mantikhoras's neck let out a loud crack and twisted violently to the side. The creature fell to the ground and didn't move. Arche felt his Mana dissipating and released his Divine Body skill, praying he hadn't given himself Mana Burnout.

He let out a few shaky breaths and checked his vitals.

Health: 379 / 420 90%	Stamina: 280 / 280 100%	Mana: 7 / 190 4%
Envenomated: 4:47:34		

He'd almost burned himself out, but he hadn't. For the moment, at least, he was still alive. As it stood, he was envenomed and, despite his regenerated Health and Stamina, felt like the mantikhoras had used him for a punching bag rather than the other way around.

Arche noticed that he hadn't received an experience prompt from the mantikhoras and looked at the creature more closely. It was lying on the ground, unmoving, but as Arche looked closer, he saw that its eyes were open and staring toward Arche with a look Arche recognized.

Fear.

Investigation has increased to **Level 3**.

+1% Chance to Spot Hidden Things (+3%)
+1% Chance to Spot Traps (+3%)
+1% Speed of Searching (+3%)

Arche dismissed the notification reflexively and stared at the mantikhoras. He could hear a small whistling as the creature's chest rose and fell. It was struggling to breathe. Understanding came with a small wave of revulsion.

He had broken the monster's neck but he hadn't killed it. It was paralyzed, slowly choking to death. Arche looked at the broken thing laying before him. He almost felt pity, but mostly he felt tired. He pulled his knife free from its arm, but the mantikhoras didn't, or couldn't, react.

"You know, a big part of me wants to just turn away and leave you like this. Choking on air and your own bile, wallowing in fear and hatred," Arche said quietly, still panting from the fight. "I think under normal circumstances that I'd do it, too, but killing you will make me stronger."

Arche grabbed the mantikhoras's head and lifted it, exposing the creature's neck.

"Don't mistake this for mercy."

Arche plunged the dagger in and twisted, severing the creature's jugular and carotid artery together. Hot blood sprayed his front, squelched between his fingers, painted the ground around them. The sharp intellect in the mantikhoras's eyes faded and Arche dropped the creature's head with a thud.

> You have slain Rakor, a **Level 27 Mantikhoras**.
> You gain 810 experience.
>
> **Slayer of the Mighty** activated!
> You gain 1,200 experience.

The experience was staggering. As great as it was, however, he was stuck. He couldn't level any further until he chose his profession and that was not something he was ready to do. Divine Body had saved his life, at the end. He needed to learn more about the skill, but he was hesitant about using it in front of other people. His inebriated display the night before didn't count. After all, he couldn't reasonably be held accountable for the rash decisions of drunk Arche. That guy was a moron. Arche's eyes went wide.

Theresa.

He whirled around and found her lying on the ground twenty strides away. Now that the fighting was over, the extent of the damage the mantikhoras had dealt her was clear.

Long slashes had laid open her torso and blood oozed out. The woman drifted in and out of consciousness, groaning all the while. If he didn't do something quickly, she would die. He Examined her quickly, trying to see how much Health she had left. His head pulsed with pain, almost bringing him to the ground as his Mana nearly bottomed out.

Theresa Eliades		
Level: 23 **Race**: Human **Age**: ? **Height**: ? **Weight**: ?	**Profession**: ? **Trade**: ? **Traits**: ? **Companions**: ? **Adventuring Party**: ?	
Health: 52 / 420 12%	**Stamina**: 207 / 375 55%	**Mana**: 260 / 260 100%

Her vitals dropped before his eyes. Arche looked around for anything he could use to bind her wounds, but his inventory had been emptied and his pants, the only clothing he'd been left with, were soaked in orange and red blood.

"I'm really sorry about this," he muttered.

He took the knife carefully in his hand and cut at the straps of Theresa's scaled armor. He pulled the armor away from her legs, revealing simple dark trousers. Taking great care to not accidentally stab the dying woman, he cut her trousers off around mid-thigh, turning what was left into shorts. Then he removed her damaged chest piece to reveal the tattered shirt underneath. He tore the scraps of trouser cloth into long strips and tied them around Theresa's middle, doing his best to cover the majority of the wounds and bind them down.

> You have learned a **Skill**.
>
> ### Medicine — Level 1
>
> *Often the only thing standing between life and death is a steady hand and a cool head.*
>
> Each level in this skill improves your knowledge of natural healing.
> Every 5 levels in this skill improves your **Wisdom** and **Willpower** by 1.
>
> +2% Effectiveness of Treatment (+2%)
> +1% Effectiveness of Identifying Ailments (+1%)

Arche brushed away the notification before he could let himself get distracted by why a skill like Medicine would improve his Willpower over time. Instead, he tried to focus on the task at hand. The weak bandages and constant pressure seemed to do the trick, as she stabilized with twenty Health left. Arche let loose a sigh of relief. They would both live, for the moment.

Until the venom took him, at least.

Chapter 19

Arche's hands were drenched in blood. He stared at the unconscious woman in front of him, trying to figure out what to do. He couldn't carry her, the jostling of forest travel would no doubt kill her. He couldn't leave her, either. They were in unfamiliar territory and he didn't know the way back to the village. He had no map, no weapons other than his knife and hers, and no equipment other than the blood-stained pants he wore. The sky was overcast, obscuring any hopes of telling the time of day other than that night had yet to fall. Despite the level-up curing his hangover, Arche still hadn't had a sip of water and had a horrible case of cottonmouth, which was exacerbated by the metallic taste of blood from the fight with the mantikhoras.

He was also still envenomated.

A glance at his vitals showed that he'd dropped over a hundred health, but he'd also gained back eighty Mana. Paying careful attention, he activated Divine Body for a single second. His Health shot up as his Mana plummeted. Checking his vitals again showed another surprising development.

Health: 364 / 420 87%	Stamina: 280 /280 100%	Mana: 18 / 190 9%
Envenomated: 4:29:16		

Using the Divine Body skill during the fight and to regain his Health had shaved over ten minutes off the timer of his Envenomated condition. He seemed to be getting health back at about the same rate he lost Mana while using the skill, but he was still losing Health faster than he was regenerating Mana. He closed his eyes, muttering as he counted.

"Twenty Health a minute. Sixteen Mana a minute. Aw, shit."

Arche pulled open his profile and dumped all five attribute points into Wisdom.

Health: 359 / 420 85%	Stamina: 280 /280 100%	Mana: 20 / 190 11%
Strength: 29 Dexterity: 22 Agility: 20 Fortitude: 18	Endurance: 19 Intelligence: 19 Wisdom: 21 Willpower: 14	Perception: 16 Charisma: 18 Comeliness: 1 Luck: 11

A twenty in Wisdom would even out his Mana regeneration with his Health loss but there was no reason to take the risk. At twenty-one, he had a safety net. The faster he could activate Divine Body, the sooner the Envenomed condition would wear off.

The adrenaline from the fight dwindled, leaving his limbs cold and tired. Arche sat next to Theresa, Examining her again to reassure himself that she was still stabilized.

"You really know how to fuck up an assassination," he muttered, chuckling darkly to himself.

She hadn't regained consciousness. Not for the first time, Arche wished he knew magic. *Real* magic, not whatever facsimile of a skill he had was. He had no doubt there was magic out there that could heal injuries or cure conditions. His Divine Body skill, though incredible, seemed to only improve his own abilities and regeneration. He wondered, not for the first time, how he had even come to learn such a skill. The vast majority of his skills had been learned by stumbling onto them but each had been rather obvious to what he'd been doing at the time. Divine Body had activated in the middle of a fight and Arche still had no idea how it worked.

The skill was part of the ever-growing list of things for which he needed answers, the top of which was the truth behind his identity before he'd lost his memories. A small, worried part of him wondered if he actually existed. His first glimpse of life, a lightless, empty space where he had been prompted for his name and told he was entering Tartarus, was still fresh on his mind even though several weeks had passed.

The thought of being nothing before that moment was terrifying but he used idioms that no one else seemed to understand and, even though he himself wasn't always entirely sure of their meanings, it had never felt like he'd come up with it on the spot. It was proof, however tenuous.

Theresa stirred. Her body convulsed, limbs thrashing, then her eyes shot open and she tried to sit up.

"Whoa, whoa, hey, take it easy."

"What...happened?"

"You got attacked by a monster. I bandaged your wounds but I'm shit at it. Take it easy."

Theresa grimaced then looked down at herself, taking stock of the state of her body and clothes.

"What happened to my pants?"

"What happened to my shirt?"

Theresa glanced up at him, taking in his bare chest.

"Fair enough." She coughed, then gasped with pain. "How bad is it?"

"I'm not sure. You got scored pretty deep but I stabilized you. Hopefully you can recover enough to move, soon."

"I'm surprised you didn't leave me."

"What good would that have done me? I don't know the way back to town."

"So you're what? Going to get directions from me and leave me here for trying to kill you?"

"Shouldn't I?"

The words came out more bitter than Arche intended but he watched her reaction carefully. She was an unknown and this whole business could have been orchestrated. It was unlikely, of course, but he couldn't rule it out.

Theresa closed her mouth and dropped her eyes. Arche watched her for a moment longer, then stood and let her ruminate while he walked over and nudged the mantikhoras's body with his foot. It had occurred to him that he hadn't looted a body since Lyssa had shown him after a fight with wolves, several days earlier. He didn't necessarily see anything of value on the mantikhoras, but in a world with invisible inventory space, he supposed that he wouldn't necessarily see what the creature carried with it. The contact made between the two and Arche's desire to view the creature's inventory was enough to open up a translucent window with what the monster had on it when it died.

Rakor's Inventory		
3x Kilograms Wolf Meat (Raw)	6x Liters Mantikhoras Blood (Requires container)	Mantikhoras Hide
Mantikhoras Tail Stinger	2x Mantikhoras Wing	24x Mantikhoras Claws

Arche's brows rose. It seemed most of the mantikhoras itself had been flagged as a usable resource. The wolf meat had likely been saved as a meal, which Arche was grateful for as it meant he wouldn't have to cook and eat the mantikhoras if they couldn't make it back to the village by a reasonable time. The blood would have to be wasted since he didn't have anything to carry it in, but the other usable parts were free game. Perhaps someone in the village could turn them into something useful.

Arche hesitated as his eyes landed on the mantikhoras's slack face.

Harvesting a clearly intelligent creature seemed wrong but to leave it was an utter waste. Maybe some good would come of the encounter. If the gear Arche could make with it saved lives, not the least of which his own, then it would be a worthy sacrifice, his own scruples be damned.

It was a savage world. He had to get used to it. More than that, he needed to take every advantage if he was going to survive. Those with power took what they wanted from those without. That part wasn't a surprise. What really surprised him was how forthcoming they were about it. It was equal parts refreshing and terrifying. Despite Lyssa's constant warnings that Tartarus did not look favorably upon the weak or the hesitant, the extent and ease at which people rose to violence was still shocking.

Arche supposed, if he had to be fair, that he also rose quickly to violence and carried it out past what was probably necessary. The monster—Rakor, he reminded himself—lying dead at his feet was proof enough of that. He wasn't sure if the barbarity of the world was having an influence on him or if this was the way he always was, but it didn't have to be the way he always would be. When he was strong enough to be different, maybe he could make that choice.

Arche attempted to move the items over to his inventory but was met by a prompt.

Warning!
You are attempting to automatically harvest materials that are too high for your **Skinning** skill. Harvesting these items in this way will severely degrade the items' quality and durability.
Do you wish to continue?

Yes	No

"Nope," Arche said aloud, immediately closing out the prompt and leaving the materials where they were.

Skinning wasn't a skill he'd learned, yet. He had some skill notifications waiting for him but a quick glance showed none of them helped here. Still, if he was going to collect these items and already had a severe penalty for doing things the easy way, he might as well get his dirty hands dirtier and try to learn something.

Arche pulled out his knife and held it loosely in one hand, trying to decide where to start. The hide was clearly the largest object and would take quite a bit of time. He decided to save it for last, hoping that the other parts would at least get him started in the right direction so he could take a chance at salvaging the hide. That left the tail, the wings, and the claws.

Arche moved to the tail, which had already been nearly severed from the encounter. He took the bulbous stinger of the tail in one hand and stared at it for a while, turning it over to look at it. Finally, he took the knife and finished cutting through the disturbingly fleshy tail, spilling a fresh gout of orange blood onto the ground. He was left holding a fairly heavy chunk of stinger, but he still felt he was missing something. Arche cut around the base of the stinger, rotating the blade around like he was carving fruit. More blood dripping onto his hands, but when he'd finished, he'd exposed a viscous sac at the base of the stinger. Narrowing his eyes, he Examined it.

Mantikhoras Venom Sac	**Rarity**: Epic **Potency**: Strong **Durability**: 1/1 **Weight**: 0.4 kilograms **Traits**: ?

Examine has increased to **Level 4**. +2% Examine Speed (+8%)

With excruciating care, Arche used the knife to sever the fleshy connections between the sac and the rest of the stinger. It took nearly twenty minutes, but he managed to extract the sac and a small tube that ran to the end of the stinger, no doubt how the venom was normally injected. He'd had to pause halfway through to use Divine Body, counting on the distance and the sunlight to mask the red glow but also not really caring whether Theresa saw. The assassin didn't even glance in his direction. As Arche held the sac, he carefully placed it into his inventory where he wouldn't have to worry about it bursting.

> You have learned a **Skill**.
>
> ### Skinning — Level 3
>
> *There's more than one way to skin a centaur.*
>
> Each level in this skill will improve your ability to harvest materials from slain creatures.
> Every 5 levels in this skill improves your **Dexterity** by 1.
> This is a subskill of **Wilderness Survival**.
>
> +1% Speed of Harvest (+3%)
> +2% Quality of Harvest (+6%)

> You have learned a **Skill**.
>
> ### Wilderness Survival — Level 3
>
> *You have taken your first steps toward being a true woodsman.*
>
> Each level in this skill helps your overall ability to survive in the great outdoors.
> Every 5 levels in this skill improves your **Wisdom** by 1.
>
> +2% Insulation (+6%)
> +2% Durability of constructed shelters (+6%)
> +1% Vitals regeneration in camp (+3%)

Two skills he hadn't been taught and they had started at level three. Lyssa would be proud. More notifications flashed, waiting to be revealed, but Arche ignored them. There would be time enough to go over all his awaiting prompts from the battle, but for now he had skinning to do. He'd also have to build a cooking fire and prepare a shelter if Theresa wasn't well enough to travel by the time he'd finished.

Arche got to work on the wings of the creature, feeling instinctively where the knife should cut in order to produce the best result. His command over the tool was hesitant but his Dexterity allowed him enough fine control that what few mistakes he made didn't heavily degrade the quality of the wings. As he worked, he let his mind wander back to Theresa.

She had accepted Callias order to kill him, yes, but she hadn't really followed through on it. She was capable, clearly. She'd lured him out and strung him up easily enough. The armor she wore wasn't cheap, whatever it was, though it hadn't been enough to save her from the Mantikhoras. A simple mercenary would be hard-pressed to have equipment like hers or be as high a level as she was.

Most of the guards that Arche had surreptitiously Examined in the village had averaged about level sixteen. Theresa was a higher level than Gigator and Elpida, and both of them struck Arche as people who'd been in more than their fair share of combat. That being said, it seemed the woman had less experience in the forest than Arche did and that didn't bode well for either of them if they were forced into an extended stay. If he could make an ally out of her, it would be well worth the effort. Plus, it'd be a kick in the teeth for Callias.

That alone was worth the try.

Arche finished with the wings, each one granting him a level in both Skinning and Wilderness Survival, then started on the claws. He gave one an experimental tug, but it held fast. Separating them was going to take some careful work. His eyes wandered back to Theresa, who frowned at the ground and clutched her side. A myriad of emotions were etched into her face, readable without the need to meet her eyes. Foremost among them was fear.

Arche wouldn't leave her behind.

She had tried to kill him, sure, and though it was a prospect he was still very much afraid of, he fully believed that if the mantikhoras had simply waited a few more seconds, she would have freed him. That had to count for something. If that made him a fool, so be it, but he couldn't get back to the village without help. Besides, if he could convince her to go public about what Callias had paid her to do, that might be enough to turn people against the smug bastard.

Arche didn't want Callias dead, per se, but he wouldn't be much inclined to douse the man if Callias found himself on fire and the only water Arche had to hand was in his bladder. To kill Callias meant that any allies the man had would be able to come after him publicly and the ensuing power struggle over the village would probably end in the death of several people, potentially including Lyssa and Helwan, if not himself. In order to assure the survival of the village, Callias had to be run out or deposed by the village itself. What happened after wasn't really Arche's concern, unless Callias tried to take revenge, which he most likely would.

Arche scowled.

He hadn't killed a person before. A few named entities, sure, but nothing that hadn't attacked him first. He wondered if he'd be able to do it if the situation called for it. It was easy to say yes, but he wouldn't know until the moment came. Arche sincerely hoped it wouldn't come to that, but Callias wouldn't take a coup lying down.

The last of Rakor's claws came free with a small, sucking plop.

Skinning has increased to **Level 6**.

+1% Speed of Harvest (+6%)
+2% Quality of Harvest (+12%)

Wilderness Survival has increased to **Level 6**.

+2% Insulation (+12%)
+2% Durability of Constructed Shelters (+12%)
+1% Vitals Regeneration in Camp (+6%)

Arche looked down at the claw in his hand. It seemed odd that despite having the body of what resembled an ape-like lion, the mantikhoras had six claws on each hand. Was it a birth defect or the number of digits the species normally had? Endless questions.

Arche closed his eyes and used Divine Body, letting the skill go as his Mana dipped below twenty. He opened his eyes and glanced toward Theresa, but she was still staring at the ground in front of her, hands holding her side. There was no way he was going to be able to hide from her view every seven minutes for the next couple hours as he burned through his Envenomated condition. It was a bizarre feeling, having his blood coagulate inside his body, only to be purged by his skill every few minutes. It was as though his joints were constantly growing stiff and painful, but instead of his joints it was all of his internal organs.

At any rate, it was time to begin on the hide. As the most complicated and potentially most valuable material to harvest—next to, perhaps, the venom sac, which he really should have saved until later for risk of damaging it—Arche had left the hide for last so his skill would be greatest and his chances of ruining the pelt would be lowest. He gave it all of his focus for the next half hour, only pausing to use Divine Body to regenerate his Health. The knife still felt a little unsure in his hand, but he was able to hold it steady and the few mistakes he did make were easily fixed. By the time he was done, his Skinning and Survival skills had raised all the way to level eight. He deposited the mantikhoras's hide safely into his inventory and returned to Theresa, who was, thankfully, still conscious and had pulled herself into a sitting position with her back braced against a tree.

"How are you feeling?" Arche asked, his voice flat and tired even to his own ears.

Theresa didn't meet his eye. She raised her hand and pointed off into the forest.

"West."

"Beg pardon?"

"West," she repeated. "The village is west."

"...And?"

Theresa let her hand fall back to the ground and closed her eyes. The wounds made her voice raspy and strained.

"You're right. I tried to kill you and you saved my life. You saved me from that monster and treated my wounds, none of which you were obligated to do. You have every right to kill me now or leave me behind. It's no less than I deserve."

Arche cocked his head, his scowl deepening. Silence spread between them until finally Theresa met his eyes. Only then did he speak.

"Nothing you just said answered my question."

Theresa blinked in confusion. "What?"

"How. Are. You. Feeling?"

"...Better?"

"Good. I'm going to get a fire going and cook some meat. Don't worry, it's wolf, not mantikhoras."

Arche began gathering up dry wood from the forest floor as Theresa watched on, confused and speechless. Within a minute, Arche had gathered a large bundle of kindling and tinder. He brought it back to near where Theresa was sitting and dropped it in a pile. He was about to light it when he remembered that they were in the Sylv. A fire could attract attention, even in daylight, and Theresa was in no position to fight or run. A small risk, perhaps, but still one they couldn't afford.

Following an instinct he couldn't quite put a voice to, Arche began digging a hole. He lacked a shovel, a lack he greatly mourned, but his relatively high skill-level in Digging proved its usefulness as the ground seemed to mold itself around his hands and intent. Within five minutes, he had managed a hole that was an arm's length deep and had made a second hole, almost as deep and about as far away with an underground tunnel connecting the two holes.

"What are you doing?" Theresa asked, utterly confused.

Arche paused while aligning his kindling in the deeper hole.

"I'll tell you in a minute," he said, then added under his breath, "when I figure it out."

Arche dumped leaves into the hole for tinder, then paused, turning back toward Theresa.

"You don't happen to have fire magic, do you?"

"Do I look like a mage?"

Arche shrugged and tried to think about what he could use to start a fire. He had a knife and there were plenty of dead leaves all around. He just needed some way of making a spark. His gaze alighted on the rocks scattered about near them. He picked up a couple and Examined them, but eventually put them back. He kept a couple that identified as containing pyrite and put them with the dry leaves until he came across one that identified itself as flintstone.

Arche grinned and brought his supplies over near the fire hole he had dug. He placed the leaves into a pile next to the hole and sprinkled the pyrite chunks onto it. Then he took the knife in one hand and held the palm-sized flintstone in the other. Holding both above the pile, he struck the steel pommel of the knife against the flintstone with a small shower of sparks. Arche grinned. He struck the rock again and again until one of the sparks successfully caught the leaves on fire.

Blowing gentle breaths, he fanned the flame until it was burning healthily, then carefully scooped up the burning leaves and placed them inside the fire hole, where it could attempt to light the kindling. Arche put his head down the secondary hole and blew through the tunnel he had dug, feeding oxygen to the flame. Within the minute, he had a fire burning, fed with air through the secondary tunnel and with flames completely concealed by the earthen sides of the hole. What was more, practically no smoke came out of the fire.

"Hah!"

You have discovered an **Advanced Survival Technique** well above your **Wilderness Survival** level without guidance. For your efforts, you gain bonus **Wilderness Survival** experience.

You have learned an **Advanced Survival Technique**.

Fire Hole

For the hunted, a fire can be both savior and executioner. This technique helps give that choice back to the fire starter.

+90% to Stealth of Fire
-50% Dispersal of Heat from Fire

Wilderness Survival has increased to **Level 11**.

+2% Insulation (+22%)
+2% Durability of Constructed Shelters (+22%)
+1% Vitals Regeneration in Camp (+11%)
+1 Wisdom

You have reached the rank of **Novice** in **Wilderness Survival**.
You receive 100 experience.

Arche laid a long, flat rock across the hole above the flames, which were now burning strongly. Then he laid out the meat. The juice sizzled on the hot rock and he used the knife to flip the meat every couple minutes until it looked nice and ready. At one point he had to activate his Divine Body skill to regenerate lost health, but if Theresa noticed, she didn't say anything. When the gurgle in his stomach grew too loud to be ignored, he tested one of the steaks by cutting into it. It had a little more pink on the inside than was preferable, but it was good enough. Arche lifted the stone carefully and placed it to the side to cool, then used a couple sticks to spear the meat. He glanced up to see Theresa was looking at him suspiciously.

"What?"

"What do you mean, '*what?*'" she demanded. "I've never seen someone build a fire like that."

"I didn't want monsters to lock in on the light or the smoke. Taking a big enough risk with the smell as it is. Do you want some or not?"

Theresa was quiet for a while, giving Arche enough time to prepare the steaks for transport.

You have learned a **Skill**.

Cooking — Level 3

Food comes in an endless variety, limited only by the creativity of those who consume it.

Each level in this skill will improve the taste and ease at which you prepare food. Every 5 levels in this skill improves your **Wisdom** by 1.

+2% Quality of Food Prepared (+6%)
+2% Chance to Discern Ingredients by Taste (+6%)

You have learned a **Recipe**.

Seared Wolf Steaks (Unseasoned)

Arche suppressed a grin at the new skills. As it turned out, being kidnapped and nearly assassinated was doing wonders for his skill accumulation and progression. If it hadn't come with mortal danger to his wellbeing, he might have considered making it a regular thing.

He held out an impaled steak to Theresa. He had one for himself while the last, still piping hot, had gone into his inventory for later. Theresa looked at the steak for a few moments, then stared up at Arche.

"I don't understand."

"Yeah, that seems to be a popular trend among people I know."

"Why are you helping me?"

Arche shrugged.

"So you tried to kill me. You changed your mind. You got in a bad situation and were asked to do something you clearly didn't want to do. What was I supposed to do when the tables were turned, just let you die?"

"Yes."

"No," Arche replied, a touch of annoyance creeping into his voice. "Look, if you try to kill me again, it'll be different, but I'm not gonna let you die here in the woods alone."

"Why not?"

"Holy fuck." Arche had to fight the urge to break something. "Is everyone here so goddamn sadistic that they just kill people or let them die with no fucks given? What the fuck is wrong with you people?"

Theresa shrank back against the tree, hissing in pain. Arche grit his teeth and tossed the steak at her. He'd taken it a step too far, perhaps. He sat down next to the fire to eat his own. Despite the lack of seasoning, it was tender and juicy and exactly what he was craving. In less than five bites, he finished it.

"You are, without a doubt, the strangest person I have ever met. But, please, don't mistake my confusion for ingratitude."

"Cool, be grateful. Eat your dinner."

Arche stood and paced around the area while Theresa ate. It gave him another chance to use his Divine Body skill with minimal risk of her seeing it. Rather than ask her how she was doing, Arche Examined her, taking care not to stare too openly as he checked her vitals.

Theresa Eliades		
Level: 23 **Race**: Human **Age**: ? **Height**: ? **Weight**: ?	**Profession**: ? **Trade**: ? **Traits**: ? **Companions**: ? **Adventuring Party**: ?	
Health: 45 / 420 15%	**Stamina**: 375 / 375 100%	Mana: 260 / 260 100%

"How did you know my name?" Theresa asked suddenly, making Arche jump. "I don't give anyone my real name."

"I have a way of figuring out most people's names. Call it a talent."

Lord Cypress's warning about people reacting negatively to knowledge of the Examine skill was still fresh in his mind. Theresa shifted uncomfortably.

"I didn't know such a thing existed," she admitted.

Arche nodded, looking to change the subject. "How are your wounds? I'm afraid I don't have anything to change the bandages with."

"They've begun the healing process. I still can't walk, but soon, with any luck. We likely won't make it back to the village before dark, but we should be able to avoid a night under the stars as long as we aren't attacked by monsters."

"That's a big 'if.'"

"I know. Also, I'm not much use in a fight in my current state."

"You don't have any of my old gear, do you?"

Theresa shook her head. "No, left that all in the tent."

Arche grimaced.

"Would you mind...walking me through exactly what happened?"

Theresa snorted, then coughed painfully.

"We left the party together, went back to my tent. You took two steps inside and passed out. I waited until the sounds outside quieted, then carried you out of the village.

I figured by the time anyone missed you, you'd be dead. I reckon I'll have a few questions to answer when we get back."

"That's likely," Arche agreed, grateful he hadn't done too bad. Still, it was surprising she was strong enough to carry him all the way out here. "We'll see if you can answer those questions before an arrow gets lodged into you."

"Your wood elf friend?"

"Yeah, she's a bit protective. She might very well be looking for us now. I just hope she hasn't gotten herself into trouble."

"You're foolish indeed, then, for throwing devotion like that away for a chance with a stranger."

Arche let out an actual laugh.

"First, You suck at compliments. Second, it's not like that. She doesn't really think highly of humans."

Theresa raised an eyebrow. "And yet she's protective of you?"

"Long story. Not all mine to tell. Just take it for what it is."

"If you insist."

Arche stiffened, not comfortable with where the conversation was heading. Theresa must have noticed the movement because she changed the subject.

"Are you going to kill Callias?"

Arche paused, gathering his thoughts.

"Do you want me to?"

"He won't suffer a voice of opposition, nor will he suffer a failed tool. His ire will be directed at us both. He will have us killed if he can."

"I'd rather avoid murder if I can help it."

"And if you can't? You've seen him 'lead.' He doesn't care about anyone's safety but his own. That's why he keeps all the guards in his own vicinity instead of sending some of them out to form watches or even build defenses for the village. If he remains in power, there will be casualties. Heavy casualties."

"I don't disagree, but I don't like the thought of killing someone for being a dick. If the village itself can rise up against him, I think we'll have a better chance of making some positive change."

"That's a lot to ask for," Theresa pointed out.

"If people want a change, they will strive for it. All they need is the opportunity. That's what I'm planning on giving them. I actually think you can help with that."

"Me?"

"Yeah. If you share with them what he asked you to do. If you tell them what he demanded of you, it might stir them into action."

Theresa gave him an unconvinced stare.

"And what if he calls me a liar? I don't exactly have proof."

"Then we go with Plan B."

"What's Plan B?"

"I ask my satyr friend to incite riot."

Theresa stared at him for a few moments, then she began to laugh. It was short-lived and quickly devolved into gasps of pain, but it was a sweet sound while it lasted. The first sweet sound he'd heard all day. Arche grinned at her.

"You ask some very intense questions, you know."

"I like to know who I work with. That way future actions are easier to predict. You've told me what you intend, misguided as it may be. And, for once, I respect what you're trying to do."

"Thanks, I think." Arche scratched his head.

"I told everyone my name was Tessalyn, by the way. If you could call me Tess when we get back, I would appreciate it."

"Are you an outlaw or something?" he asked, more teasing than serious.

"Not in these woods, but there are a few who would wish harm upon me and those I'm with. My real name getting out is just more trouble than it's worth."

"Wait, isn't Tess normally short for Theresa?"

"Most people just accept that my name is Tessalyn and let it go at that."

"Tess it is, then. I'm Arche, though I guess you already knew that."

Tess gave a small, tired smile.

"It's nice to meet you properly. I don't think I said it before but thank you for saving me."

"Don't worry about it. Thanks for not killing me."

They fell into silence and Arche took the time to go over the notifications awaiting him from the fight.

You have learned a **Skill**.

Daggermanship — Level 2

Large blades look pretty, but often the most dangerous are the ones you never saw coming.

Each level in this skill improves your ability with small blades.

+3% Damage with Small Blades (+6%)
+1% Sneak Attack Chance (+2%)
+1% Sneak Attack Damage (+2%)

You have learned a **Skill**.

Anatomy — Level 2

Knowing the makeup of creatures can lead to many scientific discoveries, but most settle for killing them more effectively.

Each level in this skill will improve your ability to assess the physical structure of living creatures.
Every 5 levels in this skill improves your **Intelligence** and **Perception** by 1.

+1% Critical Strike Chance (+2%)
+1% Critical Strike Damage (+2%)
+1% Chance to Spot Enemy Weaknesses (+2%)

Unarmed Combat has increased to **Level 4**.

+2% Damage while unarmed (+8%)
+0.5% Natural armor (+2%)

> **Divine Body** has increased to **Level 9**.

Arche frowned at the last skill notification, annoyed that Divine Body still didn't give him any hint as to what the skill actually did. He had a feeling there was more than what he'd observed so far.

"You were being honest when you said you didn't have any of my stuff, right?" he asked.

Tess nodded. "It's all back at the village."

"Well, that sucks. A better blade may have come in handy. I'd have settled for my bow. Don't suppose you have a spare?"

Tess extended her hand and a bow appeared.

"I have a shortbow and a quiver of twenty arrows. It's not much, I'm more of a dagger woman."

She offered it to Arche, who took it without hesitation. He could tell just by holding it that it wasn't as good as his, but it could have been a lot worse.

Oak Shortbow	**Rarity**: Common **Quality**: Average **Durability**: 10 / 10 **Weight**: 1.4 kilograms

It lacked the craftsmanship of his elven bow, but it would get the job done well enough.

"This'll be better than trying to stab a monster to death if we get attacked on the way back," he said.

"I'm still shocked that you managed to kill the mantikhoras. What happened?"

Arche shrugged.

"I got lucky. I had an opening and went for the throat."

"I fully believe you got lucky but I'm still shocked you killed it. There's a reason those beasts are called Crimson Terrors. A single mantikhoras can take out an entire squad of soldiers and barely break a sweat. That you killed one while injured, unarmored, and with nothing but a shoddy knife...it's downright unbelievable."

Arche gestured lazily toward the body of the mantikhoras about forty paces away, mutilated from the harvesting he'd done. "Nonetheless, it's dead and we're not. Don't look a gift horse in the mouth."

"Don't...horse? *What?*"

"Fuck's sake," he muttered. "Don't overanalyze it. Be grateful for the situation at hand."

Tess nodded, then slowly eased herself onto her feet. Arche rose as well, ready to catch her if it seemed she would fall.

"I don't think we should wait here for more predators to be attracted. As it is, we likely won't return until after dark."

Arche nodded and kicked the mound of dirt he'd excavated back over the fire, dousing it.

"Let's head back, then."

Chapter 20

The next three hours were a grueling march through the forest. Tess had hauled him a considerable distance away from the village, likely so that Lyssa wouldn't be able to find them. Their going was also slowed by her wounds, which drained her Stamina at a prodigious rate and forced them to make frequent stops to let it regenerate. It gave Arche plenty of opportunities to use his Divine Body skill and work off his Envenomed condition. He was certain that Tess had noticed the light despite his best efforts but she said nothing about it. As night fell, their pace slowed even further as they had to pick their way among the roots and bushes.

Arche took the last wolf steak out of his inventory and handed it to Tess. She took it gratefully, passing him a waterskin in return before tearing into the steak. Other than the waterskin, Tess had no rations. She hadn't expected to be gone for more than a few hours. The need for more water kept them moving past nightfall. Arche was confident in his ability to find creatures to hunt if it came to that, but without water they wouldn't last long, especially when the sun came back up.

Tess's wounds improved as they went. Her regeneration was slowed by the travel, but she was no longer in serious danger of losing her footing from pain or weakness. Instead, the only danger underfoot was the poor lighting and hidden roots. Arche was going to suggest they stop for the night and make shelter when a loud, screeching cry had him diving to the ground, bow half drawn as he tried to pinpoint the danger. Tess also fell to the ground, more out of surprise and pain than from an attempt to remain hidden.

Arche looked around wildly, but nothing jumped out to attack them. The cry came again, more raucous this time, and Arche realized it wasn't as close as it had seemed. There was something familiar about the cry, but he couldn't place it.

"Stay here."

She gripped her dagger in her hand and crawled her way into the shadow of a large tree.

"Don't worry about me, I'm not going anywhere," she grunted, one hand clutching at her side.

Arche crept forward, staying low to the ground. He kept an arrow knocked to his bow as he did his best to meld silently into the forest as Lyssa would have. Straining his ears, he heard noises. Voices and screeches, some sounding humanoid and others that sounded like they couldn't possibly be made by normal throats.

"Beastmar," he breathed.

Arche continued forward until he saw them. Four beastmar gathered near a gaping cave entrance in the side of a hill. In the dim light, Arche couldn't tell whether it was a natural cave or an opening to some deeper dwelling.

Stealth has increased to **Level 9**.

+2% Chance to Hide (+18%)
+2% Sneak Attack Chance (+18%)
+1% Sneak Attack Damage (+9%)

Arche felt a trickle of relief. If his Stealth had leveled, then his presence was probably undetected. Beastmar milled about around the cave entrance. There was no fire to see by and very little light filtered through the trees, indicating that the beastmar possessed some sort of night vision. He Examined each of them in turn, finding that all were between levels eleven and fourteen.

Examine has increased to **Level 5**.

+2% Examine Speed (+10%)
+1 Perception

The beastmar seemed about the same strength as the ones that had attacked the village before, but without armor or proper melee weapons, Arche was in no position to pick a fight. Especially since he didn't know how many more were hiding in the hill. One of the creatures used an arm that forked at the elbow into a set of two hands to smack another that had three legs that all bent backwards.

"Quiet!" the oddly armed beastmar said in broken common speech. "You keep watch."

The tri-legged beastmar made a chittering noise that sounded distinctly avian but spoke the common tongue much better.

"Pah! Nothing in these woods to keep eyes on! You ask me, we should head back and put the hurt on that settlement. Maybe grab some more people. Been too long since I've had manflesh, and there were all sorts there as well!"

Arche held very still, his hand clenched around the bow.

"Lose more tribe? They have warriors. Trust the chief. His plan good."

The beastmar's voices lowered and Arche could no longer make them out. He carefully backpedaled until he felt he was out of earshot, then made his way quickly back to Tess.

You have received a **Quest**.

Forest Abominations

You have stumbled upon a beastmar camp. They have mentioned a plan set in place to destroy the village of Buton. Stymie their efforts and remove their influence from the valley.

Objectives	Rewards
- Figure out the beastmar's plan - Foil the beastmar's plan - Slay beastmar 0/50 *(Optional)*	- Experience *(Variable)* - Removal of beastmar influence from the valley - Increased relation with the village of Buton

Time Remaining: Unknown

Arche dismissed the quest notification, feeling rather unsettled by the last line. He wished he had a map of the area but doubted such a thing existed in any great detail. He found Tess in the shadow of a tree where he had left her.

"We need to move," he hissed, still loath to raise his voice with enemies so close.

"What's going on?" she asked, rising unsteadily to her feet.

"Beastmar. We need to get back and warn the others. They're up to something. I got a quest to stop them."

"Then let's not waste any more time."

Arche ducked beneath her arm as she leaned her weight onto him. They managed to go another hour before Tess needed to stop for air.

"You should know," she said between breaths. "Even if you get the people to turn against Callias, he won't stop trying to tear you down. You're a threat to him, what you did for the village. He doesn't like that he can't control you. If you move against him openly, he'll move against you openly. And if you beat him, he'll kill you for it."

"I know. I'm working on it."

Another twenty minutes of pained walking and the trees began to thin. They broke through the treeline and stepped out onto the rolling hills of the valley, the lights of the village burning in the distance. Another half hour of walking and they were at the village. Most had already gone to bed, but a few still tended the fires and kept an eye on things. As they approached, an arrow thudded into the ground at their feet.

"Ah, shit," Arche muttered, staring at the green fletching.

Lyssa appeared two dozen strides away, bow drawn and leveled at Tess's heart.

"Lyssa, it's okay," Arche said placatingly.

"I felt you nearly die, Arche. I couldn't find you." Lyssa's voice was as hard and cold as steel.

Arche felt a chill shoot down his back. Even if he wasn't the target of her ire, the chill fury of the huntress was terrifying.

"Sorry about that, really. Things were out of hand for a little while, but Tess isn't our enemy right now. In fact, she can help us with our problem, but she needs medical attention."

Lyssa hesitated, bow still tightly drawn, then she loosened the tension and slung it across her back.

"Very well. Bring her. I will bind her wounds."

Persuasion has increased to **Level 4**.

+1% Persuasion Chance (+4%)

Arche helped Tess over to a table where the injured woman could rest. He turned back to Lyssa only to find her fist flying toward his face. The blow staggered him, dropping his Health an astounding twenty points. As he rocked back on his heels, completely dazed, Lyssa grabbed him by the shoulders and drew him into a tight hug.

"Don't scare me like that," she whispered.

Her voice sounded thin and stretched. It was more vulnerable than Arche had ever heard it. He fought the urge to rub his throbbing cheek and returned the hug.

"I'm sorry," he managed. There was nothing else he could say.

Lyssa pulled away and cleared her throat. She nodded once at Arche, then turned toward Tess, who threw up her hands in a surrendering motion, eyes wide.

"I'm sorry, too."

"You will be." Lyssa's voice had regained its steel. "Now, let's see about your injuries. Arche, go clean up. We'll talk later."

"Yes, we will. I have news that concerns the village. I think it can wait until tomorrow but be on your guard. The beastmar are planning something."

Tess shot Arche a worried glance, clearly uncomfortable being left alone with Lyssa, but Arche simply gave the woman a shrug and walked off to retrieve his equipment and take a dip in the river. It took him a while to find the right tent, going off drunken memory and the annoyed directions of a few freshly woken villagers, but eventually he was reunited with his gear.

The first thing he did after pulling on his backpack was retrieve a waterskin and drain it dry. His hangover may have been cured by the regenerative properties of leveling up, but he'd barely drunk a drop of water that day. The second thing he did was slip on his Ruby Ring of Lesser Life, feeling reassured as his Fortitude and Endurance each increased by five points. Double-checking that he had everything, he headed to the river for a much-needed bath.

The water was refreshing and the slightly overcast night gave him all the privacy he needed to strip down and wade into the river. He felt the grime and blood of the last two days wash itself away with the current as he splashed around. There was still a bit of unease that tickled his mind, reminding him of his two near-drowning events, but he did his best to push it to the back of his mind.

He wasn't certain he'd ever be completely comfortable in water again but he couldn't let such a fear dominate him for the rest of his life. He faced better chances of dying almost every day and his steady increases in the Swimming skill only improved his odds. Still, he stayed close to the bank and didn't stray out farther than his feet could touch.

After feeling and smelling much better, Arche crawled out of the river, dried off, and equipped fresh clothes. He returned to the camp, crawled into his tent, and fell into a deep sleep.

Ψ

The world was a husk of the one he knew. The ground Arche laid on was covered in ash and all life had long since choked and burned. The tattered remains of tents and tables were the only signs that a village had ever once tried to fill the smothered valley. A half dozen spewing volcanoes splashed an angry glow against the horizon, with the closest dominating the northern edge of the valley. Arche stood up, feeling the ash compress under his feet, the white powder clung to his skin and left dark stains as it drifted all about him.

"I'm dreaming."

The words felt weird coming through his jaw, as though his muscles were strained by the usage and his throat was loath to work properly.

"Not quite."

The voice was smooth and deep, as if it was often used to lull people to sleep. It sounded like a grandfather bidding a beloved grandchild to sleep well.

"You are in the Dreaming."

This time the voice was high, like a mother cooing at her newborn, but maintained the same softness.

A figure appeared. It was formless and featureless, a humanoid body wrapped in strange black robes and wearing a smooth mask of night sky that completely hid whatever true face the figure had.

"Who are you?" Arche asked, not really expecting an answer but hoping to get one anyway.

"I am the Oneiroi," the figure responded in a voice like an old crone. **"And you are an anomaly."**

Arche didn't really know how to respond to that, so he gestured about himself at the ash-covered valley.

"What happened here? What is this place? It looks like the valley, but like death has touched it."

The Oneiroi let out a child's giggle.

"Death is a vital component to Tartarus but they have not caused this. This was a part of an older design. Now it is a place for the fallen divine. By rights, you should not be here. Death spoke to me of you."

"What?" Arche took a step back in surprise, remembering his earlier meeting with a strange figure in a place much like this. "That was actually Death? Death's a person?"

The Oneiroi laughed again, a deep throaty sound not dissimilar to a dwarf.

"Death is a consciousness. An amalgamation of spirits absorbed into a single entity. The old alliances have fallen, betrayed by the last grasps for power in a dying existence. In many ways I am the same, many become one. But I am not here to explain the truths of this world to you."

Arche felt his anxiety spike. "Then why are you here?"

The Oneiroi came closer. Arche tried to step back and found he couldn't move. Out of reflex, he tried to Examine the Oneiroi, but nothing happened. He couldn't see his vitals, which were usually always visible, if somewhat ignored. Like before, none of the strange parts of the world he had come to know seemed to work in whatever shadow world he was in now.

The Oneiroi stopped directly in front of him, close enough that Arche could see stars swirling in the piece of night sky that was used for a mask. The Oneiroi reached out with a hand swaddled in black cloth and gripped Arche by the forehead.

Arche expected pain, to feel some alien presence probing his mind or forcing its way past his mental boundaries. He felt none of these. Instead, the Oneiroi leveled their inscrutable gaze against him.

"I see," the Oneiroi said at last, their voice the half-asleep murmuring of a small child. **"You are lost. A stranger without purpose arrived through violence and deceit. You were granted power by one who would see it used, forced to become part of a game that is larger than you have the awareness to realize. I am...sorry."**

Arche frowned as the voice took on a mournful timbre.

"Sorry for what?"

"You have so very far to go and peace for any lasting period will always be beyond your grasp. Your soul has been marked by one of the Twelve and that fact will bring you great power, but it will also bring great pain."

The Oneiroi released him and Arche stumbled backward.

"I cannot interfere on your behalf. Though the Twelve have no power over me, I would not risk their wrath. You have a long road ahead of you, but at the end of it you may find an opportunity that has not been granted to mortals in millennia, should you wish to take it. Take great care which path you profess to take; the Moirai weave many threads but not even they can interpret meaning."

"I don't know what you're talking about," Arche said, desperation straining his voice. "Please, I don't know what's going on."

The Oneiroi angled their head to the side.

"It is too soon. Someday you will, but you will not return to this place. Worry not, I will reassure my sibling of your condition."

"You're the only one who knows me. Please, can you tell me who I am? Will I ever be able to speak to you again?"

The Oneiroi shook their head.

"I cannot. There are truths that you are not ready to hear. We will speak again, but not for a long time yet, by your judgement. I must confer with the others. Though I will not appear to you, if you call out to me in the Dreaming, I will hear your message. Be strong, little spark. Burn well."

Arche opened his mouth to ask another question, but the Oneiroi raised their hand and Arche fell backwards into darkness.

Chapter 21

Arche woke in a panic. He was thoroughly entangled inside his bedroll, which only served to worsen his already addled mind. With a slightly muffled yell and a final, desperate jerk, Arche freed himself from the bedroll and stumbled to his feet, scanning the tent for attackers. The Tridory, lying next to him, flew to his hand with a thought as Arche whirled about, feeling as though Death themselves was reaching for him.

He was alone, not that it did much for his hammering heart. The encounter with that entity, the Oneiroi, was still fresh. There would be no convincing himself it was merely a dream.

Hot tears pricked Arche's eyes and washed down his cheeks. He'd been so close to answers, only to be denied and given even more questions. There wasn't even a hint to point him in the right direction. The Tridory slipped from his fingers and fell point-first to the ground. He'd been *so* close.

Arche held his scarred face in his hands, feeling every peak and valley as he tried to rub his feelings away. He was no closer to answers, but he was no further, either. More questions meant more opportunities. It would take time, that was all. Just time.

The Tridory stood embedded in the dirt, almost seeming to stare at him reproachfully. He stared back, biting his lip. The spear itself was full of similar questions. Where had it come from? How did it come to be here? Why could it do the things that it could do? The cold metal was silent, full of secrets but not answers.

Arche left the Tridory in the tent. He was in no mood to lug around the heavy spear all day. The xiphos was safely sheathed at his side for reassurance, slung through his belt, but he left his armor in his inventory. Hunger gnawed at his stomach and he made his way to the communal dining area. The morning sun had roused many of the villagers and they were sleepily wandering about, preparing themselves for the day ahead. Arche gathered a bowl of stew and brought it to an unoccupied table to eat by himself.

His solitude didn't last long. Helwan and Lyssa sat down across from him.

"Are you all right?" Helwan asked, concern heavy in the satyr's voice. "You look like you haven't slept in a week."

"I'm fine, just…disappointed, I suppose. Anyway, that's not important right now. I have news that can't wait."

Arche set down his spoon.

"In the forest, I found a beastmar camp. It's set into a hill, two hours' walk east from the forest's edge. Maybe less, I'm not completely sure. I received a quest after overhearing them. They're planning something bad for the village."

With a thought, Arche shared the details of the quest with them, taking another spoonful as they read the details.

"It's timed," Helwan said, his brow drawing down into a frown. "Though not explicitly."

"Yeah, which means the village needs to be made aware."

"You're going to tell Callias?" Lyssa asked.

"I have to. I don't like him, but not telling him could get people killed and I'm not about to risk that."

Lyssa nodded. "I'll tell Elpida and her group, they should be able to marshal the other guards and keep them ready."

"That's a good idea. I also think we should hit their camp. The quest specifically says to figure out the plan and foil it. We can't do that by staying on the defensive and without knowing what the plan is, we won't be able to adequately prepare for it."

Lyssa nodded slowly.

"There's a lot of beastmar listed on that quest," she pointed out. "And only three of us."

"Two," Arche corrected, looking at Helwan. "I know you're not a fighter. I won't ask you to join us."

Helwan's horse-like ears flattened against his head. "I may not be able to help you fight but I might be able to convince a few here to join you. What about your new friends among the guards? Surely they would want to join?"

"I think it'd be wiser to keep people here that we can trust, they'll make sure the village is protected if anything else attacks while we're gone," Arche said.

"Count me in," a new voice said.

Arche flinched and whirled to find Tess standing behind him. Her armor had been patched and she walked without a trace of the injury that had plagued her the previous day. Arche immediately cut his eyes to Lyssa, worried that a fight might break out over the breakfast table, but Lyssa only nodded in response. Clearly the two had talked things through the previous night. He was equal parts curious and terrified at how that conversation might have gone.

"We would be lucky to have you," Arche said.

"Excellent. I never quite got to show you what I was capable of, having been blindsided and all. I'm still getting used to the ways of the forest. City girl through and through, you know?" Tess smiled.

Arche didn't really know how to respond to that, so he didn't. Instead, he moved over to make space for Tess to sit.

"I don't believe we've been properly introduced. Helwan Panysk, at your service." Helwan rose from the table with surprising grace and executed a formal bow.

Arche and Lyssa met each other's gaze and rolled their eyes as Tess smirked.

"A pleasure I'm sure, master satyr. The name's Tessalyn, but you can call me Tess." She sat down at the table next to Arche and leaned forward onto her elbows. "I hear there's some adventuring to be done."

Arche nodded. "There is. You remember those beastmar we stumbled on? We're going to head back and try to stop whatever it is they're doing."

"Sounds reasonably noble, if a bit light on details. What about Callias? He's a threat to both of us, now."

"That reckoning is coming." Arche's voice came out in more of a growl than he intended. "But not today, not unless he pushes for it. Right now, the safety of the village is my top priority."

"Right." Tess eyed the rest of the group, settling on Lyssa. "I'm guessing you're a Ranger or a Scout, based on your armor and handiness with the bow."

"I'm a Huntress."

Tess's eyebrows arched. "A Huntress? Wow, I haven't met one of those. Heard of them, though, pretty rare. I'm curious to see what you'll be able to do. I'm a Rogue. What about you, Arche?"

Arche looked back and forth between the two women. "What?"

"What's your profession?" Tess continued. "I'm guessing some kind of Fighter, given how you took on that mantikhoras. Must be a rare one."

"I...don't have a profession."

"*What?* What level are you?"

"Erm, fifteen? I just got there."

Tess's face grew guarded as she stood up and walked away from the table. Lyssa gave Arche a curious look, to which he shrugged.

"The mantikhoras I killed was level twenty-seven. I think she thought I was more advanced than I really am. What's a profession?"

Helwan's eyes nearly popped out of his skull. "Mantikhoras? You really slew one?"

"Yeah, I've got some materials from it to prove it. I was hoping I could get a set of armor made from it. But seriously, what's a profession?"

"A profession is a path that you walk, something to define yourself as," Lyssa explained. "When you reach level fifteen, you are given the choice to pursue a profession. Until you have chosen a profession, all experience earned is held in reserve until you achieve it and leveling becomes remarkably more difficult afterward."

"So she's upset because I don't have a profession?"

"No, she's upset because of what you accomplished while being remarkably less than your potential. No doubt, some part of it is pride. She will calm down; she's already coming back."

True enough, Tess was stomping back. She gave Arche a suspicious look as she sat down, this time across from him. Helwan changed sides to accommodate her.

"You really don't have a profession?"

"I really don't."

"What about your combat skills? Do you have insanely high-leveled maneuvers? I don't understand how you could kill something that strong while being so low-leveled."

Arche gave her a blank look and smiled weakly. Tess's face dropped again.

"Don't tell me you don't know any maneuvers."

"I've got combat skills if it makes you feel better. First I've heard of a maneuver, though."

"Titan's Blood!" Tess swore. "What rank are your combat skills?"

Arche took a moment to look through his profile.

"Archery, Spearmanship, and Swordsmanship are all Novice; Daggermanship and Unarmed Combat are still Beginner."

Lyssa blinked.

"Oh."

"What?" Arche asked, turning to look at her.

"Once you hit the Novice rank in a combat skill, you can learn Novice maneuvers. They're like a specialized subcategory of skills that have their own levels and cost Stamina to use. I hadn't realized you'd hit the Novice ranks in so many combat skills."

Arche stared at her for a moment. "You saw me level up after you taught me Archery!"

"I didn't trust you, then, and I had forgotten about it in light of everything else that happened that day."

"Okay, fine, but does this mean that all this time I could have had skills, techniques, whatever they're called, and they would have helped me fight?"

"Maneuvers, and yes."

Arche rubbed his face with both hands.

"Fuck me," he groaned. "I don't believe this."

Tess's face grew hard and she glared at him like he was a rabid animal. Helwan shifted uncomfortably in his seat.

"Before we go anywhere, I would like to learn as many maneuvers as I can." Arche pushed away his bowl, now finished.

Lyssa nodded. "Easy enough. I can teach you archery and swordsmanship. Nothing I can do for the spear."

"All right." Arche slapped the table. "Helwan, spread the news and try to find some trustworthy folks that are willing to help. Lyssa, go talk to Vik and the others and let them know what's going on. I'm going to head to the tanner and see what he can do with the materials I got from the mantikhoras. Tess, do you think Callias is going to be an immediate issue once he learns I'm still alive?"

"He certainly won't be happy about it, but I doubt he'll act publicly. Chances are he'll just cut me off the payroll and leave it at that for the time being. He might try another way of finishing you off, though. I'd watch your back if I were you."

"All right, why don't you go with Helwan and take the measure of any volunteers. I'll talk to Callias directly after I see the tanner and, with any luck, we can meet back here in, say, two hours to train and prepare ourselves. We can head out first thing tomorrow. Deal?"

The others nodded their assent and they went their separate ways. Helwan was kind enough to point Arche toward the small crafting corner that had been set up for the several tradesfolk that lived among the villagers. Most of the villagers were still strangers to him, even if they now knew who he was. He resolved to get to know them better, but between Callias and everything else, he hadn't had the time to really talk to anyone.

As he approached the tannery, Arche found a very large man stroking a taut hide stretched out on a rack with some metal tool that Arche couldn't identify by sight. The man's skin was mottled, in some places appearing a dark brown and in others having a greenish tint, almost like paint had been spilled over him. He did not turn as Arche approached, engrossed by his work, so Arche used the opportunity to Examine him.

Danocles Malachinous		
Level: 9 **Race**: Half-Human/Half-Orc **Age**: ? **Height**: ? **Weight**: ?	**Profession**: ? **Trade**: ? **Traits**: ? **Companions**: ? **Adventuring Party**: ?	
Health: 640 / 640 100%	**Stamina**: 560 / 560 100%	**Mana**: 130 / 130 100%

Arche plastered a big, friendly smile onto his face.

"Hey, you're Danocles, right?"

The half-orc turned, giving Arche a full view of the man's large, flat face and fierce expression.

"Do I know you?" Danocles asked in a surprisingly mellow voice.

"My name's Arche, I hear you're good at all things leather. I have some material I was hoping you could help me refine."

"Arche," the half-orc repeated, scratching his chin with one hand. "Aren't you the one who rushed the beastmar when the village was under attack a few days ago? And the one who decided to try out-drinking the dwarves during the party?"

"My reputation precedes me," Arche said, coughing to hide his embarrassment. "Anyway, I have some unusual materials and I wanted to see if you could make something out of them."

Danocles gestured toward a nearby table, leaving behind the hide on the rack. Arche walked over and began withdrawing materials from the mantikhoras. He started with the claws, laying out all twenty-four claws he had gathered. Next, he produced the two wings, one of which had been badly damaged during the fight. Then, gauging the tanner's reaction, he produced the hide itself, and lastly the venom sac.

Throughout all of it, Danocles didn't react. With a gentle touch, he carefully sifted through each item as it was presented, examining quality and, at some points, sniffing them.

"The harvesting is rather mediocre. I might be able to add some improvement during the refinement process, but it'll be difficult and slow going. The materials themselves are not commonly available, so any armor I make from them would be stylized. The venom sac is valuable. Not much use to you, I'd wager, unless you intend to try poisoning someone. An alchemist or apothecary would likely shell out quite a few drachmae for it. The wings are nice, but not much use for them. With some time and work, I might be able to make a decorative piece for you. Or, perhaps, a glider. What did you want to do with all of this?"

Arche chewed his lip as he thought about it.

"I was hoping to get some armor out of it. A glider sounds pretty cool, too, though I don't know when I'll ever get an opportunity to use it."

Danocles stroked his chin as he took stock of everything on the table.

"Let's talk armor. How do you fight?" the half-orc asked. "Do you want light armor, like you're wearing?"

"Uh," Arche paused. "Well, normally it's up close. I don't tend to have a lot of defense, I rely more on my Agility to keep me from getting hit. Light armor has been great for that, but whenever I do get hit, it *hurts.* Do you have any suggestions?"

"Medium armor. Sacrifice some mobility for padding. It'll do you better in close fights than those elven cured hides you're wearing, but it won't be the same as wearing a full set of metal. Material such as this? I'll need to reinforce it with steel. I have a few designs in mind. It won't be quick, I'll need a few days to get the required materials and fashion it into something usable, your current armor will have to last until then."

"I imagine it won't be cheap, either." Arche grimaced, realizing he had no money to pay with.

Danocles looked down at the materials on the table.

"I'll need the entire hide to fashion the armor. The wings have no use for protection but leave them with me and I'll see what I can do. I can incorporate the claws into the design, which may improve any inherent traits in the final product. The metal will have to be paid for, which means bargaining with the dwarves. They're steep hagglers, no getting around that, but they're the only ones with workable metal right now. The venom sac can be sold to offset costs, but there are no alchemists or apothecaries here. I will make you a deal. Since you brought me the materials, I will only charge for labor and further materials required. If you allow me to trade the sac for you to offset expenses, I will take the cost of the steel and, when the opportunity to sell arises, any leftover drachmae will be split between us evenly."

Arche's eyebrows shot up at the tanner. He hadn't expected to come out of the transaction making money, even if the sac wouldn't be sold until there was a proper buyer. Danocles must have misread him, however, as the half-orc's glower deepened.

"Let no one say Danocles is a cheat," he growled.

"Not at all. I'm just surprised it's worth so much. How much drachmae do you think an alchemist will pay for it?"

The tanner shrugged.

"Depends on how well I haggle. I reckon I can get one to pay a hundred-fifty drachmae for it. Alchemists often deal in expensive reagents."

Arche nodded slowly, gathering that a hundred-fifty was a lot.

"And how much will the metal cost?"

"Again, it depends on the haggling. Steel for the design I have in mind shouldn't be more than forty drachmae. It will also depend on what the dwarves have with them. If they have a higher quality metal, I will try to obtain that instead, though it will be more expensive."

Arche nodded, starting to get an idea of how much this drachmae was worth.

"Okay, and if you had to have requisitioned all these items through normal means and sell the armor, what would be the going price for it?"

"Mantikhoras armor is not an easy find, as I've said. A full set could easily go for three hundred drachmae, and that's if it didn't retain any natural properties."

Arche let out a slow whistle and looked down at the table full of supplies.

"It's a deal. Use what you can, sell what you need to, buy what you must. I'm in."

Danocles gave a smile, revealing a few large fangs reminiscent of a gorilla. Arche grinned right back.

"Come back in four days," the half-orc said. "I should have it ready by then. Would be faster, but this village lacks a suitable workshop."

Arche left the tanner and began making his way to the only permanent structure in the entire village. A score of hired guards and mercenaries were milling about the building. To one side, Arche saw Lyssa talking to Elpida while Gigator and Vik were engaged in their own conversation. As Arche approached the door, he was stopped by two guards he didn't know.

"Hold there, friend. Callias don't like unannounced visitors," one of them said, a human man in a metal breastplate, wielding a spear and shield. "Not ones of your variety, at least. What're you here, for?"

Arche raised his hands. "I don't mean any trouble. I have news regarding the beastmar that Callias needs to hear. It's about the safety of the village."

The guard exchanged a look with his partner, a big brute of a man with dark hair. The big fellow shrugged and nodded.

Persuasion has increased to **Level 5**.

+1% Persuasion Chance (+5%)
+1 Charisma

"All right. Come along."

He led Arche inside. The building was made of wood but Arche had yet to see any downed trees near the village. It made him wonder if the lumber had been carted all the way from Ship's Shape. The majority of the building was one massive room, at the end of which was a desk. There was also an upstairs area that, from what was visible from downstairs, had a few private rooms. A door toward the back of the building suggested at least one room on the lower levels as well. The decorations left no doubt that Callias went to exceedingly great lengths for comfort and lavishness. Tapestries depicting the slaying of mythic beasts and large-scale warfare adorned the walls. Plush furniture was scattered about the room, with men and women of varying races and in varying stages of undress lounging upon them.

Arche gawked.

What he'd taken as a town hall could have just as easily been Callias's personal sex dungeon. Doing his best to look anywhere but at the people, Arche followed the guard through the throng of softly grunting undulation and toward the desk at the far end. Arche had half-expected Callias to be the one on the opposite end, but as they neared, he found a frazzled, mousey-looking human pouring over documents from behind large spectacles, completely at odds with the debauchery going on in the rest of the room.

"Yes?" The mousey man looked up at them with eyes made large by the spectacles. "How can I help you?"

"This one here says he's got important information for Callias regarding the beastmar and the safety of the village," the guard said by way of introduction.

"Really? Please, have a seat. My name is Theodorous Apostolakis."

"Arche. Nice to meet you." Arche sat, not sure what to think of the kindly, middle-aged man surrounded by a den of depravity.

The guard did not sit, but he did not leave either.

"Well met, Arche." Theodorous's voice had a note of recognition in it. "I must apologize for the state in which I have to receive you. Believe you, me, this is not a conducive work environment. Now, please tell me all about this development with the beastmar."

"Shouldn't we wait for Callias?"

Arche glanced around for the surly village leader. He was immediately distracted by a woman dressed in what would charitably be called a transparent sheet being fed grapes by a doting attendant as she stretched backwards over the arm of a sofa. Cheeks flaming, Arche turned back to Theodorous.

Theodorous, for his part, grimaced and glanced toward the door to the back room. "I am afraid Lord Buton is currently...indisposed. I am his steward and as such, I am authorized to allocate proper resources to certain issues."

Arche stared at the man for a few moments, trying to take the measure of him.

"So, he's having you run his village while he's off having a sexcapade."

"I have no desire to spend my time imagining the archon's activities, but you are correct in that I handle most of the day-to-day drudgery. Large-scale changes, I am not authorized to enact, however."

"Large-scale in what way?" Arche asked. "You mean like forming any sort of protective perimeter despite having been attacked *twice?*"

"Precisely." Theodorous did not break eye contact. "Or, for example, authorizing resources be used to develop more permanent dwellings for the villagers."

There was an edge in the man's voice, but his kindly expression did not waver.

"Please, you said there is an emergency?"

"Yes," Arche said. "While in the woods yesterday, I stumbled across four beastmar that were guarding a cave, perhaps two hours' quick walk east of the treeline. I overheard some of their conversation, during which they said their chief has a plan to attack the village. I received a quest to put a stop to whatever it is that the beastmar are planning and I intend to do so. I have already gathered two others who will join me and we are searching for more."

"And you have come here hoping for sanctioning?" Theodorous asked.

"Not in the slightest. I've come here to warn Callias—well, you, now—that there is imminent danger and that you should prepare. If we fail, the beastmar will attack. If we do not try, the beastmar will attack. The village needs to be ready."

Theodorous put down his spectacles and rubbed his eyes.

"Very well. I will organize the guards to be extra cautious. I will also institute a bounty for each beastmar slain until the attack. I can't offer much, and Archon Buton will likely be furious when he finds out, but I can give two obols per beastmar."

"I'm not asking for money, but what's the exchange rate between obols and drachmae?"

"The current exchange is six obols to a drachma," Theodorous explained. "In the city, you'll find there's an additional layer with four drachmae becoming a tetradrachm, but out here we decided that the use for such currency would be minimal at best. Regardless of whether you want the pay, it may incentivize some help. It will at least underscore the gravity of the situation."

"All right. Three beastmar to a drachma," Arche said, nodding along. "How would you like proof of kill? Ears? Thumbs?"

Theodorous smirked. "Nothing so crude will be necessary. A moment."

The man closed his eyes, and about half a minute later Arche received a prompt.

You have received a **Bounty Quest**:

Hunt the Beastmar

A bounty has been placed on the beastmar near the village of Buton. Until the start of the next attack against the village, a bounty of two obols has been placed against each beastmar, with an unspecified monetary bonus on any beastmar leaders.

Objectives	Rewards
- Kill beastmar 0/?	- 2 obols per beastmar slain
- Kill beastmar leaders 0/?	- Bonus per beastmar leader slain

"I'm not complaining," Arche said, "but won't having a bounty like this mean more of your guards will go off and try to hunt the beastmar?"

"Some may," Theodorous admitted. "But the sum is not great and the danger is real. Because of the risk you are incurring to help the village, I did not feel it was right to let you do so without some kind of reward. I only wish there were more that I could do."

Arche stood from the table and Theodorous stood as well.

"You should be aware, Theodorous, that Callias wants me dead. Helping me might get you in trouble with him."

Theodorous gave a polite smile and gestured at the busy desk in front of him. "Even Lord Buton is aware of the value I offer him. Without me, he would be the only one left to do the papyruswork."

Chapter 22

Arche pulled his bow back farther than what felt safe to do. The wood of the bow creaked under the strain and he felt like the thing would snap at any moment. Arche focused on the tremors coursing through his hands and willed them to be still. Breath shuddered out of him like a river of air, the beat of his heart tapped a rhythm to the growing pressure against his fingers. In the negative space between breaths and heartbeats, he let go. The arrow sprang from his bow and sped toward a tree in a blur of movement. The shaft nearly disappeared into the trunk with a crunch of splitting wood.

Penetrating Shot has increased to **Level 3**.

+4% Penetration (+12%)
+4% Damage (+12%)

Arche shook his tired arms. In addition to the basic Stamina cost of thirty that the maneuver required, it also increased the Stamina cost of keeping the string pulled back. The sun was barely visible over the western forest and Lyssa called for a break. For the last six hours she had drilled him relentlessly in two Novice level maneuvers, Penetrating Shot and Power Attack. The maneuvers had been difficult to learn, requiring not only precise mechanical activations but also the mental intent to perform them. He could have pulled back the bow for Penetrating Shot as often as he wished but unless he had the desire to perform the maneuver, all he was likely to do was break his bow.

Arche pulled up the list of maneuvers, a submenu on his skills page, and lamented the fact that learning the maneuvers wasn't enough to progress his main skills to the next level.

Maneuvers		
Archery		
Penetrating Shot	Level 3	+12% Penetration +12% Damage Cost: 30 Stamina
Swordsmanship		
Power Attack	Level 5	+25% Damage Cost: 35 Stamina

"You've progressed well," Lyssa said after he reported his levels. "When you reach the Student ranks, more maneuvers will become available to you, so don't wait to let me know."

Arche nodded. "I will. I also need to find someone who can teach me how to use a spear properly."

"I'm sure there's someone in this village who can use a spear. Though there isn't time to have you trained before we leave."

"I know, I know. I'll add it to the list."

Arche hefted the Tridory and eyed it. He was tired of having to carry it around everywhere. The inability to inventory it proved to be a massive inconvenience compared to everything else in Tartarus. He really had to figure out a fix to carrying it by hand everywhere. Maybe if he found out more about how it worked, he'd be able to inventory it. It was, once again, a problem for future Arche. No matter how much he learned about what it could do, he couldn't shake the feeling he hadn't even scratched the surface of its capabilities.

"We should head to dinner," Lyssa said. "Perhaps Helwan and Tess have found volunteers."

Arche nodded. "Yeah, let's hope they're ready for whatever we're getting into."

They walked into the open dining area and spotted Helwan and Tess at a table, waving them over. Two strangers sat next to them. Arche Examined both as he and Lyssa approached.

Odelia Andromedina		
Level: 16 **Race**: Halfling **Age**: ? **Height**: ? **Weight**: ?		**Profession**: ? **Trade**: ? **Traits**: ? **Companions**: ? **Adventuring Party**: ?
Health: 280 / 280 100%	**Stamina**: 170 / 170 100%	**Mana**: 740 / 740 100%

Abraxios Oskopadous		
Level: 19 **Race**: Tengu **Age**: ? **Height**: ? **Weight**: ?		**Profession**: ? **Trade**: ? **Traits**: ? **Companions**: ? **Adventuring Party**: ?
Health: 320 / 320 100%	**Stamina**: 200 / 200 100%	**Mana**: 800 / 800 100%

Their Mana levels were much higher than he'd expected. Helwan must have found mages willing to join them and Arche's pace quickened at the idea of learning secondhand magic. As he approached, he was able to get a closer look at them. Odelia had dark hair in a braid and a diminutive profile, even sitting down. She was even smaller than the dwarves, whose height topped out around Arche's naval, and seemed to be no taller than his hip. Abraxios, however, was perhaps a hand's width shorter than Arche and, most notably, was completely covered in tropical feathers and dressed in a swirling blue robe with no hood or sleeves. He'd never heard of a tengu before, but it seemed they were an avian race, similar to how Gigator's sauros race was reptilian.

He sat down at one end of the table, Lyssa settling in next to him, as Helwan stood up to make introductions.

"Arche, Lyssa, allow me to introduce Odelia and Abraxios. Odelia is a Life Shaman and Abraxios is a Storm Dancer. Odelia, Abraxios, this is Lyssa, a Huntress, and Arche. He doesn't yet have a profession, but don't let that fool you. I've seen him carve his way through beastmar without breaking a sweat."

Both Odelia and Abraxios paused momentarily when they saw Arche, their gazes lingering on his face but not quite meeting his eyes. Both looked away after a moment, as if trying to hide their momentary lapse in propriety. Arche tried not to grind his teeth. He was getting really tired of how people reacted to his scars.

Abraxios moved to clasp Arche's forearm, giving Arche a view of a small hand that was nestled among the multicolored plumage. The tengu looked like he would be more at home in a jungle rather than a forest or valley, but Arche did not feel it was his place to ask about it.

"A pleasure. We have heard some of Helwan's songs these last few days," Abraxios spoke in a voice that croaked and chirped oddly, as though their language was not quite suited to his larynx. "We have also been told about some of your quest, though I, for one, would like to hear it from you directly."

"Nice to meet you both!" Odelia said cheerfully.

Her voice was high and, despite a face darkened and beginning to wrinkle from years under the sun, Arche had a hard time rationalizing that he wasn't in the presence of a child.

"The tales Helwan has been spinning have been turning my head, I must admit. Did you really fight a revenant in a lost dwarven ruin?"

Arche blinked in surprise. "'Fight' is a generous word. 'Survived' would be more accurate. As far as the quest details go, sure. Pass some of that fish and I'll tell you anything you want to know."

As they dug into the dinner, Arche gave them the rundown of traveling through the forest and stumbling upon the beastmar camp. Tess helped fill in any details he had missed. They decided not to share the fact that Tess had kidnapped Arche and brought him to the woods with the intention to kill him, instead saying that they had been in the woods for 'reasons' and refused to elaborate further. Arche finished off with his meeting with Theodorous, the sanctioned quest he'd received, and the bounty that now existed for beastmar. He shared both quests with the newcomers.

They listened with rapt attention, asking only a few questions for clarification as the story unfolded before them. When it was finished, everyone's plates were empty and cold. They sat in the light of the bonfire, as the newcomers digested both the meal and the information.

"That is quite the tale," Abraxios said, wiping his beak against a folded cloth. "I am not quite thrilled by learning our quest takes us underground but I have some magic that will still be available."

"I've never heard of a Storm Dancer. What do you do?"

"I am not surprised." Abraxios let out a rapid trill. "It is a specialized profession of anemancy, or air magic, as you might know it better by. My people have high affinity for anemancy. Storm Dancer means I have access to lightning and wind, as well as certain speed bonuses."

"So you're a Mage? Lightning and wind, eh?"

Abraxios shrugged and nodded. "Similar, yes. Mage is the basic spellcasting profession. The farther from the center you travel during the Professing, the more rare and specialized Professions you will find. A Mage has affinity for at least one of the four basic magic schools, but often have at least two: hydromancy, anemancy, gaiamancy, and pyromancy. They draw their power through rituals and incantations, often requiring years of study, but that effort is rewarded by powerful magic. An anemancer, however, is a specialist in air magic. They forego the other schools of magic, but they learn air magic more quickly and it is often stronger. During the Professing, if you go far enough you can unlock specialized professions, as I have done. They tend to open doors that are not offered by the more general class of Mage."

"So during this Professing, the rarer and more powerful professions are farther away from the center, and the direction I go will help dictate which professions are available?" Arche asked.

"Oh, yes," Odelia piped up. "I always wanted to be a healer. When I went for my profession, I could have chosen Healer and dedicated myself to the study of science and medicine, but I felt something inside me call for nature and the wilds, so I pushed on and found the Shaman profession, which requires great affinity for gaiamancy. Through it, I was able to obtain a specialized profession which focuses on using aspects of nature to heal, so now I'm a Life Shaman, a mix of biomancy and gaiamancy, which has its own unique properties."

"Fascinating. So you just find a profession that speaks to you and," Arche snapped his fingers, "just like that, you're now a professed whatever?"

"Not quite," Lyssa said, jumping into the conversation. "If you have the potential for a profession, but lack the requirements, it gives you a Profession Quest, where you must either achieve a specific act or complete whatever prerequisites the profession requires, after which you become that Profession. The rarer the profession, the harder it is to meet the requirements, which is why most people settle for professions close to the Origin."

"The Origin?"

"The starting point of the Professing," Tess said, picking up where Lyssa left off. "Usually there are three Professions that surround the Origin, at least for those that pick combat-based professions. Warrior, Rogue, and Mage. After that, it changes from person to person, but not much. Some Professions will be locked to you based upon your natural affinities or, in some cases, racial Professions may be available or unavailable."

Arche lowered his head into his hands, causing the others to chuckle. Abraxios slapped him good naturedly on the back.

"This much is the same for everyone," the tengu said. "There are many options, but you will know the right path when you see it. It will call to you as much as you call to it."

"Right," Arche said. "Well, I'm level fifteen, so I'll have to pick one before I can level up."

"It's not a decision to make lightly," Odelia said. "It's your quest, if you think you're ready to take it on, all I can offer is that I can try to keep you alive."

"I'll drink to that."

The others fell into quiet conversation, mostly involving the beastmar as neither Abraxios nor Odelia were involved in the previous attack on the village. Arche listened for a while before excusing himself. The night was still young, but he retired to his tent anyway. The next day would be a long one, and he wanted to ensure he was well-rested for whatever horrors would be coming their way. A profession was important but it could wait.

Chapter 23

Arche awoke before dawn. A restless energy had settled about him. No dreams, good or bad, had interrupted his sleep, so he took that to mean the Oneiroi was continuing to impart their 'gifts.' Being awake early meant he could triple-check his equipment to see if he had everything he needed. More specifically, he could get rid of things he didn't need, like the horde of treasure he'd been carrying since the dwarven ruins.

"Too bad this frontier town doesn't have a bank," he muttered.

With the absence of an easy way to store his valuables, the best thing to do would be to head to the village market when it opened and see if anyone was interested in buying ancient dwarven treasure. He hefted the Tridory and exited the tent. A dull glow over the horizon heralded the coming dawn and his companions would be up and about soon.

"Ready?"

Arche turned in surprise and found Lyssa standing next to him. The hood of her cloak was up and the rest was pulled tight around her against the morning chill. *Most* of his companions would be up soon, he corrected himself. He had forgotten that Lyssa didn't need as much sleep as the others, thanks to her elven nature.

"Yeah, thought I'd resupply before we head out. I'm running low on rations and other gear. You?"

"Just waiting for everyone else to wake. The sunrises are beautiful in this valley. Do you have coin?"

Arche shook his head. "No, some treasures I'm looking to sell, but no coins yet."

"Then we'll use mine. I sold a few baubles for drachmae already." Lyssa's face drew into a frown. "I must say, I don't like this system of trade."

"What's wrong with it?"

She gestured aimlessly to one side.

"It's selfish. What use is money, here? Favors and reciprocation would be better. Greed runs rampant with accumulation of wealth, but a community working toward a common goal brings itself together to survive."

"Is that how the elves do it?"

Lyssa scratched at one of her clipped ears absentmindedly. Arche cursed inwardly.

"It is."

"Might be all well and good for an isolationist group, but I think the intent here was to establish some sort of trade back with Ship's Shape. To do that, they'll need coin. A favor isn't worth much if the person you owe it to is too far away to do anything for."

Lyssa waved her hand dismissively, ceding the point.

"How much treasure did you sell?"

"A quarter of it, perhaps. I thought the treasure from the dwarven ruins would be worth most to a dwarf, and we can't exactly eat gold."

"Not with that attitude." Arche grinned. "I'll bet there's some 'Dragonkin' trait or something out there that's got people eating precious metals and gems."

"I've never heard of a dragon consuming their horde before, but not all dragons gather treasure in a conventional sense. Perhaps there's some dragon out there who has a horde of confectionaries."

Arche held the Tridory out toward the sunrise and closed one eye, pretending to gauge the distance.

"Then after our quest we should sally forth without delay! There are dragons to slay and sweets to steal."

Lyssa snorted and fell in-step with him as they walked toward the market. Since there were no other buildings aside from Callias's den of depravity, the merchants of the village had instead gathered together to display their wares under canvas roofs strung up to keep the sun off. Despite the early hour, many were awake and setting up for the day. Unlike the crafters, who were more fixated on their work than selling their services, the merchants were a cheery bunch who smiled and waved them over, hoping to sell some of their stock.

A dark-skinned human displayed various sized bags, lanterns, and a variety of camping equipment. Lyssa engaged her in good-natured haggling and, after a few minutes, coins were exchanged, leaving Arche and Lyssa with fifty meters of sturdy rope for each member of their crew, enough honeyed nuts and jerky to last two weeks, and four new waterskins. Lyssa opted for a few small bowls of vegetable stew instead of jerky.

Arche paid a dwarf a drachma and two obols for a pickaxe, managing to haggle down from the three drachmae the dwarf had initially demanded. Arche wanted it in the event that they found any precious ores inside the cave and had the time to unearth it, or in the event that they would have to break rocks and his shovel wouldn't be enough to do the job.

You have learned a **Skill**.

Bartering — Level 1

By crossing words with a dwarf over an old, favored pickaxe, you have stumbled upon one of the oldest trades in existence. Though you're certain you talked the dwarf down to a good price, you'll never really know until you learn how much things are actually worth.

Each level in this skill improves your ability to haggle.
Every 5 levels in this skill improves your **Wisdom** and **Charisma** by 1.

+1% Chance of Improved Prices when Buying or Selling (+1%)
+2% Estimation of Price (+2%)

Arche blinked in surprise.

Most of his other skill descriptions had gotten straight to the point and left off. They didn't recap how he'd earned the skill and they definitely didn't insult him while doing it. Arche dismissed the notification with more than a touch of annoyance.

Lyssa left him to wander as she inspected the wares of an elven bowyer. Arche looked around the growing throng of villagers, trying to decide if there was anything worth the fistful of drachmae she'd given him. As he turned, he saw a couple of women looking at him and whispering.

Arche tensed, one hand subconsciously resting against the hilt of his sword. More assassins sent by Callias, perhaps? Upon second look, however, the girls were not in any fashion that befitted combat, wearing sleeveless dresses that were belted high over the stomach, shawls wrapped around their arms. Upon seeing that he had noticed them, the girls blushed and turned away, hiding smiles behind their hands.

It seemed their attention was to be taken quite literally at face-value. He turned away, wishing he had a hood he could pull down over his face. The cloak Lyssa had given him had not aged well in the hard days through the Sylv. Between storms, briars, and sleeping on the forest floor, it had been torn and stained a dozen times over. It could be patched, but Arche didn't have the skill to do that and it would have been quite the effort.

As he turned, he caught sight of a tailor setting up a few wooden mannequins to display his wares for the day. He was a small fellow, about half Arche's height, but finely dressed. One of the items on display was a forest green cloak with, most importantly, a hood. Arche approached the tailor immediately.

"How much for the cloak?"

The tailor peeked his head around one of the mannequins. At first, Arche had taken the vendor for a halfling, but there were clear differences. This man was of a similar size but had large ears and, contrary to the halflings' youthful appearances, intense wrinkles that indicated extremely advanced age. His hair had thinned and his waist had thickened, but he had a kind, grandfatherly face. Curious, Arche Examined him.

Baldwic Tsaoussis	
Level: 17 Race: Gnome Age: ? Height: ? Weight: ?	Profession: ? Trade: ? Traits: ? Companions: ? Adventuring Party: ?

Health: 240 / 240 100%	Stamina: 130 / 130 100%	Mana: 190 / 190 100%

"Cloak?" The gnome moved around the mannequin to better regard him. "Oh, my! Yes, ahem, indeed. The cloak is a Mundane, I'm afraid, though excellent craftsmanship. It's currently priced at two drachmae and five obols."

Arche opened his mouth to agree, but something in the gnome's wording made him pause.

"What's a Mundane?"

"Why, a non-magical item, my boy! If you're looking for magic cloaks, I have some in my tent here. Afraid I won't have a wood-and-stone shop for quite some time, given that all building materials have been confiscated."

The gnome led Arche inside a large tent behind the mannequins, filled with chests and displays with a small, cordoned area near the back that was clearly a sleeping quarters. The gnome opened up one of the chests and began removing different cloaks from inside.

"Hang on," Arche said. "Did you say Callias confiscated all the lumber and stone in the village?"

"He did indeed. That's right, I remember you now. You and those other two came after, during the second attack by the beastmar, didn't you? Well, it's no surprise that you wouldn't know. We spent the first week here clearing out a few trees and leveling the ground a bit between these hills. Got a fair bit of materials from it as well, but once Lord Buton built his town hall, he confiscated the rest while he 'decided what next would be best for the village.' I wouldn't be surprised if he was trying to figure out how to sell it back to Ship's Shape, not that they would need the shipping from a little village like this."

Arche blinked several times, digesting the information as the gnome continued pulling out cloak after cloak of all colors.

"There we go," the gnome said. "Oh, dearie me, I've forgotten my manners. My name is Baldwic. My friends call me Baldy; my better friends call me Wic. I've learned to respond to both over the years."

Baldwic rubbed his head as if to lament the loss of his hair.

"Arche. Pleased to meet you, Mister Wic." Arche clasped the gnome's forearm, having to stoop slightly to do so.

Wic smiled.

"You catch on quick. I like you. Now, let's see about a cloak. A good cloak can make all the difference. It will either be people's first impression, or what makes it such that they won't see you at all. Which do you prefer?"

"The latter."

"Ah, the noble art of stealth, or is that the stealthy art of pickpocketing nobles? I always get those mixed up. Anyway, I have a few cloaks that should do nicely."

Wic gathered up a good portion of the cloaks and dropped them into a chest, where they promptly disappeared into the inventory space.

"Now, given our surroundings I would recommend one of the green or brown cloaks, though if you are planning on going incognito in the city, I would suggest one of the dark gray cloaks."

"You put back some of the black cloaks, what was wrong with them?"

"While very stylish, black is not actually a good color for sneaking. Few things in nature are so dark, and in the light of the moons it is very apparent when something is actually black versus something that is merely dark."

"Oh." Arche paused to think. "I'd like something that could improve my stealth in the forest, but I imagine I'll be making my way to Ship's Shape at some point. Do you have something that improves stealth all around?"

Wic stroked his chin as he thought about the question.

"Magic items are often a balance between utility and specialization, as I'm sure you're aware..." the gnome trailed off, gauging Arche's puzzled reaction, "...however I'm an old gnome and I like to talk, so I'll tell you anyway. The more specialized a magic item is—that is, the more specific the criteria are that it affects—the stronger the enchantments on it typically are. In plainer speech, a cloak that only improves stealth in a forested environment will be stronger than an all-around stealth cloak of the same caliber. Now, do you think this makes them more expensive than an all-around stealth enhancement, or less?"

Arche thought about it for a moment.

"More?" he answered. "Because it's more niche of an item and the improvement is larger?"

"Wrong!" Wic smiled. "A wonderful thought, and if we were talking mundane machinations, you might be correct, but there is an ingredient I failed to mention. The materials to make all-around enhancements are often much more difficult to find or create than those with targeted activations. Take this environment for example. You may think that a forest-based stealth enchantment would be all you need for this area. That is, of course, until you step onto the mountain yonder and find that every beast and monster is suddenly aware of you. Or if you head underground and find that your green cloak that lets you blend into foliage is like a beacon to the grayscale tones that the cave creatures are used to."

"So the more utility a magic item has, the more expensive it is when compared to a specialization?" Arche asked, frowning.

"Precisely! And, sadly, the weaker it is when compared to a specialization. A cloak that gives a thirty percent bonus in forests might be worth as much as twenty percent all-around. A significant difference, I'm sure you'll agree."

"And what kind of price range would those cloaks fall into?" Arche asked, very aware that he only had a handful of minted drachmae on him.

"A few hundred drachmae," the gnome admitted. "But I have some more affordable items as well."

Gears began to turn in Arche's mind. "What's the best all-around stealth cloak you have, and it's cost?"

Wic thought for a moment, then turned and produced a beautiful emerald cloak. Despite the green color, as Wic shook it out, Arche's eyes lost track of it for a few moments.

"This is my pride. Acquired her three years ago and haven't parted with her since. I call her the Emerald Ghost. Take a look at her stats for yourself."

Wic passed the cloak to Arche, who received a prompt as he took it.

Emerald Ghost	**Rarity**: Epic **Quality**: Masterwork **Durability**: 100 /100 **Weight**: 3 kilograms **Traits**: +20% Passive Hide, +40% Active Hide, Repairing, +6 Charisma, +4 Comeliness

Arche gaped in unabashed shock. There was so much to take in that he didn't know where to start. The 'Repairing' tag was as good a place as any.

Repairing
An item with this trait will regain durability and clean itself over time. The regeneration rate of durability is variable, based upon the total durability and quality of the item. An item reduced to 0 durability is destroyed and beyond the help of this trait.

A cloak that would repair itself *and* keep itself clean? Arche's fingers twitched; he wanted it. No more trying to ignore the smells that pushed up against his face while he was trying to sleep. No more fiddling with frayed ends, watching his cloak slowly unravel around him. Arche had to work hard to close his mouth. Not only was the active bonus equivalent to twenty levels in Stealth, but it gave an improvement to his attributes equal to two entire levels. Arche's hands shook as he handed the cloak back.

"How much?"

Wic took the fabric back and looked at Arche sadly.

"More than I'm afraid you could afford. A cloak such as this? I would have to set its price firmly at four-hundred drachmae. Were we in the city, I could get several times that, but here? That is the lowest I could go, and it's very nearly at-cost. For anyone else here, I'd have set the price at eight-hundred, but I saw what you did in the battle. More lives would no doubt have been lost, perhaps my own among them, had you and your friends not been there."

Arche tried hard not to let his disappointment show. Lyssa had left him with about twenty drachmae, which was, as he was beginning to understand, rather substantial, but still nowhere near the price point of a quality magical item. However, Lyssa still had quite a bit of coin left over even after their morning shopping, and all that was gained from selling only a few relics from the dwarven ruins. He met the gnome's firm gaze and gave a smile laden with avarice.

"Well, my friend, I just so happen to have a cache of valuable items. I think one or two might be worth that price tag. Care to trade?"

Arche scanned through his inventory, skipping over the metalwork and going straight to the collection of jewels and precious gems that he had acquired. What he was really hoping for was a nice one-to-one trade, but he'd be willing to part with a few gems for the cloak. Finally, he found what he was looking for. A beautifully carved emerald the size of his thumb. Wic picked it up and looked it over, then set it back down. He looked at Arche with wild eyes.

"Where did you come across such an item?" the gnome asked in a strained voice.

"A little something I picked up in my travels," Arche said, smiling coyly.

Wic took several deep breaths, his eyes darting back and forth as he did mental calculations. Finally he nodded, more to himself than to Arche, and pushed the cloak.

"We have a deal. The Emerald Ghost is yours. If you *ever* need your clothing tailored, please know that I am at your disposal."

Arche took the cloak in hand and nodded, smiling. "I do imagine I'll need more clothing if I ever make it to the city. As it is, most of the clothing I have gets torn or bloodied fairly frequently, so you'll probably see a lot of me in the days to come."

Bartering has increased to **Level 8**

+1% Chance of Improved Prices when Buying or Selling (+8%)
+2% Estimation of Price (+16%)
+1 Wisdom
+1 Charisma

Arche pulled the cloak over his armor and lifted the hood, leaving the gnome to wonder at the emerald as he stepped out of the tent and breathed the fresh morning air.

"I would bet the rest of the hoard that I seriously underestimated how much that emerald was worth," he muttered.

There was nothing more to do about it, now. He got what he wanted and hoped he would never find out how much it had really cost him.

No one turned to regard him, or even indicated that they had overheard him, though the market was fairly busy. After his interaction with Wic, Arche decided he would wait until he had someone else present before he went to the dwarves to try to pawn off his treasure. He made his way back to his tent, marveling at how people barely paid him a second glance.

Once inside, Arche pulled out his shovel and started digging. Armed with the proper tool for the job, it took barely less than a minute to make a sizable hole beneath his bedroll. Once deep enough, he opened up his inventory and started piling heaps of treasure down into the hole. When all his treasure was deposited, he filled it, stamped down the loose dirt, and placed his bedroll over it. Arche didn't particularly expect anyone to go through his things but given that Callias had already tried to kill him once, it was best to take precautions. With the job done, he left the tent and went off to find his friends.

They were waiting near the edge of town. As Arche walked toward them, he found that melding into the crowd was easier than ever. Arche activated his Stealth skill as he approached his group and the difference grew even further. No one noticed him at all. Even when he came up to the others, all waiting for him, none of them looked directly at him. None, that is, except for Lyssa.

"I see you've bought a toy."

Abraxios, who stood between Lyssa and Arche, cocked his head. "Eh, what? I have bought nothing."

Arche smiled and lowered the hood, standing right behind the tengu. "Yeah, it was worth every obol."

The others' reactions were as immediate as they were drastic. Abraxios's wings extended as he nearly took off in surprise, Odelia fell backward with her quarterstaff held out in front of her in a warding gesture, and Tess had a throwing knife in one hand, already cocked back and ready to throw. Only Lyssa had not reacted, a smile quirking the corners of her lips as she shook her head at the others.

"Malaka," Tess spat, sheathing her knives. "Why would you go and do a fool thing like that?"

"Because it was funny?" Arche smiled at her.

She scoffed and turned away.

"I hope you save your next joke for the beastmar," Odelia said, picking herself off the ground and dusting off her robe. "My hands are trembling."

"A cloak of incredible quality," Lyssa said, nodding her approval. "This will go a long way toward your stealth training, Greenstick."

"I apparently have a long way to go if you could still see me. Nobody else did."

"I am trained to spot things that are hard to see. Especially things that move. It is part of being a Huntress."

"And an elf," Tess muttered. "Warn a girl next time, would you? If for no other reason than that we don't accidentally kill the party leader."

"Wait"—Arche held up a hand to pause the conversation—"I'm party leader?"

"Well, yes," Abraxios said. "It's your quest, after all. You discovered it; you should take the lead."

"I...all right. Are we ready to get this show on the road?"

The others stared at him.

"Are we ready to go?"

A chorus of agreement filtered back to him and he sent out party invitations to all of them, watching as their icons filled a corner of his vision. He couldn't see their vitals, but he would be able to sense if they were injured or know if they died. It felt a poor facsimile of the Companionship he shared with Lyssa, but there was nothing to do about it but bear it.

Besides, there were beastmar to kill.

Chapter 24

Abraxios, they soon learned, could move faster than any of them if he wanted to. His light-boned avian physiology and mastery over wind meant that his flight speed was unmatchable by anything the rest of them could replicate on the ground. The tengu had decided to loosen his nerves after Arche's surprise entrance by taking to the skies and scouting for beastmar. Arche could not help but feel a soft pang of jealousy as the tengu soared almost effortlessly, manipulating the currents of air around his feathers. It was a kind of freedom Arche would never know.

He hefted the Tridory and set off, leading the way. None of the others asked him why he carried the spear instead of inventorying the heavy weapon for ease of travel and he was grateful for it. As it was, it made a fairly decent walking stick as they pressed on toward the forest, though the sharp sauroter dug into the ground and left little pyramidal holes.

The walk along the valley was peaceful. Odelia engaged Lyssa in quiet conversation, staged far enough back that Arche couldn't hear what they were saying. Instead, his attention was captured by Tess, who had quickened her pace to walk next to him.

"Callias is more furious than ever," she said quietly. "That bounty you finagled and the details of your quest finally reached him. I wouldn't be surprised if he tries to kill you the moment you get back. Wouldn't be surprised if he tries before then, honestly."

"We'll deal with it as it comes. Has he threatened you?"

"Not directly. I've been staying near others. No one I trust, mind you, but it's enough that I wasn't isolated. Kept roving blades away, but they might see this expedition as the perfect opportunity to rid themselves of us. I barely slept last night, don't know how you managed."

Arch's expression darkened. It was bad enough they were walking into overwhelming odds, now they had to worry about Callias sabotaging them as well? Typical.

"Do you think he'd actually send mercenaries after us while we're fighting the beastmar?"

"I wouldn't discount it. He hates you. You make him look bad. Publicly."

"He looked terrible long before I arrived. I'm just the only one willing to call him out on it, apparently."

"Seems he's taken that personally. He's hardly used to being challenged."

"With any luck, he won't have the time to get used to it."

With the mood sufficiently dampened, they reached the tree line that marked the Sylv. Abraxios landed among them, interrupting any further private conversations.

"No monsters that I could see in the valley, though the trees block my vision of the forest."

"All right." Arche turned to get everyone's attention. "I know this might seem like too little, too late, but what we're going to do is exceedingly dangerous and there's no guarantee that we'll come back from it. If anyone wants to turn back now, I won't hold it against you."

The quartet of faces looking back at him were mildly taken aback, making him wonder if he had somehow put his foot in his mouth.

"Where you go, I follow," Lyssa said, echoing his own words from when they had left Dawnwood.

"Yeah, you're not getting rid of us that easily. You just want the bounty for yourself!" Tess jabbed his chest with an accusatory finger. She was smiling, likely for the benefit of the others, but it didn't mask the worried glint in her eyes.

Abraxios and Odelia turned to each other and shrugged.

"We knew what we came for," the tengu said. "Let's hunt some monsters."

"For the village!" the halfling woman cheered, raising her staff into the air.

Arche looked around at the members of his adventuring party and couldn't help but smile. Their enthusiasm was infectious.

"When I saw them last time, there were four of them. We'll have to be quiet on the approach or they'll hear us when we get close."

"Wait a moment," Odelia said.

The small woman chanted something under her breath, then jabbed her staff into the ground. A green light flashed and settled onto the five of them. Arche saw a green light surrounding his vitals even as he watched the glow settle onto his skin, feeling coarse and hard. The icon coalesced into a symbol of a tree. Focusing on it, he was able to pull up the spell's description.

Barkskin — Level 8

+5.2% Physical Resistance
+10.4% Magical Resistance
+10.4% Hide Chance in Forests

Barkskin — Level 8: 01:37:20

Odelia's eyes fluttered a moment, then she smiled at them.

"That took a fair bit out of me, casting that on five people. No one get hurt for the next ten minutes, all right?"

They set off into the woods, moving quickly and quietly. Arche led the way, retracing his steps. He had a feeling of where they needed to go, as though his feet were walking an invisible path and knew whenever his brain took them slightly off course.

Wilderness Survival has increased to **Level 12**.

+2% Insulation (+24%)
+2% Durability of Constructed Shelters (+24%)
+1% Vitals Regeneration in Camp (+12%)

Arche chewed his lip. The skill didn't mention anything about retracing steps. It seemed there were additional bonuses that weren't apparent in his skill descriptions. He'd have to look into that later, Lyssa probably knew something about it.

For now, there were beastmar to kill.

They'd made good time, much faster than he had guessed. His Barkskin buff still had around forty minutes left before it would need to be reapplied. It would be best to have Odelia recast it before entering the cave proper, but it would be enough to handle whatever perimeter guard the beastmar had set up. Arche held up a hand, signaling the others to stop and, for once, they seemed to understand what he meant. Arche crept forward as quietly as he could and glanced over the rise.

Three beastmar guarded the cave, each looking incredibly bored. One, a humanoid, leaned against the hill and picked at its nails, a rather large endeavor considering it had no less than seven hands. The other two had animalistic bodies, one resembling a cow and the other a lion, and were curled on the ground as they kept a lazy eye on the forest around them. Arche retreated from the rise and conferred with the others, keeping his voice to a whisper.

"Three. Two on the ground, but they're awake. Third is by the cave. If we hit them hard, we might be able to get them before they sound the alarm."

Arche drew his bow and nocked an arrow to it. He turned to the two mages.

"Does all your magic come with glowing light?"

They nodded.

"All right, you two hold off for now, then. I don't want to give away our location before we have to, but if you see a place you can step in, do so." Arche turned toward Lyssa and Tess. "Lyssa, you focus the one with the arms, you'll know the one. Tess, take the lion. I'll get the cow. We'll go on my signal since you both probably have faster reactions than me."

They both nodded and Tess faded away into the forest, completely disappearing from Arche's vision due to what he could only assume was her Stealth skill. Lyssa knocked an arrow to her bow and nodded, getting into position on the rise. Arche followed her up, focusing in on the bovine beastmar. Arche counted to fifteen to give Tess time to get into position, then drew back his arrow and focused on his Penetrating Shot maneuver. The bow bent beneath his grip and the wood creaked. The lion beastmar perked up, head swiveling as it scanned the treeline. Arche released the string and his arrow sprang forward, immediately followed by Lyssa's.

The cow beastmar's throat exploded, sending up a spray of black blood. The beastmar opened its mouth to bray a warning, but only low, wheezing breath came out. It shuddered, limbs unsteady as it tried to rise and fight, but the blood spurted from its wound, painting the ground around it. Thanks to the maneuver, his arrow had punched straight through its neck and stuck into the ground behind it, still quivering.

Lyssa's arrow was even more impressive. It spun through the air, picking up speed as it went. It took the many-armed beastmar in the nose. Black blood splattered across the hill and the forest floor as the spinning arrow stuck in the beastmar's face and kept spinning. Arche couldn't tear his eyes away. He felt a tremor run through his stomach, a slight quiver in his throat. The beastmar died before it had a chance to scream. Nothing was left of its face, just a bloody mass of pulp.

The world swayed and Arche stumbled, his vision swimming. Lyssa's hand on his shoulder steadied him before he fell, the touch breaking whatever trance he'd been under. He looked away from the beastmar, already knowing that it would be haunting his dreams for a long time to come.

The final beastmar scrambled to its feet, readying itself to let out a roar. Just as it began, a knife sailed through the air and slit the powerful looking beastmar's vocal cords. It recoiled in pain and confusion as the roar became a low, breathy gurgle. Two more knives flew from the underbrush and thunked into the lion beastmar, one where its heart ought to be, and another higher up on its torso, where it began to look more human. The beastmar took a few unsteady steps, then fell to the ground. The clearing before the cave had been turned into a sticky mess of black blood.

Arche inventoried his bow and hefted the Tridory, running down the rise to post up next to the cave mouth, in case any beastmar ran out of it. They had been fairly quiet, but he had no way of knowing how many, if any, beastmar were inside. Tess joined him on the other side. Lyssa covered both of them with her bow from the ridgeline, Odelia and Abraxios standing near her in case they were needed. When nothing happened for two full minutes, Arche waved them down.

They gathered outside the cave entrance. Arche had Odelia recast Barkskin on them, resetting their timer back to an hour and forty minutes. The friendly halfling blinked a few times when the casting was done, swaying on her feet. Abraxios steadied her with a hand and she gave him a tired smile. Arche took the moment to quickly go over the notifications that had appeared during the short battle.

> **Archery** has increased to **Level 13**.
>
> +2% Damage with Ranged Weapons (+26%)
> +2% Accuracy with Ranged Weapons (+26%)
> +1% Range with Ranged Weapons (+13%)

> **Penetrating Shot** has increased to **Level 4**.
>
> +4% Penetration (+16%)
> +4% Damage (+16%)

> **Leadership** has increased to **Level 5**.
>
> +1% Persuasion Chance (+5%)
> +1% Reputation Gain (+5%)
> -0.5% Reputation Loss (-2.5%)
> +1 Wisdom
> +1 Charisma

Arche bit back the grin at seeing his Leadership skill hit level five. So many of his skills could improve his attributes, if only he had the time to dedicate to their training. He would have to set some time aside soon. The more he could train, the more effectively he could assign his precious level attribute points.

> You have slain a **Level 11 Beastmar**.
> You gain 220 experience.
>
> Lyssanderyli has slain a **Level 11 Beastmar**.
> You gain 110 experience.
>
> Your party has slain a **Level 11 Beastmar**.
> You gain 55 experience.

<table>
<tr><td colspan="2" align="center">Experience is held until a Profession is chosen.

Choose a Profession?</td></tr>
<tr><td align="center">Yes</td><td align="center">No</td></tr>
</table>

Arche dismissed the prompt and closed his notifications window.

"I'm ready," Odelia whispered, bringing him back to the present.

"Wait." Abraxios looked at the rest of them, his head cocked slightly. "I just realized, none of you can see in the dark, can you?"

"I can," Lyssa said as the others shook their heads.

Abraxios nodded. "A moment."

He shook his staff and enunciated a strange word of power. A dark blue light seeped from the staff and settled over Arche, Tess, and Odelia. Arche struggled not to recoil as the light flew into his eyes. He shut them tight, feeling like someone was blowing intently on his face, but the magic paid no mind to his eyelids. When he opened them, everything was in startlingly clear detail for as far as he could see. He saw an icon of an owl next to the tree that signaled Barkskin and focused on it, pulling up details on it.

<table>
<tr><td align="center">Owl Vision — Level 19

Perception +9
Low-Light Vision: 35.7 meters</td></tr>
<tr><td align="center">Owl Vision — Level 19: 35:39</td></tr>
</table>

"That should help in there," the tengu chirped.

Arche didn't notice a change, at first, then Tess turned to look at him. Her eyes had turned bright yellow, with massive black pupils the size of a marble. Their mouths dropped in unison and he could only assume that his eyes had changed as well. He shut his mouth and swallowed, forcing himself to turn back toward the cave.

"Clock's ticking. Let's go."

Arche hefted the Tridory and entered the hillside, the rest of the party at his back. Five paces inside, Arche realized the area was much larger than he had previously expected. He'd feared that the inside would be a horde of sleeping beastmar that, upon their entrance, would wake up and maul them. This, thankfully, was not the case. Instead, what awaited him was a perilous bridge, some thirty strides across, stretched over a chasm that extended downward into darkness, past his ability to see. The far side of the bridge ended some ten strides below them and led into a tunnel, preventing any further scouting from where they stood.

"What the fuck?" Arche breathed.

The massive interior gaped back at them and he winced as his voice echoed off the walls.

> You have found a **Dungeon**.
>
> *The Vivitorium of Hekáte*
>
> **WARNING!**
> Your **Dungeoneering Level** is too low to view **Dungeon Information**.

Arche read the message twice, then looked at the others. They stared back at him, clearly wondering why he had stopped. Only Lyssa was also reading a notification, her eyes unfocused for a few moments. She locked eyes with him and nodded, adjusting her grip on her bow. He nodded back, turned to the bridge, and took the first step forward.

Abraxios laid a hand on his shoulder, stopping Arche, and gestured at himself, then down the chasm. The moments stretched out between them, one after the other. Arche squinted at the tengu, blinked, then nodded.

Abraxios took off, winging down into the darkness and was quickly out of sight, his wings made no noise, even in the still air. It took a full minute before they saw the tengu flying back up toward them. The tengu landed on the far side of the bridge and signaled for them to be quiet before waving them over. Arche made his way first, stepping carefully in the center of the bridge.

The whole structure was in a state of disrepair and there were several holes that threatened to twist an ankle or, in a worst-case scenario, could allow someone to slip through completely and fall into the darkness below. There was no guard rail to the bridge, only a flat expanse of stone bricks wide enough to accommodate two people standing abroad, though that would risk one falling.

Arche's first step was tentative. He didn't trust the bridge one bit. At any moment, the stone would give way beneath him and he would be dropped into nothing. He would fall into the blackness and be swallowed up by it, likely to die a painful death at the bottom.

But the bridge did not give way.

The stone held beneath his feet, so he took another step, and another. His heart pounded in his ears all the while. He tried to take deep breaths, but they ran ragged through his chest, pushing in and out far too quickly. All he could hear was the pounding of blood in his ears. To make matters worse, the incline of the bridge made him look down the entire way.

A hand touched his shoulder and he nearly cried out, stopping himself at the last moment. He turned to find Tess looking at him with concern. She nodded encouragingly at him, but it was no help to him. Her nodding wasn't going to save him if he fell. Arche gritted his teeth and walked a little faster.

He had made it about halfway across without issue when a loose stone caught his foot and he tripped. Unable to help himself he let out a startled cry as he fell, his heart about to burst from his chest. The stone pressed against him, holding him up. Tess grabbed his legs to prevent him from rolling or tumbling off the bridge, but his panic had dislodged some small rocks and sent them tumbling down into the abyss.

Everyone stared as the stones fell into the darkness and vanished from sight. Arche forced himself to look away from the yawning abyss and focus on Abraxios, who frantically waved them forward. Arche clenched his jaw and scrambled to his feet, staying low to the bridge as he ran toward Abraxios. He said a silent prayer of thanks that he had managed to keep ahold of the Tridory. This was the last place he wanted to test the limits of the Return trait.

After an eternity, or at least a minute, he made it to the other side of the bridge. The others arrived shortly after, seeming none the worse for wear. Abraxios gestured for them to move into the passageway attached to their side of the cavern, only speaking once they had all entered.

"We must move quickly. There were signs of many beastmar at the bottom and I'm certain they'll hear when the stones hit the bottom," Abraxios said.

"What else did you see?" Tess asked.

"This place is a network of tunnels," Abraxios replied. "I saw many of them as I flew downward. Inside it is confined. It is not my preferred method of travel, but in these tunnels, we can fight on our terms."

"And remove their numbers advantage," Arche said, nodding as he caught his breath. "Outside, we'd have to fight all of them at once. In here, we can funnel them, two or three at a time."

"Then let's not wait for them to come find us," Odelia piped up. "Let's go."

They set off, moving at a brisk jog down the twisting passageways. Arche was grateful for the Owl Vision buff. Without it, he would have been hopelessly lost in the darkness of the tunnels. Every now and then they came across a bioluminescent patch of moss that threw its light across the tunnel for quite a distance, thanks to their enhanced eyesight, but though it was more common the deeper they went, it wasn't always present. Arche wondered if it would grow in the village, perhaps providing a method of nighttime illumination that wouldn't need fuel to burn. He decided to save those thoughts for another time.

The tunnels gradually became smoother, the worn stone gave way to a more polished, crafted passageway that twisted and turned ever deeper underground. The hours crept by, one after the other in the endless dark. Odelia and Abraxios recast Barkskin and Owl Vision whenever the timer got close to running out. Arche wagered it was late morning, by a rough estimate of how many times the spells were recast. The lack of adversity was a kernel that had settled in his stomach. Every scrape of a shoe or quiet echo set his teeth on edge. Still, they encountered no beastmar, no monsters, no mildly disgruntled rats or snakes. Everything was quiet and still.

Like a tomb.

Arche fought a shudder, still dwelling on the macabre thought when he turned a corner and saw a door. He stopped dead in his tracks. Tess walked into him and grunted in quiet surprise.

"Wha—?" her question was cut off as he raised a hand in answer, pointing towards the door at the end of the hallway.

The door was ajar and slick with fresh blood.

Chapter 25

Arche crept toward the open door, Tridory extended in front of him and ready to stab at anything that so much as flinched in a threatening manner. Blood pooled out into the passage from somewhere beyond the door. Arche took a deep breath in and noticed he couldn't smell it. With Owl Vision giving him an extra nine Perception, his total was at twenty-six. He hadn't been able to stop smelling the mustiness of the Vivarium, but the liquid ahead didn't have the tell-tale warm, iron scent. Instead, it was acrid and made his nose-hairs curl.

"What is that?" he muttered, sniffing again to get a better sense of it.

He crept forward, then knelt in front of the liquid. He prodded it with two fingers and sniffed again.

"Oil."

Arche stood and nodded at the rest of the party stacked up behind him, then peered inside the room. The walls were embedded with glowing crystals, each shining a different color, creating a disorienting kaleidoscope of light that illuminated what appeared to be a fairly advanced laboratory.

Cobwebs hung from beakers and graduated cylinders, many of which were cracked or broken. Some larger, more specialized equipment that Arche couldn't put a name to stood against the walls, broken or deactivated. Arche stepped deeper into the room, frowning as he looked around. Something about the equipment in the room made him pause, tugging at memories he couldn't quite vocalize. Everything about it felt wrong. The clearly intricate machinations seemed like they had no place in the world above. They were far more advanced than anything he had seen so far, even in Dawnwood.

"Arche?"

He didn't respond. One of the unbroken beakers had caught his attention. It was filled with a viscous liquid, the color of which was impossible to tell with the haphazard lighting of the room. The beaker was topped with a cork stopper, which Arche made sure to leave in place as he picked it up and squinted at the liquid inside. It was translucent, allowing him to see straight through.

A distorted humanoid face, drawn in a soundless scream, stared back at him.

Arche dropped the beaker with a muffled cry and stumbled backwards. It shattered on the ground, spilling liquid across the floor. Directly across from Arche, somewhat hidden by the lab equipment surrounding it, a large vat held the severed head of a human he had seen distorted through the beaker.

"Malaka," Tess swore as she also caught sight of the vat. "What is this place?"

"I don't know." Odelia eyed the broken equipment littering the room. "The Mana here is twisted. Unnatural."

"We should leave," Lyssa said, her voice sounding somewhat strangled. "We are not meant to be here."

"I agree." Arche stared at the severed head. "This place is wrong on a visceral level. I've got half a mind to burn it down."

"I don't think that would be wise, considering where we are," Abraxios said.

"Yeah, you're probably right. Still doesn't feel right to just leave it like this, though. It might not have been used in a while, but I can just imagine what a place like this could do in the wrong hands."

"Have you seen a room like this before?" Lyssa asked, suddenly interested.

"I don't know," Arche replied. "Maybe? Parts of it look familiar, I think. Let's take a look around before we go. There might be something we can use in here."

They searched through cabinets and drawers for anything that might prove useful. Odelia found a bottle with a yellow liquid inside, holding it up for the others to look at. No one recognized it until Arche used his Examine skill on it.

Potion of Agility	Rarity: Uncommon Potency: Weak Durability: 2 / 2 Weight: 0.5 kilograms Traits: +10 Agility Duration: 1 hour

"It's a potion of agility," Arche said, sharing the rest of the details with them.

Everyone looked at him with surprise. Lyssa's look was especially sharp.

"You have apothecary experience?" Tess asked.

"Well, no..." Arche trailed off, immediately uncomfortable under the weight of the attention he was receiving.

"Then you've seen one of these before?" Odelia asked as she put the potion into her inventory.

"Not exactly. Look, I can't really say how I know, I just do."

Lyssa narrowed her eyes in a way that said, *'We will discuss this later.'*

Arche looked around the room for anything else of note. His eyes landed on a structure that stood from floor to ceiling, the front of which was covered in cracked glass that spiderwebbed throughout. A handle on the front allowed the glass to be lifted upward. Arche walked toward it and lifted the glass. As soon as he did, the whole structure shifted, its supports worn away through years of decay. Inside, a shelf full of beakers and vials slid forward, caught by the glass door Arche was in the process of lifting. The beaker at the front had a label that faced toward him, reading 'trinitroglykos.'

His memory sparked and fear clenched his stomach.

"Everybody out!"

The Tridory clattered against the ground as Arche used both hands to keep the glass door shut, trying to keep the shelf inside as steady as possible.

"What's going on?" Lyssa asked, immediately at his side.

"The shelf inside broke. At least one of those beakers contains a highly volatile explosive. I need you to get everyone out of here, *now!*"

Lyssa turned and made a violent gesture at the rest of them, who began filing quickly out of the room and back into the passageway.

"You too, Lyssa. Get out of here."

"I'm not leaving you behind, Greenstick."

"You're gonna have to. Leave the door open, get them far away, farther than you think you'll have to go. I'll follow as soon as I can."

"That's insanity. We'll find some way to reinforce the glass, bind it shut."

"There isn't time. The slightest jostle could set this stuff off. It's a miracle it hasn't already exploded."

Lyssa set her jaw.

"Then let me hold the glass. You can get to safety."

"Being the brave fool is my job," Arche snapped. "You're faster than me but I'm more durable. Neither of us can outrun the explosion but I can probably survive it. Even if I'm wounded, my skill helps me heal. And let's face it, Lyssa, if this goes wrong, they'll need you a lot more than they'll need me."

"Don't talk like that," she growled.

The shelf inside the vat shifted slightly and Arche clenched his teeth. Sweat lined his forehead and palms as he struggled to keep the unwieldy structure as steady as he could.

"We don't have time to argue, Lyssa. Go. Keep them safe. I'll be right behind you."

Lyssa hesitated another long moment, her face a battlefield of conflicted emotion. Then she knelt and picked up the Tridory.

"You had better be."

With that, she was out the door, her footfalls making no sound as she sped over the stone floor out of sight. Arche turned his full attention to the glass door. It had already been damaged before he had touched it. Spiderweb cracks spun outward across its surface. Now, with pressure placed upon it both by him and the shelf, it seemed like it was no longer up to the task. There was an ominous crack as the spiderwebs deepened. Arche let out a silent prayer, hoping the others had managed to get far enough away. He prepared himself for what was next.

Divine Body pushed strength and vitality through his body as he let go of the vat and turned away. Everything seemed to happen in slow motion. With a single step, he vaulted over an island countertop in the middle of the room and headed for the door. As he reached it, the glass broke behind him. Forcing himself to move faster, he grabbed the heavy metal door and slammed it shut behind him, bracing himself against it. The explosion hit the door and traveled through it, reverberating into Arche. His Health plummeted, only to shoot back up again, instantly regenerated by his Divine Body skill, but the explosion didn't stop there. The strength of the blast broke the hinges and sent Arche flying backwards down the hallway, holding onto the heavy door like a massive tower shield against the fireball that raged forth.

Arche's Mana was nearing zero but he couldn't deactivate his Divine Body skill. His Health yo-yoed up and down as the regeneration warred against the damage he was taking, trying to keep the force of the explosion from liquifying his organs.

The door hit a wall, sending him flying. He lost his grip, perilous as it had been, and was thrown ahead of the door as it ricocheted off the walls and ceiling, still propelled by the fireball. Arche hit the ground at an angle, bouncing and landing mostly within the confines of a side passage. His head cracked against the stone, dazing him. Arche felt something hit his leg, then his Mana hit zero and everything went dark.

Ψ

"GAH!"

The gasp tore itself from Arche's throat as consciousness returned.

Pain consumed him. His leg felt as though it had been lit on fire and shoved into a block of ice while twisted backwards at the knee. He tried to sit up and hands immediately landed on his shoulders to restrain him.

"Steady, Arche."

"Don't move. Odelia is attempting to repair the damage to your leg."

Arche saw a glimpse of his leg and found that his earlier assessment was only partially correct. His leg was neither on fire nor on ice, but it was twisted backwards in a nasty break. It also had one or two new joints between his ankle and knee. Bile rose at the back of his throat as he allowed himself to be pushed down. Waves of hot agony flooded through him, robbing him of all his sense except touch and pain. Never in his life had he imagined there could be so much pain. Odelia's magic brought only moments of reprieve before the pain came roaring back. Something pressed into his mouth and he bit down, muffled screams and sobs tearing out of him.

Arche felt hands on the side of his head, lifting it as something soft was placed beneath it. The hands didn't leave as another surge of pain caused his entire body to seize. Delirium crept into his mind and the darkness was close behind it. A pair of tear-filled eyes looked down on him from above, but with his swimming vision he couldn't tell if they were green or brown. Then the sweet release of unconsciousness claimed him.

Ψ

Nausea was the first thing Arche felt when he woke. There was still pain, old friend that it was by that point, but all he wanted to do was empty the contents of his stomach all over the stone floors. The only problem was that as his abdomen and throat flexed, nothing came out. His stomach cramped and he felt burns along his esophagus that explained what the issue was.

He'd already thrown up everything he had and had nothing left to give.

"Hey, you. You're finally awake."

Arche grunted, waving off Lyssa's comment as the world spun beneath him. Steeling himself as best he could, he chanced a look down at his leg. Blood soaked it and the ground around it, but it was at least pointing the proper direction. It was also wrapped in a pulsing, arboreal shroud that looked like the stalk of some gargantuan plant.

He croaked, his throat almost completely dry. "I remember hitting the wall. What happened to my leg?"

"The door hit it as you made the turn. You nearly lost it, but Odelia was able to get to you almost immediately. Drink this."

Arche felt a waterskin pressed into his hands. He uncorked it and drank deeply, coughing as it wet the irritated tissue in his throat. When he'd drunk as much as he could, he corked it and handed it back. He looked around for the others, then realized they were alone in the passage.

"Where did everybody else go?"

"Scouting for beastmar. The explosion wasn't exactly quiet. They will be back soon now that you're awake."

"How do they know I'm—" Arche stopped as Lyssa put her thumb and finger into her mouth and let forth a brief, shrill whistle that echoed along the stone walls. "Oh. Guess we're not trying to be quiet anymore."

"How do you feel?"

"Like I tried to outrun an explosion and lost."

"I have questions about what happened back there, but they can wait for later. I saw the light you emitted in the tunnel. The others will likely think it was fire from the explosion, so you don't have to worry. Do you have any lasting injuries?"

Arche checked his vitals and winced.

Health: 373 / 495 75%	Stamina: 311 / 355 88%	Mana: 26 / 190 14%

Barkskin — Level 8: 29:47 **Owl Vision — Level 19**: 4:20 **Nature's Embrace — Level 24**: 2:08 **Mana Burnout**: 16:29

"Fucking burnout. I've got to figure out a way around that. Mana's gone, Stamina's good, Health is all right, but I'm not going to be much use for about fifteen minutes."

His eyes flitted to Nature's Embrace but he was too tired to pull up the details, assessing it to be whatever Odelia had done to his leg.

"Maybe when we get out of here, Odelia or Abraxios can help you with your Mana issue."

Lyssa stood and hauled Arche to his feet.

"Why would they be able to help?"

Arche grunted in pain as he shifted his weight onto his leg.

"They're mages. If anyone has a work-around for Mana Burnout, it would be a mage."

Arche blinked.

"That's brilliant."

One of Lyssa's ears twitched. "They're coming."

Arche nodded in response, quickly going through his notifications for anything important.

Broken Leg Movement Speed reduced by 75%

He was *distinctly* aware of that particular debuff, but it was handy to see exactly how that had affected him. Thankfully, the debuff had disappeared after Odelia's healing.

Divine Body has increased to **Level 10**. You have reached the **Rank** of **Novice**. You gain 100 experience.

Experience is held until a **Profession** is chosen. Choose a **Profession?**	
Yes	No

Arche dismissed the notification as a shout from down the passage and the sound of fighting echoed back toward them. Lyssa cursed, drawing her bow and nocking an arrow in one fluid motion. Arche leaned heavily against his Tridory, cursing his Mana Burnout. With his regeneration slowed and his head pounding fit to burst, there was no way he'd be able to fight for longer than a minute.

"Stay behind me," Lyssa ordered.

Her tone brooked no argument. Arche gathered up his bag and waited behind her, listening to the sounds grow louder and louder. In less than a minute, Tess came into view. The Rogue was holding Odelia in her arms and sprinting toward them. Abraxios was not far behind, using his wings to propel his feet down the passageway toward them, twisting occasionally to fire a lightning bolt backwards, the air crackling with static.

"How many?" Lyssa called out over the rising din.

"Too many!" Tess shouted back, voice full of panic. *"Run!"*

Chapter 26

Two feelings gripped Arche as the beastmar horde drew nearer: pain and fear. Pain in his leg, which hadn't fully healed and cost him Health with every step, and fear of the sort that every hunted prey knows. Lyssa carried him under the shoulder but they were far too slow to get away.

The air crackled as Abraxios discharged more lightning. Odelia, the smallest and slowest of them, clutched to Tess with a white-knuckled grip as the golden-haired Rogue ran ahead, trying to find some refuge or, barring that, a place to make their stand.

"This way!" Tess called out, her voice loud and desperate.

Arche cursed his Mana Burnout condition and hobbled on as fast as he could, every step sending shooting pains up his thigh and into his groin. Lyssa practically dragged him along but doing so left Abraxios as the only one capable of slowing down the enemies behind them.

The tengu let out a fierce, avian shriek that reverberated off the walls and down the passageway, louder than what seemed possible. Arche and the others cried out in pain, the noise impacting them like a physical force despite the tengu facing away from them. Tess disappeared into a side room, hauling Odelia along with her. Lyssa dragged Arche into it and set him down against a wall. Abraxios slammed the door behind them.

Arche wheezed, trying to catch his breath. His Stamina was down to twenty percent.

"What's wrong with him?" Tess demanded.

"Mana Burnout," Odelia replied before Lyssa could say anything.

The halfling woman hurried over to Arche and placed the back of her hand against his head. Arche, for his part, was doing everything he could to keep from dry heaving. His head felt as though he were beating it against a wall and his stomach had settled somewhere near his throat, which was bobbing dangerously as he struggled to keep his gorge down.

They had landed in a room full of rotten wooden boxes that looked like it had been ignored for the better half of a century. The smell of mold was strong, but with any luck it would mask their scent.

"I don't understand, though," Odelia continued. "I never saw him cast any magic. How could he have burned through his Mana?"

"Later." Lyssa cut in. "Can you fix him?"

"The leg? Yes, with time. The head, already done. The burnout? That's well beyond me. How is he using Mana without having formed the proper channels for it? Doesn't he know it could kill him?"

"I'm right here," Arche groaned, his voice gruff and hoarse.

He held the Tridory in a vice with both hands and used it to get his feet under him. Lyssa grabbed his arm and helped him into a standing position.

"Who taught you magic?" Odelia demanded. "Whoever it was should be Honor-Broken. How could they not have taught you how to channel your Mana?"

"I wasn't...taught," Arche managed, his breath coming heavily.

"What?" This time it was Abraxios who demonstrated his disbelief. "A spell is not merely a gesture or a word that you can will into existence through effort alone. It takes years of study and practice to learn the arcane theory that goes into spellwork. Trying

to use magic without understanding it…why, you'd be lucky if anything happened at all and *anything* could happen."

"I clearly don't understand," Arche grunted. "So if we could skip the part where you two explain how much of a dumbass I've been and tell me how to fix what I've been doing wrong, I'd appreciate it, because it doesn't sound like we have a lot of time."

"What spell have you been casting that's bottoming out your Mana?" Odelia asked.

"It's not a spell, really," Arche hesitated, then grunted as his leg sent a wave of fresh pain upward. "It's a skill I learned by accident. I was up against an enemy I couldn't beat. A force took over me and burnt off all my Mana almost immediately, but with it I managed to fend off a revenant long enough for us to get away."

"That's, erm, a lot to unpack," Abraxios said, cocking his head to the side. "What skill is it that you are using?"

Arche hesitated, glancing between them. Tess threw her hands up in frustration.

"Malaka! We can't help if we don't know."

"Fine. It's a skill called Divine Body."

The others blinked and looked at each other, each wearing the same blank face. With the exception of Lyssa, the consensus was clear: none of them had heard of it before.

"What does it do?" Odelia asked.

Arche shrugged.

"Makes me strong and fast. Replenishes my Health and Stamina."

"Hmph, that explains the mantikhoras," Tess muttered.

"Sounds like an incredibly powerful skill," Abraxios said slowly. "However, if you are letting it use all of your Mana at once, you are searing it throughout your body's natural Mana paths. Mana must be channeled in a very careful manner, a manner that normally takes weeks, if not months, to cultivate. Your skill seems to do some of that work for you, which can be the only explanation for why you have not killed yourself with it, but it isn't doing everything for you. You must learn to control it, rather than have it control you."

"That sounds great and everything, but you've yet to get to the 'how' portion."

"Practice," Odelia said, something akin to regret in her voice. "There is nothing else for it. If we survive today, I'm sure Abraxios and I can teach you the basics of how to unlock the Mana Manipulation skill, but I'm only in the Student ranks so my instruction won't be of much benefit other than how to get started."

"Enough talk," Lyssa interjected before Arche could ask another question. "They are coming. Not as many of them as before, but more than a dozen. Arche, are you able to fight?"

Arche peeked at his vitals. His Stamina had nearly bottomed out and his Mana Burnout timer still had over five minutes left. His Health had also dropped to sixty percent.

"No," he gasped. "But I'll give it what I've got."

"That's sweet, Greenstick, but stay behind me and try not to get yourself killed."

"Fine. They're weak to fire. Their fur and skin burns quickly."

Lyssa nocked an arrow to her bow and turned toward the rest of them.

"Abraxios, find a vantage point from which you can shoot lightning. Odelia, take this camp oil and pour it near the door. Make sure you spread it over a wide area, then get back and ready whatever healing spells you have left. Tess, be ready to engage with any who break through. Be ready for things to go awry."

The others scrambled to obey Lyssa's orders while Arche sagged against the far wall behind her, impressed at how effortlessly she had taken command and formed a strategy. Odelia had barely finished emptying her third flask when the door flexed inward. The halfling woman jumped back as the door flew open and beastmar began to tumble into the room.

Lyssa's first arrow ripped through the leading beastmar's head, killing it instantly, and wounded the one behind it. The beastmar's corpse collapsed in the doorway, slowing down the ones clambering in behind it. Abraxios fired a bolt of lightning at the ground, igniting the oil and creating a thick, dark smoke that billowed up, filling the narrow confines of the room. Howls of pain, fear, and fury echoed off the stone walls as the beastmar caught fire. Arche gritted his teeth, barely able to stay on his feet.

Tess launched herself in and out of the fray with the grace of a dancer. One moment, she was lunging forward to deal a devastating blow to an exposed side or throat, the next she was twirling and dancing backward out of danger, the swiping claws and thrusting weapons of the beastmar catching only air. The fluidity of her movements reminded Arche of Lyssa's flowing style, but there was something brutal in Tess's strikes. Stab, step, twist, spin, stab. Each attack was designed to disable or to cause pain, only a few lucky blows to a neck or a heart actually killed. Arche's brow furrowed as he watched her, then he clutched at the wall as a sudden gust of wind nearly blew him over.

Abraxios swept his wings, funneling air into the fire, which roared up with sudden life. Burning oil splattered against beastmar crammed into the passageway outside, their shrieking howls dominating the sounds of battle within.

Good luck did not last forever, as Tess was the first to learn. One beastmar surged from behind its companions, knocking them aside to bear down on the Rogue. She sidestepped to avoid bisection via enormous axe, but failed to avoid the kick that launched her across the room. She landed near Arche, limbs akimbo, eyes wild and unfocused. A pained croak gurgled from her as she struggled to breathe. Arche fell to his knees next to her, the Tridory clattering against the stones as he fought against his own weakened body to get Tess back on her feet.

The Rogue's absence from the front line let several beastmar push their way forward, past the inferno. Lyssa drew forth two kopides and leaped into the fray. While Tess struck like a viper, leaping forward and backward with her strikes, Lyssa moved in circles like a great storm. She used the weight of the swords as ballasts to swing her body around first one way, then the other, often amputating limbs as she danced along their line.

The press of the beastmar was greatly slowed by her efforts, but too many had already forced their way past the still-burning door and into the room. Odelia fell to her knees, trembling as emerald light flowed down her arms and into the ground. Thick vines shot out of the floor around the doorway and started whipping about wildly, throwing beastmar aside. Tess used the opportunity to jump back into the fray, dragging her knives across the throats of the fallen beastmar while Lyssa pressed the others back against the thrashing vines. The few beastmar that had yet to run into the room were hacking wildly at the vines while trying to avoid the fire. For the first time, it looked like they might actually win.

Then the wall exploded.

Large chunks of stone blasted into the room, several of which hit Arche and sent him flying. He hit the opposite wall and pain descended on him again. A roar—louder than battle, louder than thought—filled the room. Heat flooded the space, sucking the breath from Arche's lungs and replacing it with scorched wind. Arche dragged his arms over his head as the wall crumbled around him. Once the stone settled, he could hear the yipping and barking of beastmar retreating into the distance.

Not without great effort, Arche picked himself up out of the rubble, noticing with a spike of excitement that his Mana Burnout debuff was gone. His excitement was immediately replaced by a wave of pain and exhaustion as he noticed his Health hovering at twenty percent. His arms and legs were a mess of bloody scrapes, embedded with bits of stone. A brief glance around the room told him the rest of the group wasn't fairing much better. They were scattered about the room, either laying unmoving or slowly rising to their feet.

Lyssa was the first to recover. She placed herself between the rest of them and the new threat. Arche's gaze moved from his Companion to the monster itself. Amid the settling stone dust stood an enormous lion, easily twice as large as it should be. Its size was hardly the strangest part, however. What really made Arche's blood run cold was the goat head that grew alongside the lion, splitting its neck into two. The monstrous beast padded into the room, tail whipping about almost lazily, green and scaled, with the tip culminating in a serpent head with fangs the size of Arche's hands.

The creature leveled its gaze onto Arche, a glint of intelligence in each set of eyes. The lion head opened its jaws impossibly wide, an amber glow building in the back of its throat.

"Aw, fuck."

Instinct took over and Arche threw himself to the side as a spout of flame shot forth from the monster's maw. It bathed the rubble where he had been standing, turning the rocks a glowing, cherry red. He landed heavily, bruising himself on the pointy rocks. His breath was ragged, not quite recovered from the aftereffects of Mana Burnout and his injury.

An angry, feline hiss echoed throughout the room as he picked himself up. Lyssa had engaged the beast, spinning with her kopides as the creature swiped massive paws through the air or lunged with one of its three heads. A gust of wind signaled that Abraxios had rejoined the fray. The tengu whipped his wings about in some martial form and, despite the fact that the tengu was across the room from the monster, slices opened up over the creature's body with every deft movement.

Arche wanted to help but the Tridory was no longer with him. He must have dropped it when he was sent flying. Arche twisted his head around, searching around for it frantically, but it was nowhere to be found. Likely it was buried beneath the rubble when the creature crashed through the wall. Arche moaned inwardly, hoping that his paltry amount of Mana would be enough.

Taking a steadying breath, Arche held out his hand and concentrated. His head throbbed as eight Mana drained almost instantly, but the rubble across the room shifted and the spear shot out toward him. He caught it, immediately gritting his teeth against the renewed headache as he braced himself to get involved.

Tess was off to the side, launching knives at vulnerable points along the beast's side, but whether it was the sheer size of the creature or an abnormally thick hide, the blades weren't penetrating deep enough to do much damage. The creature spun, its snake-tail whipping outward faster than Lyssa could dodge. She caught the fangs against her blades, but the force of its strike knocked her off her feet and sent her flying toward Arche.

He was moving before he knew what had happened, closing the distance across the uneven terrain. He caught her, remembering to drop the Tridory just in time, and her momentum knocked him off his feet. They tumbled to the ground, a tangle of body parts. Arche grunted as Lyssa landed on top of him, sucking air between clenched teeth as she pressed down on his bruised ribs and wounded leg. Lyssa groaned and stirred, stunned from the impact. Arche carefully rolled to the side and laid her down beside him. Pain flared in a dozen new places, but looking at Lyssa's dazed, slackened face, a new feeling took hold of him.

Rage.

Arche snatched up the spear and turned toward the beast, which had brought the weight of its attention onto Tess. The Rogue was doing her best to keep her distance, her eyes darting back and forth as she looked for a way out, but the monster had cornered her. Lightning coursed through the air as Abraxios tried desperately to distract the creature, but the electricity washed harmlessly over the creature, barely fazing it. Odelia crawled to Lyssa's side. The halfling's left foot was bent at a bad angle but she gritted her teeth through the pain and conjured a spell. Lyssa's naturally reddish-brown skin glowed with a soft, viridescent hue as open wounds sewed themselves shut.

The creature's lion-head opened its mouth wide—too wide, like an unhinged jaw—and Arche knew he wouldn't be able to close the distance in time. It seemed to have grown tired of Tess's stabbing knives and decided to eat her whole. Tess shrank back into the corner and covered her face with her arms. The monster stood above her, poised to strike at any moment as its mouth opened larger and larger.

Arche hoisted the Tridory into an overhand grip and launched it forward with all the strength he could muster. The effort brought him to his knees. The monster roared in pain as the spear sank into the creature's flank. Tess used the distraction to leave her corner. She rolled out of the way of a late swipe and came up near Abraxios. The creature's attention affixed on Arche, who staggered to his feet.

"Easy." He plastered a smile on his face as his stomach nestled somewhere near his feet. "Good kitty."

The furious growl emanating from the monstrous creature promised a slow and painful death.

"Fuck you, too."

Arche rolled to the side as a massive paw slammed into the ground where he'd been standing. He popped back up and immediately fell backwards with a cry to avoid the snapping maw of the goat head as it bit at him. He landed on his back, cracking his head painfully against the debris. Bright spots flooded his vision.

The creature spun and the snake tail lunged for him, fangs gaping, too fast for him to move out of the way. Arche clenched his teeth and waited for the pain to come, but the strike never landed. One of Tess's daggers sailed neatly through the air and stuck the snake head clean through. The whole tail went limp.

The creature howled from its goat head as its lion mouth gaped again to spew forth fire. Arche stumbled to his feet, blinking furiously to clear the spots from his vision. Between his Mana headache and his multitude of injuries, he was lucky to be standing. That said, his luck was fading quickly.

It hadn't quite run out, however, as he was on the same side of the creature as his spear, which still protruded from the beast's flank. Arche dove for the weapon, grabbing hold of the shaft just as the goat head clamped down around his torso, lifting him into the air. Arche gasped for breath as the tremendous force of the bite drove the wind from his lungs. The goat head's teeth weren't sharp enough to break through his armor—which kept the creature from tearing a chunk out of his side—but the sheer, crushing force snapped several of Arche's ribs with loud cracks.

In a panic, Arche ripped the Tridory out and stabbed at the monster again and again, opening up a half dozen wounds in the creature's side, though none were particularly deep nor dangerous. The goat-head shook him like an alligator, sending the Tridory flying. Arche could do nothing but hope his armor would hold and his limbs wouldn't mangle. Just as he was sure the creature would shake the last bit of life from him, the goat-head went suddenly limp and he fell to the ground. The world swirled and darkness crept around the edges of his vision. A trio of arrows protruded from the limp goat head, each deep enough to pierce its brain.

Arche was tired. More tired than he had ever felt. A great weight had settled into his arms and legs, and his eyes wanted nothing more than to shut and rest for a few hours. Lights flashed toward the bottom of his vision, the only thing he could see in the darkness. Flashing Health, flashing Stamina, flashing Mana. All three bars were nearly empty, some scant points in each, but Arche was past the point of really caring. A chill filled him and the floor seemed suddenly the most comfortable place in the world. If he could just keep lying there for another five minutes or so, he was sure he'd be able to finish killing the monster.

Just five minutes of rest.

A hand grabbed his shoulder, pulling at his armor. It felt distant, numb, but it was enough to keep him from falling asleep. Arche's head lolled and his eyes opened. Odelia looked down at him, tears streaked across her cheeks as she pulled desperately at him, trying to get him away from the fight. It was a vain effort, Arche was far too heavy for the halfling woman to budge. She balled up one fist, muttering something. A moment later, she uncurled her fist to reveal a yellow light. She pressed the light against Arche's chest and great, racking coughs forced their way out of his lungs.

His Health, Stamina, and Mana all rose by fifty-six points. Instead of a pleasant experience, Arche's bones popped painfully back into place. He would have screamed if he'd had the breath to do so but his lungs were too busy reinflating, repairing the holes his broken ribs had torn. A few seconds later, he was able to breathe, if painfully. His body felt like it was covered in biting insects trying to burrow into the marrow of his bones to unleash their venom, but he was no longer tired beyond care. The healing magic had brought feeling and awareness back to him, but at great cost.

Odelia collapsed next to him, breath shallow and drenched in sweat. Arche had no idea how to help her. Helpless anger flooded him. Anger at the creature and at himself, his own uselessness.

Arche snatched the Tridory off the ground and looked for the beast. It was not hard to find, but the sight of it made his blood run cold once more. It had cornered Abraxios, Tess, and Lyssa and kept them in place by spewing a gout of flame. Abraxios had taken point and was diverting the flames to either side with a powerful gust of wind, but the sheer heat was cooking the trio. Abraxios was the picture of concentration, a single errant ember would ignite his feathers into a conflagration of doom.

Crouching low to the ground, spear brandished, Arche activated Divine Body and lunged forward, crossing the entire width of the room in a single bound before plunging the Tridory into the monster's neck. He deactivated the skill as the flames, which had poured relentlessly only moments before, sputtered and died. Without removing the spear, Arche pressed the third button on the shaft and the head of the spear, now firmly embedded, broke apart into three prongs, slicing open flesh into a gaping hole. Arche wrenched the spear out and activated Divine Body once more, leaping high into the air. He spun, flattening himself horizontally as the creature recoiled.

Arche landed on the cross-section where the lion and goat heads diverged and drove the head of the trident deep into the back of the lion's skull. The bone gave way with an awful crunch as the great beast shuddered once and fell to the floor, dead. Arche ripped the trident out and deactivated Divine Body. As soon as the skill's empowerment left him, he collapsed.

Everything seemed far away, everything but pain. Slowly, Arche became aware of someone holding him and wiping something across his face. When consciousness fully returned, he almost wished it hadn't. He was sitting at a quarter of his maximum Health and could feel the full extent of every point he had lost. A notification caught his attention and he opened it.

> You have slain a **Level 36 Chímaira**.
> You gain 1,800 experience.
>
> **Slayer of the Mighty** activated!
> You gain 2,100 bonus experience.

> Experience is held until a **Profession** is chosen.
>
> Choose a **Profession?**
>
> | Yes | Yes |
> | --- | --- |

Still dazed, Arche stared uncomprehendingly at the notification. Without waiting for his answer, the prompt closed itself and a new one appeared.

> *Initializing...*
>
> *Ready for transport.*
>
> *3...*
>
> *2...*
>
> *1...*
>
> **Welcome to the Professing.**

Chapter 27

Arche floated in a vast, dark void. There was no sensation. No twist of wind, despite his breathing. No smell, no sight, no taste. The place was alien and all too familiar. As his bare feet settled down onto what felt like cold stone, Arche had a sudden realization.

This place, whatever it was, had born him into consciousness.

What had that been...nearly a month ago? Arche could scarcely believe that time had gone by so quickly. He was no longer wearing his elven leathers and boots, but was back in the crude, cotton clothing he'd first woken up in. Something rippled at the corners of his vision and he turned to look, seeing a set of doors flicker into existence as though someone had pulled a curtain back to reveal them. Four doors in total, each staring back at him from cardinal directions, if this place even had cardinal directions.

Arche stepped up to the first door. It was made of some sort of cherry wood, stained a dark red with burnished steel accents. The knob to the door was that of a dagger handle and, as Arche looked closer, he could see that the door was engraved with tiny carvings of more weapons than he could name. A notification appeared over the door as he approached.

Combat

Arche looked at the door with a considering eye. If this was where he was to choose a profession, a combat profession was the most attractive choice. Still, it would be foolish to choose it without even looking at what else was available. He took a step back and the message over the door faded. Arche turned to the right and approached the next door.

This door was a rich purple and had a texture that resembled fabric rather than wood, stone, or steel. Unlike the straight frame of the combat door, this one was twisted and gnarled with a plethora of angles and shapes. The door itself was rounded at the top and had a paintbrush hanging from the frame.

Artisan

Arche nodded to himself and moved on to the third door. This door seemed more sterile than the other two. It was made from white metal with a circular window of glass at head height. The window was circular, like a porthole, and as Arche peered through it, he saw absolutely nothing. There was no frame to this door, but at the bottom was a sort of steel kick-plate. There was no handle or knob to the door, but a thin silver sheet of metal on one side seemed to indicate him to push. Something about the door seemed familiar to Arche but he couldn't recall ever seeing a door like that.

Scholar

Arche grunted and, with one last attempted look through the window, turned away to inspect the last door. This door was the plainest of all. Even the sterility of the Scholar door had its own quiet elegance and intellect of craftsmanship, but this door was made from mud and sticks. Granted, the mud was smooth and the sticks had been debarked and aligned in very neat vertical rows, but there was no denying that it was using the least quality of materials when compared to the other three.

Labor

Arche stepped back to the center and turned slowly, looking at each of the doors in turn. Combat was the obvious choice. Still, he couldn't shake the feeling that there was something else, something just beyond his senses. He looked carefully at the void, peering into the darkness between doors and even upward, but there was nothing out of place.

"Come on. What am I missing?"

A small knock echoed in the empty space. Arche spun around, searching for the source. It seemed almost to have come from the ground, but where? He took a step to reexamine the void spaces between doors and stumbled. Something beveled on the ground had caught his toes. Arche dropped to his knees and searched with his hands.

Something was sunk into the floor and hidden by a cloak of void. Upon finding it, the void pulled back and revealed a plain, wooden door with no knob or handle. The only giveaway, which Arche had stumbled upon, was the slight lip between the door itself and the ground around it, which was still covered by blackness. The door was made from dark wood and had no special markings on it. It almost appeared as a simple board that had fallen onto the ground and been forgotten. No prompt appeared as Arche knelt in front of it, a fact that only made it more interesting to him.

Arche looked back up at the combat door, biting his lip as he wrestled internally with his decision. If he chose this strange, hidden door, there was no guarantee that he'd be able to reverse his choice if he'd made a mistake. A combat profession spoke to him, but would he really squander this new option after all the trouble to hide it? Perhaps it was fate, perhaps it was luck, perhaps it was nothing at all.

"I really hope I don't regret this."

Arche stepped onto the door and stamped his foot. Without delay, the door swung down and he dropped through the floor into nothing. His jaw clenched to keep him from crying out but there was no rush of air that he normally associated with falling. Instead, it was as though the ground had simply risen up and consumed the doors around him and he was once more surrounded by an endless void. Pure absence.

Just as before, his feet touched cold stone. There was no indication of how long he'd been left in limbo. It could have been minutes or days. Arche turned, trying to get some grasp on his surroundings but there was nothing. A message appeared in his vision, seeming to float several feet in front of him.

You have found the **Door of Hidden Potential**.

Instead of restricting yourself to the choices ahead of you, you found a different path and decided to follow it wherever it might lead.

The choices you will be provided with have been tailored to you.

<u>**Choose wisely.**</u>

The notification disappeared as suddenly as it had appeared, leaving Arche feeling more apprehensive than reassured with its closing remark. He flinched and brought his hands up defensively as he realized he was no longer alone. A multitude of dark figures surrounded him. Three of the closest figures came into view as the void pulled back from them and Arche realized with a start that they all looked the same.

Each was a man with dusky, sun-tanned skin and messy, dark brown hair. Dark eyes stared back into nothingness, looking beyond Arche to some distant, nonexistent horizon. Their faces stuck out the most. Scarred was an understatement. Not a finger's breadth of skin was left unmarked. Pink, raw flesh crisscrossed with scars, both jagged and linear, stretched from hairline to the hollow of throats.

Arche locked eyes with the man in front of him, clearly a warrior type wearing heavy, stylized armor with a spear and shield. His throat closed up. This was his face staring back at him. He'd known that he had scars, known that they were intense from the reactions of others, but he hadn't known the extent of the damage.

In truth, he had avoided looking. He didn't want to know.

There was a layer of deniability that not knowing had granted him. He had been allowed to forget about it. People like Lyssa and Helwan had gotten used to him and he didn't feel self-conscious around them, but staring into his own reflection and realizing the extent to which he had been marked, how could he stand to face them now? How must they have seen him, all this time? He could have lived with being ugly, but disfigured was a hell even the ugly couldn't imagine. This was beyond some cruel casting of cosmic dice. Something had done this to him. This had been deliberate.

Arche covered his face with his hands, tears streaming down his cheeks. It was foolish. It shouldn't mean anything to him. How he looked had nothing to do with his capabilities, nothing to do with who he was, but he couldn't shake the shame, the despair.

It was *his* face.

It was everything that people saw when they looked at him. It was the only thing he saw himself, now that he could look. He felt the lines with his fingertips, traced the bumps and valleys he had worked so hard to forget.

Arche wished he'd never seen himself. How could he ever hope to earn the trust of others? A monster killing monsters will never change what it is. Who would follow his face into danger? Who would believe it would bring them anything but death? A mask would cover it, with the exception of the lines that crawled down his throat. He could hide his face from the rest of the world. An escape. Some façade he could present that would secret him away from judgement, leaving only a mysterious curiosity in its wake.

With no small degree of effort, Arche pulled his hands away and stared into the identical face peering blankly back at him. Hiding from his own face wasn't practical, he knew that. It didn't matter if no one else saw it, he would still know, and taking steps to hide it would only cement it in his own mind. He couldn't run from himself. No, this was something he would have to deal with. It might take a long time before he could truly become comfortable with it, but what choice did he have? He had to play with the hand he was dealt and live with the face he'd been given.

Arche drew a deep, shuddering breath and stared his own face down. This wasn't a calamity. His looks didn't matter, his actions did. Cognitively, he knew that, but it was a hard thing to feel. Maybe, *maybe*, somewhere down the line he could look into investing points into Comeliness. He didn't know if that would get rid of the scars or diminish them, but surely it would help, especially since his starting Comeliness score had been a whopping 'one.'

Mentally tearing his attention away from the replica's face, Arche focused on what his doppelganger was wearing in greater detail. Anything to distract himself from the rabbit hole of self-pity he'd spiraled down. The armor was quite a bit heavier than anything Arche had worn, looking like cast bronze. The breastplate was stylized to resemble a heavily muscled chest and the bare arms that poked out indicated the metal muscles were an accurate indication of what lay beneath. This version of him clearly had invested heavily in Strength with a Fortitude to match, if the thickness of the torso was any guess. A message appeared over the doppelganger's head.

<table>
<tr><td colspan="2" align="center">Warrior

The path of the warrior is not one for the faint of heart.
A warrior will stand up to any foe on any battlefield.

This profession favors the front lines of conflict and grants bonuses to Strength, Fortitude, Endurance, and Willpower.

This is a Common profession.</td></tr>
<tr><td colspan="2" align="center">Choose Warrior as your profession?</td></tr>
<tr><td align="center">Yes</td><td align="center">No</td></tr>
</table>

Arche shook his head. It sounded great, but there were too many other options to narrow down a choice yet. There were the other two figures that he could see, and a multitude of silhouettes that he could barely make out hiding behind the swirling void itself. Warrior might be a good choice to fall back on, but it was generic and its bonuses would likely also be generic. There was a benefit to being an all-around fighter, but they often died to skilled specialists. At the very least, knowledge was power and it would be foolish to make such an important choice without at least considering other options.

Arche looked over to another version of himself, one wearing dark leather armor and a cloak. Two bandoliers of knives stretched from shoulders to hips. It was a tad excessive, like the figure was trying a little too hard to pass off a mysterious aesthetic.

Rogue

The path of the rogue is one of stealth and subterfuge.
A rogue will think their way around any problem that may arise but won't hesitate to slide a blade into any problem that gets in their way.

This profession favors the clever and grants bonuses to **Dexterity, Agility, Intelligence,** and **Perception**.

This is a **Common** profession.

Choose **Rogue** as your profession?

Yes	No

Sneaking around was great, but it wasn't his style. Arche enjoyed the bonuses his cloak gave him and he liked getting the drop on monsters, but that wasn't who he was. He smiled as he considered that Theresa had likely been presented this same choice and decided it *was* for her. He wondered which parts of the description had most drawn her to it and was once again thankful she had decided not to kill him, though he could have done without the dagger in his side.

Arche turned to the last visible doppelganger and gave it a thorough once-over. Unlike the other two, this one wasn't wearing armor. Instead, it wore fine, form-fitting robes that were at once respectable and attractive. The expression on the figure's face was one of quiet confidence, and the eyes glimmered with a hidden depth of knowledge that the other figures had lacked.

Mage

The path of the mage is one of research and the cultivation of Mana.
A mage is never more at home than when solving a problem none have bested and are often leaders among their scientific communities. Their command of the basic elements of magic has earned them much respect.

This profession favors the pursuit of knowledge, a journey that is never quite finished, and grants bonuses to **Intelligence, Wisdom,** and **Willpower**.

This is a **Common** profession.

Choose **Mage** as your profession?

Yes	No

This was the easiest dismissal Arche had faced yet. His thoughts turned to Helwan, who had claimed, among other titles, to be a mage. Arche didn't have the patience or the access to a scientific facility required for a path like scholarship and a life of quiet research was not in his cards. He could guess why this path had been chosen to fit him.

It seemed to be all about asking questions and that felt like all he ever did, but he wanted answers to those questions, not to keep asking them forever.

Arche turned back to the others and took a few steps toward the Warrior, knowing that whatever profession he picked, it would fall under the Warrior archetype. The figures waiting behind it shimmered and he grew excited. As that excitement grew, so did an odd feeling in his center. It was small, at first, but every step magnified it. It wasn't quite an ache, rather it felt like someone had tied a rope around his organs and connected it back to the Origin. The more he pulled away, the worse it felt.

Arche understood why people chose the core professions instead of branching out to see what else laid beyond. It wasn't beyond his ability to bear but it was a pull somewhere below his solar plexus that was extraordinarily uncomfortable, like something was trying to suck his innards out his back with a straw.

As he passed the Warrior, three more figures came into view as the void pulled back. The first was the most surprising. It towered over him, a full head and shoulders taller, and was an absolute beast of a man. His head was shaved and a plaited beard sprouted down from his chin toward his unarmored torso. A vest hung open over a loose, linen shirt that did little to hide the bulging muscles beneath. Arche found it hard not to stare at this mountainous version of himself.

Barbarian

The path of the barbarian is one often undertaken alone.
Civilization rejects you as you walk the natural world, reveling in its power and its secrets. This profession favors connection with nature and nurtures a resilience that is deeper than flesh, though its practitioners often find themselves misunderstood by those who have not walked the same path.

This profession grants bonuses to **Strength**, **Fortitude**, **Endurance**, and **Willpower**, but suffers reductions in **Charisma**.

This is an **Uncommon** profession.

Choose **Barbarian** as your profession?

Yes	No

The physical aspect of the profession had a lot to be desired, but as Arche read over the prompt again, he realized that becoming barbarian would likely alienate him from his allies. It required a lot of commitment and, even though the rewards were great, the price didn't seem worth it. Shaking his head, he turned and moved to the next profession.

This version of himself was regaled in a muscled cuirass of hardened steel, with matching greaves and a cheeked helmet that sported a black plume running vertically like a mohawk. The stylized warrior wielded a spear and shield, with a sword belted at his side. The stiff posture and stony face gave Arche the indication that this was a soldiering profession. The accompanying message did not disappoint him.

Hoplite

The path of the hoplite is one of service.
Found in the strongest armies in Tartarus, the Hoplites are warriors that wield destruction with their spears and shields. Their formations have broken the fiercest hordes and they are most dangerous when in large numbers.

This profession favors those who desire the rigidity and reliance of military life and provides bonuses to **Strength**, **Intelligence**, and **Charisma**.

This is an **Uncommon** profession.

Choose **Hoplite** as your profession?

Yes	No

A surprisingly tempting option. Strength, Intelligence, and Charisma were all good attributes to invest in, and keeping them high going forward was a priority. That said, Arche didn't have any intentions of joining a military and it seemed like the profession relied on having other Hoplites to fight alongside. Moving along, he looked to the last doppelganger on the row.

This version of himself was wearing haphazard armor from head to toe, none of it matched, but all of it looked rather expensive. There was a cocky glint in the double's eye and a full coin purse hanging from their belt next to a jeweled xiphos.

Misthios

The path of the misthios is one that follows the rivers of currency.
Misthioi are mercenaries, blades for hire that know any task can be performed for a price. Shrewd in their calculations of people, diligent in their duties, a misthios knows that their reputation is their life and that without it, they will starve.

This profession favors those willing to do the dirty work for a bit of coin and provides bonuses to **Wisdom**, **Perception**, **Charisma**, and **Luck**.

This is an **Uncommon** profession.

Choose **Misthios** as your profession?

Yes	No

That was an easy dismissal. Coin was nice, yes, but it was not his life's purpose to pursue money. He had more that he wanted to accomplish than doing jobs for others. He pressed forward, midway between the hoplite and the barbarian.

The queasy feeling intensified, no longer a minor annoyance he could cast to the back of his mind. Arche had to concentrate on suppressing the feeling just to keep from throwing up. It was worth the effort. The void pulled back and revealed three more professions for him to choose from.

The first figure wore leather armor and sported a completely shaved head. His hands bore metal gauntlets constructed from interwoven metal plates with spines extending from the knuckles. Hardened muscles lined the man's form, but there was a litheness to his posture that several of the other muscle-bound professions had lacked.

<table>
<tr><td align="center">**Pugilist**</td></tr>
<tr><td align="center">*The path of the pugilist is one with as many opportunities to fall as there are to rise.*
Many know arts of fighting with only their own limbs but few have ever truly mastered the attempt. The Pugilist is one such master that prides efficiency and effect over the artistic and spiritual sides of the martial arts.

This profession favors those who wish to be unequaled in combat even while disarmed, and provides bonuses to **Strength**, **Dexterity**, and **Agility**.

This is a **Rare** profession.</td></tr>
<tr><td align="center">Choose **Pugilist** as your profession?</td></tr>
</table>

Yes	No

Fighting with his fists had always been comfortable. It was an aspect of himself that Arche wanted to explore further, but it wasn't one he was willing to profess. He grunted as he turned away, the pull in his center vying for his attention.

The next doppelganger wore form-fitting robes of exquisite material and craftsmanship. A thin sword, similar to Vik's Starpoint, hung from the double's belt. Beneath the fine clothing, chain-linked armor was sewn into the clothing. What was most surprising, however, was that the face reflecting back at him looked almost normal. While it still had his scars, they had faded into a network of small silver lines that looked roguish, almost handsome.

<table>
<tr><td align="center">**Duelist**</td></tr>
<tr><td align="center">*The path of the duelist is one of fame and glory.*
A true artist with a blade, a duelist can make their name recognizable across the entire span of Tartarus by doing what they love: competing.

This profession favors the quick, the accurate, and those hungry for glory, and provides bonuses to **Dexterity**, **Agility**, **Charisma**, and **Comeliness**.

This is a **Rare** profession.</td></tr>
<tr><td align="center">Choose **Duelist** as your profession?</td></tr>
</table>

Yes	No

Once again, Arche found himself tempted. Being a master of the blade was nice enough, but the promise of being able to change his face was a powerful motivator. With more than a little effort, he tore himself away. He hadn't yet looked through all the options and he knew deep down that it wasn't the right fit. He also knew deep down that the uncomfortable pulling sensation was getting worse. He needed to move faster while he could still withstand the sensation.

The next version of himself wore crimson scale mail with a helmet that covered his entire face and was stylized after a dragon. In his hand was a lance easily twice as long as the Tridory, but he hefted it without any hint of unwieldiness. Despite the discomfort of the situation, Arche's interest was piqued.

Dragoon

The path of the dragoon is one that has nearly fallen back into legend.
These warriors gain their strength from the bond they form with dragons. They are protector and enforcer and are elevated beyond the squabbles of their fellow humanoids, having been granted a small degree of enlightenment on their journey. To fight a dragoon is often to invite death from above, as each dragoon is empowered with abilities from their bonded dragon, but you might just have to fight the dragon as well.

This profession favors those who seek a higher calling and who wish to seek out life above the clouds, and provides bonuses to **Strength**, **Dexterity**, **Agility**, and **Wisdom**.

This is a **Rare** profession.

Choose **Dragoon** as your profession?

Yes	No

Arche had no doubt this profession had only been revealed because he had gone through the Door of Hidden Potential. The other two Rare professions were great, but this was so obscure and enticing that he could easily have never come across it.

The major drawback was, of course, that he didn't know any dragons to bond with, and that was the lifeblood of this profession. It was great on paper, but the journey to find a dragon and bond it could take years, assuming he survived the process. No, circumstances did not favor this profession, even though it tugged at his heartstrings. Who wouldn't want a dragon friend?

Arche turned away from the clone and moved forward again, between the duelist and the dragoon, on to the next tier. With luck, tying the archetype to the dragoon might show him more professions that would otherwise be lost, but he wasn't quite willing to give up options similar to the duelist. His breath came in short gasps, like someone was pushing down on his diaphragm. Still, he managed to continue on and see the next set of professions waiting for him.

The first was a version of himself wielding two curved blades, more akin to scimitars than to kopides, and had him dressed in linen wraps. Most notably, his eyes glowed a soft blue. Taking a closer look revealed the profession itself.

Spellblade

The path of the spellblade is one of dedication and power.
These mystics empower their weaponry with magic, to devastating effect. Masters of a unique brand of enchanting, the spellblade can create their own weapons and can empower them with many specialized spells from every branch of magic.

This profession favors those who have a connection to both combat and magic, and provides bonuses to **Dexterity**, **Agility**, **Intelligence**, and **Wisdom**.

This is an **Epic** profession.

Choose **Spellblade** as your profession?

Yes	No

Arche's interest was piqued yet again. A spellblade sounded like the perfect mixture of physical combat and magical progression, but it had one glaring problem: Arche still didn't know any magic. Based on what Odelia and Abraxios had told him, magic was difficult to learn and fairly uncommon. There was no guarantee that picking the profession would teach him any spells or be of any immediate use to him. With some sadness, he moved on to the next profession.

This version of himself was dressed in thick, heavy armor emblazoned with numerous symbols. He wielded a greatsword easily larger than his entire body in one hand, while the other held a shield embossed with symbols similar to the ones adorning his armor. Strength and determination were evident on this double's face, but there was an additional shine in his eyes, something more akin to enlightenment.

Paladin

The path of the paladin is one of devotion.
These holy warriors use oaths made to an ideal to unleash power. Whether they lift a hand to heal or a fist to destroy, none can doubt the power that comes with this path. Through faith and devotion to specific tenants, the paladin can singlehandedly accomplish what entire kingdoms cannot.

This profession favors those who have a connection to something greater than oneself, and provides bonuses to **Strength**, **Fortitude**, and **Wisdom**.

This is an **Epic** profession.

Choose **Paladin** as your profession?

Yes	No

Arche frowned. Single-minded devotion to a single ideal was much too rigid for him. It had a simplistic side to it, and though there was clearly power in such simplicity, there was no room for nuance. For as much power and freedom as the profession would offer, it also restricted him into a very specific path. One that he wasn't sure he would like.

Still gasping for air, he moved on to look at the last profession of the tier. This one had him dressed in dark armor, with a face visor shaped like a grinning skull. A dark spear hung across his back and he exuded menace.

<table>
<tr><td colspan="2" align="center">Death Knight

The path of the death knight is one of power and perseverance.
These knights have turned to necromancy as a source for power, in augmentation of their physical selves. Through ritualistic practices in which they kill and reanimate portions of their bodies, the death knight conquers both life and death. Notoriously difficult to kill, death knights are often outcast from civilized society, finding welcome with other denizens of undeath.

This profession favors those who seek power and dominance over death, and provides bonuses to Strength, Endurance, Fortitude, and Intelligence.

This is an Epic profession.</td></tr>
<tr><td colspan="2" align="center">Choose Death Knight as your profession?</td></tr>
<tr><td align="center">Yes</td><td align="center">No</td></tr>
</table>

Arche turned away from the Death Knight immediately. He hadn't found a profession that suited him just yet, but there was nearly nothing about the class that reflected him, aside from the bonus to his attributes. Still, the Door of Hidden Potential must have seen something down that path that would call to him and the mastery over death was something that deeply interested him, but using necromancy was the wrong way to go about it. He could still see Lyssa's reaction to it in the Necropolis of Pygmaia. It was clear the practice was abhorred and pursuing it would likely drive a wedge between them, something he was not willing to risk to satisfy his own fears.

With this tier out, the only path left was forward. Arche considered for a moment which profession to progress past, knowing that each one influenced the other options he would get. Death Knight was out, so would he progress past Spellblade to get more magically inclined options, or go with Paladin? The choice was hefty but the lasso around his organs told him to choose quickly. More spell-based professions would still have the issue that he didn't know any magic, so he moved past the Paladin, hoping the tier beyond it would have whatever he was looking for.

With every step, the feelings of discomfort intensified. Each movement was stiff and dragging, as though he were wading through mud as he forced himself onward. The twisting of his bowels made him gag and retch. His mouth and throat filled with spit, ready for him to vomit up his guts.

As he readied himself to give up, three figures were, at last, revealed by the void. Arche turned to the first, his vision swimming. The clone's robes constantly flickered and changed colors. Blue, then red, then purple, then yellow, then green, then black, then starting all over again in a kaleidoscope of color. It was doing nothing to reassure his stomach. There was a round sigil on the profession's chest but it was empty and smooth, as if waiting for something to be engraved.

<table>
<tr><td colspan="2" align="center">Acolyte</td></tr>
<tr><td colspan="2" align="center">The path of the acolyte is one of service and devotion.
The gods, distantly removed as they are, are still holders of great and divine powers which they bestow onto their champions. Dedicating oneself in service to a god and gaining their blessing is required in becoming an Acolyte, which will unlock a sect of Divine Magic congruent with their patron. This profession is a relationship, as opposed to a bond or pact, and can be lost if the Acolyte falls out of favor with their chosen deity.

This profession favors those who wish for guidance and reassurance in a chaotic world, and grants bonuses and reductions dependent on the chosen deity.

This is a Legendary profession.</td></tr>
<tr><td colspan="2" align="center">Choose Acolyte as your profession?</td></tr>
<tr><td align="center">Yes</td><td align="center">No</td></tr>
</table>

Divine Magic? Like his Divine Body skill? Arche reeled from the implications and from the metaphysical hooks in his organs. This profession might give him answers but it had already given him something to look into. He would find out who these 'gods' were and, if he was lucky, find some answers about himself along the way. However, he couldn't, or wouldn't, do that by making himself beholden to such a thing.

Arche turned toward the next version of himself. At first, it appeared normal, wearing simple, form-fitting clothing. Then he realized there were aspects of it that were not altogether human. The eyes were yellow instead of brown, the teeth and fingernails were long and pointed. The doppelganger's skin was mildly reflective and had small, flesh-colored scales. It was hard not to be a little repulsed.

Summoner

The path of the summoner is one of experimentation and dedication.
This profession has long lied dormant despite the great powers it grants to those brave enough to choose it. Summoners have the ability to siphon the essences of creatures they kill and, upon gaining enough mastery, can augment their own abilities with the aspects of those essences. The most powerful summoners can create minions out of those essences and enchant them with life, for a time, or bind magical creatures in servitude, answering to the summoner's whims. This profession favors those who desire power and aren't afraid to make sacrifices to get it.

This profession provides bonuses to **Intelligence**, **Wisdom**, **Willpower**. Additional bonuses or reductions may be provided by this profession based on chosen augmentations.

This is a **Legendary** profession.

Choose **Summoner** as your profession?

Yes	No

Arche turned away. He wanted to be powerful, yes, but this was a step too far. The body augmentations were reminiscent of the Beastmar and the latter half of the description mentioned the enslavement of magical creatures. No, it was too geared toward corruption, if not of mind, then of morals. The thought of it made Arche queasy, though that may have been his squirming insides.

The last version of himself stood without armor or weapons, only simple robes. Looking at it in comparison to the others, he was almost disappointed with how normal it seemed, considering he was on the 'legendary' tier of professions. The identifying notification left his preconceived notions to rot.

Battle Lord

The path of the battle lord is one of devastation and beauty.
A battle lord can master any weapon, including themselves, and can lead a small force into overwhelming odds and emerge the victor. Combat comes easy to them, leading is like breathing, and death follows any foolish enough to stand in their way.

This profession favors those who wish to lead and who wish to master any combat form they choose, and provides bonuses to **Strength**, **Dexterity**, **Agility**, **Endurance**, and **Charisma**.

This is a **Legendary** profession.

Choose **Battle Lord** as your profession?

Yes	No

This was a profession he could wield. One strong enough to change the world. But was that what he wanted to be remembered as? One who killed and compelled others to kill? Arche wasn't sure, but there were no more figures beyond, no higher tiers to climb to. He had to make a choice because just standing still was an effort. If he lowered his guard, he was certain that whatever was pulling on his center would snatch him back to the beginning and he would either have to choose one of the Common professions or suffer this fate all over again, if the choices would even remain the same. The figures in the void had seemed to be moving, after all.

Arche gnashed his teeth. He felt like he was missing something, something huge. Each of these Legendary professions promised power he could barely comprehend, but they were all wrong. All of them. The door had said his choices would be tailored to him but there hadn't been a perfect fit.

That either meant he had no true profession or he hadn't yet reached the end.

Arche took a step forward and bile forced its way up his throat. He coughed, splattering yellow into the void as his body shook from the effort, but he kept moving forward. His vision faded around the edges as invisible, serrated hooks latched themselves into him, pulling him backwards, but he held to what he was doing with single-minded determination to keep his consciousness from slipping. He stumbled, now side-long with the Battle Lord, and fell. Every muscle spasmed and trembled. His nerves fired sporadically, making him twitch, writhe, and convulse from pain. Still, between juddering movements and shakes, he clawed his way forward.

Arche reached his hand past the Battle Lord and two figures appeared. There had been no silhouette, no indication that they had ever been there. One moment: nothingness, void. The next, beautiful existence.

Unlike the others, these moved. They stepped forward together and lifted Arche onto his feet, carrying him forward. One wore a strange set of armor and had an aura of power. The other wore the same crude clothing as Arche, but cleaner. His skin glowed faintly, seemingly of its own accord, gently shifting colors.

The glowing double raised a hand and pointed toward Arche's chest. The gesture looked almost like he wanted to shake Arche's hand but it was too close and too high for him to grasp comfortably. The hand exploded with light, blinding him, who was already struggling to stay conscious.

Arche screwed his eyes shut, feeling the burn of more bile forcing its way up his throat. Something shifted in his chest and he peeked one eye open, seeing that the light had faded somewhat. The glowing version of himself had stuck his hand into Arche's chest and was fishing about for something.

The sight of this was more than Arche could take and he barely managed to twist his head to the side before vomiting yet again. The pulling feeling in his center faded. Arche took a deep, shuddering breath and found that other than the remnants of an irritated throat, he felt fine. The figures stepped away from him and simply stared at him.

"Thanks," Arche muttered, not able to speak any louder.

The figures did not respond. Now that he was no longer being wrenched back by the hooks, they stood unnaturally still, like the other versions he had already passed. He looked at the figure in armor, the one that had reached him first.

Ancient Hero

The path of the Ancient Hero is one that has never been walked in Tartarus.
Elsewhere, they have accomplished incredible feats, slain terrible monsters, and performed great acts of service, tales of which still live on, thousands of years later. This profession favors those who are willing to do what is good for all of Tartarus, even if it comes at great risk to themselves.

This profession provides a bonus to all attributes.

This is a **Mythic** profession.

Choose **Ancient Hero** as your profession?

| Yes | No |

Arche was stunned. It was an incredible choice. A boost to every attribute and a promise that his name would live on long after he died. That was hard for anyone to turn down.

He turned his eyes to the glowing figure.

Demigod

The path of the Demigod is often thrust upon the individual, not chosen.
Perhaps somewhere in your family lineage a deity was involved, or some deity sponsored you at some point during your life. Whatever the case, you have been given some degree of Divinity and unlocked access to this profession. Further travel down this path will reveal what powers lie dormant within you but have caution. Some will hate you for what you are, others will resent the attention you receive, and still others will want to use you for their own ends. This power is yours, however, and though it must be awakened fully before you can gain the benefits of this profession, it cannot be taken away from you.

This profession provides a bonus to all attributes.

This is a **Mythic** profession.

Choose **Demigod** as your profession?

| Yes | No |

Arche's breath caught in his throat. Finally, a path toward answers. The profession wasn't just incredibly powerful, but it encouraged—no, *rewarded*—him for learning more about himself. The choice, at last, was obvious. He wasn't here for power, glory, or fame. More than anything, he wanted to know who he was and why he was here. If a god had been involved in his life at some point, no matter how distantly removed, that was a start. Maybe they could provide him with answers if he found them.

"Yes," Arche said to the void. "I am a demigod."

All the various versions of himself faded into smoke, reabsorbed by the void. Arche was met by a sudden barrage of notifications.

You have chosen the **Demigod** profession, a **Mythic** profession.

Unlocking your Profession…

Error!
*Subject does not possess fully awakened **Divinity**.*

Error!
No deity bypass observed.

Error!
Parameters not met, engaging system backup.

You have been ~~offer~~[*e/r*] <u>given</u> a **Profession Quest**.

Unlocking Your Potential

You must complete the quest in order to claim your profession.
All leveling will be halted until you have claimed your profession.

Objectives	Rewards
- Reach a Divinity of 100% (20/100) - Do not die	- Claim your profession

Accept this **Quest**?	
Yes	Yes

Quest Accepted

Profession Unlock parameters defined…

*Returning to **Tartarus**…*

Initializing…

3…

2…

1…

Welcome back.

Chapter 28

Arche opened his eyes. He was on his back, dazed and in more than a little pain. Thankfully, the feeling didn't last long. Soft, greenish-yellow light surrounded him. The faint scent of flowers filled the otherwise musty room.

"Are you all right?" Lyssa asked.

"I...I think so?"

"You got a profession, didn't you?" Tess said. "Picked an interesting time to do your Professing."

It wasn't a question but Arche nodded anyway.

"Yeah. But that doesn't matter right now, it's locked behind a quest. Is everyone all right?"

Odelia took that opportunity to pipe up. "Nothing ten minutes or so can't fix. I think we're mostly surface wounds."

"Speak for yourself," Abraxios said, lifting up one wing to show the wilted and singed feathers. "This kind of damage will take weeks to fix. I won't fly right until I've had a chance to molt. I really thought it had us there."

The tengu gave Arche a sidelong look. "That is, until you did...whatever it is that you did."

"Divine Body," Tess said in a playfully deep voice, waving her hands in a foul mimicry of Arche. "It makes me strong and dumb."

"Hey," Arche replied, feigning annoyance. "I don't need any skills to be dumb."

"Don't I know it," Lyssa muttered.

"Hey!" Arche held up a hand to stop further banter. "How long was I out?"

"Only a minute or two," Odelia reassured him.

"We need to plan our next move." Lyssa moved to the destroyed wall.

She peeked into the adjoining passageway, cocking her head to listen for the sounds of approaching beastmar. Satisfied, she returned, shaking her head to indicate a lack of alarm.

"We still haven't figured out what the beastmar are planning or how to put a stop to it. That's our number one priority." Arche eased himself upright and found a seat on the rubble as Odelia moved back and forth between the rest of the party, using her biomancy to seal open wounds with a yellow glow.

"I think we need to go farther down, as much as I hate to say it," Abraxios chimed in. "When I scouted it out before, I saw a lot of passages far below. This place is big and being entirely underground means it's probably bigger than any of us know."

"We could take a beastmar captive, next we fight them, and make them take us to their leaders," Arche suggested.

"Absolutely not," Lyssa replied.

Arche looked at the Huntress in surprise.

"Something the matter?"

"They're abominations."

"And you're not willing to even consider that we use one to our advantage?"

"How would we know that it isn't walking us into a trap? That it wouldn't gladly throw away its life to kill us?"

Arche thought about that for a moment.

"Well, no way of knowing about a trap, but the ones from before ran away when the chímaira showed up, so they clearly have some sense of self-preservation."

"They fear fire," Abraxios said. "Many of them hesitated to enter when the oil was ignited, and several cried out who were not caught in the mess."

"Shit, I forgot about that. What happened to the fire?"

"It's buried beneath a thousand kilos of stone. If it hasn't smothered, it will burn itself out," Odelia replied.

"Wow, uh, a thousand. That's...a lot?"

The others rolled their eyes collectively. The synchronicity was impressive but they had other concerns.

"Anyway. Back on topic. Unless someone has a better idea than wandering these tunnels for days and hoping we don't get lost, I think our best bet is taking a prisoner and making them show or tell us where to find the rest."

Lyssa frowned but said nothing. No one else objected.

"All right, good talk."

Arche stood, still feeling unsteady. Odelia had done much to heal him, but with his profession locked behind a quest, he still hadn't been able to level. His Stamina and Mana were low.

The others stood as well, Odelia having seen to it that everyone was fully healed.

"So, who's ready to make some noise?"

"One moment." Lyssa knelt and touched the corpse of the chímaira.

A moment later, the chímaira sagged inwards into itself, its hide and all heads gone, along with several other various body parts. Arche balked slightly at the display, wondering how high Lyssa's Skinning skill was that she could skip the process at, presumably, no loss in quality. She noticed him gawking and raised an eyebrow in response.

"I'm a Huntress, what did you expect?"

"No, you're right. You're absolutely right. I should have seen that coming."

They filed out into the passageway, heading away from the cave-in Arche had caused. They walked for longer than was necessary, each of them wanting to put the room behind them. Arche led the way as he was best suited for front-line combat. It was also his idea, so he felt it was only fair that he be the tip of the spear. As he walked, his thoughts turned to levels.

Arche vaguely remembered Lyssa mentioning levels were harder to get once someone chose a profession. His Slayer of the Mighty Trait had made leveling a breeze, so far, but that was only for as long as he fought and personally killed creatures that were a higher level than him. As it stood, his profession was locked until he increased his Divinity, whatever that was.

It had to have something to do with his Divine Body skill, but he didn't get the feeling the relationship would be quite so straight forward as leveling it. It could be tied to the skill itself, the number of times he activated it, how long in total he had channeled it, learning more about how it worked, the circumstances in which he used it, or any number of other factors. There was no telling without trial and error, and the last thing he wanted to deal with was more Mana Burnout, especially after Odelia's and Abraxios's warnings that improper usage could kill him or cause irreparable damage. There would be no quick fix leveling to save him until he had unlocked his profession.

There was one silver lining about the whole situation. For as long as his level was capped at fifteen, monsters that he killed that were stronger would give him bonus experience, which would all come rushing back to him upon completion of his profession quest. There was a tightrope to power in front of him: hunt and kill dangerous creatures, but don't die while doing it. It wouldn't be easy, but it could be lucrative. Arche shelved those thoughts for another time. Power had never been his goal and it was time to focus.

"All right, this should be far enough," he said, coming to a stop. "How are we going to draw them out?"

Abraxios parted his beak in a strange, avian smile.

"Just leave that to me."

The tengu stepped forward, in front of Arche and several steps past. The tengu held his wings out to either side, the feathers brushing against the wall. Then he brought his hands together in a thunderous clap accompanied by a fierce cry that echoed throughout the enclosed stone space.

Arche opened his mouth in an alarmed shout but couldn't hear any noise come out. The world had gone from unthinkably loud to eerily quiet in the space of a breath. Abraxios snapped two taloned fingers together and the noise returned.

"Sorry," the tengu said. "I forget you wingless ones have never braced a thunderstorm."

"Of course we have," Lyssa replied, her eyes still closed as she massaged what was left of her ears. "They're not that uncommon."

"I meant from inside the clouds."

"All right, enough with the humble-brags," Arche cut in. "Did it work?"

Abraxios nodded. "Oh, yes. Those who were not stunned upon hearing it will come to investigate."

"Great. I guess this is a bad time to ask what happens if too many come."

"If too many come," Odelia said wearily. "Then I will cave in the passage."

"Perfect," Tess sang with a fake smile. "Because that won't be problematic in any way."

Arche moved to the front of the group and readied himself, bouncing on his toes. After being relatively helpless for most of the previous fight, he felt restless. More than that, he felt angry. He'd been forced to sit and watch, drained of everything, as his friends had fought and almost died against overwhelming odds. He'd been helpless to stop it. Worse than helpless, they'd had to worry about protecting *him*. His presence had been actively bad for them.

Not this time.

Arche hefted the Tridory into an overhand stance with white knuckles as he heard the scrabbling of too many feet in the distance, echoing down the passage toward them. Adrenaline and anger mixed deep in his belly, creating a hot blend that traveled throughout his entire body. He was glad they were coming. Glad he had something to fight. Something he didn't have to hold back on. Something to slaughter. It was time to paint the caves with their blood. Time to revel in their massacre.

Arche didn't know when he had started moving, but he found himself running through the passage. The others called out his name from behind, shouting for him to stop, to come back, but there was a pulse in his veins that spurred him on, a thrill. His blood was up and his vision was red. What lay ahead was the answer to all his problems, for the time being. The enemy was approaching and he was ready for them. Here, at last, was something he could do.

Something he could kill.

Arche rounded a bend in the passage and saw the beastmar approaching. The passage was long and straight, thirty paces at a glance, and wide enough that two of the multi-legged beastmar could run abreast, or three of the normally proportioned ones, but they would have great difficulty fighting on top of one another. Arche dug inside himself and channeled a sliver of his Divine Body skill, directing it into his arm. His arm glowed with a bright, red light, lighting up the passage. He skipped a step and threw the Tridory. With his suddenly enhanced Strength, the trident flew impossibly far for how short the ceiling was and punched through the first beastmar unfortunate enough to block its path.

The line of advancing beastmar buckled as those rushing behind tripped over their fallen comrades. Arche never stopped, continuing his rush forward. With a small expenditure of Mana, the Tridory flew back toward his open hand as he closed the distance, dripping with black gore.

An arrow sped past his head, burying itself into the throat of a beastmar and it went down in a tumble of flailing legs. Arche slammed into the horde, thrusting and stabbing with his spear before turning it like a quarterstaff to block or displace. As confined as the passage was, the stack of injured or dead beastmar slowed the rest down, who pushed against their brethren, knocking them off balance in turn and making them easy prey to Arche's spear.

And prey they were. Hot anger flooded Arche's hands and feet, giving him strength. Everything, every repressed emotion came tearing out of him with frightening intensity. The beastmar were strong and hateful, but most were not especially fast. Arche wielded the Tridory in both hands, constantly adjusting his grip to change his reach. One moment, he was fully extended to tear out a beastmar's throat, the next he was right up on them, hand practically gripping the blade as he used the Tridory to disembowel, to stab, to rip. Tess appeared beside him, adjusting her movements to flow with his as her daggers made short work of anything that slipped inside of his spear.

"Malaka! What is wrong with you?"

Her voice was quiet beneath the blood pumping through him. It didn't matter. There were beastmar to slay. Arche thrust forward at a relatively humanoid beastmar wielding a large kopis. The beastmar deflected the spear thrust to the side and into one of its allies, before sliding the small sword against the shaft and toward Arche. Arche let go with one hand, channeled Divine Body into his arm, and lashed out with his fist faster than the beastmar had expected.

Crimson light bathed the narrow corridor.

The creature brought the kopis up into the path of Arche's fist. Arche saw the motion and snarled. A little bit of steel against the full weight of his Divine Body? Child's play. He threw even more Mana into his fist and pushed through. Knuckle met blade and persevered. The sword shattered and Arche's fist continued through, found the beastmar's face, and shattered that as well.

He deactivated the skill a moment later, his Mana flagging at less than half. With it gone, much of Arche's anger faded as well. It washed out of him, leaving him cold and tired. Still, the beastmar came.

The full weight of his stupidity bore down on him. He'd abandoned his allies and rushed toward the enemy, giving up any strategic position they might have had and forcing the rest to follow along after him or abandon him to a deserved fate. Stupidity was too kind a word.

"You're right to be mad," he grunted, narrowly blocking a spear thrust. "I shouldn't have run off. I couldn't stop."

"What are you talking about?" Tess spun behind Arche and came up on his other side, driving a dagger into a beastmar's armpit.

"Later, please."

He thrust the Tridory up toward the necks of a two-headed beastmar, but somehow managed to thread both through the prongs of the spear instead of skewering them.

With the press of a button, both heads were severed as the trident condensed back into a single-pointed spear.

"No! No, we cannot finish this later. Why are you being so reckless? This isn't just your life down here. All of us followed you and I want to know that you're not leading us to our deaths."

Arche hesitated, just for a moment. It was enough for a beastmar to rake its claws down his arm, drawing hot blood. He stabbed it through the face in response but the damage was done.

"Not intentionally."

An arrow skipped off the ceiling and hit a beastmar in the eye, making it howl and scrabble at its face even as Arche stabbed it in the chest. He almost missed the opening, as distracted as he was.

"Holy shit, what a *shot!*"

Even as it fell, another took its place in what seemed an endless supply. Arche gnashed his teeth, feeling the fighting spirit rise again. A thin wind blew around him and Tess, buoying them and making their movements faster and more precise.

"How many are left, can you tell?" Arche gasped, his attention completely taken by a beastmar with two spears that was trying its best to turn him into a kebab. One of the spears slashed his leg, but he managed to pin the other to the wall with one arm and slam the blade of the Tridory into the beastmar's chest.

A large fist emerged from the swelling mass of beastmar and collided against Arche's chest, knocking him back and off his feet. The Tridory ripped free from his hand, lodged in the ribcage of the beastmar he had killed. Tess danced backwards toward him, trying to slow the press of monsters but she couldn't keep them at bay by herself.

"Eight." Tess ducked a swipe from a hand that had at least seventeen claws.

She twisted to the side and stepped off the wall in a graceful maneuver that let her reach high enough to slash the throat of the beastmar towering above her.

"Seven."

Arche got to his feet. He drew his xiphos in a fluid motion, then jumped back into the fight.

"On your left!"

He wished, not for the first time, that he had picked up a shield somewhere along his journey, but he had to make do with what he had. Activating his Power Attack maneuver, he brought his forearm up and channeled Divine Body to give him the extra strength needed to arrest one beastmar's arm against the wall. He brought his sword down and managed to sever the entire arm.

The beastmar screeched but Arche wasn't done. Twisting and thrusting the xiphos into the creature's other shoulder, Arche severed the tendons and rendered the limb useless. The beastmar lunged toward him, trying to bite him with a face that was a foul cross between a man and a frog. Arche lost his footing and landed on his back. The beastmar descended onto him, biting and gnashing. Arche grabbed it by the throat to keep it from tearing into his face and used his feet to kick it over his head, back toward Lyssa and the others behind him.

"Keep that one alive," he barked, not waiting to see if the others were listening.

The move had left Tess to fend for herself against two smaller beastmar simultaneously and their combined assault had proven more than the dexterous Rogue could handle. She let out a cry of pain as claws tore into her side, though she exacted her retribution in blood. Arche dropped the sword and summoned the Tridory to his hand. It impaled two beastmar as it flew to him, ripping through their bodies like they weren't even there. An expertly placed arrow from Lyssa took another in the throat, dropping it before it reached either of them.

Arche thrust his spear into a beastmar's stomach as Tess's throwing dagger caught the last in the throat. At long last, the fight they had picked was over. A host of notifications awaited Arche but he shelved them all for later. He picked up his fallen sword and placed it safely into his inventory. He winced at the few wounds he had accrued but none of them seemed serious. He was slowly staining his clothing red, but the bleeding was only trickling a few health every five seconds or so and would stop before long. Tess let out a wet, raspy cough.

Arche turned toward her and froze. The Tridory slipped from his hand and clattered against the floor.

The armor around her side had been torn open and there was a jagged slice of white poking through a gaping wound. One of her ribs had snapped away. Tess slid to the ground, both hands trying desperately to hold her insides back as a puddle of blood grew around her. Arche was at her side a moment later, his hands over hers.

"Fuck! No, no, no, no, no, stay with me."

He put pressure on the wound, his panic rising. This was far beyond anything he knew how to deal with.

"Odelia! Stay with me, Tess. *Odelia!*"

The halfling knelt next to Tess's other side, her hands weaving complex spell patterns. Tess's breathing grew ragged and painful. Her face quickly losing color. Arche kept his hands on the wound until Odelia pushed him out of the way. Brilliant light burst forth from the halfling's hands and sank into the gash in Tess's side. Arche held her hand, his eyes darting back and forth between the wound and her face.

This was his fault. All of it. Why had he run off? What possessed him to do something so fucking stupid?

Arche's stomach clenched as Odelia worked complex spell forms over and into the wound. He had been the one to rush forward, chasing some ridiculous feeling and desire to prove himself, and all it had done was endanger the lives of his friends. It had been reckless, stupid, and pointless. There had been no thought to it. None at all.

"Come on, please. Please, stay with me."

Tess's ashen face turned toward him, slack from exhaustion. Her lips twisted into a small smile, then her eyes closed.

"No, no, no, no..." Arche felt his throat start closing up.

"She's not dead," Odelia said quickly, still pumping golden Mana into the wound. "Just lost consciousness."

Arche felt a hand on his shoulder and looked up. At first, all he saw was a blur, but he blinked a few times and his vision cleared to see Lyssa standing next to him, her face creased in pity and compassion. Arche stood; Tess's hand fell limp into the dirt. He backed away, his breath coming in short spurts. Lyssa grabbed him by the shoulders and kept him from sliding back down to the ground.

"Calm, Arche. Calm yourself."

He barely heard the words. Tess's face, her slight smile, her blonde hair stained red, all of it was burned into his memory. Her blood coated his hands, as surely as if he had dealt the wound himself. It was too much. He couldn't...

The emerald light faded, startling Arche out of his spiral, and Odelia slumped to the ground, her Mana spent. The halfling took a couple labored breaths before speaking.

"I've done what I can to staunch the bleeding, but the wound is deep. It damaged several organs and I'm out of Mana. I'll continue doing all I can for her, but it's up to her, now."

Arche held his face in his hands.
"What did I do?"

Chapter 29

"Arche, it's not your—"

"Bullshit. Yes, it *fucking* is my fault."

They had retreated down the passage from the others. Not quite out of earshot, but far enough to not be in the way. Abraxios was keeping an eye on the beastmar they had captured and Odelia was tending to Tess, who had yet to regain consciousness. The Life Shaman's Mana regeneration was truly prodigious; it seemed she could cast a new healing spell every half minute, but even still, Tess's survival was a coin-toss.

"You need to be there for her."

"I'm the reason she's like this. The best thing for her is for me to stay away before I do any more harm."

Lyssa's eyes flashed with anger. Faster than Arche's eyes could track, she shoved him up against the wall and spoke with a grit to her voice that Arche had never heard before.

"You played a fool; this is the price. You don't get to run from that. Go to her, Arche. She needs you. Whatever happens, you will be there because she needs you to be there. She followed you this far, do not betray that."

If she hadn't pinned him to the wall, he would have crumpled. Everything had gone so wrong so quickly. He'd fucked up—*god*, he'd fucked up—and he couldn't explain to anybody, not even himself, why he'd done what he had. Things had gone well enough for so long that he'd forgotten how dangerous the world really was. Even after almost dying to the chímaira, even after all his close calls, he'd let himself get caught up in his emotions instead of thinking. Tess was paying the price when it should have been him lying on the floor, bleeding out.

Arche found his feet under him, took a shuddering breath, and nodded. Lyssa let him go, her own expression growing inscrutable. He followed her back to the others and sat on the stone floor, taking Tess's hand in his own again. Her skin was cool to the touch, as if she were already dead, but a subtle, arhythmic rise and fall in her chest showed she still lived. For the moment.

He pressed her hand to his chest with both of his, willing heat back into it. Helpless was too small a word for the emptiness inside of him. He felt small, like a child confronted by the inevitability of death. He wanted to retreat inside of himself, curl up and push everything out. He wanted it to be him on the ground, being operated on, so at least if he died it would have been his own fault and no one else would pay the price for his mistakes.

Cold droplets splashed across the back of his hands. Arche realized he was crying. He didn't know if he'd been crying the whole time or if he'd just started, but when he rubbed his face against his shoulder, his cheeks were slick. A flash of green light, another healing spell. Odelia's face was flushed and sweaty from the effort of constantly draining Mana, though her evident control and skill with magic must have staved away all risk of Mana Burnout.

The light triggered a memory, one Arche had almost forgotten. An experience from a dream, when he had met a strange figure who had extinguished a green candle from a world similar to Tartarus but not quite the same. Arche didn't know if he'd be able to contact the being, or even if it would be able to help, but it was something.

Arche rearranged himself into a poor-man's lotus position and straightened his spine. He held Tess's hand in his own, focusing the full extent of his attention on her. He tried to trace a path from his heart to hers, willing his mind to open up and accept her in its awareness, like it accepted the Tridory. When he called out to the spear to return to him, he got the vaguest sense of where it was. The slightest hint of direction, of something existing outside of himself. He tried to find Tess in that same way, calling to her with sheer will.

He had no idea if what he was attempting was even possible. He was skating by on half-baked instincts, desperation, and the barest seeds of hope he was too afraid to let grow. The alternative was to do nothing and that wasn't an option.

For several minutes, he felt nothing but her hand in his, her weak pulse beneath his fingers. Then his mind brushed against something. He felt her. She was an awareness on the edge of his mental boundaries. Her mind's walls were like stone but they were weak, deteriorating. His own were mud, shoddy and unkempt, but he could still feel her through them, however faintly. He focused on his own walls first, fashioning a gate that would allow him to exit and others to enter by his desire, and reinforced the walls around it, turning that portion of his mind into hardened stone. Strangely, his Mana dipped as he manipulated the mental construct. He felt he could continue strengthening the borders of his mind, but it would take considerable time and effort. Time he didn't have.

With a command, he lowered the gate to his mind and forced his consciousness to leave its safety, stepping out into the ephemeral nothingness that stood between his walls and Tess's. The negative space was unexpectedly aggressive in its expanse. Arche was struck with sudden fear as he became aware of the sheer expanse that awaited him in this new domain. It was almost enough to make him turn and bolt back into the safety of his mind, but his purpose kept him where he was. He forced himself closer to Tess's mental walls and reached out his consciousness to brush against them. They shuddered at his touch but he kept the contact, trying to project reassurance and support.

He felt instinctively that he would be able to break through her walls if he tried, given the weakness of her condition, but he also felt the shock from doing so could kill her. He was in the untested waters of ephemerality, where instinct and logic clashed. There were secrets out in the nothingness that could never be revealed in the physical world. He could discover things no mortal mind could conceive, but to go that far would be to lose himself as well, leaving his body behind forever without hope of ever finding his way back.

Arche ignored the impossibilities and focused on Tess's mind alone. He pushed more complex emotions toward her. His gratitude for sparing his life. His guilt for what had happened. His burning need to do something, anything, to help her. A few stone blocks tumbled away in front of him, leaving a gap large enough for him to slip inside.

Tess had let him in. That simple fact nearly broke him.

His consciousness filtered into her mind and her emotions washed over him. Fear was near the top. Fear of death, fear of pain, fear of betrayal, fear of being alone. All of it came crashing down on Arche's consciousness even as Tess herself appeared to be trying to hold it back, in vain.

'It's all right, Theresa. I'm here.'

Arche projected reassurance. He was with her, he wouldn't leave her. In those moments, he could hide nothing from her and she could hide nothing from him. Their lives coexisted. She saw his every memory, his every mistake and every triumph, from the time he had woken up in the woods to that very moment. She saw his profession trial and the choices he made, she saw his first encounter with Lyssa and how he'd nearly died to a diseased wolf, and she saw how he had stood up for Helwan and given him a chance when it would have been easy to let the satyr die.

In return, he saw her life. He saw her grow up in the house of a merchant lord, doted on by servants. Saw her rebelliousness as she would slip away from the house and her caretakers to go play in the city with her friends. Tasted the nectar of stolen fruit, pinched from stalls for childhood dares. Felt the deep laughs of clever jokes and the solemnity of pacts that only the young can make with their entire hearts.

He also saw darkness. A betrayal at the hands of her friends. She was stolen away and held for ransom against her father. She had been abused, tortured, and led to believe she would die. Two months she was kept captive, waiting for her father to rescue her, for his guards to come sweeping in and take her to safety. Her friends had used her trust to lure her somewhere her father couldn't find; their own fathers wrote the ransom note. Five thousand drachmae for her life. A life that was belittled and tortured with every passing day. A life that was violated and degraded. A life that came to wish for its own end.

She was twelve.

The ransom was paid and she was freed, but the scars were heavy upon her mind. She bore their weight everywhere. She did not eat, she did not speak. Sleep came only upon exhaustion's beckoning and it was restless. Her father was patient with her, at first, but grew angry by her sixteenth birthday. He didn't understand how deep the scars went. Didn't understand how shattered Theresa's mind had become. All he knew was the price he had paid and that what he'd received wasn't the same girl that had been stolen. She felt her father's resentment for what had become of her and Arche felt it through her.

At seventeen, she left her father's house.

She wandered the streets for days, sleeping in alleyways and stealing from stalls like she had as a child, but she did not go unnoticed. The local thieves' guild, Hekatonkheires, had taken an interest in her and sent her an invitation. Here, the memories became shiny, hopeful. She had joined, reluctantly at first, but grew to appreciate what they provided her with. They taught her skills and gave her the confidence she needed to look after herself. She had forced herself to be strong, to be self-reliant, because she never forgot what had been done to her, and she never trusted anyone the way she had trusted her childhood friends.

Ten years passed as she worked for the Hekatonkheires, then the guild was attacked by a rival, the Keres, and her chapter was destroyed. Theresa had barely escaped with her life. She spent the next year scrounging up what she could, running from the Keres, who still tried to hunt her down, and finally found a place in the expedition to create the village of Buton. The shininess faded.

Arche saw Callias Buteo approach Tess, offering her coin and an ultimatum. Kill Arche and be paid a hefty sum or be left to fend for herself once again. So far from the city, the only home she knew, she had no choice. The forest was a death sentence. She knew nothing of Arche, either, other than that he had shown up and fought. It was his life or hers, and she had long since refused to place other lives above hers. He saw the party from her perspective, how she had maneuvered drinks into his hands, danced with him, led him away from the party and the prying eyes of Lyssa. How she had waited until he'd passed out, robbed him, then dragged him deep into the forest where none would find his body.

Then she had made her fatal mistake. Instead of simply killing Arche, she had decided to speak with him first. She was a thief, not a killer, and she needed reassurance that Arche deserved the fate coming to him. After their talk, she had decided he didn't.

Then he had saved her, both from the mantikhoras and the forest itself, when she was too weak to carry herself back to the village. Saved her when it would have been the easiest thing in the world to let her die. When she would have deserved it. When she would have done it, had their positions been reversed.

There was an emotion wrapped up in that memory. One too complex and ethereal for Arche to recognize, but it was strong. Joy and fear, guilt and attraction. All roiled together in a seething mass, until he couldn't tell them apart anymore.

Arche's heart broke for her, for the struggle that had been her life. He didn't know if she had shared her life purposefully or if it had been a side-effect of allowing his consciousness into her mind, but he was grateful for the trust. Now that he was here, he was unsure of what to do, but he knew he needed to find a way of contacting that being. The one that claimed to be Death. He reached his consciousness out toward the world he had only seen in his dreams.

At first, nothing happened. Then, slowly, he felt his consciousness bleed into that strange world. Tartarus, but not Tartarus. Arche's eyes opened and he became aware that, for the first time in several minutes, his consciousness was connected to a body. He stood, trying to get a sense of his surroundings.

He was still underground, but the rock was red instead of gray. The passage continued for a long way in both directions before eventually disappearing into nothing. Several dim, green candles floated around him.

"What's going on? Why can't I see my vitals?"

Arche turned and found Tess lying on the ground. Her positioning was the same as it had been but she was conscious and moving. Her armor was gone, replaced by the same crude, white clothing that Arche also wore. He helped her to her feet.

"I entered this world once in a dream and saw a creature here that affected the dead. It was the only thing I could think of that might help."

"I'm...dead, then."

"Not if I can help it. I didn't actually know you would come here, too. Not quite sure how I managed that. Not quite sure how I got here myself, actually. As far as I know, I didn't fall asleep."

Tess looked at him for a moment, then nodded as if to herself.

"That was you, in my head. I didn't know if I had dreamed it." Her face fell. "So...you saw."

"I did. I'm sorry."

Tess turned away.

"I suppose that was my choice. I didn't want to die alone. Sorry you had to see all that, bet it wasn't what you were expecting."

"I...I know it doesn't mean anything coming from me, but it wasn't your fault. Any of it."

Tess looked at him, eyes wide and discerning. She cocked her head and gave him a small smile.

"It doesn't mean nothing. I'm pretty sure I'm still dreaming, though."

"You should not be here."

The voice swept through them like a chill wind. Arche and Tess whirled to find a figure standing near them. An amorphous helmet covered its face, shifting between humanoid features and a smooth, metallic surface. Two eyeholes cut deep into the mask, the only permanent blemish. Arche shuddered under the weight of Death's glare. Two white pupils surrounded by sclera as black as the void. The figure took a single step toward them, its interlocking black metal plated armor making a chinking noise as it moved. The black cape at its back billowed despite the lack of wind.

"You said that last time," Arche said as the being advanced.

"It was true then. It is true now."

The entity's voice was mellow and smooth, like it had lived a thousand lifetimes and was now simply bored. No, bored implied it had something better to do. It was as if the creature cared for nothing, despite the words it spoke.

"Arche, who is that?" Tess's voice quavered as she spoke, a sound that Arche had never heard from the normally implacable woman.

"I am the end that comes for all things. I am become Death."

The being said this plainly, without boast or pride, as if they were simply commenting on the weather.

"And I have come for you, Theresa Eliades."

"No." Arche moved between them. "You want her, you go through me. I don't care if you are Death."

Death raised a gauntleted hand. Every muscle in Arche's body froze. His nerves fired erratically but he couldn't move despite every instinct telling him he'd been thrust into an ice bath of pointy needles. Death drew closer to him, peering at him with those horrible, inverted eyes, any emotion hidden behind the ever-shifting mask.

Arche was left with no choice but to stare back into the uncaring eyes in front of him as they searched his, seeming to scour into his very soul, which was a very real possibility. After several long moments, Death pulled away.

"You have fire, spirit. I can see why you were chosen. But this is not about you. Theresa Eliades, it is time."

"To...die?" Tess's voice shook. "I'm not ready."

"No one ever is, young one, but I come for them all, in the end."

Arche raged, still held prisoner in his own body. He was helpless, again, and the one being he had sought out to try to deal with was also the thing that was going to take Tess away. He struggled against the invisible chains binding him, but he couldn't even exert enough control over his own body to blink. There was a deep, aching, tearing pain in his chest as Death stepped past him.

Help me.

It was a desperate plea, laden with all the sorrow in Arche's heart, all the weight of his mistakes.

Help me. Please.

"What are you doing here?" Death's voice was confused, the first emotion the entity had shown, but Arche was grateful for the delay.

There was no reply that Arche could hear but Death responded anyway, as though carrying on a conversation.

"You are weak. Perhaps you have forgotten yourself. You should be resting with the others before I come for you myself. Again."

Silence again. Arche burned anew, this time with curiosity. Everything that was going on was happening behind him, and he could only hear part of the conversation. It was maddening.

"Speak not to me of the knave king. You would spend that debt now? For these mortals? Not even for your own life, but for theirs...very well. But know this: I shall grant it only this once. Interfere again, and I will come for you."

There was a sound like a flapping cape and Arche could move again. He whirled around, hoping to catch a glimpse of whoever had intervened on his behalf, but saw only Tess. She collapsed, apparently likewise frozen. Arche rushed to her side, scanning the passage to make sure that they were actually alone before returning his attention to her.

"What's wrong?"

"I can feel it," she hissed. "My side. Titan's Blood, it hurts. What happened? I don't understand."

"Death spared us, it seems. We can talk later; we should get back to the real world. I think this means you're going to live."

"Lucky me. Why did no one mention how much this was going to hurt?"

Tess groaned, loud and guttural. Her eyes clenched shut as her entire body seized. Arche grabbed her hand and tried to focus on returning to their bodies back to the tunnel with the others. He felt a pull in his center, not dissimilar to that from the Profession Trial, and succumbed to it. The world around him blurred and he shut his eyes against the motion.

He was floating in space.

No, not floating. He was *hurtling* through space. He could see nothing, feel nothing, but he knew he was traveling. Too much had happened in much too short a time for him to explore the feeling. He only hoped that wherever he landed, it wouldn't hurt.

Chapter 30

"Hold him steady, Lyssa. Don't let him crack his head against the floor!"

Arche tasted bile and blood. It seemed he had not only lost the contents of his stomach but had also apparently bitten his tongue. He also seized uncontrollably as his nerves and muscles fired rapidly and randomly, making him thrash about like a fish fresh off a line. Lyssa had one hand beneath his head and the other on his forehead, stopping him from busting open his skull as he convulsed. His mind already pounded and he wasn't in any hurry to see what kind of dent his face could put into solid stone.

"Calm yourself. You are in control. Exert your will."

Lyssa's quiet voice gave him something to hold onto. He flexed his inner will, feeling out the constraints of his own body in a similar way as when he had brushed against Tess's mind. He had an awareness of self that would have been unfathomable just an hour prior. The spasms dissipated as his mind felt the limits of his body and demanded it to fall in line.

As his movements calmed. Lyssa removed her hands from his head and let him sit up. Arche promptly twisted to the side and spat out a large globule of spit flecked with vomit and blood. The taste lingered, but he could live with that. He could even live with the pain of his lacerated tongue, which still bled, so long as it meant Tess was still alive. He turned toward her, worried about what he might find when he saw her.

Had he succeeded? Failed? Could he bear to know?

His eyes met hers and he let out a sigh of relief. Tess panted and grimaced with pain but was very much alive. Their eyes met and his blood froze. There was something there, deeper than the pain she was going through.

She was terrified of him and he had no idea why.

Arche looked away. Whatever was in her eyes wasn't something he could face. Not now. He waved off Lyssa's questions and sat against the wall opposite Tess, his head pounding mercilessly. A multitude of notifications flashed in the corner of his vision and he welcomed the distraction, turning away as Odelia went back to casting her healing spells.

You have learned a **Skill**.

Psychic Link — Level 1

Obol for your thoughts?

You have learned how to expand your consciousness past the confines of your own mind.
Pushing your consciousness in this way expends Mana over time.
Every 5 levels in this skill improves **Wisdom** and **Willpower** by 1.

-0.5% Mana Cost (-0.5%)

> You have discovered a **Trait**.
>
> **Psychic**
>
> You have the ability to glean insight into the world around you. The benefits of this ability may change depending on how you use it. Be warned, not everyone will take kindly to a surprise connection.
>
> +25% **Willpower**
> +10% **Charisma**

The new skill wasn't particularly surprising, given what he'd done, though he couldn't help but feel like he had been extremely lucky nothing had gone wrong. That space between his mind and Tess's had been terrifying. It would have been so easy to lose himself in that space, and their minds had practically been touching. He would have to be exceedingly careful using the skill going forward, but he resolved not to be so afraid of using it that he never learned to master it. It was his first epic-tier skill, if the color palate was anything to go by.

He had no idea what the limits of this new skill were and a similar idea of the dangers, but it was too enticing to not pursue, when he had the time.

> **Spearmanship** has increased to **Level 15**.
>
> +2% Damage with Spears (+30%)

> **Spear Throwing** has increased to **Level 8**.
>
> +3% Accuracy of Thrown Spears (+24%)
> +2% Range of Thrown Spears (+16%)

That was a bit of a surprise. Spearmanship and Spear Throwing had both gained multiple levels. Those were serious improvements from the fight, which was surprising, but it must have been a mixture between the fight itself and the tactics he had employed. Did he get more experience in skills by adjusting the circumstances in which he used those skills? It made a degree of sense, but it seemed very...esoteric.

Arche wondered if anyone studied the circumstances surrounding skill use and how it affected the improvements. He wished he had an idea of how much skill experience he actually had, that would have made calculating everything so much easier, but it would also distract him from things that were happening around him. One more rabbit hole to dive into.

He was faced again with the conundrum that had bothered him from the first skill he had learned in this world. He wanted desperately to know how everything worked and to figure out the most optimal way to master everything, but he didn't have the time or resources to dedicate to such study. There was too much he didn't know and he had barely scratched the surface. To make things worse, his personal progress would remain stagnant until he managed to unlock his Profession.

Arche continued looking through his notifications, realizing he had never looked at the after-action report from the fight. With a thought he pulled it up.

You have slain **12 Beastmar**.
Your Party has slain **26 Beastmar**.
You gain 5,420 experience.

Experience is held until your **Profession** is unlocked.

It was quite a bit of experience, but it may as well have been nothing. What meant the most was how many they had killed. Arche checked his quest progress, seeing that, indeed, thirty-eight beastmar had been killed, with the thirty-ninth having become their prisoner.

Arche's gaze flicked to the injured beastmar. Its gaze was locked on him as it sat against the wall, its one remaining arm limp from where Arche's sword had severed the nerves. Abraxios was keeping an eye on it, ready to blast it with lightning if it moved too quickly.

The beastmar had dark, gray fur and lighter skin. It regarded Arche with fear and fury. He had crippled it and it knew that its life was likely soon to be over, but it had the intelligence to hate him for it. Arche could use that. He wasn't quite ready to interrogate it for all it knew, though. He needed a few more minutes for himself and there was no way that Lyssa would let him move on without him explaining what he'd done. As it was, she was helping Odelia treat Tess, but she was throwing glances back toward him, which he did his best to ignore.

A few notifications still flashed in his vision so he pulled them up.

Divine Body has increased to **Level 12**.

Divinity has increased to **25%**.

Arche froze, staring at the last message. His Divinity had increased, but how? Was it because he'd leveled his Divine Body skill or was it because of what he'd done for Tess?

"Fuck me, just more questions," he muttered, rubbing his eyes.

It was a good thing, he decided, because he was closer to getting his profession, but he only had a general idea of what to do to increase this new parameter and he sincerely hoped he wouldn't have to petition extraplanar entities on the regular just to unlock his own powers.

That would be unfair, not to mention time-consuming.

A pair of legs stood in front of him. Looking up, he met Lyssa's green eyes boring into his own. They left no room for his protestations, so he let out a breath and let her pull him to his feet.

"What happened?" she asked, her voice made it clear that she would accept no distractions until she got answers.

"A lot, and I don't understand the half of it."

"Then start with what you do."

Arche took a deep breath.

"All right. So you know how I used to have bad dreams? Sometimes in dreams I see a different world. It seems to be parallel to this one and I've met people there. Well, people being a loose term because they seem more like super-powerful entities, maybe even deities."

"Deities?" Lyssa asked slowly, as if sounding out the word.

"You know, gods?"

"What's a god?"

Arche stared at her, his mouth slack.

"I...I don't know if I know how to explain that concept. Incredibly powerful beings? Creators and destroyers of life itself? Sound familiar?"

The look of absolute confusion on Lyssa's face was priceless. If Arche himself hadn't been so dumbfounded and confused himself, he would have burst out laughing. Instead, he was caught in a web of bewilderment to which he was actively contributing.

"Anyway, I met one harvesting the soul of a dying person back when we first found the village. Tess was dying, so I thought I would try to bargain with it for her life. Only problem was that at an earlier time I met another such entity that called itself the Oneiroi and it prevented me from traveling there in my sleep. Not to mention, I can't exactly fall asleep on command like that."

Lyssa blinked several times with each new wave of information.

"So if you couldn't get to that realm, what did you do?"

Arche shrugged.

"I tried. But first, I..." Arche paused.

Lyssa had warned him about traits and how it was dangerous to share if you had one. He trusted her implicitly, and the others he trusted with certain knowledge, but he had only really known Odelia and Abraxios for about a day. Tess, well, they had things to talk about when or if they ever got some privacy. Lyssa's initial warning about traits still echoed in his head, there were those that would try to kill him just for the chance at taking his traits.

Arche dropped his voice to an almost inaudible whisper, leaning in so that only Lyssa could hear.

"I discovered a new trait. Turns out I'm psychic."

Lyssa, to Arche's relief, didn't make a huge deal out of that information, but she did grab his arm and lead him down the passageway to have some privacy.

"Tell me everything."

"I've had a tenuous connection with the Tridory, but I thought that was just because I had bonded to it, but now I think that's only part of it. I managed to project my consciousness outside of my body and into Tess's."

Lyssa's fury was so sudden and great, that Arche tried to step back and smacked his head against the wall.

"You did *what?*"

Arche threw up his hands placatingly, hoping to cut off Lyssa's ire.

"I knocked. That was all. She chose to let me in."

Lyssa's face softened slightly, but her eyes still blazed.

"Proceed."

"After Tess let me in, I focused on what I remembered of that parallel world and that entity that I met. I managed to travel both of our consciousnesses there and was able to speak with the thing, which might be Death itself."

"Death is a person?" Lyssa frowned. "I'm not sure that's a reassuring thought."

"Definitely not, can attest. I initially intended to try bargaining with it but it made itself pretty clear from the get-go that it was there to collect her and wasn't going to be distracted. I interfered and it froze me, somehow. It was about to take her when someone else showed up. I couldn't see or hear them but Death spoke with them. Apparently, some favor was called in to spare us and that's when we woke up here."

"Something from that world intervened on your behalf and wouldn't let you see it? That's troubling."

"You're telling me." Arche looked back toward the others. "I think we need to finish our business here and get out. There will be some fallout with Callias because of the bounty-quest Theodorous gave us but I think we need some downtime to figure out what the fuck is going on and what we're going to do about it."

"Agreed." Lyssa rubbed her eyes. "I'm growing tired of this dungeon, it feels like for all we've gone through, we're no closer to reaching its end."

"Then let's get some answers and finish this fucking thing."

Arche took a step toward the beastmar but Lyssa grabbed his shoulder and held him back. He frowned a question at her but she met his eyes with a look of fierce determination.

"Allow me. I will question it; I want you to probe its mind."

Arche blinked in surprise.

"You want me to use my new trait to rip information from the mind of a prisoner without their consent?"

"Is that going to be a problem?"

Arche paused.

"Not this time, but I want to make sure you know what you're asking me to do."

Lyssa let out a sigh and nodded.

"I know, and I won't ever ask you to use it on a person, but my instincts tell me that thing will be either unwilling or unable to help us without your newfound insight."

"I'll follow your lead."

Lyssa turned and walked back to the others, making a beeline straight for the beastmar, who growled at her approach. Arche followed a half step behind, moving to stand next to the creature as Lyssa bore down on it. She withdrew a kopis from her inventory and held the curve of the blade against the beastmar's throat.

"Where is your leader?" Lyssa asked in a flat voice.

The beastmar continued its growl and made no effort to answer. It was mostly humanoid, despite elongated limbs it still had the basic assortment of two legs and two arms. Rather, it *had* two arms until it had attacked Arche.

Lyssa moved her sword down to the beastmar's exposed groin.

"Tell me where to find your leader, or I will cut you."

"Foolish she-elf," the beastmar spoke with a voice like falling stones. "The master will destroy you and all your ilk."

"The scum speaks. Wonderful. If you think your master can defeat us, then let him prove it. Tell us where to find him."

"You will die without ever seeing the light above. The darkness of our caverns will consume you. We will sup on your flesh and our newborns will suckle the milk of your bones."

Lyssa's gaze flicked toward Arche, who inhaled deeply and placed one hand on the beastmar's head. He extended his consciousness outwards, pushing against the gate he had constructed in his own mind and allowed his awareness to enter that space between minds. Once again, he felt the emptiness. A void that stretched beyond understanding, farther than even Tartarus could reach. Full of questions never voiced and answers that had transcended comprehension.

His consciousness brushed against the beastmar's mind as Lyssa threatened it again.

"This is your last chance before things get painful. Tell me what I want to know."

"My people will consume you. You think you scare me with threats of pain and death? You know nothing of my people, and soon you will know nothing but the taste of worms as they burrow into your corpses."

Arche didn't bother waiting for Lyssa to signal him. He hardened his consciousness into a point and attacked, battering against the mental walls of the beastmar. The beastmar reacted physically to Arche's assault, its defiant grin turning into a moan of anguish as Arche slammed his mind against the creature's mental defenses.

"Where is your leader? What do they have planned?"

With every strike against the mental walls Arche managed to map out more of the perimeter of the creature's mind. Like some strange form of echolocation, every strike brought back a host of information that Arche interpreted intuitively. The defenses of the beastmar's mind were not dissimilar from Arche's own, made from some kind of mud substance that chipped away with every strike.

It was a frightening mirror to his own mind. Arche promised himself that he would take the time to shore up his defenses when he next had the chance as the mud walls of the beastmar were barely keeping him at bay.

In less than a minute, he pierced the barrier, creating a small hole into the beastmar's mind. He kept striking, widening the hole until he could filter down his consciousness into smoke and slip through.

Sensation bombarded him. Memories bled through their newfound connection. Arche recoiled, trying to shove the memories away and erect a barrier around himself. It wasn't a counterattack, not exactly. It felt rather similar to what had happened with Theresa, but he didn't want to experience this creature's entire life. He was searching for very specific information and didn't care to learn about its formative years. One interesting piece of information, however, was that the creature had not been born a beastmar.

The awareness from back then was dim, almost a shadow, but from what Arche was able to piece together the beastmar was originally a creature called a troglodyte, a small, cave-dwelling creature with a strange insectoid diet that was apparently capable of running extremely quickly. Anything further, including how the troglodyte had become the beastmar, was blocked when Arche had erected the mental defenses around himself.

He'd managed to wall himself off before he shared anything of his own life with the creature, to his relief, but now he was encircled by a shoddy construction of mud with no awareness of what was going on in the mind outside. Arche pushed himself up against the barrier in all directions, forcing the mud to strengthen and reinforce itself, transmuting it into wood.

Arche pulled back, satisfied with the current strength of his mental fortifications despite the increased focus they now required. Narrowing his will, Arche focused on one small portion of the wall, forcing the wood to grow translucent and allow him a peephole to see. It took a considerable amount of effort and Arche didn't get it on his first try. Nor on his second, which nearly lost him the entire barrier, but on his third he managed to change a tiny piece of the wall and grow it until he had a translucent window the size of a porthole with which to look into the mind of the beastmar.

Now that he had no longer truly melded with the beastmar's mind, it appeared different. Rather than an ineffable, ethereal substance with which his own consciousness had permeated, the beastmar's life was spread before him like a twisting river of white-gold light that looped and twisted throughout. With some effort of focus, Arche was able to move his consciousness alongside the river, traveling forward through the beastmar's life without absorbing the memories within.

Shortly, he came upon a point where the white-gold light muddled into a blue-black mess. He knew he should keep going, that this was too far back in the beastmar's life to be relevant to their current situation, but curiosity got the better of him and he peered in at the river of this creature's memories, which flowed through the translucent wooden window he'd created and flooded his barrier.

Fire. Heat all around. Run. Needed to run. Friends ran. Family ran. Terror. Dark ones. Murder. Darkness. Fear. Pain. Captured. Taken away. Magic. Great magic. Powerful dark one. Torture. So much pain. Mangled limbs. Death.

Arche expelled the memory from his fortifications, his consciousness reeling from what he'd seen and felt. Someone had stolen this creature away and experimented on it, turning it into what it currently was. The 'how' was hazy, concerning some kind of magic he had never encountered before. The troglodyte had been transformed in what had clearly been a traumatic process that involved dying and being revived. The magic involved in that immediately made Arche worry because, so far, the only power that came close to that was wielded by the entities from the other world.

Arche filed the information away for later examination and continued traveling along the memory river, forcing his consciousness to fly quickly until he reached the near past. At a greatly enhanced speed, Arche sifted through the beastmar's memories, mapping out the dungeon as well as marking the areas they congregated in. He was careful to keep a leash on what he allowed in so it wouldn't overwhelm him. He was even more careful not to let anything about him pass back to the beastmar. It might have been paranoia but he had the feeling that, without his barrier, he would leave himself vulnerable to a counterattack, even if the mind he was invading wasn't inherently psychic.

Arche withdrew from the river of memories and floated to the edge of the beastmar's consciousness, searching for the breach he had made upon entering. He found the hole without much difficulty and squeezed his consciousness through, keeping hold on his defenses. The vastness of the empty space between minds called out to him again, trying to tempt him, but its ethereal voice was muted through his barrier. Relief flooded through him as he slipped back inside his own mind and shut the gate behind him.

Psychic Link has increased to **Level 2.**

-0.5% Mana Cost (-1%)

Arche opened his eyes to find everyone staring at him. The beastmar was in front of him, unconscious. He removed his hand from its head and it slumped to the ground. Arche met their eyes—all except Tess, who refused to look at him—and offered an uncomfortable smile.

"I know where we need to go."

Chapter 31

"Did you get what we needed?" Lyssa asked.

"Yeah, we need to—"

"No, I'm sorry, what was that?" Abraxios cut in.

Lyssa and Arche both turned to the tengu, whose head swiveled back and forth between them. Odelia looked uncomfortable but didn't say anything. Tess stared at the floor, trembling. She wasn't looking at anyone but it felt like she was especially not looking at Arche.

"I thought we were past the point of keeping secrets," the tengu continued. "And I thought we had made it clear. If we're going to do this together, we need to be honest with each other. I am willing to overlook certain...eccentricities, but that was abhorrent."

Odelia gave a small nod and Arche raised his hands placatingly.

"You're right. You're right and I'm sorry, that wasn't fair of me."

"Arche..." Lyssa warned.

Arche spread his arms wide to gesture at the passage around them.

"We trust them or we don't. If we want to finish what we started here, it will take all of us." He turned toward them. "I'm psychic. I found out when Tess and I woke up. I told Lyssa and she asked me to help get information from the beastmar. Now I'm telling all of you."

It did not escape Arche's notice that every person in the room stiffened at the word 'psychic.' Abraxios actually took a threatening step toward him, eyes narrowed in suspicion.

"Do you intend to harm anyone present?" the tengu asked.

Arche's blinked. He was so taken aback by the ridiculousness of the question that he forgot to answer until Abraxios made a trilling noise that must have been the bird-person equivalent of clearing one's throat.

"No," Arche said emphatically. "I don't want to hurt any of you. Look, I know I haven't made the best decisions while I've been down here, but really I just want to finish up these quests and head back to the village where maybe I can figure out some of the weird shit that's been happening to me."

Abraxios turned and nodded toward Odelia, then turned back to Arche and caught his eyes. Arche found the large, avian, yellow irises to be very arresting when the full weight of the tengu's glare was affixed to him.

"For now, I will trust you because you did not attempt to alter my thoughts. If you ever probe my mind without my consent, I will kill you. It will be swift and violent."

Arche shrugged.

"Yeah, no, that's fair. Loud and clear. You've got my word, I won't probe any of your minds without your consent. Now, can we all settle down so I can work on how we're going to pull this quest off?"

Odelia and Abraxios nodded, so Arche continued.

"All right. Does anyone have paper and something to write with? I've got a pretty good idea of the tunnel system, but I want to write it down while it's still fresh in my head."

"What about the beastmar?" Lyssa asked.

"Let me finish writing out the map," Arche said. "When I'm done, we can put him of his misery."

Lyssa nodded as Odelia produced a sheet of papyrus from her inventory and handed it over along with a short charcoal stick. Arche began outlining passages, noting the accompanying notification but dismissing it almost instantly to focus on what he was doing.

You have learned a **Skill**.

Drawing — Level 1

Whether it be sketching, doodling, or designing, this skill covers it all. Not to be confused with 'Painting.' That's totally different.

Each level in this skill improves your ability to draw.
Every 5 levels in this skill improves your **Dexterity** by 1.

+2% Speed of drawing (+2%)
+2% Quality of drawing (+2%)

By the time he finished the map, several minutes later, he'd gone up to level three and received yet another skill.

You have learned a **Skill**.

Cartography — Level 1

Mapmaking is a noble profession into which you have dipped your toes. The creation of maps is a highly sought-after but often very dangerous skill as the best maps are made from firsthand experience.

Each level in this map improves the quality of maps you can produce.
Every 5 levels in this skill improves your **Dexterity** and **Wisdom** by 1.

+2% Speed of mapping (+2%)
+2% Quality of mapping (+2%)

You have created a **Crude Map** of the **Vivitorium of Hekáte**.

"Here," he held the map up, calling the others over.

He spread it out in front of them and pointed toward a passage near the middle of the elaborate system of passages.

"This is us, here."

He dragged a finger down to a network of larger tunnels and caverns.

"And this is where the majority of the beastmar live. I'd estimate recent numbers to crest a hundred-fifty."

Lyssa bit her lip. "Too many," she muttered.

"Yes, but there's good news," Arche said. "That count is from about a week ago."

"Before the attacks on the village."

"And before the thirty-eight we've killed here."

"Thirty-nine."

Every head turned toward Tess. It was the first time she'd spoken since she woke up. Arche furrowed his brow, checking his two related quest logs to verify that the count stood at thirty-eight. Tess drew a knife and fell on the unconscious beastmar. The knife went up, down, up, down, stabbing throat and face, turning everything into a bloody mess.

Arche noted the fifty-two points of experience from the party kill and blinked away the notification, wishing his surprise was as easily dismissed. Everyone else was in as much shock as he was, eyes wide and mouths open as Tess dragged herself to her feet. Only Lyssa looked on with a grim smile.

Arche swallowed hard.

"All right. Thirty-nine. Erm, back to the plan...if we follow this route, we should get into the vicinity of these bigger rooms here within a couple hours. The beastmar roam around haphazardly, but often in smaller groups of five to seven. Given the recent number of killed beastmar, I'd estimate their numbers to be about five dozen. Still a lot, I know, but there's good odds they won't all be grouped together and that gives us a chance. For the most part, they don't use magic, so we have the advantage on that front.

"Unfortunately, this one didn't know what the chief was planning, so I couldn't scratch that off the list, but the chief will be in one of these larger rooms here. The chief isn't a magic user, but his right-hand beastmar is, so we'll need to be extra careful and try to weed out as many of the others as we can before picking that fight. Or we take him out in a heavy blow and then try to lose the inevitable pursuers who, let me remind you, know this area much better than we do."

The others nodded along, but Lyssa was the first to offer up her wisdom.

"What about other larger monsters like that chímaira we fought. Do you have any idea how many of those there are?"

"Those, apparently, are like a kindred beast to the beastmar but not allied with them. The beastmar we fought earlier were terrified of the chímaira we fought. Similar hybrid creatures do have some claimed territory, but the map only lists what was in the beastmar's head and he, as far as I'm aware, never ventured into monster territory. Where we were attacked technically isn't monster territory, but if I had to guess I'd say that the chímaira heard the explosion and came to investigate."

"So, what's the plan?" Tess asked. "We get there, then do what?"

"We'll have to get some eyes on them to know what we're up against. I'm certain there will be a way to draw things out. This big room here," Arche pointed to the largest cavern on the lower levels of the map, "is connected to that huge air shaft that leads all the way back up to the beginning of this place. The one you flew down, Abraxios."

"I recall seeing some beastmar at the bottom, but I didn't fly too closely. The whole area made my feathers stick up and I didn't want to risk getting spotted."

"Dropping rocks on them from above is probably out, but if shit really hits the fan you can get yourself and Odelia out of there."

Everyone stopped and looked at him, with the exception of Lyssa, who continued examining the map. Arche shrugged, suddenly uncertain.

"What? We're heavy and you two have history."

"No, *that* makes sense," Tess said. "That other thing didn't."

"Oh. You know, when a potentially bad situation gets as bad as possible. Like shit hitting a fan and getting everywhere."

The rest just stared at him.

"You get used to it." Lyssa smirked.

Arche folded up the map and sent it to his inventory.

"All right. We've got a few hours of walking, let's go."

He summoned the Tridory into his hand from where it rested against the wall and used it as a walking staff, the sauroter at the bottom digging into the stone ground with every other step. The others followed along behind him.

Fifteen minutes later, Arche became aware of someone walking next to him. He glanced over to see it was Tess. The others had backed off a little to give them some privacy. The look of terror she'd given him was still heavy in his mind. Arche glanced away.

"I'm sorry," he said quietly.

"For saving my life?" she asked dryly.

"No, I...I'm sorry I got you into that situation. And I'm sorry about everything that happened in here." Arche tapped his head. "I want you to know that I didn't know what I was doing. I was flying on instinct, no idea what would happen. I didn't mean to look into your past, I didn't even know that would happen, but mostly I'm sorry that I didn't give you the choice to share what you wanted to, when you wanted to. You didn't get a chance to choose and if I could have done it differently, I would have."

Tess didn't respond for a long time. The seconds dragged into minutes.

"You worry a lot about how other people feel," she said finally.

"Shouldn't I?"

"Why would you? Most don't. They're too busy trying to preserve themselves to consider others. It's one of your more endearing qualities."

"Thanks," Arche said slowly. "I'm confused."

"That makes two of us, then. I don't have answers for you. Whatever you did stirred up a lot of memories. Memories I thought I had buried. I need some time to process them. Time I don't exactly have while we're stuck down here."

"Yeah, of course. Take whatever time you need."

"I also got a good look at your life, you know. I know what profession you chose and everything else that's happened to you."

"I suspected as much. Only seems fair, or as close to fair as I could get considering my life is considerably shorter than yours."

"I want you to know that I will keep your secret, if you ask me to, but I can't promise I will stick around when this is all done. I'm in the business for life security and personal safety. You're the walking opposite of that. That being said, I like you. I also hate you for what happened to me. Like I said, a lot to process. I just didn't want you to get your hopes up about me."

Arche snorted.

"Wow, you Tartarus girls really don't hold back, do you? You should make whatever decision is right for you. You deserve to put your own needs first, but if you decide to stay, know that you're welcome. And as for my profession, I would like the opportunity to share it in my own time, if you're all right with that."

"I'm all right with it, but the others may not be."

"They'll have to get over themselves, then. My profession is locked right now, so it's not like telling everyone helps right now anyway."

"True. Listen, no matter what they say, you don't actually owe anyone information about yourself. Your profession is your business, your traits are your business, and there are plenty who would kill you for either."

"Thanks. I get it, some knowledge is dangerous here, but keeping secrets from those I'm leading just doesn't sit right with me. Especially when those people are trusting me to help keep them alive."

Tess cracked a smile. "You have a good heart, even if you're naïve."

Arche gave her a lopsided grin and they fell into silence, making their way through the long dark. Heading ever deeper underground.

Chapter 32

"This is good enough. Let's stop here and get ready."

They had been walking for hours and, though Arche felt good about their plan, they were all feeling the effects of too much time spent away from the light of the sun. Arche found it difficult not to point his spear at every shadow, imagining movement in the corners of his eyes. The rest were similarly jumpy. Even Lyssa, the most composed of all of them, was abnormally stiff and watchful, a change Arche would not have noticed had he not spent practically every day of the last five weeks with her.

Their rest stop was an hour's walk from the first of the larger rooms, sequestered inside an unused side-tunnel that forked into dead ends. There was no escape if they were to be caught inside, but it was the least likely place for them to be found. Arche had initially been against camping in an area with no exit but had let himself be talked into the idea by the others, who weren't so sure they would be able to outrun the beastmar regardless.

Being deep underground, they had no need for tents so each of them laid out their bedrolls, coordinated who would be on watch, and settled into preparing their food. Dinner consisted of dried rations they'd brought with them: nuts, roasted meat, various fruits and vegetables, and water to wash it all down. It was a simple meal and did little for their dampened spirits until Odelia produced a small flagon of wine. They could not risk a fire and, indeed, had no fuel to sustain one, so they ate and settled in the darkness. Abraxios promised to renew his Owl Vision spell on them before he went to sleep, telling the others to wake him if they needed the spell recast.

Lyssa offered to take the first watch, allowing the others to get some rest. Arche took up second watch, Tess took third, and Odelia took the last. Abraxios had claimed that tengu needed more sleep than other people and so was excused from the rotation. Arche didn't particularly mind. They had more than enough bodies to keep an eye out and it had been a long, stressful day for all of them.

"How did a tengu and a halfling come to be traveling companions?" Tess asked as they ate.

Abraxios waved a wing toward Odelia, his beak buried inside a small bag. Arche eyed it suspiciously, then stifled a gag as the tengu withdrew his beak, bright colored grubs disappearing as Abraxios threw his head back and swallowed.

Odelia smiled at the large birdman fondly, smothering the expression as she wiped soup from her mouth with a small cloth handkerchief.

"We met by happenstance, actually. I was on a pilgrimage, you see, seeking to deepen my connection with nature by meditating on the peak of Mount Coeus. Fancy that when in the middle of my meditation, I hear the loudest squawking. I broke meditation to see what the fuss was and saw a huge bird diving toward the side of the mountain. I thought for certain it was some giant raptor, come to eat me, but then it crashed. I decided to investigate and that's when we met."

Abraxios's neck feathers ruffled as the group shared a chuckle at the thought of quiet, reserved Abraxios crashing into a mountain.

"I was a very inexperienced flyer. I was just beginning to practice my air magic, not yet to my profession, and I caught an updraft badly. It sent me spinning out of control, into the best accident of my life."

Odelia reached out and rubbed Abraxios's arm feathers. He let out a low cooing noise at her touch. Lyssa shifted slightly in her seat, inching away from the two, and the moment ended. Odelia withdrew her hand as though she had touched fire, suddenly very interested in her broth. Abraxios stiffened, pausing from his meal. Arche looked up from the pomegranate he'd been scooping, feeling like he'd missed something. There was a tension in the air, now, where camaraderie had been a moment earlier.

Before Arche could think up a way to alleviate the pressure, Abraxios stowed his food bag, announced he was going to bed, and walked away before anyone could say anything further. Odelia also finished her meal, putting away her utensils and retreating a short distance down the hall for privacy. Tess gave Lyssa a pointed look and rolled her eyes.

"What…just happened?" Arche asked, utterly nonplussed.

"I'll start the watch," Lyssa said, ignoring the question as she walked away.

Arche looked at Tess, hoping for answers. She rubbed her eyes and edged closer so they could speak in quieter tones.

"Just some old prejudices shaking their ugly heads."

"What?"

Tess sighed heavily and rubbed her eyes again. "Right, sorry. You wouldn't know."

Arche snorted quietly. "Someday, maybe, people will stop saying that to me."

Tess continued, ignoring his comment. "Look, a lot of people disapprove of relationships like this. Some think of it as a purity thing, others as a distrust of any who are not their own, and still others hold grudges against slights that may have never even personally affected them."

"Oh?" Arche blinked a few times in rapid succession. "Oh. *Oh!*"

"Indeed."

"But then…what happened?"

"People who have suffered persecution tend to be hyperaware of the signs of intolerance. It's really not that surprising. Lyssa indicated she didn't approve and they reacted to that."

Arche frowned.

"I didn't see it."

"Why would you? You weren't looking for it. It's not shocking that she'd be uncomfortable with interspecies relationships. Many are, and her upbringing as a wood elf would not help her in that regard."

"That seems like a heavy accusation to levy for such a small reaction."

"What about the way she reacted when you first met your satyr friend? What about the way she acted when she first met you?"

"She saved me."

"And nearly killed you in the same breath."

"That doesn't make her a bad person."

"I'm not saying she's a bad person, Arche, but she *is* an elf from a remote village. The older people get, the harder it is for them to change, and elves are both notoriously long-lived and difficult to judge on age. I've never heard of her village, but if it's one of the older elven strongholds then they might still hold onto traditions and perspectives from thousands of years ago, with all the good and bad that comes from that."

"Lyssa is not incapable of change. She's changed drastically in the short time I've known her."

"I'm not disputing that, what I'm saying is that sometimes her reactions to things are going to upset people with modern sensibilities. People who have already had to put up with a lot of difficulties for being who and what they are."

Arche looked over at Abraxios and Odelia, who were lying on bedrolls next to each other, the tengu's wing draped protectively over the halfling in sleep.

"She's not a bad person," Tess repeated. "But neither are they, and they don't deserve to be treated like they're doing something wrong for loving each other."

Arche was quiet for a while, letting the silence settle as he tried to arrange his thoughts.

"When I first met the elves," he said. "they treated me with distrust. Some of them regarded me like an exotic trinket from a faraway land, an object to be gawked at or examined. That was the nicer treatment. Others looked at me like a threat or an unpleasant smell. Lord Cypress also treated me with distrust but he gave me the chance to prove that I wasn't a threat to his people. Lyssa didn't wait for me to prove myself before she helped me. She taught me basic combat skills and got me proper armor so I could survive the task we shared. She trusted me to have her back and not to turn on her. She trusted my judgment before I had any idea of who I was. She may be a product of her environment but she's more than that."

Arche nodded toward Abraxios and Odelia.

"You can't expect the impossible from people doing their best. It's easy to take a single action or reaction and judge someone's entire personality from it, but that ignores everything. Every struggle or decision they've made. Every introspective argument. You're making assumptions about her based on her background, but you're ignoring who she is."

"Think about their lives, for a moment," Tess said softly. "In the city, it may have been more acceptable, but not everyone sees it the same way. They'll have met opposition at every turn. Don't you find it odd that there are no other tengu in the village? They're rare enough this side of Tartarus, not to mention one on his own. He's either been cast out of or willingly left his flock, something that doesn't happen without a strong reason. Most of the people that came here are hoping to start a new life for themselves, away from the obstacles of their old ones. Aren't they allowed to be disappointed when they see the same disapproval they've been trying to get away from?"

"Of course they are, but at the same time they are of this world. They know it and its people, and they know that, right or wrong, there are people who disapprove of what they do, who they are. I bet they've faced more opposition and opinions about their relationship than I can guess and they probably always will because some people will refuse to change. That isn't right, but..." Arche trailed off.

Tess nudged him, brows raised. "But?"

"But they have each other. They know who they are and they've embraced it, regardless of what others think. They have their identity and no outsider can take that from them."

Tess cocked her head, staring at him. Arche fixed his eyes on his hands.

"You envy them."

He hesitated.

"In a way. Who they are has been reinforced by the adversity they've faced. The more people tell them what and who they should be, the more they commit to who they are. Me? I'm...I don't even know. Am I a warrior? Am I my profession? Am I a magic spear's bearer? I have no idea who I am and every step I take makes me feel farther away from finding out. How can I look at people who have steadfastly proclaimed who they are and are willing to stand against adversity to prove it without being a little envious of that certainty? I know, it's a horrible thing to think. They've been through more than any person should have to, I don't want to disparage that, but it's hard to see them and not connect my own struggles to it."

"It's not a horrible thing. I think it makes you human. You want to know the person you used to be, but that isn't necessarily the person you are."

"How can I know who I am if I don't know who I was?"

"Because you exist, here and now. You are a person, sitting here on this stone, capable of thinking, making decisions, and feeling."

She flicked his ear lightly.

"Ow."

"Your reactions, your choices, your intent, your ideals. These things and more all help make up who you are. You may not know who you used to be but that doesn't stop you from being the person you are now. The person who brought all of us together. The person who's trying to save the whole village by stopping the beastmar. The person who saved me. You may think you don't have an identity, but I think you have more certainty of self than you realize."

Tess stood, stretching as she yawned.

"Now, I'm going to bed before it's my turn to go out on watch."

Arche nodded, standing as well.

"Thank you, Tess, for the conversation."

Tess flashed him a brilliant smile and his heart skipped a beat.

"Thank you for being you."

She turned and walked away, leaving him alone in the firelight, heat spreading across his cheeks and a strange ache in his chest.

Chapter 33

Persepera
The 25ᵗʰ of Elaphebolion
The Year 4631 in the Era of Mortals

The morning came without incident, or as close to morning as they could guess in the gloom of the underground network. None of them had heard anything more than the sound of rummaging rodents and insects, all of which had stayed thankfully far away from them. Arche had spent his portion of the watch casually pinching himself to stay awake. He was bone-tired from the day's events and would have liked nothing more than a full night of uninterrupted sleep like Abraxios. Still, there was a certain comfort to be taken from the solitude of a lone vigil.

When he woke the next morning, he felt as though he'd barely slept at all. He even went as far as to check his status page to make sure he wasn't afflicted with an exhaustion debuff. Sure enough, tier one. Arche stretched, blinked as hard as he could to wake his eyes, and did his best to suck it up.

"You look terrible," Tess commented.

"Oh, great, it's on the outside, too."

"You all right? Didn't get an infection from all the blood yesterday, did you?"

"If he did, it's because he didn't tell me about it," Odelia interjected. "I can disinfect wounds for a pittance of the Mana it takes to heal them, you know."

"I'm uninjured, just... just tired. What I wouldn't give for a cup of coffee."

Arche was rubbing his eyes as he said it and still felt the weight of everyone frowning at him.

"Bitter drink. Helps you stay awake."

"Sounds unpleasant," Lyssa said.

"Actually, it's pretty fucking divine, and I really wish I—" Arche stopped midsentence, realizing this was the first time he had had some feeling held over from before his memory started that hadn't faded away as soon as he tried to recall more.

"Arche?"

"I... I remember. Coffee. Of all the things that might have come through, fucking *coffee* stays with me."

Lyssa smiled. "That's good news. If one thing has stayed with you, maybe more isn't far away."

It also proved he wasn't crazy, at least about this aspect of his life, but Arche kept that fact to himself.

"Maybe," Arche hedged. "I just wish I remembered something a little more... meaningful, I guess."

"Not to interrupt a touching moment," Abraxios cut in. "But are we all ready to go?"

Arche stowed his bedroll and blanket, then grabbed the Tridory. The rest were already packed and waiting as he took his position at the head of the group.

They had spent a full day inside the dungeon, as far as anyone could tell. The darkness made it impossible to determine time by conventional means, but Arche wasn't as interested in the day already past as he was in the day still ahead of him. If everything went well, they might make it out before nightfall, assuming that their bodies still operated off normal, solar time.

"We should probably go over the plan," Arche said.

"There's a plan? I thought we were just stumbling around in the dark trying not to get killed," Abraxios quipped, turning to Odelia. "Did you know there was a plan?"

"Hush," the halfling said gently. "Let's hear him out."

"The bigger chambers are probably going to have more beastmar than we've encountered in these individual patrols. It'll also be harder to engage them in the open as they can surround and overwhelm us. Furthermore, whoever's leading them is probably in these larger chambers as well. Tunnel fighting has proven to be pretty effective in limiting what they can do but it's not without its risks to us as well."

No one disagreed, so he continued.

"As we get close, we should scout the chambers to get an idea of what we're dealing with, then set traps along the passageways and lure them back to us. The traps should injure or kill enough of them that the rest have a difficult time getting through."

"I'm all in favor of setting traps, but how? We don't exactly have the materials to do so," Tess pointed out.

"Odelia, can your gaiamancy be used to shape the stone in these passages? Stone spikes, pitfalls, that sort of thing?"

The halfling cocked her head, considering it.

"It's doable, but it'll be time- and Mana-intensive. I don't know a specific spell to path traps in stonework, so I'll have to rely on Nature Meld. The more intricate you want the traps, the longer and the more it'll cost, but basic features should be reasonably doable."

"I can help her," Lyssa said, stepping forward. "I've trapped many a beast in the forest, I can help her pick locations where traps will be most effective."

The wood elf moved over to stand next to the halfling, catching Tess's eye and giving the other woman an inscrutable expression. Arche glanced back and forth but whatever was passing between them was lost to him.

"I suppose that leaves me to go scouting ahead," Tess said, breaking eye contact to look at Arche.

"Yes, but not alone. I'll go with you. My cloak should give me the stealth bonus I need to hold my own, and if either of us gets caught then the other can still report back to the rest."

"What about me?" Abraxios asked.

"You can watch the passages we came from and ensure no patrols sneak up behind us. If any do, warn Lyssa and Odelia and hide yourselves. Tess and I will think of something. Are we all clear?"

Everyone nodded their assent.

Leadership has increased to **Level 6**.

+1% Persuasion Chance (+6%)
+1% Reputation Gain (+6%)
-0.5% Reputation Loss (-3%)

Arche felt a spark of vindication at the message, as though he was being rewarded for the plan. He couldn't trust it to mean that his plan would work, though the increases the skill brought were more than welcome. It was yet another oddity of this strange world: you could still be rewarded even if what you were trying to do failed. It was an oddly optimistic feature, starkly contrasted against the harsh life that Tartarus had promised thus far.

Tess nudged him with her elbow, bringing him back to the present.

"You ready?" she asked.

"Yeah, let's go."

They set off at a loping run. Tess led the way as her Perception and trap finding skills were higher than his, so he focused all his efforts on making as little noise as possible and stepping exactly where she stepped to avoid any traps.

They made much better time alone than when the whole group traveled. In less than half an hour of running they reached the opening to the first large chamber. Arche tracked their process mentally; the map he extracted from the beastmar still etched into his head. He wasn't entirely certain how long that knowledge would last, but he was glad he still had it. On more than one occasion during their run he'd had to correct Tess's course or give directions. Without that map, they would have been hopelessly lost in the underground complex. It was undeniably useful but the fear in the beastmar's face still ran through Arche's head. Psychic Link was easily his scariest skill yet and he wasn't sure he liked all the implications that came with it.

The opening guided them toward was not actually set into the ground floor of the cavern. Instead, it was a small, balcony-style ledge set about four spear-lengths above the ground. The distance was not insurmountable from either direction but would give them plenty of cover to peer out into the room. Both Tess and Arche fell to their stomachs and crawled toward the edge, careful to make as little noise as possible. They needn't have worried, as the sounds coming from the cavern were more than enough to mask any scrapings of leather against dirt.

Inside the cavern, the beastmar were feasting. Howls and jeers split the air and the room was illuminated by a bonfire in the very center and glowing green crystals that littered the walls and floor. Near the fire, stakes had been placed with impaled animals and people, set to roast over the flames. The beastmar themselves stood well away from the fire, clearly not wanting to set themselves alight with an errant spark.

The sheer noise the creatures made should have traveled back through the passageways, given all the stone, but it didn't. There must have been sound-dampening magic or runes at play that gave the chamber some semblance of privacy, preventing sounds from traveling too far.

Three-score beastmar filled the space below.

That alone would have been bad enough and certainly gave both of them pause, but it wasn't all. In addition to the large piles of food—the majority of which was bloodied meat—there was a huge, bone cage with a dozen humanoids inside it, huddled near the middle. Several beastmar stood around the cage, harassing the occupants with spears or long, clawed hands. One of the prisoners shifted a little too close to one side, trying to avoid the prodding tip of a spear, and was snatched by a beastmar they didn't notice. The creature yanked the prisoner through a gap in the cage while the rest of the beastmar howled and cheered. Tess turned her head aside but Arche couldn't tear his eyes away, staring in grim horror as they pulled the prisoner apart, limb by bloody limb.

Arche watched as a beastmar tossed a leg to one of its fellows and took a bite out of the quartered prisoner's severed arm, making sure that the victim, somehow still alive, could see. Arche's throat closed and he struggled to keep from running down into the fray and tearing them all to pieces. The power inside of him, the so-called Divinity, was screaming for him to use it, to vanquish these abominations who made a mockery of life. What was the point of power if not to stop things like this? With Divine Body, he would tear the hearts out of his enemies and feed it back to them. The skill practically begged to bathe in their blood.

A hand grabbed his arm and Arche shifted to strike. He stopped a moment later. Tess had buried her face against her shoulder, holding onto his arm as though she would be wrenched away at any moment. Memories of the tunnel fight flooded his mind. The desire to face the beastmar openly, to kill every last one. How that decision had led to Tess very nearly losing her life.

The rage in Arche's throat sputtered and died, but the disgust was still there, making Arche's stomach feel like it had settled somewhere near his clavicle. He was about to begin crawling back when a flash of light caught his attention. Unlike the glowing green crystals or the bonfire, this light was crimson. Arche nudged Tess and she lifted her head up and opened her eyes. He nodded toward the far wall, too distracted to give a clearer indication. Luckily, another flash of crimson showed both of them exactly where to look: the passage into the other huge cavern they hadn't yet managed to scout. Unfortunately, they didn't have a good angle and the distance was too great to make out any details.

A third flash came but Arche's attention was snared by two beastmar pulling a makeshift cart piled high with bloody meat and body parts. They neared the opening to the next cavern and were clearly uncomfortable getting any closer, exchanging looks and proceeding rather slowly. As they reached the opening, one of the beastmar dropped his load and sprinted to the side. The weight of the cart momentarily pinned the remaining beastmar, who struggled to free himself.

As the beastmar struggled, an enormous wolf-like head lunged from the tunnel, grabbed the beastmar and the cart together, and pulled them both into the tunnel. The beastmar screamed, the sound echoing back over the din, then violently stopped.

The hairs on Arche's arms tickled as they stood. If the head was analogous to the creature's entire size, which wasn't a certainty anywhere beastmar were involved, then it was the size of a building, maybe even a small warehouse. Arche didn't know how they were going to fight that behemoth, but he was certain of one thing.

This was how the beastmar were going to destroy the village.

Chapter 34

Persepera
The 25th of Elaphebolion
The Year 4631 in the Era of Mortals

Arche and Tess sprinted back the way they came, toward the rest of their group. Neither of them said anything since seeing the hound, but the primal fear that accompanied seeing an enormous, people-eating monster transcended all need for language. Arche had no idea how he was supposed to fight that *thing,* only that he had to find a way or they were all dead.

Tess had been especially introspective since they had left the cavern. Her face was a perfect mask, betraying no emotions, though Arche had enough of a sense of her to tell she was deeply conflicted behind her stoic demeanor. Arche slowed down after his Stamina was beginning to lag, dipping down to thirty percent. For a moment, he thought she was going to keep going, but she slowed as well, coming to a stop a few paces in front of him before grabbing her knees and panting.

"Needless to say," Arche said between breaths. "We're in over our heads."

Tess stared at him, as if already analyzing a response to words she had yet to say. "If we fight that thing, we're dead."

"I'm inclined to agree."

"So what do we do?"

Arche threw up his hands.

"I am open to suggestions."

There was a brief pause as they both considered their options.

"We should talk to the others but I don't see how we can defeat that."

"I think we're going to have to, not just to complete the quest but also to keep the village safe. Plus, I'm not comfortable leaving those prisoners behind."

"There are limits to what we can accomplish. To fight a force that large, we'll need help. Perhaps we should return to the village and recruit more fighters."

"Maybe," Arche hedged. "I'm not sure that'll work. We should discuss that play as a group, though."

After a couple minutes of rest, they sped off again. Arche led the way through the tunnels this time, the lack of traps they faced the first time gave him confidence that they would make it back unscathed. Whether by calculation or serendipity, they made it safely back.

Lyssa met them before they could barrel into their own traps. Arche hadn't considered that he and Tess would have had to cross the trapped passage and felt a flush of gratitude for the elf's foresight.

"I was wondering if you two were going to be gone all day," Lyssa remarked as they approached. "I was beginning to think you'd been captured."

"Captured? Us? Not likely," Arche replied with all the false bravado he could muster.

It was all he could do to keep standing.

"You're right, they would have killed you and hung you from the ceiling to ripen, Greenstick."

"I'd have caught in their throats and choked the whole lot."

Tess didn't allow herself to be drawn into the banter. Instead, she glanced back the way they had come, brow furrowed in thought. Lyssa, perceptive as ever, caught Tess's expression and turned serious.

"Follow me."

Through Lyssa's careful guidance, they weaved their way through quite a few pressure plates, false floors, and tripwires before rejoining the rest of their group.

"So," Abraxios said after they had a moment to collect themselves. "What are we up against?"

Arche and Tess launched into descriptions of the cavern and what they had seen, shoring up any details that slipped in the other's retelling. When they spoke of the wolf-like creature they had seen, the others looked hopeless.

"Titan's Bane," Odelia murmured. "What are we going to do about that?"

"What can we do?" Abraxios followed up. "We came here to fight a few bands of beastmar, not dismantle an entire army and destroy a huge monster single-handedly. We're ill-equipped for such an endeavor."

"You're right," Arche said. "This is more than you signed up for. More than any of us signed up for, really. I won't blame you if you want to leave, but I'm staying."

"Arche, be reasonable," Lyssa said. "There is only so much we can do alone. To retreat and return with greater numbers is not cowardice."

"This isn't about bravery," Arche said. "Every second we waste, more of those prisoners are going to die. I won't abandon those people. Besides, even if I go back, Callias is going to get in my way. At best, arrested; at worst, killed. Call it a gut feeling, but if he wanted me dead before, he'll want me double-dead now that he thinks I'm trying to steal his money."

"We don't have to stay here," Lyssa pointed out.

"I know." Arche ran a hand through his hair. "But I'm not just thinking about me. The quest I have practically says that if we don't find a way to stop this, then this creature will destroy the village. I can't walk away from this. Callias won't do anything to protect the village, he's already made that abundantly clear. I can't see him committing his guards now, but that doesn't necessarily mean we shouldn't try."

Arche paused, trying to gather his thoughts.

"What's your plan, Arche?" Tess asked.

"I'm staying. I intend to see this through, one way or the other. None of you are under the same obligation." He made eye contact with each of them, holding Lyssa's eyes the longest. "You can go back, take the reward from Theodorous, try to convince Callias to send his guards, or leave and try to find a better home elsewhere in the likely event that I fail."

There was quiet for several moments as everyone considered the options. Abraxios was the first to speak.

"I am sorry. I know you mean well, but this is not a fight we can win. I cannot be a part of it."

Odelia nodded. "I know you said you would stay, but we can't fight something like that. There are too many of them and I don't think any of us could rightfully fight that creature and hope to live. I can't. I'm sorry."

Arche had thought it would come to this. Expected it, even. It still felt like a punch to the gut. The loss of their spells would hurt, especially in the darkness of the underground. He extended one hand and withdrew the map of the dungeon from his inventory, holding it out to them.

"I wish both of you the best of luck. If we fail here today, get yourselves and as many as you can to safety. Callias be damned, that fool isn't worth dying for."

"We will try to rally help for you above and return as quickly as we can," Abraxios said as he collected the map.

Arche had no doubt that the tengu would attempt to do just that, but he held no hope for reinforcements arriving in time. He turned to Tess and Lyssa.

"And your decisions?"

"Where you go, I follow, Greenstick. Someone has to temper your schemes with sense."

Tess was uncharacteristically quiet. Arche could see on her face she was struggling with her decision. It was not lost on him how shaken she had been by the whole ordeal, how much she had already risked, how close she'd come to death.

"You don't have to stay," he said in a low voice, trying his best to sound reassuring. "Your choice is your own."

"I..." Tess hesitated. "I don't know. I need to think."

Abraxios met Odelia's eyes, a moment of unspoken understanding passing between them.

"We will wait a half hour before we depart for the surface," the tengu said. "After that, if you decide to leave, you must make the journey by yourselves."

Arche nodded his agreement. If they left together, they would have the best odds if they ran into any spare patrols, and the map should help them navigate back to the surface. On the other hand, a delay in leaving meant a delay in reinforcements arriving, but Arche knew better than to count on help. As long as they remained safe on the journey out, that was what was important.

"Very well. I will leave you to your preparations," Arche said, noting with mild surprise how formal his words sounded to his own ears.

Perhaps the world was rubbing off on him or perhaps this was a remnant of the man he used to be shining through. If the others noticed, they didn't say anything. Abraxios and Odelia stepped away, holding the map between them to plan their route back. Lyssa took Tess by the arm and gently led her away to talk in private, leaving Arche alone with his thoughts.

It had been such a long time since he had relatively nothing to do that he was at a loss. Their initial plan of luring beastmar back into their traps was still their best bet, as far as he was concerned. With their numbers reduced down to a reliable two and with no healing magic, they would not be able to afford open combat. That meant trickery, traps, and downright unsportsmanlike conduct.

It wasn't going to be the glorious battle that part of him craved. A little voice in his head told him to meet his foes on the battlefield and make them regret the day of their creation. To destroy them, see them cast down before him, and to hear the wailing of their wounded.

Alas, there were too many lives on the line if he failed, including his own.

Asymmetric warfare didn't provide the same rush but it was a good way to kill a lot of beastmar at least risk to himself and his allies, so it was clearly the better choice. How they would kill the rest, well, that was a problem for future Arche. Getting to that point was the problem for current Arche.

He tightened his grip on the Tridory, feeling the weight of it. The coarseness of the metal left indentations in his skin. Focusing on the sensation helped him focus on the situation, on the present and near future, and helped keep his attention from wandering. The beginnings of a plan began to formulate as he stared down the expanse of trapped hallway. He had almost convinced himself it could work when Lyssa and Tess returned to him.

"I'm staying," Tess said, meeting his eyes.

Arche glanced to Lyssa, who nodded. He fixed his eyes back on Tess.

"And this is your choice?"

"Yes. Do you have a plan?"

"I'm working on it. We should inform Abraxios and Odelia of your decision."

"Already done," Lyssa said. "They left a couple minutes ago."

Arche blinked in surprise and turned around, finding that the tengu and halfling had, indeed, gone. He even went as far as to check his Adventuring Party menu to see that both names had disappeared.

"I didn't see them go," he said quietly.

"They'll be okay," Tess reassured. "I'm not sure anything in here could stop them from running if they set their minds to it, between his speed and her ground control they could probably get out of here within the hour."

Arche nodded. He didn't doubt that they could get out on their own, but it was still surprising that after all they had been through together that they hadn't even said goodbye. He put it from his mind. Their situation demanded it.

"All right, here's the plan..."

Chapter 35

"You have the worst plans."

Lyssa and Arche stood in the mouth of the tunnel, just shy of the massive cavern. It was the first time the elven woman had seen what they were up against with her own eyes and she was not optimistic. Tess stayed behind to set off some of the traps manually. Arche didn't like the idea of them splitting up yet again and especially didn't like the idea of Tess being by herself in the dungeon but he didn't need psychic powers to know that what she'd seen in the cavern had troubled her far more than she let on.

"Great, then you can plan the next one."

"You seem to have a lot of confidence that this one will work."

Arche shrugged, keeping an eye on the entrance.

"You agreed to it."

"I said that it was as likely to work as Callias welcoming you back with open arms."

Arche flashed a grin.

"So you're saying there's a chance?"

Lyssa rolled her eyes.

"If we die, I'll kill you myself."

"That...yeah, all right. That's fair."

Lyssa flexed her hand and her bow appeared. Arche carefully set the Tridory against the wall and pulled out his own bow. He really needed to figure out a way of carrying the spear without having to hold it in one hand all the time.

Arche shook the thought free from his head. It wasn't the time to focus on quality-of-life, rather on sustainment of life. He and Lyssa were about to kick the hornet's nest.

They stalked up to the ledge, as quiet as they could be. The hubbub in the cavern had died down somewhat from last time. Some of the beastmar had fallen asleep, passed out in piles around the room. Arche felt a pang of guilt as a few more prisoners were missing from the cage. He grabbed the feeling and hardened it into anger.

They would pay. They would all pay.

He met Lyssa's gaze and saw his own anger reflected there. Without further hesitation, they nocked arrows to their strings and began raining death. Their first volley went unnoticed, felling two beastmar. Before Arche had even retrieved his next arrow from his quiver, Lyssa had shot twice more.

Each arrow found its place in some vulnerable spot, whether it was throat, eye, or heart. Arche couldn't be sure, but she was shooting at least four times faster than he was, which spoke to the massive gap in skill and capability that stood between them. Still, he was determined not to be useless. By the time the seventh beastmar died, their efforts were noticed. A loud, angry cry rose up above the natural din and the lethargic beastmar began to stir.

Arche sent a Penetrating Shot at a particularly large beastmar before surveying their situation. They had brought down or killed about nine beastmar, but there were still fifty more rallying after them. He wished, not for the first time, that he had access to magic. What he would have given for a well-placed fireball at that moment.

Sadly, wishing wasn't doing. With the approaching horde, they were running out of time. Arche stored his bow and quiver safely into his inventory and turned away to retrieve the Tridory. Lyssa hesitated, shooting twice more into the horde scrabbling up the incline, then followed Arche's lead. They raced through the underground passage, slowing every so often to shoot arrows at the frontrunners of their pursuers.

Arche remembered their first encounter with beastmar and how Lyssa had so quickly outpaced him to go fight. That display of pure speed made her current pace seem like a brisk walk, despite it being as fast as Arche felt he could maintain. If she had the inclination, she could have easily left him behind. He was grateful she was on his side. Even with the incredible benefits of the Divine Body skill, he wouldn't stand a chance against her. She was a force of nature, unstoppable in her wrath.

Passages flew past to the left and right, but Arche kept his focus on what was ahead. The sounds of beastmar stuck in his ears, drowning everything else. His heart pounded, fear and adrenaline mixed in equal measure. His muscles trembled, his breath came ragged, but still he ran. Just a bit farther, five minutes of sprinting at the max.

Something launched out of a side-passage and slammed into Arche.

A beastmar had somehow cut them off. The incredible mass of the creature knocked Arche clear off his feet, the Tridory fell from his grip and clattered away. They tumbled into another passage, this one with a steep downward incline. Arche heard Lyssa shout his name, then he was weightless.

Falling.

Flying through the black toward certain death.

The beastmar let out a howl of fear and regret. No lights lined the walls, no indication of how far he was falling or when he would hit the bottom. The air rushed by, pushing him away from the beastmar, but he grabbed hold of one of the creature's many flailing limbs and pulled himself closer. The beastmar was fully gripped by panic, its movements erratic, but Arche strained against the thrashing and buried himself in the monster's chest. Then, he activated Divine Body.

Crimson light spilled out of every pore, illuminating the tunnel as they fell. Strength flooded his limbs and he held tight, pressing himself as closely as he could. In the light, the beastmar was revealed. An enormous torso containing no less than five arms, each attempting to grab something, anything, to arrest its fall. Arche moved his grip to the beastmar's shoulder and braced himself. His other hand slid up the creature's torso, through its throat and into its head. It let out a surprised cough, twitched, and went limp. Arche withdrew his dripping hand and hugged the now-dead body.

The ground met him with a crunch.

His toughened body sank into the beastmar and, despite the softened landing and the improved resilience that Divine Body offered him, he was too dazed to focus on keeping the ability active. The light winked out and Arche was left in total darkness, his head swam as if he were still falling. With shaking limbs, he pushed himself out of the crater that was the dead beastmar's chest, managing to roll clear of it before he threw up.

He was covered in gore and entrails. The stench of it filled his nose, making him retch. He heaved again and more bile splattered against the ground. More than a little nervous at what he would find, he checked his vitals.

Health: 208 / 495	Stamina: 355 / 355	Mana: 19 / 190
42%	100%	10%

There was no doubt that without his Divine Body skill and the beastmar to land on, he would have died. As it was, he had no idea where he was. This tunnel was not included on his mental map.

He was on his own.

Arche reached for the Tridory and cursed when his hands found only empty air. It was either above him in the passage, or somewhere in the darkness around him. At ten percent of his total Mana, he might have enough to summon it, but it would hurt. Arche tried to call upon his bond with the weapon but was hit instead by a sudden wave of vertigo. He stumbled and fell to the ground, stomach heaving again. His Mana dipped five points, then stopped as he lost concentration.

Arche dragged himself away from the dead beastmar, trying to escape both the smell and the sticky pool of blood coalescing around the broken form. The ground was rough and uneven, huge stones and spikes jutted up at odd angles. He couldn't see but he had the impression he was at the bottom of a massive spike trap. He found a wall to lean against and tried to take stock.

First, he looked through his inventory. He had three torches, each of which would last an hour. There was also a bit of flint and steel to light them. The beastmar were also highly flammable, so a torch would actually be useful if he ran into more of them. He would have to wait before lighting anything on fire, however. If the light attracted more creatures to him, he would need his strength back. Divine Body was his only method of outright healing himself so he was forced to wait for his Mana to recover naturally. At his current rate, it would take him about five minutes.

The quiet of the tunnel, mixed with the oppressive darkness and aching pain of his body, lulled his mind to surrender to unconsciousness. Slumped against a stone spike, Arche found it impossible to keep his eyes open.

When he woke, his Health had risen thirty-six points and his Mana was full. Doing some mental calculations, he figured he'd been asleep for about an hour and a half. That wasn't completely trustworthy, as any number of factors could have slowed or improved it, not the least of which was the now-missing Exhaustion debuff, but it was accurate enough to go on for now.

An hour and a half stuck in a dark hole. An hour and a half that the beastmar had chased Lyssa and Tess.

With any luck, they had managed better than he had. The plan had been to use the traps they had set to slow them down, then finish off any that were left or hide somewhere. They hadn't planned for the beastmar to head them off. If something had happened to the others...

There was little use in thinking about that now. He had to appraise his situation and find a way out of the hole. But first, he had to see what he was dealing with. He retrieved the flint and steel, which consisted of a rock and a dull knife, then crawled his way toward where he thought the beastmar was and felt around for its body.

"Normally," he muttered to himself, "I'd be more reluctant about doing something like this, but you caught me in an uncharitable mood. And let's face it, I was inside you. Not much more we can really do, eh?"

It took a few strikes for the sparks to catch on the beastmar's fur but once they did, the flames spread quickly, casting a flickering, orange-yellow glow across Arche's surroundings. It was the first opportunity he'd had to take a look at himself since the fall.

He'd certainly seen better days.

Dried blood and chunky bits stained him red and black, both the beastmar's and his own but more the former. The hardened leathers that comprised his armor had been practically shredded in several places and one of his sleeves was hanging on by a few threads. The Emerald Ghost, the magical cloak he'd paid so much for, was also sporting its fair share of tears and rips, but Arche wasn't worried. As long as it retained durability, it would repair itself over time. He only hoped the cleaning aspect of the repair feature worked on bloodstains.

His self-examination over, Arche turned his attention toward his immediate surroundings. He was, indeed, in some sort of spike pit, but the spikes were much larger and set much further apart than he had expected. Instead of being clustered together, ready to impale any creature unlucky enough to fall into the pit, they were more like small trees, rising above Arche's head with enough space to walk comfortably through. The light from the burning beastmar didn't completely illuminate the space he found himself in, but Arche could see a nearby wall. On the other side, the light faded into the darkness of a larger space. The last thing he wanted was to go exploring that darkness, but he needed to find an exit. More than that, he needed his weapon.

Arche raised a hand and focused on his connection to the Tridory, willing it to return. The Mana moved inside him, channeled along his connection to the spear but the link felt muddled, as though he was trying to pull something heavy underwater. His Mana dove steadily but he couldn't tell if the spear was getting any closer or not. When his Mana was half-gone, the feeling gave way and the Tridory appeared, glinting in the firelight as it descended from somewhere above. Arche caught the spear at the haft, looking it over. It was covered in stone dust, which was somewhat surprising as the underground complex hadn't had an abundance of disturbed stone or dirt. It had actually been relatively clean.

Arche looked between the spear, himself, and the burning beastmar.

"I won't ask if you don't." He chuckled to himself. "Talking to a spear. All right, Arche, let's figure our way out of this."

He hobbled forward, bones still groaning from the impact. He rested one hand against the wall, leaning the rest of his weight against the Tridory. The flickering light of the burning beastmar didn't reach far, but Arche moved past the limits into darkness, searching for some way out. The shadow consumed him, but he trudged forward undaunted, circling around the occasional spike that rose in his path, hoping for some organic escape.

When the gleam of fire was barely visible, he decided to turn back. He'd lost so much time already; he couldn't afford to waste any more by getting lost again. Lyssa and Tess could have been captured by the beastmar, or even killed. Arche's eyes narrowed. He couldn't entertain that line of thought. He had to trust they could handle themselves. His focus was on getting out of his current predicament and getting back to them before it was too late. They had kicked the hornet's nest and now they had to deal with the swarm.

Arche quickened his pace, feeling the resentment in his muscles and bones. He needed to find a way out. A way that preferably did not include climbing back up the walls. Not only would it take forever but if he fell then he would most likely be impaled on the spikes. Recent experiences told him that falling was not a way he ever wanted to die, no matter what he was landing on.

Those concerns were banished upon finding a depression in the wall. The depression gave way to a tunnel that disappeared into the darkness. Arche followed it as quickly as his body would allow, the Tridory hefted in one hand, ready to use, while the other held the stone wall for guidance.

A quarter of an hour passed before he heard sounds echoing off the walls. The sounds gave way to low, snarled voices as he approached.

"Curse it! They hide like rats in our walls. Vermin, scattering at the first sound of danger. Find them! Split up if you have to. Flesh is always sweeter after a hunt. Show no cowardice or you will be their replacement. The chief demands their deaths."

Arche adjusted his grip on the spear. His heart thumped against his ribs until he was sure the beastmar would hear it. Being hunted wasn't a feeling he was sure he'd ever get used to, but it was better to run toward the danger than away. These beastmar stood between him and his companions and the delay could be the difference between life and death.

Unacceptable.

Arche set his jaw and tried to quell his pounding heart. Fear was a luxury he could not afford. The time for running away was past. It was time to run toward something and if he couldn't find his friends, then the enemy would have to do.

Chapter 36

Muffled footsteps echoed off the walls. The voices of the beastmar grew louder, more varied. Multiple conversations filtered through, making it hard to pick out specific words. The distortion of the sound itself left no doubt to the fact that it was beastmar speaking, so Arche had no qualms about rushing in spear-first.

For the first time in a long while, he was on his own. No companions to protect or watch out for, only enemies to fight. He thought about what they'd done to Tess and a creeping fury grew within him. Bloodlust blossomed out from his chest like heat until his fingers twitched with anticipation. Every step brought him toward beautiful violence. He would paint the entire underground complex red with the blood of his foes, watch them grovel before him as he crushed them into paste.

Arche blinked.

Anger filled him but it wasn't his. He hated the beastmar, true, but he wanted them dead, not broken. He wanted his friends safe. That was his goal. This violence and blood, he didn't care about that, did he? It was hard to tell. The feeling was powerful. He wanted to bathe in their blood, taste their fear before they died. Or did he just want them dead, no matter how?

The feelings mixed together, impossible to separate. He *did* want to hurt. To kill. He wanted to rip these monsters limb from limb, hang them from their entrails, and nail their severed heads to every tree in the Sylv. The feelings were seductive, difficult to refuse. He wanted to give in, to commit to the freedom of the slaughter. To lose whatever vestiges of himself that he had established in the last month. It was overwhelming, the desire to become conflict in the shape of a man. To let go of the pain, fear, and anxiety. To do as he was born to do. Kill. It would be so simple, as easy as breathing.

It was also unacceptable.

Arche forced himself to breathe slowly. He turned inward, focusing on the expanse of his mindscape. He had no better term for his metaphysical sense of self. Without his Psychic trait guiding him through it, opening the path for him, he wouldn't have had the first idea where to begin. As it was, there were still pockets he couldn't quite focus on and it was difficult to feel out his entire mind at once, but he had awareness enough to recognize when something was wrong.

Scarlet energy blasted Arche's mindscape but not from outside, like he'd thought. Beams of red light shot forth from a singular point within his mind, cracking the mud walls of his mental construct. Those walls represented the limits of his mind; if the energy broke through, there would be nothing protecting him from outside influence. There would also be nothing tethering his consciousness to his body. He would be lost, completely at the mercy of whatever forces lurked in the negative expanse between minds.

Arche focused on reinforcing the walls, Mana streaming into them in brilliant rivers, but the energy shifted, targeting new sections whenever he started to counteract it. He redoubled his efforts, funneling more and more Mana, trying to strengthen his walls and rebuff the rage energy. All the while, he tried to find the source, but the effort was immense. The Mana was thick and far too slow, like a glacier trying to catch a skier, but they flowed from the same direction.

He followed the energy to the center of his mindscape, where it bloomed from a blood-red pool of Mana-water. Deep below the surface, something glowed with tremendous energy. Arche dove into the pool with his mental construct, feeling the outside world slip away from him as he did so.

All that existed was Mana and energy.

The Mana reacted to him, swirling in shifting currents to wash over him, bringing with it a clarity of thought but the energy also brought anger. The pool dipped lower as the Mana drained to reinforce his walls, funneled outward to the edge of his mindscape. The red glow was below him, now, so Arche dove deeper, losing all sensation of the world outside.

As he went, anger and rage pressed upon him, trying to drown him. He should not be fighting this. This is what he wanted, after all.

To destroy. To break. To kill.

This energy was power he could use against his enemies, power he needed. Without it, he was nothing. Without it, he would die. It was necessary; good, even. He was a demigod, after all. This power was his right, wasn't it?

Arche drew on the Mana to harden his own construct. The rivers pulled back from the walls and concentrated in the avatar of his consciousness, flowing around him in a nexus of currents. A brilliant, red crystal sat at the center of his Mana pool. Large, fleshy veins grew outward from the crystal, leaching into the pool and pushing outward into the ground and the rest of his mind. The crystal pulsed, a heartbeat of power, and sent beams of energy upward, trying to break through his mind's meager defenses. Arche placed his astral hands against the crystal and tried to connect to it.

The process was surprisingly easy. It was, after all, already inside his head. The crystal radiated rage and its power. It was immense, far stronger than he would ever be. It contained multitudes, capable of consciousnesses that would shatter his fragile mind to behold. This was the source of his Divine Body skill, there could be no doubt. Whatever it was, it wasn't from him. Cohabitation was apparently no longer an option. It sent wave after wave of energy, leaching fury into his Mana and turning it bright red.

It was going to break his mind. Going to acquire him.

Each pulse rocked Arche, threatening to shake loose his defenses and consume him entirely. It whispered to him of power, of what it could do to his enemies. It roared at him to kill. It demanded blood and sacrifice and worship. As its demands grew, Arche's mind quivered. What could he do in the face of such power? It was beyond anything he'd ever experienced. He was nothing next to this unyielding hate, this undying violence. It would drown him and use him to exact a blood price against all of Tartarus. He would become nothing more than a mindless vessel to the fury.

Lost in a sea of blood.

The energy beat against Arche, crushing his construct from every side. It was growing harder to fight against it. As if it could sense his weakness, the waves of energy hit harder, came faster. He couldn't last against it. All he was would be lost in the darkness of the dungeon, never to reemerge. Arche would die and this rageful thing would live on. A face filtered in front of him, thought made form.

Lyssa.

He would never see her again. Enslaved to this maddening hate. Worse, if he did see her, there was no guarantee that this hatred wouldn't hurt her, wouldn't extend to her. He couldn't let that happen. More faces filtered through, joining Lyssa's.

Helwan. Tess. Odelia. Abraxios.

His friends. He couldn't let this hate rip them away from him. More faces joined the bunch. Vik, Gigator, Elpida, Cypress, Danocles, Baldwic, Theodorous. What would happen to them if he lost himself here? What would he do to them?

He pushed his hands through the crystal's walls and opened himself fully to it. He joined with the energy, felt the power of it, the pulsating rage, the thirst for blood. It consumed him. It would consume the world in glorious tribute.

Arche nudged it.

There was no battle cry, no defiant stand. The crystal wanted rage and blood but it wasn't Arche. When the crystal sent rage, Arche thought of his friends. When the crystal wanted blood, Arche sent back his will to protect his allies. He poured his Mana into the crystal and the waves of energy slowed. The crimson tides dulled and grew auburn, then orange.

Energy stopped flowing outward from the crystal altogether. He had tuned it to himself. Turned its power to new use, a weapon to help his friends. Divine Body was a powerful tool but he would use it to make a world worthy of his friends, not drown the old one in blood. Nearly drained of Mana, Arche fell out of his mindscape and back into his physical body.

Divinity has increased to 50%.

The message hung in Arche's vision as he caught his breath. His head pounded from lack of Mana but that didn't keep the grin from spreading across his face.

He was in control.

Howling from ahead reminded him that the beastmar were still a threat. He'd stayed still too long. It was time to move. With every step, he felt more confident, more certain of himself. The influence was suppressed and Arche was back in control over his own emotions. He doubted the fix was permanent. He didn't understand the crystal well enough to change it permanently but, for the moment, he was in charge. It could last for minutes or it could last for months. He could only hope that his Willpower would hold. Until then, his goal was unchanged.

There were beastmar that needed killing.

Arche reached into his mind again, this time focused outward. He expanded his mental awareness, imagining it as a net flung out in front of him. He connected each strand back to the walls of his consciousness, ready to pull his mind back at the first sign of danger. The psychic net didn't extend far, but in the darkness of the tunnel, barely illuminated by some bioluminescent moss, it would be a better indicator than anything else of how far ahead the beastmar were.

For several long minutes, Arche perceived nothing. He was forced to take it slow, one hand on the tunnel wall for guidance. His foot pressed a small slab of stone into the ground with an audible click.

Arche froze and looked down at his feet. There was no way to tell if the trap was ahead of him, behind him, or all around him, but stepping on it hadn't been enough to fully trigger it, likely he would have to step away. He weighed his options. Forward, back, or stay put. Not much to go on. If the pit he'd fallen into was really meant to be a spike trap, then it stood to reason that the trap would either be in front of him or around him to finish off survivors. Then again, he hadn't properly explored the spike pit and there might have been treasure he'd missed, which could mean the trap was around him or behind him. It all came down to whether or not he felt lucky. Either way, staying still was probably a bad option.

Arche stuck the Tridory into the ground and put one foot on it for leverage, then launched himself back the way he'd come. Fire erupted in the passage. The intense blast of heat washed over him, then he was out of it. Arche rolled along the ground, stamping out the embers that had caught on his clothing. He pushed himself to his feet, wincing as he saw thirty points had been taken off his Health bar, almost entirely undoing the healing that had occurred during his brief stint of unconsciousness. His clothing and armor had blocked the brunt of the flames but nothing had caught alight. Arche looked out at the still burning trap, blinking his eyes rapidly against the bright light.

The Tridory had apparently stuck into a second pressure plate and had pinned it in the active position. The flames weren't coming from spouts, as he expected, but from glowing runes placed all along the walls, floor, and ceiling. If whoever had designed this trap had included the runes both before and after the activation, Arche doubted he would have survived. As it was, the intensity of the flames was fading, white to blue to orange. Finally, the runes sputtered and died, their fires dying along with them. Arche eyed the rest of the passage warily before the last the flames died out, plunging him in darkness. The converging flames had incinerated much of the glowing moss in the tunnel and, even if they hadn't, they had killed his acclimation to the dark.

It was there, stuck in absolute darkness with afterglow burned into his retinas, that he heard shouting echo down the passage. Bestial howls signaled hunters who had prey within reach.

In spite of himself, a shiver of fear wormed its way into Arche's gut. He was alone, in the dark, potentially surrounded by traps, and was being hunted. He held his hand out to the side, calling the Tridory back to him. There was a hint of resistance as the spear ripped itself free of the floor, then it fell into his hand. With the heavy spear in hand, he felt a shadow of security, but was still at a serious disadvantage. Without knowing the number or location of additional traps around him, he couldn't move without risking his own death. All he could do was wait for the beastmar and hope that he survived the encounter.

The howls grew louder. The slapping of paws, feet, and hooves against stone echoed, heralding their arrival. Too many to get an accurate count, especially with the discordant harmonies and the fact that beastmar did not have a standardized number of limbs. Arche gripped the Tridory in both hands and cast his mental awareness outward again, taking pains to ensure that his mental walls were, if not strong, at least present. The last thing he needed was inexplicable bloodlust making him lose all caution and become a cooked dinner for the monsters.

Three tense minutes later, the beastmar entered his awareness. There were three of them and they proceeded more slowly than Arche had expected. He wasn't sure how far away they were, exactly. Thirty strides, perhaps. He had a vague sense of direction as well, which was helpful as his vision still hadn't acclimated to the near absolute darkness of the tunnel. Part of him considered activating Divine Body for the light the skill gave off but he dismissed the idea. Not only would he need to conserve that Mana in the event he actually needed to use the skill but activating it would only give him light for a few seconds, even if he tried to reign it in as much as he could. It wouldn't be enough time to do anything and it would ruin any acclimatization he'd achieved in the last few minutes. No, he wouldn't be able to gimmick his way out of this one. He was going to have to rely on strategy and luck.

Mostly luck.

"Oi! Uglies! I'm over here!"

His words echoed off the stone walls and the beastmar howled their response. They surged forward, much more quickly than before. Arche's hair stood on end as he felt them approach. They were nearly upon him when he heard a low *click* and saw the tell-tale red glow of runes.

Arche ducked, shielding his eyes as a torrent of flames shot out of the floor, walls, and ceiling, incinerating two of the beastmar in front of him. The last pulled up short, snarling at him from the other side of the flames. The runes slowly faded again, the fire dying down, but Arche was ready for it this time. He stood, twirling his spear before launching it into the conflagration. A surprised, pained yelp let him know that the attack had struck but the lack of an experience notification meant it was only wounded, not dead.

Arche held his hand out and summoned the Tridory back to him. It tore through the flames, landing warm and bloody in his palm. His psychic net told him that the creature was moving moments before it appeared, leaping through the flames at him.

"Wha—?"

The burning beastmar slammed into him. Arche's feet left the ground and he lost all sense of direction. His psychic net splintered into nothingness as his concentration broke and he lost all idea of where the beastmar was. His head hit something hard and it became difficult to think. Dazed, Arche tried to curl up, wracked with pain. A huge hand lifted him and hurled him into a wall.

There was a loud pop and pain flooded Arche's left shoulder. Heat flashed near him and feral screams bounded off the walls. It took him a few moments to realize he wasn't the only one screaming. The beastmar burned merrily and flailed about, desperately trying to douse itself. Arche met the beast's eyes and the creature stopped, then lunged toward him again.

"Shit, shit, shit!"

Arche scrambled backwards, his left arm nearly blinding him with pain. The beastmar tripped as it advanced, hitting the ground and scrabbling with three outstretched arms. Arche kicked out at it, connecting with the creature's face. It howled but one of its arms grabbed hold of Arche's ankle and yanked him forward. Arche yelped and tried to pull away, but the beastmar had too strong of a grip. The Tridory had been knocked from his grasp after the first hit and he didn't have the space to use it effectively here even if he had it. Another hand reached toward him.

Arche panicked.

Everything screamed. His arms, his chest, his legs, Arche himself, and the beastmar. The racket was unbearable. He didn't have space to pull his sword free, his left arm was limp and useless, and this creature was set on killing him even if it had to burn itself alive in the process. Arche knew in the pit of his stomach that he was going to die, alone in the dark where none of his friends would ever find him.

The fingers of his right hand curled into a fist, intent on making his final moments one of defiance, and closed instead around a sword hilt. He didn't have time to question it, he activated Divine Body and swung for all he was worth.

A heavy, wet weight fell on top of him. Arche trembled, whole body spasming as his conscious brain fought for control. Divine Body slipped away almost immediately, leaving him in complete darkness, colorful after-images still burned into his retinas. The weight pressed down on him, black blood soaking him through once more.

Arche shoved the bisected corpse off himself. Then the smell of blood, roasted meat, and feces reached his nose and he turned and heaved onto the ground next to him. The motion aggravated his injured ribs and he laid there, hurt, terrified, and revulsed.

Several attempts after he'd emptied the last dregs of his stomach, he'd calmed down enough that he could start thinking again. As much as his body wanted to go to sleep under the weight of his armor and the pain of his wounds, he knew that doing so could spell death for his friends, if not himself. Arche raised one hand out to the side and called upon his bond with the Tridory, summoning it to his hand. The action caused a tingle of pain to run through his head but the Tridory landed in his grip regardless. Checking his vitals, the reason became clear: he was running dangerously low on Mana.

Health: 144 / 495	Stamina: 84 / 355	Mana: 6 / 190
29%	24%	3%

No doubt about it, he'd seen better days. Using the spear, Arche hauled himself to his feet. His legs were unsteady, like he was standing on the bow of a ship over the open ocean. He stumbled to the side, pressing his weight up against the wall. His mind wandered away from his pain to wonder if he'd ever been on a ship, if such an endless expanse of water really existed and how nice it would be. The sea breeze running through his hair, the smell of salt, the endless expanse of blue above and below and the sun warming his skin.

The idea of it made the damp dark nearly unbearable.

"What I would give to level up right now."

He checked his Profession Quest status, knowing his leveling was blocked until he completed it.

Objectives
- Reach a Divinity of 100% (50/100)
- Do not die

"How the fuck do I do this?"

Arche tried to focus on each word but there were no descriptions, no hints.

"How am I supposed to figure out what to do? What even *is* Divinity?"

Divinity has increased to 55%.

Arche stared at the new message, then looked upward at the ceiling.

"Are you shitting me?"

Silence.

"It's just gonna be questions and speculation? I can't even get a condescending explanation?"

No.

~H

"What the fuck."

The notification appeared in the center of his vision for about three seconds, then dismissed itself. Whoever this 'H' was probably had answers to a lot more than just Divinity, if he could make them talk. It was an issue to shelve for later.

Moving forward, Arche used the sauroter of the Tridory to tap the trapped step and activate the fire runes. The hot air blasted him but he was far enough from the fire that it was only uncomfortable heat. When the flames died down, he limped across the trapped zone, leaning much of his weight against the spear and hoping there were no more traps in the passage.

The path ahead was long and dark, and he was injured, but there was still fight in him. He would fight these beastmar, down in their dark tunnels. He would fight these beings that were playing with his life. He would fight whatever he had to in order to save his friends and live free.

Chapter 37

Running was one of the few things Lyssa had always been good at. It didn't matter if it was into danger or out of it, she could run with the best of them. In Dawnwood, her speed was unmatched. On open ground, she was uncatchable. In the Sylv, she ran down her prey with all the wild power of a Huntress. Now, in the Vivitorium of Hekáte, Lyssa ran to survive.

She tore through the passages at top speed. Stagnant, underground air whipped past her head like wind as she lengthened her stride, practically leaping from one step into the next. No matter how fast she ran, though, the beastmar pursued. This was their territory and they knew it well.

When Arche had been tackled into a side-passage by the beastmar, she had been too slow to stop it. She saw them fall but could do nothing. He was gone, swept away into darkness. She waited for the notification to come, the realization to hit. She waited to be told that another person in her protection, who had trusted her, had died. That she had failed, again. That it was her fault, again.

The message never came.

Arche survived the fall. Somehow, some way, Arche was alive. She didn't know whether to laugh or to cry. As it turned out, she had time for neither. Two beastmar turned out of a side passage ahead of her. She ducked away as one swung at her with a greatsword wielded by arms that were too large for its body. The rest were behind her, their howls for blood and meat were deafening. Too many to fight. She could do nothing but run, away from the beastmar and away from Arche.

So she ran.

The twisted underground was unnaturally oppressive, with its dark passages and dead air. It was nothing like the gentle light of a woodland glade or the softness of grass in the bloom of spring. There was nothing of life in this place. Just endless death and things that should be dead. The beastmar were even more hateful than the undead she had fought at the Necropolis of Pygmaia. Something innate to their nature screamed of wrongness in words Lyssa could not vocalize. She could only seek to rectify the mistake by returning them to death, entomb them in this hypogean nightmare.

Lyssa had drilled the route through the passages into her mind, well past the point she felt comfortable navigating back, but being chased through it as she was, it was difficult not to feel lost. She had to hope she was on the right path, that Tess was waiting for her around some bend, but she didn't recognize the passages around her or remember these twists and bends. After an hour of running, with the sound of the beastmar forever echoing after her, she was forced to admit she was lost.

Her fingers twitched for her bow and swords. She could make a stand here and take down as many as she could. She could hunt these creatures and take their glory. Nearly two centuries of hunting had hardened her instincts and running away from prey was not an easy thing for her pride to allow – but she had learned the price of heedless pride. She saw the consequences of failure every time she closed her eyes.

It smiled at her from her brother's face.

Dozens of beastmar chased her. Skilled as she was, Lyssa couldn't defeat so many on her own, not in these narrow confines. She had to find Tess and save Arche. Together, the three of them could think of some way out of this mess. They'd had a plan, after all, and it had been only half mad, but it had barely started before it'd gone completely sideways.

Lyssa slowed to catch her breath.

Running so quickly had burned through quite a bit of her Stamina but there was little she could do about it. The sounds of pursuit echoed louder. Lyssa scowled down the passage. She'd taken several turns while out of sight of the beastmar; they should have been as lost as she was but it didn't sound like there were any less of them now than there had been before. They had some way of tracking her through the underground and that meant none of them were safe.

"Thrice-cursed, goat-smelling plains-walkers."

There was no recourse but to push on. She looked for any sign of familiarity, anything by which she could get some idea of her surroundings, but one stone passage was indistinguishable from another.

On and on she ran until a glimmer of light brought her sliding to a halt. Unlike the bioluminescent moss that occasionally wrapped the walls or ceiling, this glow indicated something else entirely.

Several small scratches in the stone, nearly parallel to one another, glowed with a soft, gentle light. Lyssa brushed a finger over them, feeling their coarseness and depth. She knew, without need of a notification, that it had been made by a beastmar and that it was relatively new, likely in the last day or two. The notification that did appear was much simpler.

Follow the Trail?	
Yes	No

The prompt appeared and disappeared nearly instantaneously. More scratches began to glow gold, leading the way in front of her. It was probably a bad idea. If she actually caught up to whatever had made the scratches, it would be an enemy to fight, but even stumbling upon an eventual enemy was better than being hunted like prey.

Time to run again.

The trail wound its way through intersections and across inclines. At one point, the trail even crept up onto the wall before turning sharply down a side passage. It was running, but whether it was running toward something or away was still a mystery. Lyssa chased the tracks until her Stamina flashed, the ten percent warning, then slowed her pace to a jog.

Going that low on Stamina was intense. Sweat trickled from every pore and her legs shook from the effort but she refused to walk. While it would take longer to regenerate her Stamina, the jog at least helped soothe some of her fears. She had no idea if Arche was in danger or if any beastmar had broken away from their pursuit of her and gone on to chase Tess. Their knowledge of the dungeon was better than hers and she wouldn't put it past them sweep all of the passages until she and the others were found.

Lyssa cursed Arche and his plans but there was no bite to it. He was a human and exceedingly ignorant but he was also earnest. Eager to learn and always ready to help, even against her own counseling. He was clever, and much better at interacting with the villagers than she was, but he was also annoyingly impulsive and too quick to throw himself into danger. Were he anyone else, she would have assumed he'd died. As it was, it was only because they were Companions that she knew he still lived.

Companions with a human. What a laughable thought.

It had scandalized her at first. Such bindings were rare among her people, who lived such long lives. She thought it was a punishment, some cosmic consequence for killing her brother, now she was bonded to a mortal who would eventually grow old and die.

It was the curse of the elves to know that they would outlast all others.

Arche was different, though. She was willing to admit she didn't have a lot of experience with the mortal races, having been born just before Dawnwood's isolation, but even from what she saw of Arche's interactions with them, he was an anomaly. Whether it was by virtue of his lost memories or simply the nature of who he was, he made an impact on everyone he met.

Thus, despite her best efforts, he had won her over. He was a stumbling child, too full of the youthful belief of self-invulnerability to recognize that he might be killed. It was the same attitude she had held before Gregori had died. It was that same sibling fear that gripped her now. She would find him. Find him and protect him before he got himself killed. Barring that, she would die alongside him before she buried another brother.

Wrapped up in her own thoughts, Lyssa didn't see the silhouette come tumbling out of a side passage until it collided with her. They hit the ground and Lyssa rolled away, rising into a crouch with a kopis in one hand, lips curled back in a feral snarl. The other figure groaned and sat up, rubbing the dirt out of straw-colored hair. Lyssa lowered the kopis fractionally.

"Tess?" the word was an incredulous whisper.

The figure paused.

"Lyssa? Is that you?"

Lyssa sheathed the kopis and stood, grasping Tess's arm and helping the human to her feet.

"It's me. What are you doing here?"

"What am *I* doing here?" Tess snorted. "I should be asking you that question. You two didn't come back and then there were beastmar everywhere. I was lucky to get out while I did. Where's Arche? I want to give him a piece of my mind."

Lyssa glanced away.

"He...fell. I couldn't help him. I don't know where he is, I only know he's alive." The words were more difficult than Lyssa expected them to be. They'd had to move past a rapidly rising lump in her throat.

Tess's face shifted. Emotions flitted across her face, far too quick and strange for Lyssa to understand them, but what settled seemed to be whatever passed in humans for resolve.

"If he's lost, we'll just have to go find him."

"I don't know where to start. Some distance behind me more beastmar are pursuing. This place is a maze. I cannot gather my surroundings."

"That's where you got lucky, Liz." Tess flashed a smile. "You've got me, now. Come on, I'll show you what your traps did to the first group of beastmar that ran by and we can retrace our steps."

The two set off running down the hallway. Tess led them through several turns until Lyssa was quite sure she would never have been able to find her way on her own, then before she knew it, they had emerged into the same corridor they had trapped.

What lay in front of them was nothing short of brutal.

Spikes, falling stones, pitfalls, caltrops, and much, much more had turned the passage into a bloody mess, like the shattered throat of a creature forced to swallow its own teeth. The beastmar scouting party had been annihilated.

Lyssa gazed over Odelia's work with a grim sense of satisfaction. These creatures were anathema to nature. She had hunted all manner of beast and bird, but beastmar were something else entirely. They tainted the grass that bent beneath their feet, their very existence leeching poison into the natural world. She would see them crushed before they could bring ruin to more.

"We don't have time to waste."

They stepped carefully through the remains of the trapped hallway, then on toward the cavern. Several minutes later, they found the intersection where she and Arche had been separated. Lyssa peered down into the dark, but the monochrome color and odd shapes made it impossible to judge distance. Tess also peered down, though she couldn't see nearly as far in the poor light.

"How far does it go?"

"I'm not sure."

Tess produced a torch and had it lit in seconds. She dropped it down into the darkness, watching as it shone a ring of light on the stone walls as it fell. After two and a half seconds, the torch clattered against the ground, showing a mess of pit spikes and the dark stain of a splattered beastmar.

Lyssa and Tess both caught their breath at the sight.

"That's got to be thirty meters, at least," the Rogue said.

Lyssa nodded, peering into the darkness for any sign of Arche.

"The corpse has been burned and there's a small blood trail leading away from the beastmar. It looks like he had a soft landing."

Arche! Tess hissed down into the hole, simultaneously trying to be loud and quiet.

There was no response from the pit.

"We should find a way to get down there," Lyssa said, already combing her inventory for rope.

Tess hesitated.

"I'm not sure that's the best plan."

"What are you talking about? He's down there and needs our help."

"He was down there, yeah, hours ago. But what happens if we go down there and then we get stuck? Don't forget the beastmar are still after us."

"And what if he's too injured to move or speak and, by not going down there, we leave him to die."

Tess winced.

"I hear you, I do, but what would you do if you were down there?"

Lyssa paused, considering.

"I would try to find my way out. Get back to the group as quickly as possible."

"Right. Staying still for too long in this place means the beastmar will catch up. I want to find him too, but right now we have other problems. Do you know how many beastmar fled the chamber to chase after you?"

Lyssa shook her head.

"A few dozen, perhaps. Most of the cave, but probably not all."

"Then we should circle back and hit them while they're not expecting it. We might be able to clean up the end, then find Arche once the threat is gone."

"I don't like the idea of leaving him to fend for himself," Lyssa said, frowning.

"Me neither, but you have to admit he's pretty hard to kill."

"Not for lack of trying."

Tess's cheeks reddened but Lyssa ignored it. They had more pressing matters.

"He's still alive, isn't he?" Tess asked, the question sounding more genuine than rhetorical.

"For now, at least."

"Then there's still hope. We should do what we can, not chase shadows. I have a feeling he's going to find us before we find him, anyway."

Lyssa let out a long, heavy breath, then nodded.

"Very well. Let's go hunting."

The two turned and raced down the passage, toward where the whole mess had started.

Chapter 38

Arche kept a close eye on his vitals as he trudged along the passage. His Stamina and Mana rose rather quickly. With his current Wisdom of twenty-five, he regenerated about thirteen percent of his total Mana pool per minute. Ideally, his Stamina would regenerate at a similar rate, tied instead to his Endurance, but it seemed walking while injured was enough of an exertion to slow the regeneration. Still, in under eight minutes, Arche had a fully regenerated Mana pool.

"Here goes nothing."

Arche closed his eyes and brought up his vitals. Then, doing his best to control the flow of Mana, he activated Divine Body. Despite his efforts at control, his Mana plummeted while his Health and Stamina rocketed upwards. Straining against the flow as hard as he could, he managed to last three seconds before he was forced to deactivate the skill, leaving him with only seventeen Mana and a pounding headache.

Health: 414 / 495	**Stamina**: 355 / 355	**Mana**: 17 / 190
84%	100%	9%

Arche grinned. His pain levels had gone from 'hurts to breathe' down to the more manageable level of 'don't bend over too quickly.' He'd also managed to avoid Mana Burnout, which was the real victory. He took a hesitant step forward, then another, confident now that his body was no longer mired in the agony of his wounds. Arche grinned and broke into a run, racing down the passage. Just being able to run again was freeing.

The passage eventually led to a huge, steel door. Arche pulled up short, cursing at himself. His relief at healing himself was making him reckless. There were traps here and, now that he was mostly uninjured for the first time in a while, he was racing off *again* to get hurt by more traps.

He had to be more careful. Arche narrowed his eyes at the floor and walls in front of him, trying to spot anything out of the ordinary. Nothing stood out to him, so he crept forward until he stood an arm's length from the door. It was twice as tall as Arche and broad enough for three men to walk through together without touching. A massive padlock the size of a kite shield secured the door to the stone frame. Arche rubbed a hand over the scars on his chin. Even if he had lockpicking tools or knew how to use them, this lock was almost comically massive. The key would have to be the size of a sword and he hadn't seen anything like that in the dungeon.

Arche took a step back and considered the problem. Either he could turn back and try to find another way through or he could figure out how to outsmart the locked door and see what was on the other side. Treasure was a strong possibility but it could also be a trap. Whatever was on the other side of the door was clearly either valuable or dangerous, perhaps both. He was also very curious about why such a large door was necessary. He scrutinized the lock again. It was a simple padlock with a front facing keyhole, looped through a metal bar in the door and the stone wall. What really caught his interest, however, was the shackle that ran the top of the lock.

Arche looked at the Tridory in his hand.

"I'm actually kind of glad no one else is here to see this."

Without further ceremony, he stuck the tip of the spear through the looping shackle of the lock, then pressed the second button on the Tridory's shaft. Metal screeched as the Tridory switched from spear into bident. The sharpened edges pressed against the metal, then sliced through. The lock fell to the ground with a heavy, echoing clang. Arche winced, reverted the bident into a spear, and looked at the broken pieces of lock on the ground.

"I take it back. I wish someone saw that."

With no visible handle to grasp and pull, Arche threw his shoulder into the door. The old metal groaned, grating against stone as it swung inward. Arche tensed, spear ready to stab at the first sign of danger. It was still a dungeon, after all.

He slipped through as soon as there was room. Once inside, it was hard not to gawk at the marked change in environment. Gone were the dimly lit halls and passages that had littered the dungeon so far. He was in a laboratory, similar to the one he had blown up far above, but much more advanced. Beakers and vials of liquids stood in various contraptions designed to heat, cool, condense, and melt all around the room. The room itself was massive, easily the size of a dining hall and filled with gray and white machinery. The floor was tiled, as opposed to monolithic stone, and eerie, flickering lights lined the ceiling in rows, shining a sanitary white glow onto everything.

Large tables covered in dried blood took up a fair portion of the room, but what was more interesting was the figure dressed in white, bent over one of the tables. Arche tensed, ready for trouble. The figure straightened, as if sensing his attention. A shadow crossed over them and they disappeared.

Arche blinked, then spun to find the figure standing behind him. It was a woman, but unlike any woman Arche had ever seen. She was tall, towering half as tall again as Arche, with skin that ebbed and flowed from one shade into another. Some parts of her seemed like stone or steel, others exhibited all the tones of flesh that Arche had ever seen and many he had not. She had long, thick, dark hair tied behind her head with a piece of simple cord.

"I do not appreciate disturbances in my work, spark."

Her voice was low and made the air tremble. A chill ran through Arche. Whatever this woman was, she was the same as the Oneiroi. The same as Death.

"Sorry for the disturbance," he said, struggling to keep his voice even and calm. "Miss?"

The woman stared down at him, her face impassive.

"I am Hekáte."

There was a short pause, then Arche stuck out one hand.

"A pleasure. I'm Arche."

A baffled look crossed Hekáte's face for a moment. Clearly, her name had not had the effect she intended. Ignoring Arche's proffered hand, she crossed her arms and looked down at him.

"What are you doing here, little spark?"

Hekáte's voice held a note of command, compelling Arche to answer.

"I was separated from my companions in this dungeon. Your door came up along my path, so I entered."

Arche dropped his arm when it became clear she wasn't going to shake it. Something in his mind itched. There was some familiarity to her name. He had seen or heard it before, he was sure of it, but he couldn't place it.

"You are different." Hekáte sniffed the air and narrowed her eyes at him. *"You are not from Tartarus."*

Arche frowned, cocking his head to one side, but before he could respond, Hekáte continued.

"Ah, one of my cousins has been meddling with things they should have left well enough alone. It is of no consequence to me. I have long abandoned your world for my own projects. Projects that you are interrupting, spark."

Arche faltered for a moment, grasping for something to say. "I don't mean to interrupt you, but I'm pretty confused right now. Do you...do you know there's a bunch of beastmar that live here too?"

"Beast...mar..." Hekáte dragged the word out. *"Describe these creatures."*

"Well, erm, they come in a lot of different varieties. Some are hairy, some are smooth. Some look like people, others are much more animalistic. Almost all of them have extra limbs or extremities. They tend to have grayish skin and fur."

Hekáte frowned, her head tilted slightly to one side. Her eyes unfocused as they began flitting about, as though she were interacting with some interface.

"Attend me, spark."

A shadow fell across her and she was gone. Arche turned and found her standing next to one of the tables stained with blood, near where she had been when he had first entered. He hastened over to her, one hand pressed to his nose to block out the growing smell of chemicals. Hekáte flipped through a large, leather-bound tome. She settled on a page and turned the book around, showing several masterful sketches of beastmar, some in anatomical poses and others standing in life-like postures.

"Is this the creature you speak of?"

"Yes. Why do you have pictures of them?"

Arche raised his eyes to meet hers. Hekáte grimaced and closed the tome.

"A failed experiment. I thought I had disposed of them. Clearly I have not. My guardian must have been subjugated while I worked."

"Hekáte." Arche hesitated. "I'm not going to pretend I understand what's going on here, but here's what I do know. I'm here to destroy the beastmar. They're threatening a village on the surface and have to be stopped. Did you...make...the beastmar?"

Hekáte stared over Arche's head, lost in thought. Arche was about to repeat his question, thinking perhaps she hadn't heard him, when she answered.

"Yes."

"They've caused a lot of suffering."

"That is not my concern."

"It concerns me. I'm trying to stop them, but I can't do it on my own. Now, it sounds to me like you owe a debt."

Hekáte's presence magnified until it was a physical force pressing into Arche. He braced against it as best he could but was pushed back a step under the weight of her displeasure.

"Be careful what you demand of me, little spark."

"I'm not demanding anything of you." Arche tried to keep his voice firm while doing his best not to crumple; just standing near her drained his Stamina. "I have an idea of what you are and I know that I have no way of forcing you to do anything you decide you don't want to do. But you bear some responsibility for what has happened. I am asking you to help me set it right."

Hekáte looked thoughtful, then her gaze drifting to the Tridory.

"Curious," she said at last. *"I had thought that lost some time ago."*

"You know about this weapon?"

"The Tridory. Forged by a relative of mine who always did like to tinker. Of all my large family, he is one for whom I have the most respect. That his creation has fallen into your hands...curious. That you are capable of wielding it, more so."

Hekáte's voice trailed away, lost in thought. Arche felt the silence stretch on between them, then her overwhelming presence faded. He gasped and took a deep breath, feeling suddenly lightheaded.

"Very well. I am forbidden from directly interfering in the affairs of mortals, even here, but I can provide you this. My guardian has been subjugated by these creatures. I know not how they accomplished such a feat, but there is no doubt that magic is involved. Take this." Hekáte conjured a small bone, about the length of Arche's hand, and held it out. *"This will mark you as a friend. With the guardian free, you will be able to clear out the infestation."*

Arche took the bone from her and stored it safely in his inventory.

"Thank you. What will you do when this is over?"

Hekáte smiled. *"It is time, I think, to move my Vivitorium once more, but I will wait until you have accomplished your task and left my domain."*

Her form flickered but she did not fade entirely. A copy of her appeared on the other side of the table and another behind Arche. He was surrounded, encircled by three Hekátes.

"I trust you will not fail me, little spark," the Hekátes spoke in unison.

The hair on the back of Arche's neck pricked up.

You have been offered a **Quest**.

Save the Guardian

Hekáte has bade you free her guardian and given you the tools necessary to see the job done.

Objectives	**Rewards**
- Free Hekáte's Guardian	- 5,000 experience - Increased Divinity - Favor of Hekáte

Penalty for Refusal or Failure
- Unknown (almost certainly bad)

Accept this **Quest**?

Yes	No

Arche frowned at the penalty but nodded. He would have accepted regardless, considering it would only help him, but the extra rewards were not something he was going to turn his nose up at.

"Thank you. If I may ask, though, what do you mean by 'Favor of Hekáte?'"

Each Hekáte raised an eyebrow.

"You would rather have it than lose it. This world may have forgotten its gods but that does not mean we have forgotten this world. Go, now. I have much work to do and can abide this interruption no longer."

Her words, spoken out of three mouths, were thick with compulsion. Arche found himself walking to a door with a horizontal handle near the top. Mechanically, he grabbed the handle and pulled. The door opened out toward him from the top, pivoting on some axis near the ground to reveal a chute.

"Aw, man," Arche whispered before the compulsion made him climb inside.

Arche slid down the smooth passage with a single thought running through his head.

I've really got to stop letting strange, powerful beings fuck with me.

Chapter 39

Lyssa took a deep, measured breath and sighted down the shaft of her arrow. On the other side, plus an additional fifty meters, stood twenty beastmar. On her right, Tess crouched, knives in hand, glaring at the beastmar with as much hatred as Lyssa felt. They had emerged into the cavern to see it had mostly emptied, the rest out searching the dungeon for them.

The few beastmar left lazed about, conversing in groups or sleeping. A couple sharpened blades with large, flat stones, another few harried prisoners in a cage made from bone. Arche had told her there were a dozen in the cage but that number had dwindled down to six.

They hadn't been fast enough to save those people. In truth, they'd barely been fast enough to save themselves and not completely. Arche was still lost. Lyssa's fingers clenched around the oiled wood of her bow as she activated a Student maneuver, Drill Shot. The arrow lanced through the air, spinning and shrieking like a banshee the entire way.

The beastmar froze when they heard the noise, unable to see where it was coming from as the sound echoed off the stone. The arrow struck one beastmar in the side of the head, plunging straight through to embed itself, still spinning, into another's torso. The first had been killed outright, but the other howled in agony as the arrow continued to churn inside its flesh. It wouldn't kill the second, but it removed the threat, for the time being.

The maneuver would continue drilling for another five seconds but Lyssa had already moved on to her next arrow. She stood, letting the beastmar get a good look at her, then loosed another shot. Tess activated Stealth, disappearing even from Lyssa's sight. Knives struck down unsuspecting beastmar, coming from seemingly nowhere as the Rogue flitted in and out of sight like an apparition.

Things were going better than expected, all things considered. Together, they had taken down over half a dozen of the beastmar, with another dozen well on the way. Lyssa strafed to the side, each draw of her bow spelling death for the monstrous things before her.

The air hummed and filled with static. Lyssa abandoned her shot and dove for the ground. As fast as she was, the lightning was faster. It crashed into her and blasted her away. She tumbled across the rock, feeling every nerve in her body twitch and spasm with pain. Her combat notifications triggered, giving her the information without distraction.

Lightning Bolt: 184 Damage
Stunned: 00:03

Sparks flashed up and down her body. Every attempt to move was met with blinding pain as her limbs ignored her commands to instead jerk and flail of their own accord. Three seconds might as well have been an eternity. The lightning had cost her precious time, time that the beastmar had used to catch up with her. Her bow was gone, flung from her reach by the muscle spasms.

With fried nerves, Lyssa got to her feet, still feeling unsteady. The beastmar had split into three groups. Three beastmar approached her, weapons and claws raised. Another five attempted to surround Tess, who still flickered in and out of stealth as she fought. The last three were ranged fighters, two stringing bows while a robed beastmar—the only one Lyssa had ever seen wearing clothing—chanted and waved a blue-white wand. That meant trouble, but there were more pressing concerns.

Lyssa side-stepped, dipping her head as a beastmar with large, bear-like claws slashed at her. She twisted and the claw sailed past, less than a hair's breadth from rending her flesh. Then she dove forward, rolling beneath the trampling horse-like legs of another beastmar that resembled a corrupted centaur. She brought one arm up as she came back to her feet, a kopis materializing in time to deflect a swung axeblade harmlessly to the side. Lyssa turned with the momentum and threw an elbow into the axe-wielding beastmar's face.

Over its shoulder, Tess spun and danced, knives flashing as the rogue flipped and rolled, always moving and stabbing at the five beastmar still working to encircle her. As close as the beastmar were, the Rogue couldn't disappear into Stealth any longer.

Huge hands grabbed Lyssa from behind, then she was flying through the air. She spun, trying to get her feet under her, but to no avail. She hit the ground back-first, bouncing and rolling across the stone floor. Pain lanced through her side as she fought to get her feet under her. Hesitation was death; the pain could be dealt with later.

The centaurian beastmar bore down on her, wielding a large spear pointed forward to run her through. Lyssa deflected the spear tip high with her sword but momentum carried the beastmar forward. They collided and Lyssa was thrown to the ground. Her head smacked wetly against stone.

Lyssa blinked hard, bleary as she tried to gather her thoughts. It was dark, but she couldn't hear the night insects or see the moons. Strange. She didn't normally spend the night outside of Dawnwood. It wasn't safe.

A combat notification flashed in front of her.

Dazed: 00:07

Reality wormed its way in slowly. Dawnwood was behind her, a past she would never see again. She was deep below ground, far away from her beloved forest, in a battle to the death – but in the moment, it was hard to care. She missed the open air, the forest, her brother. Anywhere was better than here.

Lyssa tried to push herself to her feet but her body was rebellious and her legs wouldn't respond. Four seconds left. Pressure gripped her wrists. Lyssa shifted, trying to wrench away but it held her fast. Something impacted the side of her face.

Lyssa blinked hard and the world swam back into focus. She was suspended, held aloft by rope that now bound her hands together, lifted by the centaurian beastmar. Its distorted grey-brown face snarled at her triumphantly. Lyssa bared her teeth and snarled back, wriggling side-to-side, trying to loosen the beastmar's grip.

A heavy fist slammed into her face, rocking her head back. Green blood flowed steadily from her nose, dripping down her face and onto the ground below but, if anything, it only made her angrier. The beastmar hauled back for another blow but Lyssa was ready. She drew herself up, pulling on the rope until her arms protected her head; she curled her legs in and kicked forward, planting both feet into the beastmar's face. It reeled backwards and dropped her. Lyssa twisted in the air, landing hands-first, and tucked herself into a roll.

Static charge rent the air and Lyssa threw herself to the side. A blast of lightning flashed above her, deafening thunder echoed off the cavern walls. Lyssa blinked, trying to clear the afterimage from her eyes. An arrow clattered against the stone ground next to her, splintering on impact. Lyssa grabbed the shattered arrowhead and turned the sharpened edges of metal against the rope tying her hands.

She had barely scratched the rough-spun when she was forced to dodge again. The centaurian beastmar bore down on her with its bloodied, fierce visage matching her own in all but color. The beastmar reared up on hind legs, aiming to trample her. Lyssa cursed and stumbled back, coming up against the bars of the cage. Her mind raced but there was no way out.

The centaurian beastmar swung around to charge her once again. Behind it and to the right, the magic-wielding beastmar and his archer accompaniment focused on pinning Tess down, whose armor was stained red from a dozen minor wounds. The Rogue kept moving forward but her movements grew slower by the moment. In her wake, several beastmar clutched mortal wounds, spilling the last of their black blood onto the rocks. The rest attempted to catch her before she reached the archers. The more immediate concern to Lyssa, however, were the three beastmar intent on ripping her limb from limb. The bear-claw beastmar charged from the right, the axe-wielder from the left, and the centaurian with the spear was in front.

No fear gripped Lyssa as the three beastmar bore down on her.

She had no weapons, nowhere to run. Her hands were bound but she held her head high. Blood flowed from her nose and she spat more from her mouth, letting loose a savage war cry that held every broken thought and feeling she'd repressed for the last ten years. She filled it with her pain, her grief, and her rage.

They would kill her – but she would have them know fear before the end.

Hands grabbed her shoulders and pulled her backward, between the bars and into the cage. She fell into a pile of tangled limbs as the beastmar collided in front of her. Iron and bone buckled and bent around the weight of impact; the whole cage gave a threatening shudder. There was a wet squelch as the centaurian beastmar's spear, which had been leveled toward Lyssa's heart only a moment ago, was too slow in moving off-target and pierced clean through the torsos of the other beastmar. They howled in agony, not dead but gravely wounded.

Lyssa felt the rope binding her hands fall away as the prisoners of the cage came to her aid. One moved forward and grabbed the spear, wrenching it from the centaurian beastmar by pulling it through the other two. A hoarse cry broke free from one of the prisoners, a dwarf, who snatched up the fallen axe of the beastmar and slipped through the bars of the cage. More of the prisoners surged forward, three running through the gaps between bars to pummel the beastmar with fists and feet. Someone grabbed the centaurian beastmar's leg, holding it fast while the dwarf swung his axe into its side.

"Die!" one of the prisoners shouted, striking out with a broken length of chain.

The tide had turned. Tess closed in on the archers, one of which had already fallen to a thrown knife. Two beastmar gave chase but they wouldn't catch her in time. The mage beastmar raised its wand into the air and barked a word of power. The air rippled outward from the wand's tip. A primal instinct told her to make herself small. She stuck her fingers into what was left of her ears and closed her eyes. The ripple crashed into her like a wall of sound. A screeching, horrible, burning noise that drowned everything. Blood dripped from her ears, squelched against her fingers. Lyssa fell to the ground, throat hoarse with screams, silent against the noise. It was too much. Too much by far.

The sound faded, echoing off the stone in a phantom cry. Lyssa gasped and smeared tears into blood with the back of her hand. The magus was far across the cavern, moving toward a passage that would lead to a smaller cavern, if Arche's map had been accurate. A dull roar echoed from behind Lyssa, coming from the tunnels that led to the rest of the complex. The other prisoners stopped and turned as well. Howls, barks, and cries for blood and battle echoed back.

The horde was coming.

Chapter 40

The smell was the first thing Arche noticed. It blasted into him, hot, fetid, and rancid. He had to fight to keep his gorge from rising through it all. The slide took him through a myriad of different turns and drops until he was utterly scrambled and confused. He'd barely managed to hold onto the Tridory without it getting stuck in a wall or accidentally impaling himself on either end of it.

The landing was squishy, which, when combined with the smell, made for a unique revulsion that Arche was sure he'd feel again in his dreams, if he survived the day. There wasn't much light, only a dim glow from bioluminescent moss, but it was enough to see the truth of things. The floor was covered in bones, some still with rotting flesh attached. More smells mingled in, excrement and other waste. A massacre in a sewer would have been more pleasant.

Arche coughed, trying and failing not to gag. He stumbled away from the mess, toward a dark opening in the rocks, making it only a handful of steps before vomiting, then stumbled on again. A tunnel stood next to the dark recess. When he reached it, the rocks rumbled. A deep, grating rasp, so heavy it made Arche's chest thrum. He spun, trying to find the source of the noise. From the recess, four yellow orbs appeared, the size of bucklers. They blinked at him, two at a time. Horror crept up Arche's spine and settled somewhere near the crown of his head.

Not orbs, eyes.

Arche stumbled back and brought the Tridory up defensively. The sound intensified until it became a part of Arche. Bones vibrated across the floor with the force of it and the moss shivered, making the light flicker. The eyes moved closer. Sparks flashed near the ground, revealing monstrous claws scraping against the stone, the sound lost to the bone-shaking growl emanating from two separate heads.

"Whoa, whoa, easy!" Arche couldn't hear his own voice.

He stumbled on something unseen and fell, landing heavily on his back. The creature advanced, not hearing or not caring about his attempts at placation.

The sound was all encompassing. Even if Arche had shouted, not a word would get through, so he cast his mind toward the creature, trying to get some sense of what he was dealing with. He brushed against a vast consciousness, larger than anything Arche had connected to before. To say a storm of emotions swirled inside the beast would not do it credit, there was an entire world of consciousness, full of agony and hunger and hatred. It swarmed over Arche, threatening to bury him in its immensity. Arche's mind cried out at the weight of it, the intensity. He tried to project peace, friendliness, but it was like flicking a drop of water into the sun. It would consume him, mind and body.

Another consciousness appeared. If this roiling planet of emotions was the sun, then the new consciousness was the moon. It was sadness and apathy, the spirit of a broken creature that no longer remembered how to hope. It was drops of water, tempering out the flames that beat against Arche's consciousness, giving him just enough respite together his concentration in a desperate cry.

'Hekáte!'

The roiling world of pain pulled back a fraction and from it came a thunderous, snarling, echoing voice.

'WHO ARE YOU TO INVOKE THAT NAME?'

Arche shuddered beneath the weight of the voice. This creature was on a completely different level. It radiated with power and fury.

'I was tasked by her to free you.'

The beast's growl intensified, reverberating around his mind in their mental link as easily as it did around the stone walls.

'YOU LIE.'

'No! She gave me proof!'

The beast hesitated.

'DECEIVE US AND WE WILL CONSUME YOU.'

Arche had never retrieved an item from his inventory so quickly. He held the bone high for each of the four eyes to inspect.

'She gave me this. Said it would mark me as a friend. I'm not here to fight you, I'm here to free you.'

'MISTRESS GAVE YOU THIS. IT SMELLS OF HER. BUT MISTRESS ABANDONED US, LET US BE ENSLAVED BY THE FOUL ONES.'

Despair flooded the connection, gripping icy fingers around Arche's mind as the ocean of anger ebbed.

'She didn't know. When she found out, she asked me to free you. Let me help you.'

'YOU CANNOT FREE US. YOU LACK THE ABILITY.'

Arche gritted his teeth. At the same time, a noise echoed faintly out of the tunnel to his side, some sort of explosion.

'Then tell me how to help you.'

'YOU MUST FIND THE FOUL ONE WHO ENSLAVED US AND BRING US THE WAND OF HIS CONTROL.'

'Then you'll be free?'

'THEN MY HOME IS A PRISON NO LONGER.'

Arche stood to his feet.

'All right, I'll do what I can. Do you have a name?'

A slight growl reverberated from the creature and it took another step forward. Arche caught his first full sight of the creature. A massive hound, three times his height at its shoulder, with two growling heads. Its fur was dark and matted in places, impossible to place the color in the low light.

'GO.'

Arche didn't argue, he just went. He picked up his spear and ran toward a conjoining tunnel in the wall. Before he slipped inside, however, he looked back at the massive hound and activated Examine.

Orthrus		
Level: ?	Profession: ?	
Race: Kerberos	Trade: ?	
Age: ?	Traits: ?	
Height: ?	Companions: ?	
Weight: ?	Adventuring Party: ?	
Health: ?	Stamina: ?	Mana: ?

It was the second time his Examine skill had failed to read a creature properly and it was no more reassuring. Vik had felt guarded from his skill but this felt more like the skill simply failed. Like this Orthrus was so far beyond Arche that his skill could not encapsulate it, not at its current level. As Arche severed the link and turned away, he could still feel four golden eyes boring into his back.

The encounter had reinforced the fact that he was still weak. Creatures of immense power dwelled in Tartarus and, as things stood, he had no chance of facing them. The beastmar, however, were a vanquishable foe.

Arche broke into a run. Lyssa and Tess would likely be in the thick of things, as headstrong as both women were. If they hadn't been attacked in the tunnels, they probably would have continued on with the plan. Arche wasn't sure of exactly how much time had passed since they were separated, but he hoped they were alive. The darkness of the tunnel gave way as he emerged into a much larger cavern. A chaotic sight met him.

Prisoners wielding crude, makeshift weapons hacked at a few beastmar near the middle of the room. Lyssa was among them, drenched in blood and looking as though she had finished wading through a veritable horde of monsters. Tess was also there, chasing down a few stray beastmar barreling toward Arche at top speed. One of them, wearing a robe, leveled a stick in his direction.

"Oh, shit." Arche slid to a stop over the loose gravel.

The air filled with static charge. Arche quickly switched his grip on the Tridory and threw it, hoping to at least distract the creature. A moment later, lightning flared from the wand. Arche flinched, waiting for the pain, but it never came. Instead, it arced in mid-air toward the Tridory, condensing into the spear point and running along its entire length. The beastmar with the wand stepped to the side and the Tridory sailed past, still crackling with electricity, before sticking the ground and dispersing the lightning. Arche stared at the spear.

"That's a new one."

Then the beastmar were on him. There were three in total. The one with the wand—the most humanoid of the three with a snarling wolfish face and dark robes—stood away from him, muttering incantations. The other two were hunched over, with huge, powerful arms like gorillas. One carried a massive bow and tried to shoot arrows at Tess, but clearly lacked Lyssa's skill in the matter. The other had dropped its bow in favor of trying to pummel Arche with fists the size of dinner plates.

Arche leaned back as far as he could to avoid a right cross that threatened to break bones. Before he could recover, a kick threw Arche to the ground. He grunted from the impact and rolled away. As he came up, a thick, black arrow from the other beastmar sank halfway into his left shoulder. Arche let out a cry of pain as his Health dropped twenty percent.

He grabbed the arrow and snapped it off, a small portion protruding out from his leather jerkin. There was no time to draw his sword. The beastmar was on him again, barking and screaming as it whaled down blows. Arche slipped and dodged, then struck out with the broken arrow. He kept the creature between himself and the other beastmar, using it to give himself cover from more arrows. Every strike left a small puncture in the beastmar's skin that oozed black blood onto the ground. Arche's own hands were covered in the stuff as he used his superior speed to stab the beastmar over and over, screaming all the while.

After an intense exchange, the beastmar stood in front of him, roaring in pain and anger. Its arms were covered in small holes to the point it could barely move. Arche stabbed upward, embedding the arrow into the creature's neck, then activated Divine Body just long enough to plant his foot into its midsection.

The beastmar flew back and collided with the bow-wielding beastmar, who had been waiting for a clean shot. They both went down in a tumble. Arche was now in the open, just in time for the wolf-man beastmar to launch its next attack.

A pale-yellow beam of light extended from the tip of the wand, bathing Arche in a conical glow. He froze, magical weights pressing on him from all sides. Steel bands couldn't have done a better job, his body simply refused to move. The beastmar raised the wand and Arche was lifted into the air. His stomach lurched, but there was nothing he could do. He couldn't even blink. The beastmar gave him an evil grin, then turned and made a motion not dissimilar to the casting of a fishing rod.

Arche went flying. He soared well above the ground, toward Lyssa and the prisoners, then over them. The ground was rushing to meet him and he was falling far too quickly. Something whizzed past his face, cutting across the palm of his right hand. He grabbed at it reflexively, fingers closing around a coarse rope. Then he wasn't falling any longer. He was suspended, still fairly high up, dangling from a rope tied to an arrow embedded deeply into the stone wall. The other end of the rope, angled sharply downwards, was held by Lyssa.

"Lyssa!"

"Hurry up and get down!" she shouted back, clearly straining to keep the rope taut.

Arche reached back with his wounded arm, grimacing at the pain, and grabbed the loose end of his cloak. He flung it over the rope and began to slide. At a manageable height, he dropped, tumbling into a roll as he hit the ground, his every injury crying out in protest. When he came up, Lyssa stood in front of him, drenched in blood and grime.

"You all right?"

"I'm just glad you're alive." She gave him a tired smile. "I'm growing weary of these caves."

"You and I both. What say we finish this and get out of here?"

"Agreed. What happened to the monster through the passage?"

Arche held out his hand and called the Tridory back to him. The trident pulled itself free of the ground and began twirling back toward him, flying across the distance with impressive speed.

"Still there. We have an arrangement. We need to get the mage's wand."

"You...*what?*"

"I need the mage's wand."

Arche caught the spear and looked at Lyssa, who already had an arrow knocked to her bow.

"Forget it, I'll explain later. What's the situation?"

"A half-dozen half-dead prisoners ready for blood, about the same number of beastmar with another horde on the way behind us. None of us have a way to counter that wandwork."

"All right, take out the other archer, then see if any of the prisoners can use a bow. Take them and prepare for the horde. The rest of us will clean up here, I'll take out the mage, then we'll see about escape."

"How are you going to get past the mage's spells?" Lyssa sighted down another arrow before letting it fly.

"Persistence."

"That won't work. He's more than capable of killing you before you get close enough to hurt him. Go get his attention, I have a plan."

Arche grinned and nodded. They broke into a run, splitting off. Lyssa toward Tess, who was forced to give up her pursuit and deal with the two beastmar hoping to sharpen their blades on her bones, and Arche toward the mage who had relaxed his retreat to cast lightning and bolts of fire at the prisoners, who were doing their best to stay out of the way of the deadly magic.

The mage saw him coming, bearing a wolfish snarl as it leveled its wand toward him. Static energy enveloped the air as a bolt of lightning shot out the end toward Arche. Arche swung the Tridory and the lightning arced into the spear, flashing and arcing down the runework of the shaft. It grew warm under his touch and he felt a burst of energy as a notification appeared before him.

You have discovered a feature of the **Tridory**.

Lightning Manipulation

Upon contact with lightning, the Tridory will activate Mode 1: Spear. During this time, it can store lightning to be discharged in an attack, dealing bonus lightning damage. Additionally, this lightning can be siphoned by the wielder to induce the **Innervated** status condition.

Innervated

+50% Reaction Time
+15% Movement Speed
+25% Lightning Resistance
+100% Stamina Regeneration

Innervated: 2:58

Arche's stride lengthened as he sped over the ground. The lightning filled his veins with energy. It wasn't painful, despite what little was left of his logical mind saying it should be. Instead, it was like he'd taken a hefty dose of caffeine straight to his veins. He felt *amped.*

The beastmar, on the other hand, stumbled away from him. Fear danced across its features for the first time. It leveled its wand at Arche again. Spouts of flame flew toward him with impressive speed and frequency, but his new reaction time made them seem slow. Still, it delayed his chase as he zigged and zagged around the fire.

Seeing that the fire was only delaying the inevitable, the beastmar howled a cry of frustration and leveled his wand at Arche once more. A small, golden glow gathered around the wand's tip and Arche threw himself to the side, grunting in pain as the broken arrow in his shoulder scraped the ground. A golden cone of energy flashed where he'd been standing, disappearing a moment later. The mage snarled and bolted toward the tunnel containing the kerberos.

Arche cursed and gave chase, gaining ground but not quickly enough. At his pace, the beastmar would get to Orthrus and no doubt set it upon them.

That was when Tess came out of Stealth and sank two daggers into the beastmar's throat. With the speed and efficiency of a professional butcher, she detached the muscles, bones, and tendons connecting the beastmar's head to its torso. Its hands shot up reactively even as its head fell to the ground, then the corpse toppled, crushing its own skull under the weight of its body.

The prisoners swarmed the remaining two beastmar, burying them beneath angry bodies. The jubilation was short-lived, however, as a howl arose from the far end of the cavern. Dozens of beastmar poured in, all rallied behind one that rose above even the largest of them. It was gargantuan, easily three times Arche's own height, and shaped vaguely humanoid in that it had the decent number of arms and legs. What set it aside was the two heads growing out of its neck, each craned toward each other and were connected by a crown of black metal that had been twisted to fit around both heads at the same time.

The beastmar formed up in a loose line, all crowded behind the leader. The prisoners yelped and backed away, converging with Arche, Lyssa, and Tess.

"Any ideas?" Arche felt his innervation fade as the electricity dwindled.

"Nothing that would help." Lyssa pulled out a fresh quiver of arrows. "I don't have many arrows left."

"Here, got your wand." Tess tossed the beastmar's stick to Arche.

He caught it and looked at it more closely. It was a thin cylinder of dark metal, carved intricately with dozens of different patterns up and down the haft.

"What's the plan?" Lyssa asked as she drew back her bow.

"Bring the wand to the monster, hope he's angrier at his captors than he is at us."

"*That's* your plan?" Tess scoffed in disbelief. "Why not just have us fall on our blades? It'd be more efficient."

"It's intelligent and Hekáte gave me a quest to free it."

"The dungeon?" Lyssa frowned.

"We have bigger issues right now."

Arche planted the Tridory into the ground, staring at the assembling horde on the other side of the massive cavern. The beginnings of a plan took shape in his head.

"Tess, take my bow."

Tess's face was instantly suspicious but she held out her hand anyway. Arche removed his bow from his inventory and passed it to her, along with two quivers of arrows.

"All our hopes depend on if the creature will help us. Hold them off for as long as you can, fall back to the tunnel if you have to. I'll be back."

Arche hefted the Tridory in one hand, the other grasping the control wand. As he began to move, Lyssa grabbed his arm.

"We need you here, Arche." She searched his face. "How do you know this monster will help us?"

"I don't."

He gestured toward the horde of beastmar. At least forty were arrayed against them.

"But I know we can't beat them on our own."

Lyssa's emerald eyes shot back and forth between the horde and Arche. She released his arm and drew back her bow, ready to fire.

"Be swift."

Arche didn't respond, he just ran. Even as the horde howled behind him and he heard the rumbling of their charge, some forty against eight.

He just ran.

Chapter 41

Arche's boots slapped against the stone as he ran. He burst through the tunnel and into the following cavern, only to be knocked off his feet by the ensuing growl as the great two-headed kerberos stood to its feet.

"Wait, wait! It's me!" He shouted, trying to make himself heard above the noise.

He held out the wand and the growling stopped. A consciousness probed his mind, surprisingly gently. Arche recoiled from the sensation, then realized it was Orthrus trying to speak to him. He opened himself to the connection and the kerberos's booming voice echoed in his mind.

'YOU HAVE BROUGHT THE CONTROL WAND. WE DID NOT THINK YOU WOULD SUCCEED IN THIS. NOT SO QUICKLY.'

'Yeah, I did, but we've got other problems. I'll free you, like I promised, but I need your help. There's a horde of beastmar out there that are about to kill some friends of mine. I need your help to defeat them.'

The growling increased in intensity.

'WE HAVE NO AFFECTION FOR THE AFFLICTED ONES BUT WE HAVE NO DESIRE TO TAKE PART IN YOUR BATTLES.'

Arche's mouth gaped.

'You're fucking kidding me. You've got no desire at all to get vengeance for what was done to you? Or even to help the guy freeing you?'

'WE WILL NOT BE EXTORTED WHILE WE ARE CHAINED BY THESE COLLARS.' The kerberos's growls intensified, driving Arche back a step. *'FREE US OR CONSIGN YOURSELF TO BE OUR SLAVER. MAKE YOUR CHOICE.'*

'I...what? That's not what this is.'

'AND YET HERE YOU STAND, WITH THE WAND OF OUR CONTROL IN YOUR HANDS. BARGAINING WITH OUR FREEDOM.'

'There's no bargain.' Arche held out the wand. *'I'm asking you to help us but I will free you regardless.'*

Two heads moved forward out of the darkness. Arche stiffened at the size of them. Each head was larger than his entire body and each could easily tear him in half with a single bite if it decided it didn't want to eat him whole. They were bound together by a thick chain attached to a collar around each head. The chain culminated in a padlock the size of Arche's head. In the center was a circular keyhole.

A feeling of trepidation crept into Arche's stomach. This creature was massive and powerful. If it decided to eat him, he wouldn't really be able to stop it. Further, he *needed* the creature's help. Without it, there was no way they'd be able to fight off the beastmar. He had the instrument of its control in his hand.

Arche stuck the wand into the keyhole and gave it a twist. There was a loud *CRACK* and the chains and collars fell away. The wand also fell to the ground, still stuck inside the padlock. He needed help, but he wasn't willing to subjugate the kerberos to get it.

'I'm truly sorry for what was done to you. I do really need your help but I won't hold your freedom over your head...erm, heads.'

Each head shook itself, as if trying to fluff fur that had been matted from the weight of the chains. Then, each set of eyes leveled on Arche.

'GO.'

Arche took a step backward.

'If there's something I can do to change your—'
'GO!'

Both heads barked as the word sounded inside Arche's head, the sound so fierce and terrible that Arche fell to the ground, hands covering his ears. Without further attempt at words, he severed the link in his mind and ran.

Bitter disappointment washed over him as he returned. He'd banked all of his hopes on the kerberos. Now, he felt that hope wash away. As he ran, a notification opened in the corner of his vision.

You have successfully completed the **Quest**.

Save the Guardian

Through bravery, recklessness, and teamwork, you have defeated the beastmar mage and freed Hekáte's pet. She is grateful, and the thanks of a goddess is worth more than material treasures, don't you think?

Reward

- 5,000 experience
- Increased Divinity
- Favor of Hekáte

Divinity has increased to **75%**.

Arche grunted the notification away. Even a drastic improvement to his Divinity and the guarantee of at least another level did nothing to improve his situation if he and his friends were going to die here. It was hard not to be furious at the kerberos. Hard not to be furious at himself, for that matter, but he knew he'd done the right thing. There were lines he wasn't willing to cross and he'd found one. He'd rather die fighting than live as a slaver, but would he rather sacrifice everyone else, too? Arche pushed the thought away. It wasn't helpful.

He came to the end of the tunnel to find Tess, Lyssa, and the prisoners all crowded around the mouth. They were armed with whatever they could scavenge and had boxed themselves where the beastmar would be forced to come at them a few at a time.

It was clear that his group was having a bad time of it. A few of the prisoners had collapsed, wounds dampening their emaciated forms while the rest tried to close the gaps in their line. At the sight, Arche's anger flared inside of him.

Damn Orthrus. Damn the entities playing games with his life. But most of all, damn the beastmar. Enough was enough.

Arche switched the Tridory into its bident form with the press of a button, then hurled it forward over the heads of his friends. Without waiting for it to land, he channeled Divine Body into his legs. He launched forward at an upward angle and came down in a long arc. The bident sank into a reptilian beastmar's chest.

A moment later, Arche hit the creature feet-first, ripping the bident out as his momentum carried him through. Arche hit the ground and rolled, came up onto one knee and thrust forward, catching another beastmar in the belly. With no time to waste, he spun, staying low as he sliced the tendons of another beastmar's leg. Two green-fletched arrows sped past his head on both sides, embedding themselves in the throat and forehead of a two headed beastmar that had been next to approach him.

Arche slapped the ground with one hand, using Divine Body to give himself an extra push. He spun into the air and threw the Tridory. The bident punched clean through one beastmar to wound another behind it.

Momentarily weaponless, Arche landed on his feet, fists raised as another beastmar with three arms starting swinging at him. Claws reached, seeking to tear into Arche's face. He used the vambraces on his forearms to brush the strike out of the way, putting the beastmar in an awkward position with its limb across its body. He stomped a low uppercut, feeling the knuckles crack against his boot. The beastmar's third limb snaked forward from its back, aiming to plaster Arche's nose across his face. It connected instead with Arche's elbow. There was a crunch and a howl as the beastmar's fingers broke.

Seizing the advantage, Arche slammed his hand into the beastmar's throat as hard as he could, then grabbed one of its arms. He twisted, swung his hips, and the creature went flying over his shoulder into another beastmar lunging to bite him. The teeth sunk into its companion instead and they went down, howling and scrabbling at each other.

Arche summoned the Tridory. The bident flew to his hand in time for him to plant the sauroter into the throat of yet another beastmar. Something hit his back and he stumbled forward, gasping in pain as his Health dropped fifteen percent. Before he could recover, a blade left an angry gash across his left arm, weaving between the gaps in his armor and knocking off another ten percent of his Health. Down to one working arm, Arche tried to thrust with the Tridory, but one of the beastmar latched onto it, weighing it down as it tried to pull it from his hands.

His breath came ragged through clenched teeth. He was in a bad way and there was only one way out. Arche activated Divine Body and wrenched the spear back, sweeping all around him with enhanced strength as his wounds physically knit themselves back together. His Health shot back up as orange light flared outward. He dropped the skill as his Mana hit twenty percent.

A knife flew past his head and landed in a beastmar's eye, taking it to the ground as the tip pierced the creature's brain. Tess appeared a moment later to pull the knife free and stabbed at another.

"Do you have to jump into the middle of every single fight?"

Arche used the Tridory to deflect a blade thrust by a humanoid beastmar, then stabbed it through the side.

"Figured I'd make a strong first impression," he grunted back, more than a little out-of-breath.

"One of these days your luck's going to run out, what are you going to do then?"

"Hope you'll come and save me, apparently."

Tess pirouetted, slashing at an exposed arm and throat with deadly accuracy. After dicing another beastmar, she stepped to cover Arche's back as he brought the offensive to a small group attempting to get in close.

"We're fighting for our lives here. This isn't the time to be flirting."

Tess flung a knife and sidestepped. The blade sunk deep into the belly of a beastmar even as its reptilian mouth snapped against empty air.

"Oh, I don't know," Arche said with a grunt as he opened a gash across a beastmar's chest. "Might not get a better chance for it."

For a moment, in the midst of combat, their eyes met. He felt something pass between them. Then the fight swept both of them up again and whatever passed was lost. Arche stabbed a beastmar through the heart, trying to put his thoughts into words.

"Dinner."

"What?'

"If we make it out of this, I'd like to take you to dinner." Arche jerked the bident free from the bones of another slain beastmar. "Something nice, just you and me. You don't have to say yes."

A loud, bestial bellow broke through the clamor of battle. The sea of beastmar parted to reveal the massive beastmar leader. Both of its heads, wrapped together by a twisted black-metal crown, glared at Arche with murderous intent. It bellowed something in a guttural, barking language and the beastmar made space around them, forming into a ring.

"Arche?"

"I know. Can you get back to the others?"

"I can't sneak with this many watching us and I can't slip past them. We're hemmed in."

Arche used the pause in fighting to get a better look at his surroundings. He had fought his way through many of the beastmar, too far out for the others to provide good cover. The beastmar had filled the gap and separated them from Lyssa and the former prisoners. In his battle fever, Arche had overextended his position and Tess had gone right in with him.

"You, fighter." The crowned beastmar's voice rasped and gurgled like its tongue was too large for its mouth. "You will die by my hand."

"I really don't like that they can talk," Arche muttered, then raised his voice to reply. "How about a wager, then?"

The beastmar around them let out a cackling, barking laugh, like an entire menagerie was told its favorite joke.

"What terms say you?"

"If I kill you, the rest of you beastmar let us all leave in peace."

Another peal of dissonant laughter came from the beastmar. The crowned beastmar held up a large axe, its spike head pointed straight at Arche.

"I accept. When I kill you, your fighters will drop their weapons and surrender."

"Give me a moment to confer," Arche called back before turning toward Tess.

"Can you beat him?" she asked.

Arche frowned and Examined the beastmar.

Eten and Nete		
Level: 26 **Race**: Beastmar **Age**: ? **Height**: ? **Weight**: ?	**Profession**: ? **Trade**: ? **Traits**: ? **Companions**: ? **Adventuring Party**: ?	
Health: 710 / 710 100%	**Stamina**: 910 / 945 96%	**Mana**: 120 / 120 100%

Arche sucked his teeth.

"Tell you what, he's one mean sonofabitch, but what choice do we have?"

Arche eyed his own vitals.

Health: 438 / 495	Stamina: 134 / 355	Mana: 44 / 190
88%	38%	23%

If it had been purely a numbers game, he didn't stand a chance. He was injured, tired, and barely had enough Mana left in the tank for a single use of Divine Body. Maybe two if he was quick about it. Conversely, this Eten and Nete creature was well-rested and unharmed, not to mention the eleven-level advantage it had over him.

Tartarus was not just a numbers game, however. Tactics, strategy, guts, and more than a little luck had helped Arche defeat monsters far more powerful. He'd had help for most of those fights, but not all of them. Now, with everyone's lives in his hands and already nearing exhaustion, he had a choice to make. The mantikhoras had been stronger, but there was something more terrifying about this crowned monster. Arche planted the sharpened butt of his spear into the ground. He wrung out his hands and rubbed his newly healed arm, still itching with fresh skin. Tess placed a hand on his arm.

"I don't like this."

"I'm not a fan of it either but at least this way we've got a shot."

"You better survive this, you know. You owe me dinner."

Arche smiled.

"Is that a yes?"

"Why not?" Her hair pulled free from her braid and fell over part of her face as she shrugged. "It sounds nice."

"Good." Arche's smile fell as he eyed the beastmar all around him. "I hope you still feel that way in a moment."

"Wha—?"

Arche moved in a single, swift motion. He grabbed Tess, activated Divine Body, then threw her. She let out an indignant curse and a loud cry as she flew over the beastmar and out of Arche's sight back toward Lyssa and the other prisoners. Arche dropped the skill a moment later but the damage was done. Pain seized his mind and his muscles spasmed and clenched, forcing him down to one knee. A small notification popped up in the corner of his vision to inform him of a new debuff.

You have **Mana Burnout**.

-90% Health Regeneration
-90% Stamina Regeneration
-90% Mana Regeneration

Mana Burnout: 12:59

He'd held on to the skill for a touch too long and his Mana had bottomed out. He was lucky he hadn't passed out from the strain and that the cooldown was only thirteen minutes, but that was thirteen minutes he was going to be at his absolute worst. Weariness and pain washed over him, centering inside his head and spreading down his body in waves.

There wasn't enough time but any time he could buy was time for Lyssa and the others to recover. Perhaps he could buy enough for them to turn the tide. He looked up at the sneering grins of Eten and Nete. There was only one way this would end.

"I accept!" He shouted, baring his teeth into a snarl.

The beastmar began shouting and barking, banging fists and limbs into torsos and against the ground. Arche pulled the Tridory free and turned to Eten, who was stalking toward him. Up close, Arche could see just how large the beastmar really was. Next to this behemoth, he felt like a child. Tentatively, Arche tried reaching out with his mind, but as soon as his consciousness expanded past his own walls, pain seared into his mind and he was met with a notification.

> **Warning!**
>
> You are attempting to use a Mana-based ability without Mana.
> Continuing to use this ability without gaining Mana will drain Health and may cause permanent damage.

"Shit," Arche hissed and closed his mind off. "Gonna have to do this the hard way."

"Come, human. Meet my labrys." Eten grinned and hefted the big axe in his hands.

Eten's second head, Nete, shouted something in a garbled tone, which caused the beastmar to cackle.

"Hi!" Arche grinned back with mock joviality. "Stupid name."

Eten lunged forward, not with the axe but with his fist, which he slammed down to drive Arche into the unforgiving stone floor. Arche stepped to the side and thrust with the bident but his movements were slow and the large beastmar had no difficulty brushing his attack harmlessly away. The big bastard followed up with a backhand that took Arche off his feet.

As soon as he touched down, Arche shot forward, trying to take Eten off guard with a quick, ferocious attack. It was the same method that had worked on plenty of beastmar who hadn't expected their prey to put up much fight, but Eten was no ordinary beastmar. The experience of battle was evident in his movements and strategy. Eten clearly had a lot more experience fighting trained opponents than Arche had, and Arche was far from a trained warrior.

The simple, straightforward thrusts and swipes that Arche prodded with were easily deflected and avoided by the larger beastmar. The whole time, both of Eten's heads stared down at Arche with bloodthirsty grins. It was meant to infuriate him and it was working, but it was far from his only issue. His Stamina fell like a stone.

In less than a minute of combat, he had already dropped below a hundred Stamina. In another full minute, he'd be completely drained, but long before that he'd be too tired to keep evading Eten's attacks. The beastmar was a powerhouse. If that hadn't been clear enough by its size, it was certainly evident in the way it threw its weight around. Arche was forced to dodge and evade as much as he could as even a glancing blow could knock him around and hurt him.

He held the Tridory out in front of him, trying to keep his reach advantage, but the massive size of the beastmar and the huge battle-axe that it wielded nearly matched him for length. His breath came in short spurts and his entire body burned from the pains of the last day.

This wasn't a fight, it was a beatdown.

"I took you for a mighty warrior, the way you fought my kin," Eten rasped. "Was I mistaken? Is this the best humanity has to offer? Pathetic."

"Trash talk? Really?" Arche rasped, desperate for breath. "Didn't even know trash could talk until I met you."

Eten growled and grabbed the Tridory. He gave it a mighty yank and swung the axe down in a heavy chop. Arche was forced to let go and throw himself to the side to avoid a killing blow. He hit the ground and scrambled away, struggling to get his feet under him. Eten was left holding both the battle-axe and the Tridory, the latter of which he tossed carelessly to the side.

"Looks like you're out of options, tiny warrior."

Eten swung the labrys, forcing Arche to fall back again to get out of the way. On the ground, his options were even more limited. Eten continued the attack, bringing the axe down in an arcing slash. Arche rolled to the side and the axe cleaved into the rock where his chest had been, digging deep into the stone and lodging itself there.

Arche rolled back and wrapped his legs around Eten's arm, using his hands to grab Eten's thumb and twist it backwards. The beastmar let go of the axe and grunted in surprise and pain. Arche felt himself rise into the air as Eten lifted his arm, then unwrapped one of his legs and used it to kick at the crown binding the beastmar's heads together. The metal dented slightly, forcing both heads to lean toward each other even further. Eten drew his arm back to throw Arche, but Arche let go and dropped to the floor before the beastmar had the chance. He landed in a basic fighting stance, his hands up.

"All right, ugly, which head should I knock some sense into?"

Eten threw a massive right hook. Arche slipped underneath it and drove his fist into the beastmar's side. He might as well have punched the stone floor, but then he hadn't really expected it to hurt the beastmar. He followed it up with a jumping palm to one of Eten's faces. For the first time, the beastmar showed pain. Eten took a step back and wiped away a small streak of black blood from its lip.

Arche used the distraction to pull his xiphos free before the enraged beastmar reengaged. Eten kicked at him, forcing him back. He tried to stab at the foot but his limbs were thick and slow and he missed entirely. Eten yanked the axe out of the stone with a screech of metal.

Arche leveled his sword at the beastmar, but he was so damn tired. His adrenaline faded almost as quickly as his Stamina. The sword was solid lead in his hand. One mistake, one foul move, and he would die.

Eten moved forward, swinging his axe in a complicated flurry of slashes. Arche ducked the first swing and spun out of the way. He slid the edge of the xiphos across Eten's arm as he moved, leaving a trail of blood. He continued weaving around the beastmar, barely staying out of the way of the deadly battle-axe. It was the flowing, dancing sword style that Lyssa had taught him. He didn't have the Dexterity or training to really pull it off but it was still effective.

Little by little, Eten's Health whittled down by glancing attacks, but it seemed to anger the beastmar far more than it hurt him. It was also too slow to win the fight. If he had an hour of perfect execution, perhaps it would have been enough, but there was no hope of that.

Arche needed to do something drastic, something desperate. Something foolish.

He faked a lunge. The beastmar brought his axe down to batter Arche's sword into the ground but his sword was no longer there. He pulled it back and stepped onto the axe, using it to spring up toward the beastmar's chest far above. Arche used the last of his Stamina to activate Power Attack, driving his sword forward with everything he had. Surprise covered the beastmar. The attack had caught it off-guard at a moment where the beastmar had been too committed to properly block or dodge. Arche, however, was also committed.

A massive, clawed hand closed around Arche's throat, suspending him in the air as his sword pierced Eten's chest where a heart should be. Eten let out a rattling gasp, the sound escaping from both heads. Arche's vision blackened around the edges. His Stamina had bottomed out, a scant couple points left in the tank, and it took everything he had just to stay conscious.

"You missed," Eten rasped, a grin spreading across both faces.

Arche couldn't speak. The beastmar's hand on his neck prevented any hope of breathing and he was too tired to struggle free. One of his hands hung limply at his side, the other was draped across the hilt of his sword. Choking, he summoned the last of his strength to raise his hand and rest it on the side of Eten's face.

With a barely audible whimper, Arche summoned the Tridory.

Pain exploded in his head and spread to the rest of his body. Every nerve was lacerated and set on fire. He had no air to scream and no strength to thrash, so he hung in Eten's grip, enveloped in utter agony, without even the ability to breathe as his very vitality drained away. Arche clutched at his connection to the spear with everything he had. He ignored the warning notifications that popped up, telling him that he was draining his Health, that he was taking permanent damage.

Eten grinned and lifted his axe, setting it against Arche's chest.

"Goodbye, little warrior."

Arche barely felt the blade's bite part through his armor, flesh, and bone. He barely heard the hoots and howls of the beastmar and the screams of Lyssa and Tess. All of his dim concentration was on the summoning.

The Tridory tore through both of Eten's heads, perfectly splitting the crown as the freshly bloodied haft of the spear landed in Arche's open hand. The beastmar's expressions didn't change, still frozen in manic grins as the light left both sets of eyes.

Arche watched his Health dwindle. The pain that had wracked him was gone, replaced by an icy coolness that radiated from his chest where Eten's axe was still lodged. A swirling bliss dogged the edges of his mind and the corners of his vision.

Arche fell from the beastmar's limp hand and died before he hit the ground.

Chapter 42

All was still as Arche and the beastmar chieftain fell. For one second, every creature paused to take in what had happened. Lyssa felt his death, felt her connection to him sever. Felt the notification that confirmed the horrible truth. She had lost a Companion.

For the second time, she had let a brother die.

A keening wail rose in the silence. It was pain and grief and every dark thought. The sound rose, haunting as it echoed off stone. The prisoners shied away from her – the sound came from her own mouth. She drew her swords and was gone before anyone could stop her. Her blades wrought devastation as she sprinted through the throngs of beastmar. Everyone, beastmar and prisoner alike, was taken aback by her ferocity.

Then battle commenced once more.

Lyssa tore her way through the beastmar as she tried to reach Arche's body. Tess was at her side an instant later, blades flashing. Lyssa ignored the Rogue, all of her focus was on getting to Arche. If she could just reach him, she could find some way to save him. To bring him back. If she could get to him, he would sit up and laugh and have some outlandish saying he knew would only puzzle her. Most importantly, he would be alive. He had to be.

The beastmar blurred before her, one into the next as she cut them down. Arche had been foolish to challenge the chief. Beastmar were abominations, they had no concept of honor. They would never have surrendered even if Arche had won uncontested, but the damned fool had fought his way out too far and been separated. She should have gone after him, but Tess had beaten her to it. If she'd gone, the rest of the prisoners would have died. Now they would all die together.

Arche had overdone himself getting Tess out of danger, Lyssa could tell by how his posture had changed. Mana Burnout. She'd never experienced it herself, having no aptitude for magic, but she knew it could cripple people for hours, even days. If he'd still had enough Mana left to use his special skill, she had no doubt he would have defeated the chief. She'd seen him do enough incredible things not to doubt him.

Now she needed him to do one more incredible thing.

A claw tore open Lyssa's cheek and her howl grew sharper. Even with all that they'd killed, there were still over two dozen beastmar. Too many to win. She reached Arche's body, Tess fighting alongside her. The wicked labrys was still stuck in his chest. Seeing it up close, Lyssa's Huntress mind assessed the damage. It had split at least four of his ribs and likely pierced a lung, if not his heart. He'd died in moments, not minutes.

Lyssa planted herself in front of his body, brandishing both her swords as she roared her challenge. A bestial howl, even to her own ears, that promised pain to any foolish enough to challenge her. As if in answer, a deep rumble echoed around the cavern, thunder in the underground. The fighting stopped and everyone looked for its source. Everyone except Lyssa, who was past caring. The few prisoners left standing ran out of the tunnel, screaming as whatever monster had been inside came out, and what a monster it was.

A massive, two-headed dog emerged from the tunnel. Both heads loosed a baleful howl, the sound so loud that every other creature stopped what they were doing to clutch at their ears and scream in response. Lyssa was driven to the ground by the noise, hands clapped against her sensitive ears as a combat notification indicated a new debuff.

<table>
<tr><td align="center">Deafened — Tier 5

-90% Hearing</td></tr>
<tr><td align="center">Deafened — Tier 5: 1:59</td></tr>
</table>

Lyssa took her hands away to find them slick with her own blood. She wiped them on the stone ground, trying to clean them or at least get enough grip back that she could hold her swords without dropping them. When she could stand with swords in hand, she found that the beastmar paid no attention to her. They had devoted the entirety of their focus to fighting the two-headed hound.

The creature stood over five meters tall at the shoulder. By contrast, the largest of the beastmar came up to the monstrous hound's knees. Its fur was a piebald of red and black, but its form, though formidable, was emaciated. Skin pulled taut over massive ribs and the hound's stomach pulled inward.

Both heads plunged downward, moving quickly for such a large creature, and each gaping maw found plenty of beastmar to eat. That was not to say the beastmar were incapable of fighting back. Despite having two heads and a huge size advantage, the beastmar turned the creature's legs into a bloody mess. There were simply too many for the hound to fight all at once.

Lyssa adjusted the grip on her swords and was about to jump back into the fray when a hand landed on her shoulder. She turned, ready to strike, but saw Tess standing at her side. The woman pointed and said something but Lyssa couldn't hear more than a garbled warble. She turned to follow Tess's gesture.

More creatures poured out of the tunnels on the far side of the cavern, but these were not beastmar. Humans, elves, dwarves, and other races charged out into the open cavern. Above them all swooped a familiar bird-like figure.

"Abraxios," Lyssa whispered, voice lost even to herself.

Lightning arced from the tengu, splitting itself to strike half a dozen beastmar. They froze and shuddered as their muscles contracted against their will. Arrows flew, felling several more who had focused wholly on trying to kill the two-headed hound. Lyssa and Tess did their part by attacking any beastmar who turned away from the monster but, for the most part, they stood watch over Arche's body as the battle played out before them.

They were joined shortly by the other prisoners. All had their share of blood and most sported varying degrees of injuries. Exhausted, Lyssa dropped to her knees. Her Stamina was spent but it went deeper than that. They had been fighting down in the dark for so long, convinced that they were going to die, and now hope had surged forth before them.

If only Arche was alive to see it.

With the two-headed hound on one side and the villagers on the other, the beastmar were quickly routed. Some of the villagers prepared to fight the hound, weapons hefted hesitantly, but it ignored them. It dragged as many beastmar as its mouths could hold back into the tunnel and disappeared entirely from sight.

The battle was over. They had won.

Tess fell to her knees next to Lyssa. Arche's skin had grown pale beneath the blood and dirt. His eyes were dull and stared past Lyssa. Whatever his last words might have been were lost, leaving behind only the memory of a short life, less than a month old. They had lived, Arche had died.

Now they both had to face that fact.

A figure strutted up, stopping a couple meters away. Lyssa looked up into the sneering face of Callias Buteo. He said something but it was garbled, unintelligible. She ignored him, rubbing her ears as the Deafened debuff counted down to nothing. Sound came back to her with a pop.

"—you ignore *me?*" Callias shouted. "Look at this mess you've caused. All this...this...this carnage. This utter *waste*. Don't even think of trying to collect on that bounty my fool of a steward offered you. I've rescinded it, the official quest will be canceled upon our return. Why, I should have you imprisoned for the mess you've made of things. For your greed, endangering the whole village in this fool's quest to attack the beastmar. You're just trying to separate me from my family's hard-earned drachmae. I should have you flogged!"

Lyssa found it hard to care about what he was saying. She thought of Arche and what he would say. The words brought a bittersweet smile to her lips and she let them pass.

"Go fuck yourself, Callias."

"How *dare* you. I see now that prison would be too kind of a sentence for you. We have neither the means, the manpower, nor the infrastructure to incarcerate you for nearly as long as it would take to teach you some manners, elf. Neither can you be exiled, for surely your foul influence would only serve to commit greater crimes elsewhere or bring trouble to us once again. Yes, there's only one thing for it, now. Guards, kill these two."

Lyssa and Tess were on their feet in a flash, weapons drawn. Callias stepped back behind the protective line. The guards, for their part, looked uncertain as they faced down two warrior women drenched in blood and surrounded by dozens of slain corpses.

"This is rash, Callias," a familiar voice said.

Lyssa turned her head to see Vik had spoken up. He, Elpida, and Gigator had maneuvered to stand by her and Tess, weapons raised toward the rest of the village guards.

"The snakes crawl forth from the woodwork. If you wish to oppose me, very well. Your lives are forfeit, too. You heard me, kill them!"

The guards formed a circle around them and closed in, spears raised.

Ψ

Arche felt lighter than he ever had before, as though his clothing and limbs were weightless. Instinctually, he tried to breathe, but no air rushed into his lungs. His chest still rose and he felt no discomfort, but there was no breath. Now that he was aware of it, he couldn't feel anything at all. Not the air against his skin or the stone beneath him. No clothing or weapons or anything. He opened his eyes.

The world had changed but it was not unfamiliar. He found he was not naked, as he had originally thought, but was wearing very simple clothing, like he had when he'd first woken up nearly a month before. He was in a hollow cave deep inside the earth, much as before, but small flames flickered around the space. Bright green sparks with shadows silhouetting them and darker orange sparks with large, grotesque shadows. They danced around each other, but the orange sparks vastly outnumbered the green sparks. Arche touched one. His hand passed straight through and, though he felt nothing, he sensed something. Someone, more specifically.

"Lyssa," he murmured.

"The concerns of the living are not for the dead."

Arche turned, the motion more of a thought than an action. His mind appeared to control his movement in this place, not his muscles. The entity he saw before him was tall and covered in thousands of small plates of interconnected, black armor. Obscuring its face was a mask of black metal that shifted, sometimes morphing into a face and other times simply forming a black mirror. The only unchanging thing about the mask were two eye-slits, revealing white pupils surrounded by black sclera.

"I know you," Arche said. "You're that being from before. You called yourself Death."

"I am."

"You told me I wasn't supposed to be here."

"You weren't."

"And now?"

"You are."

"I'd...hoped I'd get more time." Arche's voice faltered. "There's so much I didn't get to see."

"It is the wish of many to delay my meeting with them."

Arche tried to take a deep breath but no air flowed into his unsteady form. Instead, he closed his eyes and shoved his feelings down into whatever now passed for a stomach. "I never got your name."

"I am Death."

"Yeah, got that part, but that's not a name. Arguably, that's what you are. A name's an important thing. I should know, I didn't have one for a while. Surely there's something someone calls you?"

"I..." Death hesitated.

Arche was taken aback by that. Death *hesitated?* Could Death be unsure? He'd thought Death was the only thing that was ever certain. Well, that and taxes.

"I was once a being called Thanatos, but I have...evolved since then. I absorbed many of the Keres, my sisters, and have become that which shepherds all who die."

"Would you mind if I called you Thanatos? 'Mr. Death' is a little too formal for me."

"I am Death, little spark, but I have been called many things by many beings. If my old name would bring you some comfort, then use it."

Arche looked around, seeing all the different sparks moving about each other.

"Are these souls? Living ones? Is this why your kind call us sparks?"

"They are not of your concern."

"Yeah, I know, I just..." Arche sighed, wishing he could actually blow out air to vent his frustration. "I barely got to know this world. What comes next?"

"Come and see."

The thought terrified him.

"Just tell me this much. Was this it? Did I waste the only life I'm going to have?"

Thanatos cocked its head.

"Do you regret the life you lived?"

Arche blinked. He thought about waking up in the forest, about his first encounter with Lyssa, with Helwan, with Tess. All the people he'd met and befriended along the way. The party in the village, learning how to fight, the adventures, the battles, the dungeoneering.

His body was no longer real, nor were his eyes, and he was grateful, for it meant Death would not see him cry.

"No. Only that it's over."

"Then come."

Arche hesitated. Then, slowly, he extended a translucent hand toward Thanatos.

"Not so fast."

Thanatos stiffened and withdrew its hand. Death stared at something behind Arche. A presence filled the space, so thick and overpowering that Arche felt himself mired in place, hand still extended. Fear rose in him, despite already being dead, and he wanted more than anything to turn, to see who had spoken, but he didn't have to see to know who it was. It was the entity that had been playing with him this whole time. The same one who had confronted Thanatos when Arche had bargained for Tess's life.

"You should not be here," Thanatos rumbled, showing genuine annoyance for the first time since.

"Now, is that any way to treat an old friend?"

"This is too far."

Thanatos's hand flickered and a large scythe appeared.

"You are bold, indeed, if you would take up arms against *me*. Do not forget what I am owed."

"That debt," Thanatos growled, *"has been paid already. I warned you what would happen if you interfered again."*

Once again they were talking about him as though he weren't even there. He was already dead, what more could they do?

"Enough!" Arche roared. The presence weighed on him, but it no longer felt so stifling that he couldn't speak. "Somebody tell me what is going on here or I'm going to start screaming."

Thanatos looked down at him and extended a hand.

"Don't..."

Thanatos tapped Arche on the top of the head and the overwhelming presence dissipated.

"Finally, gah, what the fuck?"

Arche turned his head and looked at the new entity. The sight would have chilled his heart if he still had one. What stood before him could have been a statue, had the sculptor intended to inspire nightmares. Blood flowed in the shape of a man, taller even than Thanatos. Darkened metal fashioned into armored plates adorned the blood, each piece bore damage but was undeniable in the quality of its craftsmanship. The eyes were cold steel, reflecting Arche's own face back at him.

"I had such high hopes for you."

The blood figure sighed like a disappointed father.

"Who...what are you?"

"He is Ares. He should know better than to interfere in matters that do not concern him."

"The boy died in battle. That's as much my business as it is yours, harvestman." Ares waved a crimson hand dismissively.

"Do not test me, Ares. Your power has waned these millennia, but mine has only grown."

"Spare me your threats, Than. You do not want to raise your scythe against me."

"Ares," Arche said slowly. "I know that name. Why do I know that name?"

"Silence. You will be dealt with in due time."

"Return to your brethren, Ares. I will not tell you again."

Thanatos shifted their weight and placed themself between Arche and Ares.

"I have claimed my mark upon this one. All the other souls of Tartarus are yours but his is mine."

"That is not how the system was designed. You have no jurisdiction in this matter."

"Enough! You will not deny me this, errand keeper. You may collect the souls but it is my wars that bring them to you. I will wage a war so great and terrible that it destroys the very fabric of this 'system' you serve. Stand aside, I will not warn you again."

"I am not some pawn in your games. One of you tell me what is going on, right now."

"Silence!"

"Fuck *off!*" Arche roared. Both entities turned toward him in surprise. "I'm sick of this shit! You all interfere with our lives so easily but in all your apparent power you can't even answer a question? *Why?* Why me? What did I ever do that I got caught up in this?"

Ares and Thanatos both stared at him without reaction, which would have sparked fear into him if he hadn't already been dead.

"He...is not of Tartarus. Ares, what did you do?"

"As I said, he died in battle. That makes him my business and I have plans for him, yet. You, boy, you wish to know what is in store for you? Why you were chosen?"

Arche glared up at the pillar of blood.

"You were chosen because you are an instrument of war. You always have been. You have fought your entire life, from birth all up unto your death, whereupon I claimed you. I bestowed upon you a gift, a divine spark to fan the flames of your potential. A feat that has not been accomplished in millennia. You say you are not a pawn? You are nothing but a pawn. Your existence here is my doing and through you I will have my war. *That* is your purpose, you have no other."

Arche reeled. Thanatos, too, seemed similarly affected.

"Ares, you have broken the pact."

"Damn the pact, Than. Change is coming, it cannot be kept away forever. When that change happens, you should consider to whom your allegiance truly lies. There is still time."

"No," Arche interrupted.

Both entities turned toward him once again.

"No, I don't accept this. I won't do it."

Ares's face congealed into anger.

"Do not push your luck, boy. You owe everything to me."

"You've fucked with my entire life, every step of the way. You used me and you're going to keep using me until you decide you don't need me anymore. How long, then, before you cast me aside? A year? A month? A week? No, fuck that. What you're selling? I'm not buying. I've had enough. Push me and I'll push back."

Ares blinked, seeming genuinely surprised.

"You would wage war against *me?*"

"If it means stopping you, yes." Arche stared up with as much grit as he could muster.

Ares smiled. **"Very well. I will relish our conflict, but you *will* serve me in the end."**

Crimson light flashed and Arche was left alone with Thanatos.

"Please tell me you have some answers for what just happened."

"This has been...concerning."

"What happens now?"

"His mark is upon you. His spark of divinity and something more. I am sorry, mortal, for that title no longer accurately describes you."

"What?"

Thanatos turned away, then turned back, as if struck by a sudden thought.

"Do you truly wish to defeat him? Or were those words spoken in the brashness of anger?"

"I..." Now that the moment had passed, he was uncertain. "I don't know if I can, but whatever he's planning doesn't sound good and he doesn't seem to care who he hurts. There are still people I care about, people I need to look out for. He needs to be stopped. I'll do what I can."

Thanatos dipped his head. *"Very well. I am limited in what assistance I can provide, but I can provide this."*

Thanatos produced a single silver coin from seemingly nowhere.

"Place this obol in the mouth of a departed loved one whose soul still lingers."

Arche reached out to take it but Thanatos held it back.

"Unless the rules of the pact change, this is the only help I will be able to give. Use it wisely."

Arche took the coin.

"Does this mean I'm not dead?"

Thanatos cocked his head and, though Arche couldn't see a face, he would have sworn that Death was smiling at him.

"For better or worse, you are banished from death. I will speak with Hermes. He will determine what next steps to take. This has not happened before. I am sure whatever cost he imposes will be prohibitive, so do not make a habit of traveling to my realm. You may find it worse than the alternative."

"I see," Arche said slowly. "One more thing. Do you know who I was? Before I came here?"

"The affairs of the living are not of my concern."

"Right, right. Of course. Erm, thank you? Thank you."

Thanatos cocked his head to one side, staring at Arche with those strange, inverted eyes.

"You are an anomaly, little spark. Nonetheless, I will return you now. Someday I will see you again. I see everyone, eventually. Do not forget this. There is no escape."

With those last, ominous words hanging in the air, Thanatos reached out and rested one hand on the top of Arche's head.

Then Arche fell through darkness.

Chapter 43

"I'll kill you all, malakas! Stay back!"

The words floated into Arche's head. Feeling came back gradually. Cool stone beneath him. Heavy clothes on top of him. The piercing, icy touch of an axe being slowly pushed from his chest. Pain was gone, to his relief. His injuries had healed, his vitals were full, but it was difficult for his mind to focus. He felt pulled between two worlds.

"One more step and I will slaughter every last one of you."

Arche blinked. His vision was blurry but quickly cleared itself. What he saw didn't make much sense. Lyssa and Tess stood over him, blades drawn. They were surrounded not by beastmar, but villagers. The village guard, more specifically, behind whom was Callias Butco. Things were beginning to fall into place.

Lyssa held her swords, her bow nowhere to be seen, but there was no more fight in her. He could tell by the set of her shoulders. Tess, on the other hand, was shouting abuse and shaking, seemingly ready to start stabbing people at any moment. Others stood with them. Vik, Elpida, and Gigator, all ready for a fight. It was shaping up to be a bloodbath.

Before Arche could do anything, a barrage of notifications appeared in his vision.

Divinity has increased to **100%**

YOU HAVE DIED.

Quest Failed:

Unlocking Your Potential

Objective Failed:
Do not die[error].

ERROR…ERROR…ERROR…
SUBJECT IS NOT DEAD.
CALCULATING…
…PARAMETER MET: SUBJECT NO LONGER DEAD.
RESETTING QUEST…

You have completed a **Quest**!

Unlocking Your Potential

Hey! You stuck it through. Figured it out and made a ton of mistakes along the way. Wouldn't have killed you to ask for more help, maybe a sacrifice or two for old times' sake, but you did it your way and no one can ever take that away from you. Congratulations! Keep it up and we'll be seeing more of each other. In any case, you're too much of a variable to stay completely automated. I'm watching you.
Don't forget it.

-H.

Reward

- Claim your **Profession**

Demigod

Not everyone is gifted with a divine spark. Through heroic deeds and service, you have fanned your spark of Divinity into a candle's flame. You have become a Demigod.

<u>Your patron deity is now an irrevocable part of you.</u>

+5 to all attributes
+1 to all attributes with each new level

You have a **Disease**.

Death Sickness

Dying and coming back is a traumatizing feat. The effects of doing so should reflect the effort involved. Don't make a habit of it unless you want to draw unwanted attention. Specifically, mine. Which, coincidentally, you already have!

-H.

-50% Vitals Regeneration
-50% Willpower
Progress toward next Skill levels reset
-5,000 Experience
+25% chance of vomiting randomly
50% chance of mentally reliving your death at random moments

Death Sickness: 11:59:57

You have slain **Eten and Nete, the Beastmar Chieftain**.
You have slain 17 **Beastmar**.
You gain 4,960 experience.

Slayer of the Mighty activated!
You gain 1,100 experience.

Lyssanderyli has slain 31 **Beastmar**.
You gain 4,650 experience.

Your party has slain 19 **Beastmar**.
You gain 1,900 experience.

You have reached **Level 20**.

As a **Human**, you gain 5 points to distribute per level.
As a **Demigod**, you gain 1 point in all attributes per level.
You have 25 unallocated attribute points.

Profession Paths are now unlocked.

As the notifications appeared, Arche scanned them over for the highlights before dismissing them. As the last one disappeared, his body was wrapped in golden light. Unlike the normal flash of a level up, the five levels he progressed through surrounded him like a flare. The light settled into his chest and throat, healing his wounds until nothing remained by scars, but it did nothing for his mind fog or the horrible queasy feeling that had settled into his gut, both likely consequences of Death Sickness.

"What are you idiots waiting for? I told you to kill them!"

"Kill me yourself, you cowardly piece of shit."

Every eye turned to him as he eased himself into a sitting position, throwing off the massive axe.

"You...you..." Tess stammered.

"You were dead." Lyssa finished for her.

The guards took a step back, clearly uncomfortable with the whole situation.

"The severity of my death was greatly exaggerated," Arche groaned. "Could I get a hand up, please?"

Lyssa sheathed a blade and grabbed him under one arm. Tess did the same on the other side and together they hauled him to his feet. Arche summoned the Tridory back to his hand and planted the sauroter into the stone, leaning against it like a staff.

"Why is he ordering us dead?" Arche asked.

"Because you are—"

"Shut the fuck up, Callias. I'm not talking to you."

"He's blaming us for the whole beastmar situation. Thinks we're too dangerous to be imprisoned or exiled, so he's ordered his guards to kill us," Tess said.

"Tell you what, Callias. I think this whole village is just about sick of your shit. You want things to get done, get them done yourself. If you want us dead, try to kill us yourself. Stop being such a fucking coward or get out of our way."

"Are you challenging me to a duel?"

"Sure! If it's an excuse to punch you in the face."

"Arche!" Lyssa hissed sharply. "You are in no condition to pick another fight."

"Very well, boy, I will accept your challenge on one condition: I fight your elven friend there instead."

Silence reigned in the cavern for a long moment, broken by hysterical laughter. Arche's hysterical laughter, to be specific.

"You want to fight her? *Her?* Whatever you say, man. Lyssa?"

"Gladly."

"As the challenged, I invoke my right to choose the means by which our battle is fought," Callias continued.

"Go on, then. I've wasted more than enough time down here already."

"We shall fight unarmed, without interference of magic or outside assistance, until one of us is incapable or unwilling to continue."

"Very well. Should we win, you will abdicate your position, pending trial for your gross negligence," Lyssa responded.

"And should I win, you and your friends will be put to death. What say you?"

"I accept."

Lyssa moved forward until she stood directly in front of Callias. The two could not have looked more ill-matched. Lyssa was covered in blood, sported several active wounds, and her thin armor had been beaten and gouged a dozen times over. Callias, on the other hand, was spotless. He wore a golden, ornate breastplate with matching vambraces and greaves. There wasn't a drop of blood on his person or a single, onyx hair out of place. He was also a good head and shoulders taller than Lyssa and weighed probably twice as much.

"This armor," Callias sneered. "Was forged by some of the finest smiths this side of Tartarus. Sword, spear, axe, and arrow don't even scratch it. Come now, elf. Do your worst."

No sooner had the last word left his mouth had Lyssa's fist entered it. Callias's head rocked back, his surprise as sharp as his pain. Her other fist slammed into his exposed throat, then she grabbed his head in both hands and forced it down into her rising knee. He stumbled back, trying to regain his composure. Lyssa leaped forward and planted her foot into Callias's breastplate, pushing him back even further . Callias recovered before he fell, swinging with a wide right hook. Lyssa caught the fist, stopping it in its tracks, then kicked out Callias's leg and forced him to the ground. She kept a hold of his arm, switching her grip to be around his wrist, and twisted over him so her foot was on his back and his arm was held painfully out behind him.

"Submit."

"Never!" Callias cried.

A loud crack echoed as Lyssa broke his wrist. Callias wailed but Lyssa refused to let go. After a moment, she wrenched again, this time with a loud pop. Callias's arm elongated briefly and Arche's stomach did a turn as he realized she'd pulled the entire arm out of socket.

"Yield, or I will do worse to your other arm."

Callias screamed, his pain too great to respond in words. His head bobbed in what was either agony or compliance. Lyssa dropped his hand and his arm fell to the ground, twisted, broken, and useless.

"Do any here challenge the outcome of this event?" Lyssa said to the crowd, her words hard and daring. "Do any here wish to lay their own challenge at my feet? I have had a lion's share of blood today, but I will spill more if I must."

Silence reigned. Several of the villagers were apparently holding their breath, trying to make as little noise as possible in case they might be singled out and made an example of.

"Very well. Guards, arrest him. Let's go home."

Gigator hauled Callias up off the ground. The former village lord had passed out from his injuries, bringing blessed silence. Lyssa turned to the other villagers.

"Gather up what loot you can find and let's get out of here. And someone bring food and water for the freed villagers, they have endured more than any here."

Arche smiled as people ran to follow her orders. Lyssa looked good in command. His eyes glanced over the crowd and landed on the corpse of Eten and Nete. A tingle of fear spread through him, concentrating in the nape of his neck, but he fought it down. He was alive, somehow still alive.

The massive axe laid at his feet, his blood still wet on the blade. Arche grabbed the handle and lifted it. It was longer than he was tall but still fit inside his inventory. He made to stand and stumbled, legs suddenly unsteady. Tess appeared underneath his arm, propping him up.

"Are you going to tell me what happened?" she asked quietly.

"Yes, when there aren't as many prying ears. Over that dinner, maybe?"

"Dinner sounds lovely."

Chapter 44

The climb out of Hekáte's Vivitorium was long and arduous. Abraxios, still holding the map Arche had drawn, took the front of the company and led them out. Most of the traps were already sprung but a few still caused minor injuries. Nothing that Odelia's biomancy couldn't patch up.

Callias, on the other hand, was left to deal with his injuries. During unconscious states, the village guards dragged him along by his arms, but as he regained consciousness, they made him walk. He'd been stripped of all weapons and armor and had been gagged with a dirty cloth to stop his whining threats.

The first step out into the forest was blinding. Arche stumbled, one hand covering his eyes, the other gripping the Tridory. The sun was directly overhead and even partially obscured by the foliage, it was too bright. The air was fresh and a slight breeze wafted flowery scents toward him. Every single aspect of it, even the painful ones, made him grateful to no longer be underground. It also came with a notification.

Dungeoneer,

You have fought your way through the depths of **Hekáte's Vivitorium**, but you have not delved through all the depths have to offer.
Your dungeoneering experience has been modified to reflect this.

Dungeoneering has increased to **Level 11**.

+1% Chance of spotting hidden areas (+11%)
+1% Chance of spotting hidden enemies (+11%)
+1% Chance of spotting traps (+11%)
+1 Perception
+1 Luck

You have reached the **Novice** rank in **Dungeoneering**.
You gain 100 experience.

Murmurs rose from the gathered villagers. Arche wasn't the only one to receive dungeoneering experience from the venture, though his group had probably received the most. The trek out had taken the better part of six hours. For Arche, it had been the worst six hours of travelling in his life. Death Sickness drained his Stamina even during light activity, such as walking slightly uphill. Much of the trip had devolved into a panting mess. More than once he had to stop to vomit for no reason other than his organs trying to strangle him from the inside. Odelia had told him there was nothing she could do for his condition, though he'd refused to tell her exactly what it was, and even the rejuvenating powers of five consecutive level ups couldn't overcome Death Sickness.

Once outside, the whole company took the opportunity to sit and rest. Arche was grateful for the break. His Stamina had hovered at ten percent for the last twenty minutes. He had twenty-five points to allocate now that he was leveling again but he couldn't concentrate enough to think about where to spend them. Now that there was time to take a breath, he could feel the past few days catching up with him.

Arche had never felt so tired.

He lowered himself to the ground and leaned his back against a tree. He pulled at the collar of his shirt beneath his jerkin, trying to give his throat some room. He felt stuffy, overly warm, and the whole ordeal was making it difficult to breathe. Why was breathing so hard? It came out jagged and raspy. Sweat poured from him, even more now than when he'd been walking. His heart hammered in his chest. Heat flooded his body one moment, ice the next. Arche clenched his fists but he couldn't feel them. His heart was so loud, in his chest and in his head, at any moment it would burst. His vision blurred and the forest fell away from him.

He had no weapons, no defenses. He was so tired. The axe was coming. It sank into his chest. Pressing into him slowly, intimately, as the grinning faces of the beastmar champion looked down on him in triumph. His ribs cracked. The axe took its pound of flesh from his lungs, his heart. His blood spilled across the floor. He couldn't stop it. He couldn't breathe. His lungs collapsed, blood filling them, filling everything. He couldn't see, couldn't feel, couldn't breathe. There was only the axe sinking into his chest, killing him. Taking his life from him. Slicing his heart in two.

"Arche."

Alone. Dark and cold. The cold of the axe froze his skin as it pushed through bone. The heads of Eten and Nete grinned at him. Taunting him. Jeering at him. He couldn't stop it, couldn't stop them. He couldn't do anything. He could only die. He was going to die. He was going to die.

"Arche, look at me."

His throat was in a vice. Eten's grip around it cut off all airflow. His blood pulsed against the beastmar's grip, weak and fading. Arche's hands scrabbled at his throat, trying to loosen the grip, desperate for air. Something grabbed his hands, held them firm.

"Look at me. You're all right. I'm here with you. Tell me where you are."

"He's killing me. Oh, god. Help me...please."

Just speaking was painful. His throat was closed tight and the words came no louder than a whisper. The axe pressed into him, spilling his lifeblood over the ground.

"No one is killing you, Arche. Look around you, you're safe."

"I don't want to die." Tears ran down his cheeks. "Please, I don't want to die."

"You're safe, Arche. I'm not going to let that happen. Focus on me. Feel the world around you. You're safe."

Arche shut his eyes tight and tried to focus. Grass beneath him tickled his elbows. Soft hands held his arms, keeping him steady. He opened his eyes and blinked rapidly. His vision was blurry and his throat was sore and dry.

"Water, please," he croaked.

A waterskin pressed into his hands a moment later and he took a long, grateful pull from it.

"Thank you, I...I don't know what happened."

He wiped his eyes and saw Tess sitting in front of him. She took the waterskin back from him and drank a swig herself before stowing it in her inventory.

"In the city, they called it 'the Panik.' Mostly, it strikes the soldiers, but it can hit anyone who's suffered."

"I thought I was dying, again. I could feel that axe sinking into my chest, over and over. God, I must sound pathetic."

"It's not pathetic at all. You...you *died.* Not even the greatest healers can reverse death but you came back, somehow. That's twice now."

Arche glanced at the clearing around them. Other villagers were milling about, a few were casting glances his way. He met their eyes and they looked away, pretending they had seen nothing.

"Not here," he whispered. "Thank you, but not here."

Tess nodded.

"Are you ready to stand?"

"Yeah, I think so."

He let her pull him to his feet. Once there, she handed him the Tridory. He took it from her, leaning into it like a staff. As he did, he brought up his active debuffs. Still another six hours left before Death Sickness faded.

"Ready for our triumphant return?" Tess asked.

Arche checked his Stamina, seeing that it was barely over fifty percent despite the rest.

"Yeah, let's go run our victory lap."

The procession set off for the village. The going was slow, but they made the trip in under two hours. Any animals or monsters they may have encountered were scared off by the large gathering of people, something Arche was grateful for, as he was in no condition to fight. He wanted to sleep off the rest of the effects of Death Sickness, take a bath, and get something hot to eat, and not necessarily in that order.

As they broke through the treeline of the forest and saw the burlap tents that made up the majority of the fledgling village, a ragged cry went up. Arche's grip tightened around the Tridory and he looked around for beastmar, but instinct gave way to understanding as he realized it was a cheer, not an alarm. Around him, people ran, glad to be home. The former prisoners, especially, cheered as they ran. It was a wall of noise and Arche found it difficult to recognize it for what it was. If there was no danger, then why was his heart beating so? Why were the knuckles of his right hand white against the dark metal of the Tridory? Why was he waiting for the first arrow to fly?

People flooded out of the village to meet them. Backs were clapped, cheers were raised, and music began to play. The villagers who stayed had started preparing a feast, waiting for the triumphant return of the fighters. It was an optimistic reaction. They could just as easily all been killed, how were they laughing and smiling now? For that matter, how had they been able to feast after the attack on the village? Had everyone gone mad? Or was he the mad one? Arche caught sight of a familiar satyr amid the throng.

"Helwan!"

"Arche, you made it! Lyssa and Tess as well, oh my! This is wonderful, I'm so glad you're all right. When Odelia and Abraxios returned asking for aid, I feared the worst, but I should have known better! Nothing can defeat you three when you set your minds. Nothing!"

The excitable satyr dragged them over to a table, pouring each of them a goblet of wine. Arche sank into the seat gratefully. He was still sweating from exertion and his Stamina was dangerously low, but at least he wasn't walking any more. Lyssa excused herself and went over to Vik and his crew, exchanging hushed words and gesturing toward Callias.

Vik scratched his chin and said something, waving one hand in the air dramatically. Lyssa scrunched up her face, nodded once, then turned and made her way back.

"What was that about?" Arche asked.

"Just handling a situation," she replied, then muttered quietly, "and making a new one in the process."

"What?"

"Later."

Arche shrugged and put it out of his mind. If it was a problem, it could wait. There was food on the table and it called to him, whispering the siren song of freshly baked bread, finely roasted meat, succulent fruits, and the delicious crunch of fresh vegetables. His stomach gurgled, twisting itself with greed and gluttony. His earlier plan of sleep and bathing was banished from his mind as the smell of it reached him.

He reached out to grab a plate, then saw that his arm was covered in dried, dark blood. The magic of leveling had cleaned him, but it had done nothing to clean the Tridory. Walking all the way back to the village with the bloodied spear had gotten him filthy, again. With a forlorn sigh, he stood from the table.

"All right, I'm gonna go clean up."

His stomach protested every step away from food as he walked to the river, making sure to stay well downstream. They needed plumbing, some sort of running water. Really what they needed was houses, but plumbing was surely next. Having to go to the river every time he needed a wash was getting damned inconvenient.

Arche waded into the cool waters without bothering to remove his clothing. All of him needed washing so he would sit and soak for a while. The current was strong and steady but he was in no danger of being swept away so long as he stayed near the bank, where it was shallow enough to stand. After he'd rinsed his face and washed blood out of his hair, he removed his leather jerkin. Little more than shreds remained, the scraps hardly worth the salvage. He tossed it onto the bank, not bothering to clean it.

His shirt, similarly, was also in tatters, but it was the only one he had with him, so he tried to get the blood out by scraping over it with river stones. The following day he'd have to find one of the fabric traders and buy some new clothing. With any luck, his mantikhoras armor would be ready, as well. He couldn't help but wonder if any of his injuries would have been prevented if he'd had his new armor down in Hekáte's Vivitorium. His cloak removed its own stains, making it the only thing he had that remained spotless.

In the monotony of the task in front of him, and to distract him from his gurgling stomach, he went through the rest of his pending notifications.

Spearmanship has increased to **Level 17**.

+2% Damage with Spears (+34%)

Spear Throwing has increased to **Level 9**.

+3% Accuracy of Thrown Spears (+27%)
+2% Range of Thrown Spears (+18%)

Swordsmanship has increased to **Level 15**.

+2% Damage with Swords (+30%)

Unarmed Combat has increased to **Level 8**.

+2% Damage while Unarmed (+16%)
+0.5% Natural Armor (+4%)

Light Armor has increased to **Level 11**.

+2% Defense with Light Armor (+22%)

You have reached the **Novice Rank** in **Light Armor**.
You gain 100 experience.

When he could recognize the color of his skin, Arche got out of the river. The scum had already been swept far downstream, leaving the waters blue and unfettered. His distorted reflection stared back at him. Making the details of his face hard to pin down. He touched his left hand to his cheek, feeling the raised scars, but they were slightly less prominent. His hand fell to his chest, where Eten and Nete's axe had split his chest. The wound itself was gone, healed by whatever Thanatos had done to return him to life and cleansed by the regenerative powers of five consecutive levels. Still, he was left with a large purple scar.

"Thought you'd still be here."

Arche turned to see Tess standing next to the riverbed, a plate of food and a bottle of wine in her hands.

"Hungry?"

"Starving." Arche threw on his still soaked and torn shirt.

"Good. Then eat quickly. There's some announcement about to happen. Lyssa wouldn't tell me much about it. She didn't seem particularly happy about the situation but she also said, 'the concern is hers to bear.' Whatever that means."

Arche grunted.

"Think we should be worried?"

"Maybe? Probably? I don't know." She shrugged. "Whatever it is, I'm sure we can worry about it plenty tomorrow."

"You're right." He took a large bite of the food, grilled meat stuffed inside fresh bread. "Thank you for the food, you didn't have to."

"I know." She smirked at him and his heart skipped a beat, almost making him choke on the bread. "Don't think that I'm counting this as our dinner. It's private, yes, but you also said it was going to be nice and I plan on holding you to that."

"I'm just glad you still want to go after..." Arche made a vague gesture with his hands.

"I haven't forgiven you for manhandling me like that but I've decided to let you make it up to me."

"Oh?" Arche raised an eyebrow. "And how exactly am I going to do that?"

"I suppose you're going to have to use your imagination."

Arche chuckled. Tess graced him with a smile, then gestured at the food.

"Oh, before I forget, I brought you a change of clothes. Can't exactly have you looking like you lost a fight with an angry badger."

"You should see the badger."

Arche took the clothes, then paused.

"Are you going to turn around, or...?"

"I thought I said to make it up to me." Tess pouted, eyes gleaming with mischief as she turned her back.

Arche unequipped his old clothing and quickly threw on the new garments. They were warm and comfortable, and slightly familiar.

"Are these my clothes?"

"Yeah, you left them at my tent a few days ago, when we first met, if you recall."

"You kept them?"

"What was I supposed to do, throw them in the river? I was going to give them back, now I have. Come on, we're going to be late."

Arche shoveled in the last few bites and they made their way back toward the feast, walking in step. Hands almost touching.

Chapter 45

"Ladies, gentlemen, and all in between, may I have your attention?"

Vik stood atop one of the tables, gathering every eye and ear in the village. Behind him, on the ground, Elpida and Gigator stood next to the kneeling form of Callias Buteo.

"Today has been a day of victories," Vik continued. "But it is not all revelries. There is a serious matter which must be attended to. We are no longer in civilized lands but that does not mean we should resort to savagery. One who would seek dominion over us has succumbed to the heights of his own hubris. Callias Buteo."

An angry murmur rose throughout the crowd.

"Tyrant!"

"Bastard!"

"Piss trough!"

This last came from the vicinity of Theodorous, Callias's steward, who quickly covered his mouth and looked upward as eyes drew to his direction.

"Callias did lead the charge down into the dungeon known as Hekáte's Vivitorium," Vik continued. "But it was not to bring aid to the adventurers who had paved the way, nor was it to rescue our friends and family who were kidnapped in the beastmar's last attack. Citizens he publicly stated he wouldn't try to rescue just six short days ago. He went down there to kill the adventurers who took up his duties, all so he would not have to pay the bounty his steward set. Callias Buteo does not pay his debts and dishonors his allies."

The crowd grew even more upset.

"Hang him!"

"Exile!"

"Rip out 'is obols!"

Vik held his hands up and the crowd quieted somewhat, soothed by the charismatic moon elf.

"I understand your anger and I share it, but there is more. Down in the depths of the dungeon, we found the beastmar's lair. We saw these three adventurers, brave Arche, loyal Lyssa, and steadfast Tess, facing down an overwhelming force. Three scores of beastmar rose up to meet them and the six prisoners they had rescued, and three scores of beastmar were repelled by their combined skill and courage. Arche challenged their leader to a duel after slaying a dozen single-handedly, sacrificing himself for the others to recover their wounds and wounded, buying time for us to arrive even though he believed no rescue was coming. They fought and, though the beastmar was larger and more powerful, it lacked Arche's courage. After sustaining terrible wounds, he slew his foe."

Cheers erupted. Arche felt a hand slam against his back, turning to see a dark-haired dwarf grinning at him. He turned back and found most of the village looking at him, eyes full of admiration. His gorge rose in the back of his throat. It was too much cheer, too much happiness. Didn't they understand what had happened down there? The attention made him want to find a nice hole to bury himself in. When the crowd quieted again, Vik continued.

"When the fighting resumed, we arrived. Let me tell you, I have never seen fighting like this in all my years. Down there were monsters, massive and small, good and bad. Down there in the dark, heroes gave their lives to save their homes and their people, and through their efforts the beastmar were annihilated. Brave Arche lay vanquished, the beastmar chieftain's axe split his chest, delivering a mortal wound, even as brave Arche's spear pierced the chieftain's heads. Loyal Lyssa and steadfast Tess stood over his body, alone in a sea of monsters, and what was their reward? Callias ordered their deaths."

The crowd gasped.

"That right bastard," one quiet voice piped up.

"Oh, yes!" Vik continued, raising a fist high. "He ordered the guards to kill the very people who had fought so hard to protect us. But there was one thing he hadn't accounted for."

Vik paused, building out the tension. The crowd leaned forward, holding its collective breath.

"Brave Arche survived! He rose from the ashes of his enemy, challenging Callias to a duel. Not for himself, nor even his allies, did brave Arche challenge Callias, but for us. For each and every one of us here who came to this village with the hopes of a new life. A better life. He challenged Callias the same way he had challenged the beastmar chieftain, though no less grotesque a foe he now faced."

"Hey!" Callias objected.

Elpida cuffed him on the side of the head.

"You'll get your chance," she spat.

"Brave Arche goaded Callias into a duel but the trickster held one more card up his sleeve. He demanded the fight be against Lyssa instead. Arche had just leveled, you see, and was at full strength. Lyssa agreed to the duel, bathed in blood and heavily wounded though she was. It would be a battle not of steel or of wits, but of fists. He thought his magically reinforced armor would protect him. He thought that because his opponent was a woman and an elf, that she would be easily defeated. While he was busy bragging, loyal Lyssa struck him down with ease. Now, I bring him before you, good people."

Gigator lifted Callias and tossed him forward to land on the table in front of Vik.

"You who have been the victims of his negligence. You, who have been forced to live in tents because he refused to use the materials to build homes. You, who he would have let be slaughtered by beastmar to save his coffers. Are there any who would speak in his defense?"

The silence was deafening. Callias looked about, searching for allies. Theodorous turned around fully rather than risk making eye contact. No one raised their voice for him.

"What do you have to say in your own defense, Callias?" Vik demanded.

"You're fools, all of you. You think we're here to start a new life? You think this venture was a settling colony? We're sacrifices. All of us. You have no idea what's coming. Do you really think the beastmar are the worst things out there? No. You may have slain one enemy, but are you ready for the rest? Do what you will, all I wanted was a bit of comfort before the end. To drown myself in wine, women, and coin. Well, I've had my fill. Do what you will to me, it doesn't matter. Death will come for you all."

An uncomfortable silence fell. Even Vik, normally implacable, seemed put off by Callias's words.

"Exile!"

"Kill him!"

"Lock him away!"

Vik held his hands up for quiet. The crowd took a little longer to settle but the moon elf still held them well within hand.

"My friends, we have no facilities for incarceration. I can't speak for your hearts, but I would rather our new home not start by killing our first leader. I stand before you in favor of an exile. If you would all agree, we can pass out ballots for the vote."

"Forget your scrolls, long-ears," the dwarf next to Arche hollered, jumping up onto the table. "Any of you lot against this bastard being exiled, raise your right hand!"

No one moved.

"All for this lecherous lout to get out of our village forever, on pain of death should he ever return, raise your hand."

Every hand in the village went up. Some, like a certain steward, raised both hands.

"There," the dwarf said, turning to Vik. "Saved your parchment, same result."

"Yes." Vik drew the word out as he looked down his nose at the dwarf. "So it seems. Very well, Callias Buteo, you have been exiled. At dawn you will be escorted to the edge of town and given one day's rations. Should you ever return, you will be killed. Do you understand?"

"I'm the only one that understands," Callias growled.

"Gigator, take him away."

The sauros grabbed Callias by the back of his shirt and hoisted him into the air. Callias didn't resist, he simply glowered at everyone. His eyes met Arche's and he grinned.

"Enjoy it while you can. They'll turn on you, just like they turned on me."

Arche gave the former village lord a good view of his middle fingers.

"Shut up." Gigator slapped the back of Callias's head and the man went limp.

"Now, friends," Vik called out, recapturing the crowd's attention. "We have deposed our leader and sentenced him to exile, but there is another matter at hand that needs to be resolved. We must elect a new leader to take his place. Someone who can lead us with wisdom and strength. Someone who is not afraid to make a stand for what is good and right."

Vik turned, arms moving in a sweeping gesture.

"My vote I will tell you here and now. You will find no better leader here than loyal Lyssa."

Lyssa stood. Her fists were white-knuckled, but she stood firm and resolute. Every eye turned toward her. Many of them craned forward, expecting some speech, but Lyssa only stood, staring back at them wide-eyed. Arche had never seen her look more uncomfortable. When it was clear she wasn't going to say anything, Arche raised his voice.

"I have traveled with Lyssa for as long as I can remember," he started, the crowd shifting its attention to him. "I can think of no greater candidate for leadership. If the people will it, Lyssa, it would be my honor to serve under you."

"Archousa! Archousa!"

Arche looked around, confused, as the cry was taken up until the whole village was shouting it.

"It's the title for a ruler," Tess said in his ear.

"I thought that was 'lord' or 'mayor,'" he replied.

"Mayor." Tess frowned. "Don't know that word. Leaders are archons or archousa. Lord or lady also apply, but those are unofficial titles. It seems our friend has been promoted."

The chanting continued, though it devolved into simply shouting "Lyssa! Lyssa! Lyssa!" over and over.

"Right then, let's put it to another vote!" the dwarf from earlier shouted. "Unless you have your heart set on wasting parchment, long-ears! All in favor of this elf lass being the new archousa, raise your hand and shout her name."

Hands shot up all over the crowd. It wasn't every hand in the village, but it was close. Arche tried to get a better look at those who hadn't but there were too many people in the way.

"And are there any who would run against her, who wish to throw their own name in the ring to be the archon?" the dwarf shouted.

Not one person stepped forward.

"Then it's decided. Lyssa is the new leader. What say you, Archousa?"

Lyssa appeared rather taken aback, as though she hadn't expected to win.

"I say that Buton is an ugly name and an ugly reminder for what this village once was. I believe this place can grow into a civilization of hope that will last for ten thousand years. I name this village Myriatos."

"Myriatos! Myriatos! Myriatos!"

A notification appeared in Arche's vision.

Archousa Lyssa has declared this village to be known as **Myriatos**.

"Let's party!" someone shouted.

A cheer rose. Someone rolled out a barrel of wine and started filling goblets. Somewhere, a band started playing. Tess flashed Arche a grin.

"Shall I grab us some drinks?"

He offered her a tired smile.

"Honestly, I'm exhausted. I'm still feeling the after-effects from you-know-what and I think a night of drunken debauchery is going to end up worse than last time."

"As I recall, you had a pretty good time."

"You drugged me and nearly killed me."

"Before that."

"I don't really remember what happened before that. On account of being *drugged* and *nearly killed.*"

"Then take my word for it, you were having a good time."

"I believe it. I'll be in my tent. After everything we went through, I think a quiet night is just my speed. If you see Lyssa, tell her congratulations from me."

"Have a good night, Arche. I'll see you tomorrow."

"Enjoy."

Arche snagged a small flagon of wine off the table and walked back to his tent in the falling darkness. A full moon shone down, casting moonbeams through the clouds. Arche took a swig before entering his tent. Once inside, he removed his shirt and his boots. His bedroll was no feather bed, but it was comfortable and warm and the air was cool on his skin.

Arche took a deep breath, savoring how fresh it tasted. He wasn't particularly sure of the season, but the nights were cool enough that it wouldn't surprise him to be in the midst of Spring.

There were still two hours until Death Sickness wore off and he still had twenty-five attribute points to distribute. He decided it was as good a time as ever to start building out his profile.

Arche		
Level: 20 **Experience to next level**: 761 (89%) **Race**: Human **Age**: 27 **Height**: 189 centimeters **Weight**: 88.8 kilograms		**Profession**: Demigod **Trade**: N/A **Traits**: Slayer of the Mighty, Psychic **Companions**: Lyssanderyli **Adventuring Party**: N/A
Health: 695 / 695 100%	**Stamina**: 505 / 505 100%	**Mana**: 290 / 290 100%
Death Sickness: 2:08:48		
Strength: 39 **Dexterity**: 33 **Agility**: 30 **Fortitude**: 33 (28)	**Endurance**: 34 (29) **Intelligence**: 29 **Wisdom**: 35 **Willpower**: 15 (30)	**Perception**: 28 **Charisma**: 40 (34) **Comeliness**: 15 (11) **Luck**: 22

Arche whistled softly, doing some counting on his fingers. Unlocking his class had given him five extra points in each attribute and gaining five levels had given him an additional five points in each attribute.

"Ten points, twelve attributes…hundred-twenty points? That's…*twenty-four* levels worth of points? Holy shit."

The profession was already paying dividends and he hadn't even used it yet. All that was left was to decide where his points should go. The idea of keeping some in reserve once again reared its head at him but he quashed it. He'd been in several life-or-death situations and in none of those situations had he ever thought to himself how he should spend his attribute points. In most of them, he couldn't even risk opening his interface to retrieve an item from his inventory. Saving his points wouldn't help him, it would only stagnate his growth.

But where to place his points? He was a physical fighter, he'd proven that time and time again. Those attributes were important to keeping him alive, but arguably just as important were his mental stats. He didn't have spells, but that didn't mean he never would, and his Divine Body skill had saved his life more times than he could count. If he had the extra Mana that leveling and getting his profession had offered, he would have avoided Mana Burnout when fighting Eten and Nete and likely wouldn't have even died. That meant his Intelligence attribute needed to be addressed.

Arche poured six points into Intelligence, bringing him to thirty-five. Nineteen points left. Next, he looked at his Stamina. As it was, he was too often fighting creatures that could outlast him in a fight, forcing him to go to desperate measures to win. He threw another six points into Endurance, bringing his total up to forty, thanks to his ring. After a moment, he put a single point into Strength, bringing that to forty as well. Twelve points left to spend.

His Willpower received a massive twenty-five percent boost due to his Psychic Trait. His Charisma received a similar, if smaller, boost. Both could pay dividends down the road. His Willpower helped him maintain his concentration, increased his spellpower, and fortified his mind. The last seemed especially important after the Vivitorium and learning how to cast out his psychic awareness.

Charisma would affect his interactions with others and it was only because of the connections he had made that he had survived this long. Without Lyssa, he would have been wolf food weeks ago. He placed four points into each category.

Four points left.

A small voice in the back of his mind whispered to spend it on Comeliness. The blanket gains his class offered had brought it up to over the starting point of the rest of his stats, and he'd felt his facial scars become less obtrusive as a result, but he still couldn't justify the expenditure any more than that he didn't want to look as he did.

Practicality over aesthetic, function over visage. The mantra ran through his head. His other skills helped him survive and Tartarus truly was a dangerous world. He was uncomfortable with his face, it was true. The scars trailed a topographical map of a history he couldn't recall; it was a violation. The first thing anyone would ever see about him would be his scars. That shouldn't bother him, but it did. He had no connection to them. He had no story, no grand tale to tell of their acquisition. In a very real sense, he'd been born that way. It wasn't fair.

At the same time, however, it was something he could grow to live with. He didn't know if he'd ever be completely satisfied with how he looked. But he could learn to live with it. And, if he was very, very lucky, some days he might even forget they were there.

Arche took another drink and forced himself to turn away from Comeliness. It was pride that drove him to it. It wouldn't help him, wouldn't change his identity or make him harder to kill. It wouldn't save his friends or help him make the right decisions. It would simply make those who looked at him more comfortable and that was not his problem.

Arche took a deep breath, then dumped two points into Agility and one into Dexterity. His last point sank into Luck, for good measure. Then he let the breath out and looked over his stats once more.

Health: 730 / 730 100%	Stamina: 565 / 565 100%	Mana: 350 / 350 100%
Strength: 40 Dexterity: 34 Agility: 32 Fortitude: 33 (28)	Endurance: 40 (35) Intelligence: 35 Wisdom: 35 Willpower: 17 (35)	Perception: 28 Charisma: 44 (38) Comeliness: 15 (11) Luck: 22

Profession Paths are available.

Explore **Profession Paths?**

Yes	No

"Not tonight," Arche muttered. "I don't even know what you are, yet."

Access **Profession Paths** at any time from your profile.

It was too late, he was too tired, and he had too little information to jump down a whole new rabbit hole of this world. He just wanted to finish his wine and sleep in.

"Arche? Are you still awake?"

Well, there went those plans.

"Tess? That you?"

Arche stood and threw back the tent flap. Tess stood in front of him; long, blonde hair freed from its braid and hanging over half her face. She rubbed her hand against her arm as though she wasn't certain of what she was doing.

"What's wrong?" Arche asked immediately.

"Nothing, it's...can we talk?"

"Of course, come on in."

The wind sent a shiver down his back, covering him in gooseflesh. Tess ducked inside the tent with him. He offered her the bedroll to sit on as he folded up his cloak and rested himself on it.

"Can I get you a drink?" he asked.

"I've got one," she replied, holding out a hand and withdrawing a goblet already full of wine from her inventory.

"Huh, cool trick. Just out of curiosity, how many of those have you had?"

She raised an eyebrow at him and he raised his hands in a gesture of peace.

"Just want to know what I'm getting into here."

"I came here to talk, Arche. That's all. But, if you must know, this is my third."

"All right, let's talk."

"I'm..." Tess hesitated.

A million ideas ran through Arche's head, each stranger than the last. Was this a professing of emotions? Was she going to tell him she loved him? She hated him? That she never wanted to see him again? Was she leaving? Should he fill the silence? Probably not. Tess's face worked through several emotions as her mouth opened and closed.

"I'm not doing well. I almost died down there. I've never been that close. I *would* have died, if not for you. I don't really know how to process all of it."

Arche nodded. It wasn't about him, not really. The wine had conjured those thoughts, surely.

"I would be shocked if you did. And then I'd probably ask you for pointers."

"It was easier to deal with it down there. I didn't have to think about it. Everyone was focused on our next move, our next step."

"But we're not down there anymore. We're not fighting for our lives, so now we have to admit how close we came to losing."

Tess nodded and took a drink.

"I don't have answers," Arche said. "I don't know how to rationalize what happened to me. What's still happening to me. I set out to try to learn about who I used to be and who I am, but I'm not really any closer to learning about who I used to be than I was a month ago. And in that time I've experienced some truly awful things. But I can shrivel up and die inside or I can put one foot in front of the other and keep trudging forward."

"One day at a time," Tess said.

"Exactly. Live in the now, not in yesterday."

"That's not bad advice. You made this complicated for me, you know."

"Me?" Arche frowned. "How'd I do that?"

"That mind-meld psychic thing you did with me. It's got me doubting myself."

"Ah. First and foremost, I'm sorry. I wouldn't have done that if I had any other option. Second, I'm not sure I follow."

"I like you, Arche," she said flatly. "You're sweet. A bit bumbling at times, but you're relatively smart and you care about people."

"Oh," Arche blinked, self-consciously scratching at one cheek, feeling the scar ridges beneath his nails. "And that's a problem?"

"Yes. Because I don't know if I like you because I like you or because you implanted the idea into my head."

Arche stared at her in horror.

"Tess, I would *never*—"

"I know, I know," she said, holding up a hand to stop him. "I know you would never intentionally do that. But you yourself said you were new to those abilities. You didn't mean to see my entire life, but it happened. You didn't mean to show me *your* entire life, but it happened. For a short period of time, you and I were as close as two separate people can possibly be. You *lived* me and I lived you. How could an experience like that not draw us together?"

"I...I don't know."

"Can you honestly look at me and tell me there's no chance whatsoever that you put the idea in my mind?"

Arche looked down.

"I don't know. This...*ability*, I don't know everything it can do, yet. Mostly I've been operating it through instinct, but even I'm not sure what I'm capable of."

"So you might have influenced me without meaning to."

"I don't know. Maybe? It's possible, I think."

"And so I have reason to doubt."

"If I did, it was unintentional and I'm sorry."

"I don't blame you for it, Arche. It's just something I have to consider, now. That my feelings may not be my own, but your own feelings reflected back through me."

"I'm not going to deny that I like you, Tess. But I'm also not going to pressure you into this. We've been through hell together and you're right, our experiences have drawn us together. But I don't want that to be the reason we get together."

"No?"

"No. If you decide you want to be with me, it'll be because you want to, not because our circumstances drove us together."

Tess nodded, then frowned.

"Doesn't it bother you? Our connection went both ways, after all."

"Not really."

Tess stared at him, surprise etched into her face. Arche shrugged and scratched his head.

"Ineffable beings have been fucking with me my entire life, or at least the last month, but I liked you before I found out I was psychic. Our connection didn't change that. Even if it did, my feelings are my own if I accept them. I like you, Tess. You're clever and one of the strongest people I've ever met, and I'm not talking stats."

That got a smile.

"I do want to have that dinner," she said. "I just don't know that I'm ready for more."

"I've got time. Take all the time you need."

"Thanks, Arche."

Tess finished her drink and stood. Arche stood as well, throwing back the flap of the tent to let her leave. She paused at the entrance, so close that Arche could smell the sweet wine on her breath. She raised a hand to his cheek, her touch so light it sent chills down his back. Her finger caressed the ridge of a raised scar and he flinched, pulling away from her. The moment shattered. Tess let her hand fall and stepped past him, out into the night.

Arche watched her go, then dropped the tent flap back into place and tied it closed.

"Looks like you've got more problems than you realized, Arche old boy."

Chapter 46

"So, Archousa, huh?" Arche smirked.

He, Lyssa, and Tess sat in the village hall. Very little remained from Callias's den of drunken debauchery. Lyssa had spent the morning overseeing its deep and thorough cleaning while Arche went shopping for new clothes. Sadly, his new armor wasn't ready yet. Though it felt like they had spent weeks in the dungeon, it had only been the better part of two days and Danocles assured him that the armor still needed another full day of work before it would be ready. He hadn't seen Tess at all that morning until Lyssa called them together for a meeting and, now that he had, she wouldn't quite meet his eye.

"So it would seem." Lyssa shook her head. "Our friend Vikterandor is more capable with words than I gave him credit for."

"I'm surprised you went along with it, honestly."

"You gave me the idea and, much as I am loathe to admit it, you may be right. But I can't do this on my own and my being the leader of this village is going to come with specific drawbacks. Namely, I am exiled by the wood elves. No elven settlement will deal with us."

Arche frowned.

"Ever? There's no coming back from that?"

Lyssa hesitated, then shook her head.

"No elf has ever had their exile revoked. But that's not why I asked both of you here."

Arche and Tess glanced at each other. She looked away first, so Arche turned back to Lyssa.

"What can we do?"

"I have a village to build from the ground up. We have nothing by way of established infrastructure other than this building and I've never done this. I need help. Will you help me?"

"Of course," Arche said. "I was never going to let you do this alone."

"Sure," Tess followed a few beats later. "It's not like I have anything else going on right now."

"All right, then. I'll need to build out the leadership positions, does anyone have recommendations?"

"Theodorous," Arche said.

Both women turned to him.

"Callias's old steward. He seems capable and has a good head about him. He was holding the town together when Callias was busy whoring."

Lyssa stood and walked to the door. She opened it and exchanged a few words with a guard, then returned to her chair.

"Theodorous will be here shortly. Who else?"

"Well, there's Helwan. He'd be good in some sort of research or teaching position, or maybe a public affairs position. There's also Vik, Elpida, and Gigator. They've proven trustworthy so far."

Lyssa nodded. "I considered them already. They're in, Vikterandor said as much to me last night."

Tess looked around. "Where are they, then?"

"They're on their way. I asked you both here early to ensure we're all on the same page."

The door opened and the three warriors made their way inside, followed shortly by Helwan and Theodorous, who seemed a little uncomfortable to be surrounded by so many fighters.

"If you would all be seated, we can get down to business," Lyssa said, gesturing to the nearby chairs.

Vik eyed the chairs and sniffed. "Is that sanitary?"

"They've been cleaned. Extensively."

"Well, in that case."

Everyone took a seat arranged in a loose circle. Tess sat to Lyssa's left, Arche to her right. On Arche's right sat Helwan. Directly across from Lyssa was Vik, with Elpida on his left and Gigator on his right. Theodorous had nestled himself between Tess and Gigator.

"I've called you all here because you've all been hand-selected to help me operate Myriatos. We're dealing with very limited resources and practically no infrastructure beyond what we see here. I'm going to need people I can rely on in order to ensure the villagers remain safe and provided for. Can I count on each of you to that end?"

Everyone nodded.

"Very well. Theodorous, we will start with you."

The older man looked up sharply at the mention of his name.

"Me, Archousa?"

"Arche tells me you were the steward to the previous archon. Tell me, what loyalties do you still harbor for him?"

Arche's eyebrows lifted. It was certainly direct, if a little tactless. Theodorous seemed similarly surprised but kept his manner calm and his voice level.

"I served him for the betterment of the village, Archousa. I had little respect for the man. I have a knack for administrative work and have worked in city management before."

"I would like to formally offer you to keep your position as steward and advisor, then. I'm sure your expertise in those areas will be a vital addition to our village's leadership. Are there any opposed?"

No one raised any objections.

"As I said before, we are starting from the ground up. We will need to focus on matters such as housing, defenses, and food production. The village guards are little more than an informal militia. Our people have been living out of tents for weeks, this is unacceptable. We have no maps of our surrounding areas, no idea of what natural resources we have to work with other than this valley and the river. As it is, I worry the waste we create will pollute it."

"There are many skilled workers among the villagers," Theodorous said. "A few of the carpenters have already expressed annoyance at Callias's unwillingness to allow them to exercise their craft."

"Excellent. After this meeting, I want you to gather a few of them and pick which location in this field will be the best to start building housing. I'm sure you'll have no shortage of willing hands. I also understand we have confiscated building materials that were originally intended to build facilities. Once a location has been chosen, you are to start construction immediately. Start with a facility that can house everyone. I don't want people forced to sleep in tents any longer. Once that's done, then we can branch out to necessary structures, like a forge and a workshop. Individual housing will be made available once other necessary facilities have been constructed."

"Yes, ma'am," Theodorous said.

"Gigator." Lyssa turned to the large lizard-man. "Vikterandor tells me that you had military service before coming to work as a mercenary. Is that true?"

"I have had more than my fair share of organized battle, yes."

"Our guard force need a strong, experienced hand to guide them. Will you be their Captain?"

Gigator scratched his scaly chin.

"Yes, but I will need assistance. Elpida has had military training as well, she would make a good assistant commander."

"I have other plans for Elpida," Lyssa said. "A well-trained guard corps is necessary for protection, but I have no intention of spending the rest of my life behind a desk. My profession is Huntress and that is a part of me I am not willing to sacrifice. I also recognize, however, the risks incumbent with that. Elpida, I am putting you in charge of security. You will determine what security details are necessary for each member here and are responsible for the vetting and training of the guards you select for the job."

"Understood, Archousa. I know a few who might up to the task."

Lyssa nodded and turned to the next member.

"Vikterandor."

"I've told you, call me Vik."

"Vik," Lyssa repeated, a hint of amusement in her voice. "What little I know about your past is shrouded in mystery. Arche and Elpida, however, have vouched for you and that is good enough for me. I would like to make you my Minister of Intelligence. You will be responsible for gathering information about our surroundings as well as on our eventual enemies. I understand resources will be tight, but if major events start unfolding in Tartarus, I do not want to be the last to know. You will also be responsible for assisting the guards with investigations into any crimes that occur in Myriatos. Is this acceptable to you?"

"It's manageable. I have a few contacts back in Ship's Shape and a few other cities besides. It might take a while to get word out and back, but with some development we should be able to find a workable solution."

"Excellent. Helwan." Lyssa turned to the satyr. "I understand you had a position back in Ship's Shape, one that you may be eager to return to, considering all that's happened here."

"Allow me to stop you there. Yes, I held a nice position back at Bits and Bobbles, but I was already on my way out, I think. As I explained to Arche once before, my stunt back at the dwarven ruins would have rendered my resignation. It wasn't exactly a sanctioned expedition. At any rate, I am not quite in my adventure-chasing days any longer. At heart, I am a musician and a mage."

"And a megaloscholar," Arche added, giving the satyr a wink.

"Yes, that too," Lyssa said. "And it is for those reasons that I have a unique job for you. Tell me again, what magical abilities do you possess?

"I am an Adept Gaiamancer, a Student Phosphomancer, and when it comes to academics, I have long researched artifacts of arcane antiquity."

"I would like you to begin training others in gaiamancy. A strong magical presence will be invaluable and it is my hope that, with effort, we can start our own school of magic here."

"Me? A teacher?" Helwan's eyes went wide. "I don't know if I am perhaps the right person to do that. My personality isn't always the most, erm, captivating."

"I think the allure of learning magic with steady employment afterwards will be more than enough to captivate your future students. The affinity for magic is rare enough, we should find all who are capable and use them for the good of the village. I also want you to seek out other skilled magic users in our village and get them onboard for professorship."

"Wait, wait, let me get this straight. You're offering to teach people magic for *free?*" Tess asked.

The others seemed surprised as well.

"In my culture, we do not demand expense for what will help all," Lyssa said. "I understand that we are no longer among my people, but the people of Myriatos have already sacrificed much. I would offer them what I can in return, and the promise of payment and steady employment should be enough to keep their loyalty."

"Do you understand how much drachmae you are giving up in offering this?" Helwan asked gently. "The Lyceum Apokryfos in Ship's Shape charges a tuition of over a thousand drachmae a year."

The weight of that hung in the air until Arche cleared his throat.

"Erm, how much is that?"

"Ten months of a skilled tradesman's wages; perhaps three years of an unskilled laborer's."

"Hot damn. So magic really *is* locked behind a paywall?"

"If you want classical training, yes. Access to the Arcane Library, tutelage in areas of proficiency, magical theory, magical history, spellcraft. All these things and more are offered by the Lyceum.

"I'm not suggesting that we'll be able to compete with the Lyceum, but we can provide an alternative to our people. I see it as an investment into Myriatos's future. Participating in our school would include a basic stipend for each student along with mandatory time in service to the village. That way we're assured to get a return on our investment. When that period of service is over, a position will be offered that allows those magical services to continue to further the needs of the village."

"A practical decision, Archousa," Theodorous said. "I predict most in the village will leap at the chance to learn and practice magic, though some will not be keen to give up their current trades in order to do so."

"For those willing to make a change, we will provide the opportunity. For those who wish to remain as they are, I will not force them to change, simply offer them the choice. Perhaps down the line, we can work out a curriculum that does not require people to give up their jobs in order to learn."

"Then you have my support for the plan, Archousa. We can fine-tune the details of payment and time in service at a later date."

"Never in all my years have I heard of such a thing," Helwan said. "But then, I have not spent much time among the elves. If you believe I am truly the best satyr for the job, then I will accept your generous offer."

"Excellent. That leaves you two." Lyssa looked at Arche and Tess.

"I'm a Rogue. I'm not exactly equipped to help run a village."

"On the contrary. In my understanding, Rogues are very good at keeping their finger on economy. I would like to make you the official Minister of Commerce. You will be in charge of the village treasury as well as overseeing the market and levying taxes. You will be in direct control of Myriatos's resources."

It was Tess's turn to get wide-eyed.

"I...I don't know. I've never done anything remotely like that. Are you sure?"

"I trust you to use your wits at all times," Lyssa said. "And I trust you to honor the ideals of this village."

"How could I refuse when you've asked so nicely?"

"Good. Now, Arche."

Arche sat up a little straighter, wondering what was going to come next.

"I know you have questions about your past that may lead you far from Myriatos. I don't intend to keep you from your intended path, but your skills and battle prowess are invaluable to this village's security."

Lyssa paused, as if considering him.

"Tartarus is full of dangers, but also full of change. Dungeons can appear and disappear, and with them come threats. They are not the only concern, however. As this village grows in power, so too will the power of the monsters around it grow. We will need warriors. Not just guards to provide protection, but individuals trained to work as an elite team. People that can do the job no one else is capable of doing. People who can go and clear out dungeons or monster dens as they arise, keeping us safe before we're attacked."

Arche scratched his chin as he considered the problem.

"You need a strike team for special operations and you want me to lead it."

"Yes," Lyssa said after a moment, clearly parsing through his words. "Yes, I do."

"I'm in, on the condition that I get to pick the people for my unit."

"Of course. How large or how small is up to you but know that your unit will be responsible for preemptive defense of Myriatos. Make sure those you pick are up to the challenge. You are the tip of our spear."

Arche nodded, ideas already spinning in his head.

"So, the cabinet's been assembled, what now?"

Everyone looked at him.

"What?"

"Cabinet?" Lyssa asked. "We're not building furniture."

"Ah, where I come from, the people assigned to leadership positions are known as a cabinet. I don't actually know why. To use equative terms, though, this would be known as the Lyssa Administration, given as you don't have a surname, and we would be the mayoral cabinet."

"You say the strangest things," Gigator chuckled. "But we like you anyway."

Arche shrugged. "Anyway, that's not important right now. What's next?"

"Theodorous and I have a lot of work to do," Lyssa said. "But there is one order of business to take care of first. Myriatos is on a path to running out of money."

"Malaka," Tess swore. "Make me Minister of Commerce and then tell me we have no drachmae? Typical."

"There is also the matter of the bounty that was assigned," Theodorous piped up. "It was using Callias's treasury, which has been seized by Lyssa. Going by the quest updates, your group is owed nearly fifty drachmae."

"Give my portions to the treasury," Arche said immediately. "I don't need it right now but the village does."

"Mine as well," Lyssa said.

Both looked at Tess, who hesitated, then sighed.

"Fine, take mine, too."

"Excellent. That will go a long way toward relieving some financial burdens. I will speak with Abraxios and Odelia to determine what they wish to do."

"There's something else," Arche said, drawing everyone's attention. "The treasure from the dwarven crypt. We grabbed a bunch of it. I'm sure most of it is probably worth a fortune. We could take that to Ship's Shape, sell it off for coin, buy any needed supplies and bring it back to Myriatos. That would probably hold us over for as long as it would take to set up our own internal economy."

Lyssa considered the idea for a moment, then nodded.

"I agree. The way is too dangerous to go alone, however."

"I will accompany him," Helwan said. "I should really tender my resignation to Lady Oyl in person, and she may be able to help identify aspects of his spear. Additionally, I am well familiar with the city and may be able to secure some contacts within the Lyceum Apokryfos who might help me in setting up our school."

"And as the freshly minted Minister of Commerce, such a trip would be along my purview. I can talk with some of the trade guilds in the city and see if there are any deals to be made. There might not be much now, but once we learn more about what's around us we may have goods to sell."

"It's settled, then," Lyssa said. "We'll take a few days so Theodorous and I can create a list of what the village needs, then we will send you off. Perhaps we should plan a return trip to the ruins, first, but we still have no certain way of killing the revenant. Until then, I suggest you settle into your new roles and do the best you can to prepare. Additionally, the upstairs has several rooms. As my 'cabinet,' I would extend these rooms to each of you. They may accommodate you better than those tents outside."

Everyone stood, preparing to leave, but Lyssa raised a hand to keep Arche and Tess behind. They waited patiently as the others filed out, or in Theodorous's case, went over to a small desk on the side of the room to begin organizing the village's resources.

"Until more suitable accommodations can be met, I have turned my bedroom into a study," Lyssa said. "It's more private than this room. Please, follow me."

Arche and Tess exchanged glances, then followed Lyssa to the back of the hall and into a medium-sized room. Gaudy tapestries hung from the walls and the furniture was intricately carved out of rich, dark wood.

"I haven't yet had time to dispose of these," Lyssa said, gesturing. "Perhaps you can take some of it with you to sell when you go, but that's not why I called you here."

She leveled her piercing, green eyes at Arche.

"What happened?"

Arche cleared his throat and sat down in the desk chair.

"All right, get comfy."

He told them everything. How the fall had nearly killed him, his survival, and his trek through the tunnels. His fight with the beastmar near the flame traps and how it had nearly killed him. He told them of Hekáte and the quest he received from her. He spoke of the kerberos, Orthrus, and its lair. About his motivation behind joining the fight and the circumstances surrounding his death. Then he spoke of Thanatos and Ares, and how the latter's claim to him apparently superseded the former's. He told them about how he couldn't die, about the toll dying would take on him, and the threat that the price would only grow steeper the more he died.

Lastly, after internal deliberation, he told them of the coin that Thanatos had given him.

"You have an artifact that can reverse death?" Lyssa asked incredulously.

"Yes. Thanatos made it clear this was a one-time use item and that it would only work on the recently deceased."

"Never speak of it again," Tess warned, moving to the window then the door to check for eavesdroppers. "Such a thing would have every thief and brigand in Tartarus coming after you. Everyone's lost someone they want to bring back, the limitation wouldn't stop them from trying."

Lyssa nodded.

"I agree. Such a thing is unheard of. You would do well to keep it a secret, always."

Arche nodded.

"I debated telling you two, to be honest. But I've tried to be upfront with both of you and I see no reason to stop now."

"Thank you." Lyssa's brow furrowed. "What do you suppose this Ares wants? You mentioned something about a war, but with whom?"

"I'm not sure. The world, perhaps? Or maybe whatever governs it. He seemed to relish conflict. He's the source of my Divine Body skill. He's the one that's been influencing my entire life here, but there's something fundamentally wrong about him. He's like conflict incarnate."

"Then we would do well to be extra cautious around him. Such a being likely has underlings and I can't imagine they would be peaceful."

"We better hope that Gigator does a good job training those guards, then. We may need them sooner, rather than later."

"Peace never lasts long in Tartarus."

"Are we sure we're ready to pick this fight?" Tess asked.

"Ready? No. But I don't think I have a choice," Arche said. "We'll have to prepare quickly. First things first, however. We have a trip to Ship's Shape to plan, and if past experience is anything to go off of, I'm sure there will be a multitude of ways it goes wrong. I'm not so sure that we can't get past the revenant and the village could use the income from those dwarven relics. I think it's time to pay a second visit to those ruins."

"Good luck," Lyssa said. "We're all going to need it."

Arche sat back in his chair and glanced out the window. The sun was shining over the village and people were busy going about their daily lives. Theodorous had apparently left his desk as he was talking to carpenters and masons, gesturing toward the valley, and Helwan was deep in conversation with Abraxios and Odelia. Hope started to well in Arche's chest. Hope that they were finally doing something right. He turned away from the window to look back at the others.

"All right. Let's get to work."

FINAL STATS

<table>
<tr><td colspan="3" align="center">Arche</td></tr>
<tr>
<td>

Level: 20
Experience to next level: 761 (89%)
Race: Human
Age: 27
Height: 189 centimeters
Weight: 88.8 kilograms

</td>
<td colspan="2">

Profession: Demigod
Trade: N/A
Traits: Slayer of the Mighty, Psychic
Companions: Lyssanderyli
Adventuring Party: N/A

</td>
</tr>
<tr>
<td align="center">

Health: 730 / 730
100%

</td>
<td align="center">

Stamina: 565 / 565
100%

</td>
<td align="center">

Mana: 350 / 350
100%

</td>
</tr>
<tr>
<td align="center">

Strength: 40
Dexterity: 34
Agility: 32
Fortitude: 33 (28)

</td>
<td align="center">

Endurance: 40 (35)
Intelligence: 35
Wisdom: 35
Willpower: 35

</td>
<td align="center">

Perception: 28
Charisma: 44 (38)
Comeliness: 15 (11)
Luck: 22

</td>
</tr>
</table>

Skills		
Acrobatics	Level 10	Novice
Anatomy	Level 2	Beginner
Archery	Level 13	Novice
Bartering	Level 8	Beginner
Cartography	Level 1	Beginner
Climbing	Level 1	Beginner
Cooking	Level 3	Beginner
Daggermanship	Level 2	Beginner
Dancing	Level 2	Beginner
Digging	Level 12	Novice
Divine Body	Level 12	Novice
Drawing	Level 3	Beginner
Dungeoneering	Level 11	Novice

Examine	Level 5	Beginner
Investigation	Level 3	Beginner
Leadership	Level 6	Beginner
Light Armor	Level 11	Novice
Medicine	Level 1	Beginner
Menial Labor	Level 12	Novice
Performance	Level 2	Beginner
Persuasion	Level 5	Beginner
Psychic Link	Level 2	Beginner
Skinning	Level 8	Beginner
Spear Throwing	Level 9	Beginner
Spearmanship	Level 17	Novice
Stealth	Level 9	Beginner
Swimming	Level 3	Beginner
Swordsmanship	Level 15	Novice
Wilderness Survival	Level 12	Novice
Unarmed Combat	Level 8	Beginner

Pronunciation Guide

Arachnean (uh-RAK-nee-en)

Arachtaurs (uh-RAK-tars)

Arche (arr-KEY)

Callias Buteo (cuh-LIE-us byoo-TAY-oh)

Charomera (kayr-oh-MAYR-uh)

Chímaira (khy-MAYR-uh)

Cypress (SY-priss)

Elaphebolion (ehl-aff-eh-BO-lee-on)

Elpida (ehl-PEE-da)

Gigator (GEE-ga-torr)

Gregorinandiir (GREH-gorr-ih-NAN-deer)

Hadespera (HAY-dee-spayr-uh)

Hermera (her-MAYR-uh)

Kopis/Kopides (co-PISS/co-PEE-dez)

Kýklops/Kýklopes (kee-KLOHPS/kee-KLOH-pez)

Kyrzzgtk (KEER-zig-tik)

Lyceum Apokryfos (lye-SEE-um uh-PAW-krih-fose)

Lyssa/Lyssanderyli (lih-SUH/lih-san-DAIR-ih-lee)

Maeotian (mee-OH-tee-an)

Mantikhoras (man-tih-CORR-az)

Moirai (MOY-rye)

Myriatos (MEER-ee-uh-toz)

Nyxspera (niks-PAYR-uh)

Oneiroi (oh-NEE-roy)

Persepera (pur-seh-PAYR-uh)

Pygmaia (pig-MY-uh)

Sylv (SIHLV)

Velgilar (vell-GIH-larr)

Vikterandor (vihk-terr-AND-orr)

Xiphos (ksee-FOS)

Content Warning

The work you find here may not be suitable for all readers. I have done my best to approach every subject with care and precision, but I do not hold my punches when I feel the story calling for it and I do not believe myself above error. We are all warriors in this game called life, but not every warrior is ready to fight the next battle. Below are some of the beasts you can expect to find here:

- Coarse Language
- Death of a Loved One
- Disturbing Descriptions
- Fantasy Racism
- Graphic Panic Attacks
- Graphic Violence
- Grief
- Mention, but not depiction, of Sexual Crimes
- Murder

I would advise parents of children under 14 to vet this book to determine if it is suitable for their child's age group. This book was not intended for a young audience.

Acknowledgments

Lao Tzu is attributed with the quote "a journey of a thousand miles beings with a single step." This story has taken me on a multi-year journey and the first step of my next adventure is sharing it with all of you. It was not created in a vacuum, however, and I owe recognition to the people that helped me make this world breathe life.

First and foremost, I have to bring attention to my wife. Her feedback, her insight, and her brilliant ideas are an ever-present source of inspiration. I am the man I am because she inspires me to be better than I was. In all worlds, in all timelines, all that I am is yours, from the first violent explosion of life until the lonely end.

Second I would like to thank my parents, especially my mother, who not only taught me to write but encouraged it. I have been telling stories since I was a child, but it wasn't until recently that I found the courage to pursue storytelling seriously. Throughout it all, they have always supported my creative endeavors. I could not have asked for more wonderful parents and I am truly grateful.

Third, I would like to thank my beta readers, who gave lovely feedback. I have read this story nearly two dozen times in the four years it took from conception to completion and your feedback was necessary to point out things I would have otherwise missed. Seeing your enjoyment as you experienced this world I have known for so long gave a jaded heart some hope.

Last, but certainly not least, thank you, dear reader. I hope that you were able to find some joy in the world of Tartarus, dangerous though it may be, and if I could ask one last thing of you, please leave a review on whatever service you received the book through. I don't have a team behind me, so I don't have the luxury of dedicated marketeers. Your review makes a world of difference in giving my book the exposure necessary to make it into the hands of new readers. Whether positive or negative, your thoughts matter. Regardless, thank you.

For future works, check out my website at www.erebusesprit.com. To be notified of upcoming projects and get sneak peeks, sign up for my mailing list there (don't worry, I post rarely).

Thank you,
Erebus Esprit